my

'2014.

ANNA

HER

ODYSSEY
TO
FREEDOM

BY ERIC J BROWN

Brown Eric J (Eric John) 1947 –
  Anna: Her Odyssey to Freedom

ISBN 0-9684384-3-1

  Immigrants-Canada-Fiction. 1. Title

PS8553.R68497A75 2002   C813'.54   C2002-901103-5

PR9199.3.B6977A65 2002

Printed and Published by
Magnolia Press
Box 499
Entwistle, Alberta
T0E 0S0

Dedication

This work is dedicated to all those brave souls who risked life and limb to escape from tyranny and oppression. May the wisdom we gain from their experience cause us to be more vigilant in safeguarding the freedoms that we so often take for granted.

Other Books Written by Eric J Brown

Ginny – A Canadian Story of Love & Friendship 1998
Ingrid – An Immigrant's Tale 2000
The Promise 2004
To the Last Tree Standing 2006
Third Time Lucky 2009

First Edition   March 2002

Second Printing May 2002
Third Printing September 2002
Forth Printing October 2003
Fifth Printing April 2006
Sixth Printing November 2009

Acknowledgments

It is a well-known fact that no book is produced alone and that the author is only a part of a team that translates the dream into reality. With this in mind, I would like to thank my team members.

Firstly, I would like to thank Edith Ferrier and Charlene Rozgo for their constructive criticism while proof reading this work.

Secondly, I would like to thank Lillian Ross for her fine job of editing and providing her well-considered review for the back cover of this work.

Thirdly, and most importantly I would like to thank Dr. Anna Gipters Rudovics whose own extraordinary life story served as an inspiration for this work. She has generously loaned herself as invaluable resource in proofing this work in trying to keep it as historically accurate as possible. She has also abundantly supplied me with materials such as books and videotapes, to give me a glimpse of her homeland of Latvia. Without her input this work would not have been possible.

Finally, I would like to thank my good wife Isabella for her continued support and patience during the long hours I spent developing this work. Her service as a first line critic is an invaluable asset to all my writing endeavors

Latvia

As an independent nation, Latvia has only existed in recent history. Over the centuries, their neighbours such as the Teutonic Knights, Swedes, Poles, and finally the Russians ruled the Latvian people.

Modern Latvia, like its next-door neighbours of Estonia and Lithuania, was born from the chaos of the Bolshevik Revolution in Russia. These three tiny republics nestled on the eastern shore of the Baltic Sea, enjoyed twenty years of freedom until they were repossessed by neo Russian Empire of the Soviets during the monstrous regime of Joseph Stalin. During the following Red terror, tens of thousands of Latvians were either executed outright or sent to a slow death in the Gulag. During one terrible day of June 13, 1941 more than 13,000 Latvians were rounded up and deported to Siberia in cattle cars. Family members were separated from each other and many did not survive the long torturous journey. Shortly after this atrocity a new conqueror appeared, making Latvia and its neighbours subjects of the Third Reich. While most of the Latvian people welcomed the invading Germans, with open arms, as deliverers from harsh Soviet rule, Latvia's entire Jewish community was obliterated during the Nazi occupation.

As the war wound down and Germany began to lose, the Soviets returned with a vengeance. An estimated ten per cent of the Latvian population fled with the retreating Germans, rather than live again under Soviet rule. Latvia, as a so-called republic of the USSR, continued to languish in the darkness of Soviet repression until 1991 when the Soviet Empire collapsed. As Latvia and its neighbours Estonia and Lithuania, once again bask in the sunshine of freedom, they hope desperately to one-day, join the European Community as their best assurance of escaping permanently from the shadow of the Russian bear.

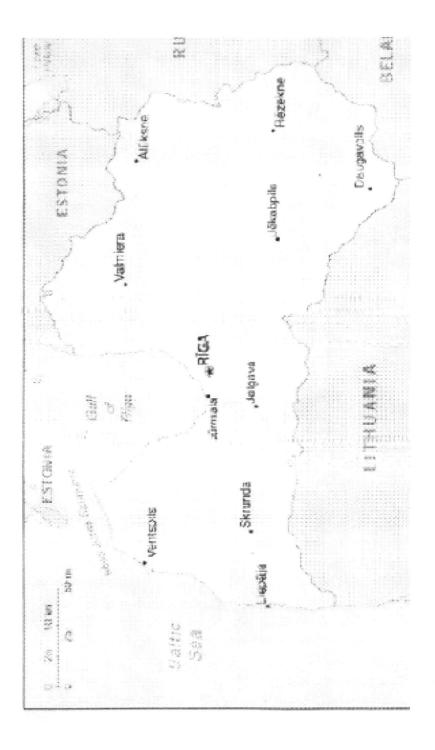

Author's Note

All unaccented conversations spoken by Anna until she gets established in Canada in Chapter 18 can be assumed to be in either Latvian or German, as Anna is fluent in both languages. I have however, inserted several German and Latvian words and phrases into the conversations at various points for the sake of colouration. While most words have been footnoted to give the reader their meaning, some widely known German terms have been left without footnotes. Other words are self-explained by the sentences around them. The accent that Anna used when she was just starting to learn English was combined from carefully listening to people who spoke with either strong Latvian or German accents.

 An apology to any Latvian readers of this work. The author, while aware that virtually all Latvian masculine names end in 's', and that the s is dropped when that person is addressed by his name, he has chosen to keep the 's' on the end of the name at all times. This is done to avoid confusion with non-Latvian readers who may otherwise see the dropped 's' as a spelling mistake.

It is also important to note that in reference the Nazi police system in those chapters that take place during the Nazi occupation of Latvia, the difference between the SS and the Gestapo. Often these two instruments of terror are confused. The SS or *Schulzstaffel* was a special police force created and managed by the insidious Heinrich Himmler. It was known by the twin lightning bolt (actually stylized SS symbols) worn on the sleeves, the deaths-head insignia on their caps, and the black uniforms of the officer ranks. They were sworn to a personal oath to Adolph Hitler and were generally bullies who performed such nefarious duties as operating torture chambers, running concentration camps or rounding up *undesirables*. The Gestapo, a branch of the SS, was the plain-clothed "Secret Police." who spied upon the citizens of the Reich watching for any evidence of heresy or opposition to the Nazi rule.

Preface

Over the years the author has spoken with numerous people who experienced the horrors of both Communist and Nazi oppression. He felt the terrors they suffered and marvelled at the daring escapes they made in their bids for freedom. While he could have chosen any one of several Eastern European countries who had the ill fortune to suffer both Communist and Nazi rule, the author chose Latvia, one of three tiny Baltic nations that had their independence stolen by the Soviets.

The author had the good fortune of making the acquaintance of a remarkable person of Latvian origin, who lived through these terrible times. Upon hearing her own amazing story, it gave him inspiration to contrive his own story of a young woman fleeing from tyranny. While the author's fictional character, Anna, is also a Latvian, her story is a compendium of that of several Eastern European refugees he had met over the years. Also the author's description of Red Army soldiers in Berlin during the closing days of the war - both in their barbaric treatment of civilians and their total ignorance of such basic elements of civilization as bicycles and plumbing, is also taken from eyewitness accounts.

While this work is a fiction, and the terrors of one woman's flight from tyranny are totally outside of the author's own experience, the author has striven to be as realistic as possible. He hopes that his tale of Anna's epic journey does justice to all those thousands of brave souls who travelled through hell on Earth to reach sanctuary in the New World.

Thus, as we are taken along Anna's harrowing odyssey to the *Promised Land* of Canada, we who were fortunate enough to be born and raised here should feel very thankful.

PART ONE

OPPRESSION

Chapter One

It is not easy living in the shadow of the Russian Bear," Andris read aloud as he sat behind his desk going over his daughter's article. "Will the Bear see our peaceful little country as a drop of honey and devour us again?" Andris chuckled as he continued. "I worry that this is a particularly hungry bear with his big black mustache."

Andris put down the sheet of paper and looked at his pretty, seventeen-year-old daughter with her large bright eyes and wavy brown hair. "A very clever article Anna," he chuckled. "Are you sure you don't want to be a journalist rather than a doctor?"

"Quite sure Father," Anna smiled sweetly. "I think it would be quite rewarding to know that I had the power to heal someone who might otherwise die."

Her father chuckled at his youthful daughter; she seemed so old and wise for her years. Andris Lindenbergis was the editor and manager of a small weekly newspaper that was printed and distributed around the Latvian capital of Riga. Although Andris was a passionate Latvian nationalist, he was partly of German origin. His ancestral name Lindenberg had been changed to Lindenbergis along the way to make it sound Latvian. Andris used his paper to constantly remind his countrymen to be wary of the Russia or the USSR as it was now called, which might burst across the border and once again devour the tiny nation of Latvia. He chuckled at Anna's allusion to the Russian symbol of the Bear as having a big black mustache. There was however, little to laugh about in this oblique reference to the all-powerful Soviet ruler whose very name meant Man of Steel. He had heard many horror stories about what went on in that dark forbidding land beyond the barbed wire border that separated their countries.

Presently the door opened and a young man stepped in. He smiled at Anna and said, "I thought I might find you here."

"Hello Valdis," Andris smiled.

"Hello Mr. Lindenbergis, " Valdis smiled. "I though I might drop by and offer to escort Anna home. That is, unless she is too busy."

Anna smiled crookedly at Valdis, and Andris said, "Are you too busy my dear?"

"Are you going to print my article Father?" Anna asked.

"Yes, it is a good article. It will help remind our people to be vigilant."

"Then I will walk home with Valdis," Anna smiled as she moved over beside the youth.

Valdemars Zirnis, a lad with a mop of curly blonde hair, known by the name Valdis, was a youth, a year older than Anna, but like her was in his final year of school. They had become secondary-school sweethearts as of late, although Anna's determination to go on to college prevented her from allowing this relationship from becoming too serious.

Anna and Valdis walked down a main thoroughfare in Riga. Its streets bustled with an odd mixture of automobiles and horse drawn vehicles. Their hands occasionally brushed, but never clasped as they talked of pleasant things.

"So you will be working in your father's newspaper all summer then?" Valdis said as they walked along.

"Yes. Father says that if I help write articles and do other errands around the office, he will help pay my entry to the university next year," Anna replied.

"And be a doctor," Valdis scoffed. "I can't imagine spending my life patching up people who are dying. All that blood."

"We all have our dreams of things we want to do," Anna replied. "What are you going to do, now that school is over?"

"Get a job and earn enough money to go to Canada."

"Why are you running away to Canada?" Anna scolded him. "Canada is some remote place on the other side of the world."

"For the sake of adventure I suppose," Valdis shrugged. "I am a bit afraid of the future. Sooner or later the Russians will take us over again, or maybe the Germans. They seem to be slowly gobbling up the countries around them."

"We should have more faith in the future than that. As Father says, Latvia is our home. We should stay here and help build it up. The Russians have left us alone thus far, and the Nazis have made no threats

"Oh Anna, you are so optimistic," Valdis laughed.

"You will have to learn to speak English if you go to Canada," Anna added. "They say it is a hard language to learn."

"I can learn it. After all you are studying German and it is related to English."

"Yes the Schmidt family is teaching me German so I will be fluent in the language by the time I go to college."

Presently one of their classmates, a lad named Evalds Ivankovs, came by and joined them. Evalds Ivankovs was a shy serious lad who had a powerful fascination with their huge next-door neighbour of Russia.

"Hello Anna," he smiled, and as an after-thought also said hello to Valdis, as he stepped along side them. "Is it really true that you want to be a doctor?" Evalds asked in a mocking manner.

"Yes. So, what of it?"

"I don't understand why a woman would want to be a doctor anyway," Evalds mocked.

"You'd have me be a housewife with a dozen children in tow?" Anna shot back.

"Now, Evalds," Valdis chided. "Anna has a right to choose her life. You have a very old-fashioned outlook on life. My cousin Zaiga is studying to become a lawyer."

"Didn't you know that Latvia is one of the most socially advanced nations in the world as far as women's rights go," Anna reiterated.

"They say you are studying German with the Schmidt family," Evalds continued.

"Yes I want to be very proficient in that language."

"Are you training to be a Nazi spy?" Evalds scoffed. He stuck up his hand in mock salute and said, "Heil Hitler."

"Don't be silly, Evalds. I'd never become a Nazi. I have also learned to speak some Russian but that doesn't make me a Communist."

Evalds grew silent as they walked along as if something Anna said had disturbed him.

"So what are your plans for the future?" Valdis asked him.

"Oh I have plans," Evalds replied secretively.

They walked along for a few blocks saying little. Then a man, perhaps in his thirties, came along side Evalds, and slipped a pamphlet into his hand. He spoke to Evalds, in a low voice. "Be sure to come to the meeting tonight, Comrade."

As the older man continued on, both Anna and Valdis looked curiously at Evalds with the mention of the word comrade. Anna tried to steal a glance at the tightly rolled pamphlet.

"What have you got there *comrade*?" Valdis mocked as he reached for the pamphlet. He pulled it out of Evalds's hand, but Evalds snatched it back. Anna caught a glimpse of a picture a formidable personage with a thick black mustache on the front and some wording that said something about "Comrade Stalin."

"Are you involved with the Communists, Evalds?" Anna recoiled in horror.

"It's better than being a Nazi," he said to Anna in an accusing tone. "Everyone knows that all you can think about are the Germans." Evalds then abruptly turned and walked away from them.

"He's crazy," Valdis remarked as Evalds headed down a side street.

"The great Stalin indeed," Anna said contemptuously "Father told me about him. It seems that not a week goes by and someone gets shot trying to cross the barbed wire into Latvia. It is said that in Russia, the police come to your house in the middle of the night to arrest a family member and he is never seen again."

"That is why I'm glad I am going to go to Canada" Valdis said. "It is far, far away from both the Nazis and the Communists. It is a peaceful place where one can prosper without fear of being invaded."

"How do you know this?" Anna snapped.

"I read history too, you know. After all, I got the next highest mark to you in school."

"Enough of this talk about politics" Anna sighed. "Let's talk about something else."

"Okay, would you like to come to the seashore with me on Sunday evening for *Ligo svetki*[1] and we can watch the sun go down over the sea," Valdis ventured.

"We will have to take the special train to the seashore," Anna teased.

"It is only about forty kilometres to the beach. Besides, we can see all the bonfires and all the song and dance."

"I was going to stay home and help Mom. We will have many people calling on us and she will have to have the *Janu Siers*[2] and beer ready."

[1] *Ligo svetki* – A Latvian celebration honouring the passing of the summer solstice also known as *Jani* or John's Day.

[2] Janu Siers – John's cheese, a special cheese served on John's Day.

4

"Surely your sister can help her. We have to enjoy some of the life before we go our own way."

"I suppose I could concede," Anna teased, though she was inwardly excited at his request for a date. "If Father will allow it."

They strolled across the main bridge spanning the broad expanse of the Daugava River, which cut through the heart of Riga, to Anna's home on the other side. It was a small two-storey house in the section of the city that housed many people of the intelligentsia and professional people. Valldis's family also lived in this neighborhood. She turned and said, "Well goodbye Valdis. I will see you Sunday evening."

"Is that you Anna?" her mother called as Anna entered the house.

"Yes Mother," Anna replied as she strolled into the house in a carefree manner.

"Was that young Valdis who saw you home?"

"Yes Mother."

"He is a fine young man you know." Her mother said coming into the foyer. Lita Lindenbergis was an attractive middle-aged woman with wavy brown hair through which ran wisps of gray. In many ways she was an older version of Anna.

"Yes Mother," Anna sighed. She knew her parents had sized up Valdis as a potential husband. Then, to forestall any further suggestions, she added. "He is planning to go to Canada once he has earned enough money for the passage."

"To Canada?" Her mother said incredulously.

"He wants to go for the sake of adventure."

"Uncle Janis and Aunt Katrina are coming over for supper." Lita said as she checked a pot cooking on the stove.

"Oh, it will be nice to see them," Anna replied

Just then her eleven-year-old sister Liesma entered the room with an armful of dishes. "We have a letter from Karlis," she said excitedly. "He's in Finland now."

"Finland! What's he doing there?" Anna exclaimed.

"Your brother likes to travel around," Lita laughed. "The last time we heard from him he was still in Tallinn."

As they went about getting the supper organized, Andris came home. "Hello Father," Liesma smiled. "Guess what, Karlis is in Finland."

"In Finland!" Andris said with surprise. "He was doing a good job sending me information about life in Estonia. They are in the same predicament as we are in regards to the Soviets."

"Apparently so are the Finns," Lita said, tossing him the letter. "Janis and Katrina are coming over for dinner tonight. They are in Riga on business."

"Is Uncle Janis rich?" Liesma asked

"He is wealthier than I," Andris laughed. "He owns an importing business over in Liepaja."

"He's even been abroad," Anna sighed.

A while later Janis and Katrina arrived. "It's good to see you, brother," Janis cried extending his hand to Andris, as Andris let him in the house.

"Come in, come in," Andris beckoned. "What brings you to Riga?"

"I am leaving Latvia," Janis replied cheerfully.

"Leaving Latvia?" Andris asked in disbelief

"I am taking my family to Canada for a new life. We will celebrate *Ligo svetki* one more time then we'll be on our way."

"Why are you leaving Latvia? Things have been going well in Latvia in recent years, since President Ulmanis took over.[3]"

"Things may be well for now," Janis continued, "but we are a tiny country caught between the Soviet Union and Nazi Germany. As a newspaperman you must know that we exist only at the mercy of these two giants?"

Andris also had vague feelings of foreboding about his country. While both the Soviets and the Nazis recognized Latvia's right to exist, tyrants who could not be trusted, ruled both nations. Still, as a passionate Latvian nationalist, Andris could not conceive the notion of leaving his home-land.

"Is Canada a big country, Uncle Janis?" Liesma asked, running up to him. He caught her up in arms and replied, "The province of Alberta, where we are going, is big enough to hold a dozen Latvias."

"Canada must be as big as Russia."

"Not quite, but they say it is the next biggest country."

[3] Karlis Ulmanis ruled Latvia from 1934 to 1940 as a benevolent dictator. The country enjoyed much prosperity and stability during his regime. It is a time fondly remembered by most Latvians.

"I was talking to Valdis today," Anna said quietly. "He is talking about going to Canada also."

"Valdis?" Andris puzzled. "Why would he want to go to Canada?"

"For the sake of adventure, he said, and he is also concerned about the future."

"He is a young man. He belongs here, helping us build a future," Andris said indignantly.

"Where are you going in Canada again, Uncle Janis?" Anna asked.

"To a place called Kasper Beach in their province of Alberta. It's near the end of a lake and there are several other Latvian families living in the area. You should come too, Andris. Maybe you could set up a newspaper over there."

"My place is here," Andris insisted. "I think it is almost treasonous to leave Latvia when we are doing so well."

"Enough politics for now," Lita called from the dining room. "Dinner is ready." As the men moved toward the table she reiterated, "And no politics at the dinner table."

They settled down to a perfectly delicious meal of roast goose as a sort of going-away party for Janis, Katrina and their family. Dinner conversation centred on Anna and her dream of becoming a doctor. They talked about how brave it was of Anna to choose a difficult course like medicine.

After dinner, when everyone gathered in the living room, Liesma offered to entertain with the kokle.[4] She strummed the instrument and sung softly. After a couple of songs, Liesma paused and everyone clapped. Katrina said the music was beautiful.

"If you will excuse me," Anna said, rising from her chair. "I hate to leave you Uncle Janis and Aunt Katrina, but I must keep my appointment at the Schmidt house."

"The Schmidt house?" Janis asked.

"This German couple, Klaus and Erna Schmidt, have been giving Anna German lessons," Andris explained. "They say she is very good."

"Why are you studying German?" Katrina asked.

"It is an important foreign language, and I enjoy learning other languages. I can even speak and write a little Russian." Anna replied, and as she headed for the door she said farewell in both languages.

[4] kokle – a stringed musical instrument used in Latvian folk music

Klaus and Erna Schmidt lived in a well-to-do part of Riga and they, like most Baltic Germans, seemed to be rich. They had, nonetheless, agreed to teach Anna comprehensive skills at conversational German so she could become proficient in the language that was her favourite foreign language. In exchange, Anna would do housework for them.

On those three nights when she took lessons, all conversations were conducted in German from the time she arrived until the time she had left. Even their teenage children, Ernst and Gerda joined in. Ernst was two years older than Anna and was planning to go to Germany in the fall. Gerda had gone to school with Anna and knew her personally. They spoke Latvian at school and on the street, but during the evenings at the Schmidt house, Gerda spoke German along with the others. Anna, like her brother Karlis, had a natural gift for being able to easily grasp a foreign language. He had studied Russian because of its relative importance in this part of Europe and had taught Anna how to speak and read the language. Now she was trilingual, as the Schmidt's informed her that her working knowledge of German was very advanced.

That night after lessons, Klaus informed her, "Tonight we will give you some extra exposure to our language. I am tuning the radio into a station at Koenigsberg."

"Yes, we will get to listen to the Fuehrer speak," Ernst said excitedly as everyone drew chairs around the radio set. The Schmidt's were most interested to hear a replay of a major speech by Adolph Hitler in Berlin that day.

The program began with the shrill voice of Goebbels introducing Hitler followed by the mass chanting of, "*Sieg Heil.*"

Then came Hitler's own speech that began quietly and worked itself into frenzy, glorifying the German nation and savagely denouncing both the Jews and Bolsheviks. The Schmidt's paid rapt attention, while Anna found it somewhat unsettling. There was more chanting following the speech, then the massed crowd broke out in a powerful rendition of *Deutschland Uber Alles*. Anna went home that night feeling decidedly uneasy. She was bothered that one person could have such a hypnotic hold not only over the crowd, but the entire nation of Germany. She was also concerned that the Schmidts whose family had lived in Latvia for about three generations still saw themselves as Germans rather than Latvians.

Sunday evening Valdis came for Anna. *Ligo svetki* and the following John's Day were a special time for Latvians. Latvia, like other northern European countries, also celebrated the passing of the longest day, and the two events, one Christian and the other pagan were combined. Andris agreed to allow his daughter to go to the all-night festival as he had a high regard for Valdis. He was confident his daughter would be in good hands. Most of their classmates, including Evalds and Gerda, were also there. They, along with many other people on the beach, played games and sang folk songs through the long summer evening of the solstice. Some brought picnic snacks of sausage and cheese. Anna, like many others, managed to bring some *Janu Siers* that was so special for this festivity. Others lit bonfires on the beach and many including Valdis wore a *Janu Vainag*⁵ on their heads. Anna wore a floral wreath around hers.

Two of Anna's close friends, Taska and Lana passed them by, decked in bright floral wreaths around their heads. They gave knowing smiles and cheery hello's as they passed by Anna and Valdis.

"Have some of my cheese," Taska offered with a smile as she gave a slice to both Anna and Valdis. Of her two friends, Anna felt closer to Taska as Lana at times appeared too reserved.

"Let us all sing *Ligo* in honour of *Jani*," Anna suggested. The four of them sang a few refrains of a popular melody with the *Ligo* refrain, before Anna's two friends went their own way.

Later, Anna and Valdis sat side-by-side on a bench watching the sun slip down over the horizon It seemed to linger, shining from the northwest along the length of the Gulf of Riga turning the water a sparkling orange. Slowly it slipped over the horizon. The world had now slipped into twilight with a broad bright band across the northern horizon and would remain that way until the sun reappeared in a few short hours time in the northeast across the breadth of Latvia. The dusk around them was lighted with dozens of bonfires both on the beach and on the hills above it as revellers all over Latvia celebrated the *Jani* festival.

Many bonfires blazed all along the beach, and some of the bolder young men, including Valdis took sport in leaping over them. They moved from fire to fire visiting with various people including those who

⁵ *Janu Vainag* – John's hat, a wreath of oak leaves worn on the head during the *Jani* celebrations

were strangers to them. They would often stop to share a song and some food. It was a joyous occasion of great camaraderie.

As they milled through the throngs, they noticed Evalds lingering on the sidelines.

"Look at Evalds," Anna remarked. "He doesn't seem to be enjoying himself at all."

"Yes, he's not even wearing his *Janu Vainags*" Valdis added.

"Hello Evalds," Anna said in a friendly tone as they came near him. "You don't seem to be enjoying yourself."

"Yes," he sighed. "*Ligo svetki* doesn't seem the same any more."

"Doesn't seem the same?" Anna puzzled. "Here have some cheese." She gave Evalds a slice from her dwindling supply.

"Have the communists brainwashed you so much that you can't even enjoy *Ligo svetki*?" Valdis taunted. "You're not even wearing a *Janu Vainags*."

"Don't worry about my life," Evalds snapped. "You should be worrying about your own." He turned and walked away from them.

"What a fool he is," Valdis remarked. "If they catch him messing around with the communists they'll arrest him."

"Forget about him for now," Anna said. "Tonight is not a night for serious discussion." She and Valdis clasped handed and walked over to the nearest bonfire to join in the merriment. As they walked away, Anna noticed, out of the corner of her eye that Lana came up to Evalds with a cheery voice to try to get him to let his guard down.

As they arrived home the following morning, well after sunrise in a tired dreamy state, Anna thought back over the evening festivity. She thought of Evalds and how his nature seemed to be changing. She reflected on the moments when she and Valdis watched the sunset over the Gulf of Riga. It seemed that as she watched the sun set that evening of the solstice of 1939, Anna had a gnawing feeling that the sun had set on Latvia.

Chapter Two

As the summer slipped by them, Anna worked busily in her father's newspaper office. She helped with general office duties, sometimes wrote articles and sometimes she even helped deliver papers with her bicycle. Her articles in the paper were even more poignant than those of her father, as they urged Latvians to be wary of their giant next-door neighbour. She hoped that by the following year, she would have enough saved up to attend the medical faculty of the Latvian State University in Riga. She spent a couple of nights a week with the Schmidt family perfecting her working knowledge of written of German. Karlis sent lengthy letters from Finland describing the Finnish way of life and how Finland, in common with its three neighbors to the south, held concern for the long-term intentions of Stalin.

Valdis got a job at the docks unloading the ships that came up the Daugava River to Riga and saved his money diligently. He declared that within a year he would have enough to buy passage to Canada. He continued to see Anna regularly though their future interests were clearly diverging.

Evalds became a full-fledged member of the underground Communist Party and spent much of his time, distributing pamphlets and trying to convince the Latvian people that joining the Soviet Union was their best protection from the Nazis.

On August 23, Anna turned eighteen. It was a cheery bright morning as she walked to work with her father. The others at the office also wished her "Happy Birthday."

Everything was cheery that morning until Andris announced solemnly, "I just got a dispatch from the wire service. German Foreign Minister Ribbentrop is in Moscow. There is even a photo of him signing a treaty with Molotov under Stalin's watchful eye. That does not bode well for us."

"Why is that Father?" Anna asked as he handed her the dispatch so she could put the news in her father's paper.

"If the Nazis and Bolsheviks are talking instead of calling each other names, they are up to something."

"Maybe they're talking peace," Anna said hopefully.

Andris snorted. "Two wolves will share a carcass, but they will not become vegetarians."

A week later Andris' warning was echoed as the Nazi war machine entered Poland without warning and, Britain and France declared war on Germany. The Soviet Union not only stayed neutral, but also moved in to take a large piece of eastern Poland once the Germans had effectively crushed all Polish resistance.

"What did I tell you?" Andris reiterated. "We're next! Those two scoundrels, one in Berlin and the other in Moscow have divided up Europe."

"In whose area does Latvia lie?" Anna wondered.

"We are very close to Russia and I fear that they will reclaim us," Andris said gravely. "It seems that Stalin wants to retrieve all territory lost during the Bolshevik Revolution."

Later that fall President Ulmanis announced that he, under the threat of war, had to allow part of the Soviet fleet to be anchored at the Latvian ports. He assured everyone that they would not be bothersome to the Latvian people. Their neighbors in Estonia and Lithuania had, likewise, been obliged to accommodate the Soviets. Although the latter's military presence in Latvia was inconspicuous, there was a general feeling of foreboding throughout the country and it seemed that the Communist Party was getting bolder in spreading its propaganda about the *great Soviet Union* and its *wonderful leader* Comrade Stalin. Andris, however, continued to fearlessly warn about the Soviet menace.

One evening in late autumn when Anna arrived at the Schmidt house for her German lesson, she found them packing up.

"You are leaving Riga?" Anna asked anxiously.

"We are leaving Latvia tomorrow," Klaus said. "Our Fuehrer has advised all Germans living in the Baltic countries to return to the Fatherland and most German families have already left."

"I've already been accepted to train as a pilot in the *Luftwaffe*," Ernst said proudly.

"Does this mean that the Russians are going to take over Latvia?" Anna asked. She was very concerned about what the Schmidts had said

"All I know is, that the Fuehrer wants all *Volksdeutsche*[1] under his wings." Erna said

"Now I will never complete my German lessons," Anna sighed.

"You are quite fluent in the language already," Erna assured her. "You could almost pass as a German."

"I will miss your company. It was so interesting coming over here and speaking German and learning the German ways." Anna said. "And I will miss you, Gerda, as a friend."

"I will miss you also," Gerda said. "If you ever get to Germany, look us up."

"To where in Germany are you going?"

"We are moving to Berlin," Klaus said. "I have been offered a prestigious job there by my cousin. And like Gerda said, you are always welcome at our house."

"Well I should be going then as you are too busy to give me a final lesson," Anna said, somewhat downcast.

"Your lessons are complete anyway," Erna said.

Anna and Erna hugged briefly then Gerda hugged Anna. Klaus shook her hand and everyone said *Auf Wiedersehen*.

Anna left that evening regretting that she would have no more German lessons and she would miss the pleasant company of the Schmidt family. It was disturbing, that while both Klaus and Erna had been born in Latvia; they answered the siren's call of the Fuehrer.

Later when Anna told her father of the Schmidt's departure Andris reiterated. "They are abandoning us to the Russians. President Ulmanis is wrong. We should have resisted. It says in the news dispatch that Stalin made the same demands of Finland but they refused."

"Then what happened?" Anna asked.

"The Soviets have invaded their country, but the Finns are fighting back."

As the so-called Winter War in Finland unfolded, Andris played up the Finnish resistance. In an article in his paper issued in early December, he chided Latvia and its neighbors for not standing up to the Soviets.

The following morning after the article was released, when Andris and Anna arrived at the newspaper office, they found the building had

[1] *Volksdeutsche* – a term referring to Germans born and living outside of Germany proper.

been broken into. They ran frantically from room to room to find the furniture had been overturned filing cabinets wrenched open, and worst of all the printing presses were smashed and none of Andris' other employees showed for work that day. Many would inform him later that they had quit.

"Communists," Andris muttered. "Only they would have reason to do this. I wonder if your friend Evalds was in on it."

"If Evalds was in on it, he's no friend of mine." Anna spat.

Valdis appeared on the scene wearing a despondent look.

"What is the matter Valdis?" Anna asked with great concern.

"I lost my job. I got into a fight with another worker who called you a Nazi because you are against the Soviets. The boss, whom I think is a communist, fired me. Everyone is so afraid these days."

"Oh no, you'll never get enough money to go to Canada," Anna said.

"Do you think we are traitors?" Andris asked.

"No I think you are very brave. But look at your shop, they've destroyed it."

"You can help us if you like," Andris said. "I can't pay you very much, but I need a hand to clean this up and start over. But first I must report this to the police."

The police listened with polite concern and a few officers looked over the damage, promising to try to find out who was responsible.

"The communists were," Andris insisted.

"You can prove that?" the police officer asked.

"Who else would do such a thing?" Anna added.

"We'll look into it." The officer said. "However, you must know that the government frowns upon too much criticism of the Soviets. We are living precariously next door to a giant."

"Is the government afraid of the truth?" Andris argued.

"Well, I am just warning you for your own good," the officer said as he left.

When the officer left, Valdis said, "Don't count on them finding anything. Everyone is afraid that the Russians will conquer us."

"I suppose you are right, but we must try to carry on." Andris said gravely. "They say that those who carry the torch of freedom have the toughest row to hoe."

The local radio news that day spoke of the war in Finland, speaking cautiously at how the Red Army had been temporarily stalled, blaming the winter weather. Andris and Anna went home for lunch bringing Valdis along. When they arrived, the mail was waiting for them. It included a letter from Karlis. He spoke from the vantage-point of an on-the-spot reporter at the front.

Since I have acquired a working knowledge of Finnish, I have grown to understand these determined people somewhat. They have developed a fierce national pride that is truly incredible. Many Finns have told me that they will die fighting before they will let the Russians retake their country.

I was at the front near Vipuri[2] and I listened to a commander addressing a company of soldiers. They were standing at attention in their white uniforms with skis strapped to their feet. He whipped them into a patriotic frenzy about defending their fatherland from the Russians. When he had finished, the soldiers all raised their rifles in a loud exclamation. They then sang the Finnish national anthem with great gusto while their white flag with the blue horizontal cross, fluttered in the icy breeze. The commander ordered them to go forward and make every bullet count. The whole episode was so stirring that I almost volunteered to join the Finnish Army on the spot.

The troops, gliding silently on skis, fanned out into the coniferous forests to the east with rifles on their backs, and some of them had only a handful of bullets in their pockets. These people were quite prepared to go out and face the mighty Red Army in spite of impossible odds.

"Trust the Finns," Andris said as he folded up the letter. "They're a very fierce lot to contend with."

"So what are you going to do now?" Lita asked. "They wrecked your office."

"I'll try to pick up the pieces. I must carry on and tell our people about the Finns. It may inspire them to resist the growing encroachment of the Soviet menace."

"Latvia is small in comparison to Finland," Valdis said.

---

[2] Vipuri – A city in southeastern Finland captured by the Soviets during the Winter War.

"Maybe if the Estonians and Lithuanians stand up with us and we all work together with the Finns we can hold the Russians off." Andris said confidently.

"What about Britain and France? Would they help us?" Valdis wondered

Andris replied with a snort, "they didn't even help Poland. If they won't help Poland or even Finland, they surely won't help us."

Andris continued to warn against the growing menace of a possible Soviet takeover of their tiny country. His small newspaper was much more virulent than the larger newspapers in Riga in respects to the Soviet menace. All through the winter his weekly paper continued to function haphazardly against vandalism and other threats. The still underground communists were particularly enraged at his articles, some of which were penned by Anna. In her articles, Anna especially railed against the Communist traitors within Latvia. Valdis continued to help them in between working odd jobs, as he had no luck in finding a secure well-paying job that winter.

One day in the spring, Valdis was set upon as he walked home from working at Andris' office. It was a gang of youths with red armbands led by Evalds.

"Why are you helping those imperialist lackeys the Lindenbergis?" Evalds demanded.

"They stand up for Latvia," Valdis retorted.

"They'll sell Latvia to the Nazis," Evalds shouted.

"I doubt that, but you'll sell Latvia to the Soviets," Valdis shouted back.

"Our future is with the Soviets. Only if we're incorporated into the USSR will we be safe from western imperialism."

"You're crazy," Valdis said as he turned away from them.

"I am warning you Valdis Zirnis," Evalds called belligerently. "If you hang around those people, things won't go well for you when we take over.

"At least I'll have my dignity," Valdis scoffed. "I won't be a robot like you."

"You really don't understand," Evalds sneered. With a nod, his companions surrounded Valdis and began to rough him up. He was punched in the face and nearly bowled over.

"Is this how your Communist paradise will be?" Valdis asked defiantly through a bloodied mouth. As he again turned to walk away, Valdis was tripped and fell flat on his face.

"What is going on here?" Andris demanded as he and Anna came running onto the scene.

"It is none of your business, you imperialist lackey," Evalds said menacingly.

"Evalds! What has become of you?" Anna demanded. "I used to know you as a friend."

"That was before," Evalds said. His face quivered for a moment, then he added, "I have no friends. We are all comrades."

"You poor misguided young man," Andris said pitifully. "I feel very sorry for you."

"Well I don't feel sorry for you," Evalds said his voice growing harsh again. "Stop printing those lies about the Soviets and our great leader, Comrade Stalin."

Andris just shook his head and said to Anna and Valdis, "Come let's go home."

"Come on comrades," Evalds said to his companions. "We will deal with these enemies of the Party another day."

"What has become of Evalds?" Anna asked gravely, after a time of walking silently.

"They brainwashed him," Valdis offered.

"Political cults are no different than religious cults, they pick on the young and turn them into zombies," Andris sighed a weary tone that suggested great wisdom.

"There is no doubt about it," Andris told his family that evening. "The Russians are going to take us over and force communism on us. I should have followed Janis and got us all to safety in the west. Now, because I used all our money to repair my shop, I don't even have the means to buy us boat passage to Sweden."

"Could we go by train to Germany?" Anna asked.

"It's hard to get tickets to anywhere. Everyone is fleeing. All our German citizens have left and the intellectuals from the university have all fled abroad," Andris said soberly. "Besides, I have used up most of my money."

One evening, the following June, when he was returning home late from work, Andris was also set upon and badly beaten on one of the main thoroughfares of Riga by a gang of thugs whom he suspected to be communist sympathizers

That night as he lay on his bed nursing his multiple bruises and broken ribs, he called Anna to his bedside. As she carefully entered the room, he told her to close the door. Anna could sense he had something very dreadful to tell her.

"Draw a chair up beside the bed and sit down," he said calmly with wheezing breath.

"Yes Father," Anna trembled.

"I have something very straight and terrible to tell you and you must listen carefully."

"Yes, Father."

"First, I have to apologize for not following the advice of Brother Janis and going to Canada with him. I should have taken us all out of here the day the Red Army was allowed to set up bases here, but I was too stubborn."

"You believed in Latvia, Father," Anna said in a small voice. "No one can blame you for that."

"I was a fool," Andris continued gravely, in a gasping voice. "Small countries like Latvia exist only at the whim of larger countries around them. When the large countries want them out of the way they are put out of the way."

"Finland is still free."

"Just barely and if Stalin wants that country bad enough he'll take it too. The point is Anna, I feel that the Soviets will soon officially take over all three Baltic nations. When that day comes, the NKVD[3] will come for me for I will be high on their list of enemies."

Anna swallowed with tears in her eyes.

"They may come for you too, but you must not let them take you," her father continued relentlessly. "You are young and brave. You must escape."

"What about Mother, Liesma and Karlis?" Anna asked, holding back tears.

"I advised Karlis earlier, when we could still trust the mail, to stay in Finland, or go to Sweden, but not to come back to Latvia. Your mother and Liesma may be left alone and will learn to adapt, however painfully, to the new order, but you my dear Anna. I fear for you."

"Why?" Anna choked.

[3] NKVD – The name of the Soviet secret police during Stalin's regime

"You were involved in writing articles about the Soviets. You wrote some of my most pointed warnings. Remember the Bear with the big black mustache?"

Anna smiled weakly.

"That Bear never forgets his enemies. They may think you to be too insignificant at first and they may even try to brainwash you into doing their bidding but you must resist." Andris smiled weakly and continued. "Think what a powerful tool their propaganda department would have if they turned you into one of them."

"What will I do, Father?" Anna asked sorrowfully.

"Survive. Watch events carefully. When it is obvious that the Reds are about to take control, you must be prepared to leave this house and never come back. I can only pray the Reds won't be interested in bothering my family, but if they do, you must flee Anna. Help your mother and Liesma if you can, but you must not let them take you. Go and hide in the streets. There will be others like you and plenty of people who will be sympathetic. Young Valdis will probably be with you. He will help look after you."

Anna smiled. "You and Mother always had Valdis and I matched."

"He's a fine young man, but unfortunately I will never live to see if our wish comes true."

"Oh Father don't say that," Anna sobbed.

"Listen Anna," Andris gasped, his sore ribs throbbed with a stabbing pain. "I cannot change what will be, but promise you will not let yourself be captured by them. If they don't shoot you, they'll make you wish they had. You're a strong girl Anna. You can survive. You must survive. Find a way to get to Sweden, but survive so you can one-day, tell the world what these monsters are about to do to Latvia."

"Yes Father," Anna sobbed. She carefully hugged her father and Andris hugged Anna as tightly as he dared in his condition.

"Father, should I cancel my plans to attend the song festival over at Daugavpils next week on June 17th?" Anna wondered. Anna wanted very much to attend this important festival.

"No, by all means go. If the Soviets come during the festival, you can lose yourself in the crowds. And if they do choose this time to strike, you must not come home lest they be watching for you." Andris began coughing and blood trickled from the corners of his mouth. Anna called for her mother and Lita tended to her husband.

Anna did attend the festival at Daugavpils, a city in eastern Latvia over two hundred kilometres from Riga, near the border. Anna travelled with her friends Lana and Taska but Valdis stayed back at Riga. They arrived at the city late Saturday to be ready for the festival the following day. Daugavpils was decorated for the great event and the spirit of celebration was in the air. It seemed to Anna that there was also a sense of urgency and strange foreboding hanging in the air.

"I feel as if there is cloud hanging over the festival," Anna said to her friends as they bedded down at a hostel for the night.

"Why do you say that?" Task asked.

"I overheard people talking, both on the street and in the lobby. Something is going on at the Russian border."

"Ah, you worry too much," Lana laughed. "We are supposed to be having fun at the festival, not worry about the Russians."

"I suppose working for a newspaper gives me too much information on the world news for my own good."

"Well if they come, they come," Lana sighed. "There is nothing we can do about it. Evalds said the Soviet Union is a workers paradise."

"Evalds!" Anna spat. "Don't ever mention his name around me. He's a traitor."

"Take it easy," Lana said. "I was just repeating what he said."

"Like you said earlier," Taska interjected "we came here to have fun, not argue about politics or boyfriends."

The three of them settled down for the night without further discussion and went on to the festival the following day. Anna was determined to enjoy herself and looked forward to hearing reassuring words from President Ulmanis, as it was customary for the Latvian president to personally address the festival at its closing.

That Sunday, as the festival wound down and the President was due to make his appearance, it was announced that he was unable to attend but would address the gathering via radio.

"That's odd," Taksa ventured. "The President always addresses the festival in person."

"Something is wrong and I don't like it," Anna said ominously.

"Oh Anna, you worry too much," Lana scoffed.

As the President's speech was broadcast through the PA system, Anna felt it carried a sense of urgency and an uneasy feeling swept over the gathering. President Ulmanis ended his speech by urging all Latvians to remain calm and united and then asked them to sing the national anthem in closing. Tears were streaming down many people's faces as it was sung. The anthem was spontaneously sung through three times as there was a powerful sense of impending doom hanging over the gathering.

Anna and her friends left early, travelling by train, and by the time they arrived back at Riga, columns of Red Army troops were moving across Latvia assuming their positions as a full-fledged occupation army. When she arrived home, Anna and her parents hugged each other with a kind of desperation.

"I hear the Russian Army is invading our country," Anna choked

"They say President Ulmanis was touring the streets of Riga today to try to reassure everyone." Lita said calmly.

"I was listening to the radio earlier on," Andris added somberly. "The program was abruptly changed and a new announcer said there were spontaneous demonstrations of people welcoming the Red Army."

"I find that hard to believe," Anna said. "Who would welcome the conquerors of our country?"

"This is all staged by the Russians," Andris said glumly.

"So what do we do?" Anna wondered. "You won't be allowed to continue with your paper."

"Like I said before," Andris sighed heavily. "I am probably high on their list of enemies."

Later, as they finished dinner, Valdis came to the door. He said desperately upon greeting the Lindenbergis family. "Columns of Red Army troops have begun to enter Riga, marching up *Brivibas Bulvaris.*[4]" There are tanks in the street,"

"I hear there were demonstrations and people actually welcoming the Russians," Andris said dryly.

"Ha!" Valdis snorted. "I saw those demonstrations. They were all strangers and they were chanting their slogans in Russian."

"They probably were Russians," Anna said. "It is all a staged takeover."

"Then you should get out of here," Andris said gravely, facing his daughter. "They will be coming for me soon, and maybe all of us."

---

[4] *Brivibas Bulvaris* – A main thoroughfare in Riga.

Lita and Liesma looked worriedly at them.

"Where will I go Father?" Anna wondered aloud, with a small voice.

"Come with me," Valdis said. "We can hide at my parents' place."

"Go with Valdis," Andris said gravely. "He will take care of you."

"Take some things with you," Lita said. "You will need a change of clothing at least."

"I don't want to leave you," Anna sobbed.

"It's just a precaution," Andris explained. "If, after a few days go by and nothing happens, then you may return. If your mother and Liesma have to flee also, two can escape more easily than three. There is a good chance they will be left alone as they are innocent."

Although her heart was heavy, Anna quickly went upstairs and gathered together some extra clothing and a few toiletry articles.

"Goodbye Father," Anna sniffed as she hugged her father.

She turned to her mother and Lita said somberly, "Goodbye Anna dear. May God keep you safe."

They hugged tightly for a long moment before she hugged Liesma in turn.

Anna and Valdis stepped into the street, and Anna looked back forlornly for a moment before they continued on their way.

Valdis took Anna to his parents' place. Since they believed they had done nothing to attract the attention of the Reds, Anna would be safe here. Nonetheless as a precaution Anna was taken to the basement. She was told she would have to spend much of her time here and that she had to stay out of sight when anyone came to the door.. The basement was warm and dry and they made up a cot for Anna to sleep in. She did not sleep well as she worried about the fate of her father. In the morning Valdis brought breakfast down to her

"Am I getting special service?" Anna smiled upon seeing Valdis.

"One can not be too cautious these days," Valdis said. "There are soldiers patrolling the streets and everyone is frightened."

"Father thinks he is high on their list because of the articles in his paper," Anna said gravely. "I am worried about him."

"I can go call on your parents today if you wish."

"I'd like that," Anna said. "If it is safe for you to do so."

"It should be. I have done nothing to get on the wrong side of the Reds," Valdis replied confidently.

"You associate with people who have though," Anna said

"I'll take my chances," Valdis grinned boldly. "But we should be leaving soon."

"I trust that your parents would rather have me out of the house."

"They would feel more comfortable if you left during the day. You may come back again after dark. Everyone is afraid of their own shadow now with the Red Army occupying our country."

"I will thank them for keeping me overnight." Anna replied.

While Anna thanked his parents, Valdis checked outside to see if their house was being watched. He was convinced that all was clear and he and Anna slipped out the back door and headed down the street.

"I will go over to your parents' place and see how they are doing," Valdis said, after they had gone a few blocks. "You go on to the city centre and wait for me at Cathedral Square. Mingle with the crowds and pretend you have a purpose other than hiding. And don't get close to any soldier or policeman."

Curiosity compelled Anna to go by her father's newspaper office. As she approached it, saw an Army truck backed up to the front door. Soldiers were busy loading his printing equipment and filing cabinets into a truck. Anger at seeing her father's equipment being confiscated, caused Anna to overcome her caution as she ran up to the truck shouting, "What are you doing?"

One of the soldiers turned to her and speaking in Russian told her to go away, as this was not her concern. Anna was about to argue the point but bit her lip. If she said any more, they might question her concern. Sickened at the sight of her father's business being dismantled, she turned and walked away.

Valdis caught up to her near Cathedral Square and Anna asked desperately of her family.

"They are well as can be expected," Valdis replied. "They asked about you."

"They are destroying Father's newspaper," Anna replied. "I went by there and they are loading all of the presses and filing cabinets into trucks."

"He knows," Valdis replied. "He went to his office this morning, but the trucks were already there, so he quickly turned around and went home."

"Can I dare to go home?" Anna wondered.

"Your father says to wait another day or two, then maybe sneak home in the evening."

Anna smiled. She was thinking of her father's caution.

Anna stayed at the Zirnis house for the next two nights. There was much confused talk of a new government being organized and red banners, some with images of the three communist heroes, Lenin, Marx and Stalin, were beginning to appear on the buildings along main thoroughfares. Pictures of Stalin were both larger and more numerous than those of the others. Some bore in bold Latvian, the caption, *Lai Dzivo Stalins*[5].

The following night Anna dared to go home. As they sat over tea and cake, Andris commented about the new government, suspecting that President Ulmanis had been reduced to a puppet of the Soviets.

"They even had another big demonstration honouring our new government," Lita added dryly.

"I saw that demonstration," Anna said gravely. "It was more like a funeral march. The people were being herded along by Russian soldiers, some of them were even crying."

"They know that this is the end of Latvia," Lita added.

Liesma began to play the kokle and sing softly. She only half understood the gravity of the conversations but could sense that all was not well in the world around her.

Lai Dzivo Stalins – Long Live Stalin

Chapter Three

In mid July elections were held to elect a new government, and everyone was compelled to vote. Andris, Anna, and Lita went to the polls. If they or anyone failed to vote, their passport[1] wouldn't get stamped and this would go on their record. When Andris saw that there was only a single candidate from the Communist Party on the ballot, he scrunched his ballot into a ball and walked out of the polling station, and dropped his destroyed ballot in a garbage can on the sidewalk. Lita scribbled across hers and dropped it in the box and in turn got her passport stamped. Anna, who witnessed her father's actions turned and walked out, joining her father in not voting.

"You didn't vote?" Andris asked in surprise.

"No. Neither did you," she grinned.

"No. I couldn't," Adnris replied. "I will not vote for communists."

Lita came out of the polling station to join them. "You two are fools. They'll arrest you, as the evidence will be on your unstamped passports. Anna, go back in there and vote. At least save yourself."

"No. I will not sanction the theft of Latvia by the Soviets any more than Father will." Anna said defiantly as they started down the street.

"Andris, make her go back and vote," Lita urged him.

"I did ask you to survive," Andris said to his daughter. "Refusing to vote for the Reds is not a good way to do it."

"We are in this together," Anna said defiantly. "You said earlier that we are both probably on the NKVD wanted list."

"For sure you will be now. Please go back and vote. Spoil your ballet like I did." Lita pleaded. "That way they'll at least stamp your passport."

They both looked at Lita and smiled.

"Either vote or run and hide," Andris said. "Don't make it easier for them by letting them arrest us both at the same time."

Anna grinned crookedly at her father.

She noticed Valdis coming down the sidewalk on the other side of the street and answered quickly, "I'll go and hide."

[1] All Latvian citizens over the age of sixteen, even before the Soviet conquest, had to carry personal identification known commonly as passports

"Such a brave and foolish child," Lita sighed as they watched Anna cross the street to meet Valdis.

"The Reds will have their hands full in trying to deal with those two," Andris chuckled.

"Can you hide me out again?" Anna breathed urgently as she caught up to Valdis.

"What have you done now?" he laughed.

"I didn't vote. Father scrunched his ballot up and threw it in the garbage, and I just walked out of the polling station without bothering to pick up a ballot."

"I didn't even go to the polling station," Valdis said. "Mother and Father went to vote and said there were only Communist Party candidates on the slate, so they spoiled their ballots."

"So did Mother," Anna replied.

Valdis' parents again hid Anna out in their basement for the night. They all listened to the radio broadcast and heard the Soviet news agency TASS brazenly declare that ninety-seven per cent of the electorate in all three Baltic nations voted for their nations to become Soviet republics.

That night at midnight, Andris rose from bed to answer a knock on his door. Curious as to who might be calling, Lita peered out through the bedroom doorway at the top of the stairs. To her horror, she watched two uniformed men grab Andris still dressed in his housecoat and whisk him out the door. They never saw him again.

Early the next morning Valdis' father advised Anna to leave. If all was well she could come back again after dark. Anna was grateful and left right after breakfast. Valdis went with her.

"I should go and check if all is well at our house," Anna said as they made their way down the street.

"Is that wise," Valdis replied. "They may be watching for you. I'll go and check for you. Go down to the main square and mingle. I'll meet you there."

As Anna made her way to the centre of Riga, she noticed red banners everywhere. They bore slogans about workers and images of working men with raised fists. Over the window of an old bookstore by Cathedral Square, hung a huge portrait of Stalin that was easily four metres high. Anna gazed up at the image of the ruggedly handsome man with his dark eyes and thick mustache. *'How serene he looks,'* Anna thought. *'It is hard to believe that such a monster is hiding behind that benign façade. I can now understand the truth in the saying that the devil is handsome and masquerades as an angel of light.'*

There were a large number of soldiers and police about in Cathedral Square. The familiar police looked confused and forlorn. In the crowds were also a number of grim-faced men in black leather coats. In the past the sight of a policeman gave Anna a feeling of security, but the sight of these police made her decidedly uneasy. Some of them were busy setting up a public address system on a hastily made podium. A banner above it read. *There will be a meeting here at 1300 hours, where the new situation will be explained to you. All citizens are expected to attend.*

Anna shuffled around the square, occasionally meeting up with some friends. All seemed to be subdued. When her good friend Taska came up to her, Anna noticed that her smile of greeting was very restrained.

"Hello Taska," Anna said in an almost morose tone.

"Hello," Taska replied.

"Who are these people in the black leather coats, they give me the shivers," Anna remarked.

"My father said they are part of the NKVD." Taska replied flatly. "Father had to go in hiding to avoid being captured by the Soviets. He says the Reds will get rid of real policemen like him."

"Oh my God," Anna replied. She thought of her father and a knot grew in her stomach. "There are still a few of our policemen around, although they look lost."

"They will be made either to work for the Reds or made to disappear," Taska said gravely. "My father is hiding because he a local Chief of Police. The Reds will go for rank first. What I would like to know though, where is President Ulmanis? He hasn't been seen publicly since the seventeenth of June."

"I think he knew that the Russians were about to take control of our country," Anna said gravely. "They probably arrested him."

After a time, Valdis appeared. Anna smiled upon seeing him but he wore a grave expression on his face. Drawing her away from the others, he said to Anna. "They took your father last night."

"T-took Father?" Anna asked in a frightened voice.

"The police came for him in the middle of the night," Valdis said gently, putting his arm around her.

"What about Mother and Liesma?" Anna sobbed as her voice broke.

"They are still all right. She sends you her love but advises you not to come home just yet in case the NKVD is looking for you as well."

"There is supposed to be a meeting at the square at 1 P.M. or 1300 hours as they call it. They are supposed to explain things to us."

"I wonder what kind of lies they will tell us," Valdis snorted.

They gathered at the square to listen to the official explanation for the Soviet presence in Latvia. As Communist Party officials gathered on the podium, Anna noticed Evalds among them. He had a smug look on his face as he looked out over the crowd.

"I see that Evalds has wormed his way right in there," Valdis said out of the corner of his mouth.

"Yeah," Anna replied scornfully.

The speaker, whose spoken Latvian was perfect, explained that Latvia had voted to become a Soviet Socialist Republic, closely affiliated with the Soviet Union. The speaker, went on to say that Latvian citizens would be expected to attend all political meetings and demonstrations so that they might better understand socialism and the great purpose of "our glorious leader, Comrade Stalin." The people on the podium chanted with raised clenched fists, "Long live Stalin."

The speaker continued, "We communists believe all people are equal and should address each other as either citizen or comrade. The decadent terms Mr. and Mrs., sir and madam are to be abolished for we are all comrades. Since Latvian people like to sing, we have a new song for them reflecting the international brotherhood of socialism." The soldiers and Party members then began to sing the rousing communist anthem, *The International*. It was sung over, and the crowd was induced to join in. Soon even the most reluctant were singing and followed the Party members in waving their clenched fists. As the singing went on, the speaker shouted into the microphone, "Workers of the world unite. You have nothing to lose but your chains. Long live Comrade Stalin."

The crowd was induced to march around the square, singing and waving their clenched fists. Red banners were distributed among them to wave as they marched. Then as the crowd was being led down a main street, Valdis pulled Anna aside and they ducked down an alleyway before police could notice them.

Valdis what are you doing?" Anna gasped

"We are not robots," Valdis gasped also, as he caught his breath. "The communists have taken over. They probably shot President Ulmanis."

"Just like Father," Anna said in a small voice.

"We don't know that for sure," Valdis tried to assure her.

"They took Father, just like he said they would," Anna sobbed. "We'll never see him again."

She sobbed on Valdis's shoulder for a time before regaining her composure. She asked in a voice of frightened desperation, "Where do I go?"

"Let's go to my parent's place, I am sure I can convince them to hide you out a while longer," Valdis said assuredly.

"Oh Valdis, I don't know how I could survive without you," Anna said with a teary smile as she squeezed his hand.

Anna continued to stay at the Zirnis house. As each passing night brought no inquiries or midnight visits by the police, looking for Anna Lindenbergis, Valdis' parents let down their guard a little more. Soon she was allowed to eat upstairs with them, albeit, behind closed curtains. Anna and Valdis continued to attend some political meetings, but tried to avoid the attendant street demonstrations.

One afternoon in early August as they walked along the sidewalk, Anna said, "I wonder if I should try to go home tonight?"

"It is probably safe. They must know that you and I are together a lot and they haven't come to our place looking for you."

When darkness descended over Riga, Anna went home. She knocked lightly at the backdoor of her father's house and Lita opened it a crack to see who had knocked.

"Anna!" she gasped as Anna slipped in through the crack. "Oh Anna it is so wonderful to see you." Lita hugged her daughter fiercely for a long moment. Then holding Anna at arm's length, she asked soberly. "Is it safe for you to be here?"

"I think so," Anna said, though her eyes darted wildly around for a moment. "I've been hiding at the Zirnis house all along and no one has come looking for me. Has anyone come here looking for me?"

"No, but remember what your father told you." Then Lita said. "Sit down please, I will make you a cup of tea."

Just then, Liesma carefully entered the room and upon seeing her sister, she rushed to embrace Anna. "Are you coming home to live?" Liesma missed her big sister.

"Just for tonight," Anna said with a forced smile. "Are you taking care of Mother for me?"

"Yes, and I baked some *speka piragi*[2]."

"It will be good to taste your bacon buns again," Anna said smiling at Liesma. "Mrs. Zirnis can't make them like you or Mother can."

"So, what do you think will happen to our country now?" Lita ventured, as they had tea and *speka piragi*.

"Latvia will become part of the Soviet Union." Anna answered flatly. "It is almost there now."

"What happened to President Ulmanis?" Liesma asked. She didn't fully comprehend what had occurred, these past weeks.

"The same thing that happened to Father," Anna said abruptly. "They probably shot him."

"Now Anna, you shouldn't say such things. Especially in front of Liesma," Lita said softly.

"It's true," Anna sobbed. "What has happened to our world. A month ago we were still a happy family. Now Father is gone and I am hiding in fear of my life."

"I'll play the kokle if you like," Liesma offered, as she wanted to turn the conversation away from the unpleasant reality of their world.

"Yes dear that would be nice," Lita said wearily. Liesma could always soothe the anxious mind with her sweet melodic songs.

"Yes, I would love to hear you play it again," Anna added.

They all went into the living room and Liesma began to play and sing. Soon Anna and Lita joined in as it was a pleasant escape from the harsh reality of their world gone bad.

The following day, which was the fifth of August, the announcement that everyone dreaded came over the airwaves. The *peoples* governments of Estonia, Latvia and Lithuania had all asked and were offically admitted as republics of the USSR. That evening Anna went home again with the intent of staying overnight this time.

---

[2] *speka piragi* A Latvian dish consisting of buns with chopped bacon mixed into the flour.

"Anna, you shouldn't have come back!" Lita exclaimed, as she let her daughter in the backdoor

Anna hugged and kissed her mother then replied, "Since they don't seem to be looking for me, I decided to sneak home again. Maybe I can even live here again"

"I would love to have you come home, but remember your father's words," Lita said gravely. "Have you heard the news?"

"Do you mean the big lie that TASS told the world, that the Latvian people asked to join the Soviet Union?" Anna scoffed.

"No that the Soviet conquest is official, they will clamp down harder than ever. You must go and hide. We may all have to hide."

"Liesma and I will have to leave this house tonight and try to find safety with some friends."

"I will go with you," Anna said.

"You'd be better with Valdis. Two of us can hide better than three."

A car pulled up outside, Liesma peered around the edge of a curtain and exclaimed in horror, "There's a *Melna Berta*[3] outside"

"Quickly Anna, go upstairs and hide," Lita said giving her a shove.

Anna sprang up the stairs as a loud knock was heard on the door. Lita opened the door and three burly uniformed men and a plainclothes-man pushed their way in.

"Evalds!" Lita gasped at the sight of the young man she had known since his childhood.

"Lita Lindenbergis," Evalds said in harsh monotone, acting as if Lita was a total stranger to him.

"Yes sir," Lita said fearfully.

"You will not address me in that manner. I am Comrade Commissar to you." Even though Evalds was only an assistant commissar, he liked to flaunt the name. He was, however, uncomfortable at being ordered to arrest a family he knew personally as a means of testing his loyalty to the Party.

"Yes, Comrade Commissar," Lita replied in a flat voice. She was horrified that Evalds could act so indifferently to her.

"And you," he said harshly to Liesma.

"Yes Comrade Commissar," Liesma said in a small, frightened voice as she clung to her mother.

"Lita Lindenbergis," Evalds continued with his robot-like voice.

. [3] *Melna Berta* – Black Bertha, a police van used to round up so-called enemies of the state.

"Records show that you have a son named Karlis and another daughter named Anna. Where are they?"

"Karlis is in Finland as far as I know," Lita replied. "Anna is somewhere in Riga I think."

"You think?" he continued in his harsh unfeeling voice. "It is known that she was here last night."

"Yes sir," Lita began, then she quickly said, "I mean Comrade Commissar."

Evalds raised his arm as if to strike her and said, "you used that word again." Then Evalds said, "May I see your passport?"

Lita fetched it and Evalds flipped it open. "So you did vote. However, neither, your husband nor Anna voted" he said flatly. "Your husband and older daughter are declared enemies of the state. You, as the wife and mother, are under suspicion of harbouring fugitives. Therefore, both you and your daughter will be taken into custody. You have twenty minutes to pack some personal belongings. One piece of luggage each."

Lita trembled with the thought of being arrested. She and Liesma would have no chance of escape. However, if they were asked to bring clothing she could hope that they wouldn't be executed.

"While you are packing we will search the house just in case you are hiding the one called Anna."

"Are we being deported?" Lita dared ask in a small voice.

"As wife of a malcontent, you may harbour thoughts detrimental to the state. This will of course have to be corrected."

As the uniformed men fanned out to search the house, Lita dared ask again, "What will become of Liesma, if I may ask, Comrade Evalds? Surely she is innocent."

Evalds looked sharply at her for trying to be personal then answered in his expressionless voice. "If you are found guilty, she will become a ward of the state."

Evalds and one of the police went upstairs and Evalds went into Lita's room. He overturned the bed and pawed through the clothes closet. Anna was hidden in the far corner of the closet and as Evalds began raking the clothing racks a dress fell down, helping to conceal her. Evalds looked at the pile of clothing under which Anna hid for a long moment, pressed his boot against it and kicked at it, but made no effort to lift the clothing. Anna could feel the pressure of his boot but the thick padding of fallen clothing helped blunt the blows. Finally Evalds turned away as he met Lita at the doorway, he said. "You may pack your things now."

He stood in the doorway of the room with his back to the interior and supervised the search of the other rooms. From his vantage he could see Liesma gathering some things together with a look of terror in her eyes. He lit a cigarette.

Lita ducked behind the closet door. It opened in a way as to make a barrier between her and Evalds should he turn around. She pulled back some clothing and found a wide-eyed Anna looking out at her in utter terror. Anna let out a sigh upon seeing her mother. Lita slipped a necklace, upon which hung a locket, from round her neck and gave it to Anna. Anna wanted to protest, as she knew it was her mother's special locket.

Lita said in a low whisper, "The locket may bring you luck. If I keep it the Russians will only steal it. Liesma and I are being arrested."

Anna nearly cried out but Lita cautioned her to silence then whispered, "They are looking for you."

Anna remained silent but gave her mother a look of tearful gratitude as she clutched the locket in her hand. Lita covered Anna up again and rose from the closet clutching a few articles of clothing that she stuffed into a bag. Evalds still stood in the doorway with his back to her. One of the uniformed men said to him, "We can find nothing Comrade Commissar."

"Very well then, Lita and Liesma Lindenbergis, it is time to go," Evalds said turning to face Lita. "Yes Comrade," Lita replied, switching off the bedroom light as she came into the hallway. Evalds looked at her, then into the darkened room toward the closet, then back at her again, with a peculiar look on his face.

'He knows Anna is in the closet,' Lita thought. *'He's giving her a chance to escape. Perhaps there is still a little humanity left in him after all.'*

Anna remained cowering under the pile of clothing, clutching her mother's locket for a long while after there ceased to be any activity downstairs. She was terrified that one of them may have been left behind to watch for her. Finally she crept out into the darkened room. She crawled on her hands and knees to the hallway and peered down the stairs. The light in the living room was on, but the curtains were still closed so she crept down the stairs and checked the kitchen and bathroom to make sure that no one was in the house. She climbed again to the top of the stairs and sat down in the eerie silence to assess her situation. As the silence seemed to roar in her ears, she thought of her mother and Liesma with a deep pain in her stomach. Were they all right? A year ago they were all happy with a future to look forward to. She was going to be a doctor, now she couldn't imagine how or where she, as a fugitive, could continue to study. A month ago, the family was still whole, even though they knew that grave danger threatened their country. Now all was lost. Anna buried her head in her lap and wept abundantly.

After a time Anna regained her composure as she heard her father's voice echo in her mind, *'Anna you must survive. Don't let them take you.'*

Anna sniffed as she clutched the locket. "I will survive Father, I promise," she sobbed as she kissed the locket. She put the locket around her neck and tucked it under her blouse. Anna rose and went into her room where she changed her clothing and gathered a few more pieces for her stash at the Zirnis place. She then went down to the kitchen where she stuffed some preserves and other items of food into her pockets. She thought of going over to the Zirnis house, but if she were now wanted the police would go there to look for her and might already be there waiting for her. She shuddered at the thought that the Zirnis family could have also been arrested. The horrible thought that Valdis could have been arrested and she would never see him again occurred to her. Anna crept, back upstairs, to her darkened room. Since her house had already been searched, this might be the safest place to be for the present.

For all of the next day Anna stayed in the house only occasionally daring to peek out through a corner of the curtains. Her mind was numb with terror. Perhaps she should have voted but it was too late to think of that. She was now an enemy of the state.

That evening, Anna stole out of the house with a change of clothing tucked under her coat and her pockets full of food from her mother's kitchen. Cautiously she began working her way over to the Zirnis house. She had to see whether they were still there or had been taken like her mother. When she arrived, the house seemed strangely dark *'Oh no, they're gone, arrested like Mother and Liesma,'* Anna shuddered, as a terrible reality occurred to her. *'I'll never see Valdis again, I really am alone.'*

Anna thought she heard a faint noise, then suddenly a bright light flashed on and a voice said. "There she is!"

Anna turned and bolted back through the maze of back alleys from which she had come. As one pursuer closed in on her Anna pulled one of the tins of sardines from out of her pocket and threw it at him. She heard a cry of pain as the tin glanced off his forehead. This stunned him enough for her to duck out of sight. She reached a bridge spanning the river and ducked under the abutment. As Anna struggled to catch her breath, she heard voices and footsteps as her pursuers ran over the bridge, but none thought to look under it, at least for now.

Anna slipped out from under the bridge and made her way along through the shadows just as she heard her pursuers coming back. On their return, Anna noticed that they did check under the abutment, but she was far enough away now and well enough hidden in the shadows that she could carry on in hope of finding some sort of shelter for the night.

Anna entered an unfamiliar part of Riga known for its collection of small shops that were owned by members of the Jewish community. She saw a small pawnshop with the light still on, so she went inside. The proprietor, a bald-headed little man, looked up upon her entry and said, "May I help you?"

"Uh, yes," Anna faltered. "I need a place to stay."

"I run a pawn shop not a boarding house," the man replied.

"Please comrade, sir," Anna stumbled. "I have nowhere."

"Which am I," the man continued, "comrade or sir?"

"Sir, I think," Anna ventured. Then out of desperation she blurted. "Look they shot my father and arrested my mother and sister."

"How do I know you are not a spy?"

"If I were sent here as a spy, would I come stumbling in here like this?"

"You have a point there. What is your name?"

"Anna Lindenbergis. My father had a small newspaper critical of the Reds."

"You're Andris Lindenbergis's daughter?"

"Yes." Anna said, her eyes glancing around. She was still uncertain of her relative safety.

"I used to read his paper. How did you escape?"

"Father warned me in advance. He told me that I must survive and not let them take me."

Presently a pleasant-looking stout woman came out of the back.

"Golda, this is Anna Lindenbergis. She needs a place to stay. She is running from the Reds?"

"We can't keep her Jacob," Golda said firmly. "We have no room. Besides if we are caught harboring a fugitive, we'll be next to be either deported or shot."

"You have a point," Jacob said. Then, turning back to Anna he continued, "However, we can let you stay the night in the cellar, but you must be out in the morning. If the police come meanwhile, I'll tell them you stole into our cellar without our knowing."

"Of course," Anna said. "I don't want to see you get into trouble. If someone comes to your shop, I'll run away."

"That's good because a lot of Party members and soldiers come to our shops to buy things they can't get anywhere else." Jacob said. " The head commissar said we could keep doing business as usual if we mind our own business."

"And don't harbor fugitives."

"Precisely."

"Maybe I should go," Anna said heading for the door.

"Stay," Jacob said. "You can stay the night."

"Come," Golda beckoned. "Best you get out of the shop before someone comes."

Anna followed Golda to the living quarters at the back. She lit a lamp and she and Anna headed into the cellar. It was a cold dank place and as they started down the stairs Golda said, "Maybe you should sleep in the attic above the store."

"Please," Anna gasped. Anna did not look forward to spending a night in a dark musty cellar that probably harboured mice. Golda led her to a narrow nearly vertical stairway that led to the cramped upper story. She was taken to a small room directly above the pawnshop. A tiny window let in light from the street side and among the litter was a lumpy cot mattress.

"You can use the mattress," Golda said. "I will see if I can find blankets. Now you can hide here for the present, but if someone comes into the store you must be still and you can not have a lamp or someone will see a light up here and get suspicious. Now I must get back down-stairs."

"Thank you for your kindness," Anna smiled.

Golda grunted as she went back down stairs. Anna arranged the mattress and discovered a floor grating, probably for ventilation purposes, directly above the middle of the shop. It was a small square vent probably not more than twenty centimetres square. This would be ideal for viewing purposes.

Just then two Red Army soldiers walked into the pawnshop and Anna's heart fell. She wondered how she might escape as she watched them. They were unarmed and seemed to be in good humor as they looked around the store, fingering various items. One of them picked up a pocket watch.

"How much," he said to Jacob in Russian.

Jacob gave the price in Latvian money.

"What's this?" the soldier laughed. "We pay in rubles, and I'll give you two rubles for this watch."

"Make it two rubles and twenty-five kopecks," Jacob said quickly.

"Typical Jew," the other soldier laughed, " always wants more."

The first soldier nonetheless produced the necessary coins. He put the watch on as they left the store. Anna breathed a great sigh of relief.

Anna lay for a long time, her mind was a blank as the pain of anguish gnawed at her stomach. Finally she pulled out the locket and held it in her hand. "I survived today Father without being caught," Anna said softly. She opened the locket. Inside was a photograph of her father as a handsome young man. Tears began to stream down her face as she thought of her father and how he probably died horribly in the torture chambers of the NKVD

Chapter Four

Jacob awakened Anna early the next morning with a sense of urgency. "I cannot keep you here," he explained. "The NKVD has investigated several homes already, checking to see if people are hiding enemies of the state, and they will come to mine."

"We would like to help you," Golda reiterated, "but we are only keeping our business at the whim of the Reds. If they find you here, we'll all be taken away. I was talking to a neighbour who saw a Black Bertha come down our street last night."

Anna shuddered at the mention of these ominous vehicles, then said, "I'll leave immediately. Thank you so much for having put me up over night."

"You may come back in a few days' time if you need a temporary place to hide," Golda said, "but our whole neighbourhood is in peril."

"You are too kind," Anna smiled.

"I feel terrible about not being able to hide you, but you will always be welcome back later when things settle down."

"Thank you again," Anna said as she turned and slipped out the backdoor.

That morning Evalds reported to his commissar with a grave look, afraid because he had failed to capture Anna. Even though Anna was now a declared enemy of the state, and Evalds a servant of the same state, he still held lingering feelings for her as a friend. He had strongly suspected she was in the closet when they searched the Lindenbergis house, but chose to let her go. He hoped that the Party would forget about her as being too insignificant. His superior however, was obsessed with her capture.

"Did you find Anna Lindenbergis, Comrade Ivankovs?" The commissar asked.

"No Comrade Commissar," Evalds said meekly. "We almost had her when she came to the Zirnis residence as we anticipated, but it was dark and she gave us the slip."

"I am disappointed, Comrade," the commissar frowned. "I had hopes of elevating you to a full commissar by autumn."

"I will try my best Comrade Commissar, but why is Citizen Lindenbergis so important to us? She is just a youth not quite twenty years of age."

"You've read the articles she has written in her father's newspaper?"

"Yes, Comrade, but . . . "

"She not only wrote slanderous articles about us, but she did not vote. She is defiant."

"Yes, Comrade."

"The Party cannot tolerate defiance. Not even from a youthful woman running around at large. If left alone she could one day be a nucleolus of discontent." The commissar explained. "If she was merely a teenage hooligan, then we would let her go, at least until we have dealt with all the more important adult enemies."

"It just seems like a waste, Comrade Commissar, that we concern ourselves with her when there are many more important people to deal with."

"Think of her, Comrade Ivankovs, as a spark that has escaped from the fireplace and has landed on the carpet," the commissar sighed heavily. "Unless that spark is snuffed out, it will burn the house down."

"Yes Comrade Commissar. I have planted informers among her friends. Having been acquainted with her all my life. I know who her friends are."

"The NKVD will assist in tracking her down," the commissar said. As he noticed Evalds's face drop, he added, "She is to be taken alive, and you will then assist the NKVD in persuading her to mend her ways and join us. If she cannot be persuaded, she will meet the same fate as her father, and you comrade, will have failed."

"Yes Comrade Commissar," Evalds swallowed. He knew he must do his best to capture Anna from now on, as the Party had little tolerance for weakness and failure.

Meanwhile, Anna walked through the street of central Riga, looking for a familiar face. She stayed in the crowd as much as possible and avoided going near to any police or soldiers. Everywhere, it seemed, were giant portraits of Stalin or red banners bearing Party slogans. Tears welled up in her eyes as she looked up at a flagpole and saw the red flag with the hammer and sickle, flying in place of the flag of free

Latvia. She thought of several friends with whom she might be able to stay. Then she spotted the two friends with whom she had gone to the song festival.

"Anna!" they cried in unison as she ran toward them.

"Taska, Lana!" Anna exclaimed. "It is so good to see you."

They embraced Anna, and Taska said, "Let's go to the park. We can talk there."

As they walked through a nearby park, far away from any possible prying ears, Taska said in a low voice, "I heard they got your parents, but you escaped."

"How did you hear that?" Anna asked, looking around.

"I heard," Lana added. "I saw Evalds yesterday."

"Evalds, that traitor," Anna spat. "He was with them when they took Mother and Liesma. If you continue to associate with him you are no friend of mine."

"He stopped me on the street," Lana said undaunted by Anna's venom. "He was driving a big Party car. He told me that if I should see you, I was to tell you that if you turn yourself in, they'll release your mother and Liesma."

Anna stopped short, as her first instinct was to save her mother and sister.

"Don't believe them," Taska said, catching her arm. "It's a trick so they can have your whole family. My father is hiding because he was a policeman, and they've taken all our policemen away."

"Your mother and brother are still safe?"

"Yes."

"Uncle Lukas disappeared because he worked for President Ulmanis," Lana said, looking fearfully around.

"So where do you stay?" Lana asked.

"Nowhere," Anna replied. "I have nowhere to stay. I was thinking of going to one of your places and asking your parents if I could stay there."

"You could probably stay with us," Taska offered, "but you better not come over until after dark, and use the backdoor. Mother says you can't trust anyone anymore."

"All right I'll come over after dark," Anna smiled.

"We should scatter lest we attract attention," Lana said, looking over her shoulder. "However, you can probably stay at our place, after you've stayed at Taska's for a while."

"Thank you both very much. It's good to have friends like you." Anna hugged them both before she went on her way.

Anna arrived at Taska's house after dark. She walked through the tiny courtyard at the back, past the conservatory and knocked at the backdoor. Taska opened the door and quickly let her in. Taska's mother provided a supper of bread, cheese and sausage for Anna and explained, while Anna ate, that she should sleep in the conservatory. "If a Black Bertha does come for you," she explained, "you would have a chance to escape."

Anna was given a blanket, and Taska decided to sleep out in the conservatory with her. It was a warm summer night so the windows could be open for fresh air. The tiny conservatory was barely big enough for Anna and Taska to sleep side-by-side on the floor. The potted plants on the shelves above them gave a pleasant odour.

Anna and Taska had barely settled in when they heard a vehicle stop on the street in front of the house.

"Hurry Anna, get your clothes and get out of here. It might be a Bertha," Taska said in an anxious whisper as they heard a knock on the front door.

As Anna gathered her clothing, two men went by the conservatory to the backdoor and knocked there also.

"Go Anna, sneak out while they are looking in the house. I will look for you immummiw."

Anna crept out of the conservatory and into the alley as the two men entered the house from the back. Taska cowered down in the blankets inside the conservatory. Anna stole carefully for a couple of blocks then turned and ran blindly down side streets and back alleys until she found sanctuary in an abandoned building. Here she rested and collected her thoughts.

'The world has gone mad,' she thought. *'Is there nowhere I can hide? How did they find out so quickly that I was with Taska?'*

The following day, Anna spotted Taska by the Freedom Monument and without speaking they walked into Esplanade Park located near the monument.

"I have some food for you," Taska said, handing Anna a paper bag. "Mother sent a loaf of bread and a piece of cheese."

"The NKVD didn't arrest you?" Anna asked, as she took the bag full of food.

"No. The police searched our house and demanded to know why I'd want to sleep out in the conservatory. I think we convinced them that you weren't there." Taska said gravely.

"Did they mention me by name?" Anna asked.

"No. They just said they were informed that we were hiding a fugitive."

"How would they know I was there? It was dark when I arrived, and I tried to make sure no one saw me."

"Lana," Taska said suddenly. "She admitted that Evalds was talking to her and she knew you were coming to our house."

"Would Lana betray me?" Anna wondered. "I have known Lana for several years and thought of her as a friend, but then I thought I knew Evalds also.

"It is possible. She has a peculiar nature at times, and she is fond of Evalds," Taska replied.

"Now I can't dare to come back to your house to hide." Anna said glumly.

"Mother says it is best you stay away for a few days, because they didn't arrest us, we are either being warned or they are setting a trap. She will however, give me food to take to you."

"It's a good thing it is summer," Anna laughed weakly. "I can sleep outside at night if I have to."

"I feel like joining you," Taska added.

"No, you still have a safe home to go to. At least it will be safe if I stay away."

Anna looked around and suddenly cried, "There's Lana coming down the walkway. She's looking around for us."

"I don't think she saw us," Taska said breathlessly as they ducked around the corner of the nearby monument.

"I'll slip away," Anna said. "You can meet her and see if you can find out anything."

Anna spent all day among the crowds. She met two of their school acquaintances and both were frightened, as each seemed to know someone who disappeared in the night. The police, inquiring of Anna's whereabouts had already approached one of them. None offered to take Anna in, though one friend slipped her some food out the backdoor. That night Anna slept on a park bench. The following day she watched for Taska but Taska didn't appear until afternoon and she brushed by Anna in a crowd slipping her another bag of food, as she said. "We can't talk now. We are being watched. Our house is being watched. Yes, I think Lana is an informer." Taska quickly moved on. Anna was despondent. If Taska was afraid to keep her, she really was alone.

That evening as Anna sat on a park bench near a wooded area of the park, a familiar voice called out her name from behind Anna turned around and upon recognition exclaimed, "Valdis!"

"Anna, it is really you!" Valdis cried as he stepped out of the bushes. It was obvious that he had a painful limp.

They hugged for a long moment.

"I wondered if I'd ever see you again," he gasped, still hugging her.

"And I thought I'd never see you again," Anna replied, clinging to him "It's been a nightmare. I am wanted by the NKVD. You can trust no one."

"I came back to be with you, to protect you," Valdis gasped, as he winced and sat down on the bench favouring one leg.

"I came back to your place the night after they took Mother and Liesma but the house was dark and they were waiting for me. I was barely able to get away from them. How did you escape?"

"I spoke with your mother and Liesma while on the train."

"On the train?"

"Your Mother, Liesma, my parents and many other people were packed into this cattle-car and it was said we were being deported, possibly to Siberia."

"Siberia, oh no!"

"That's where Russians always ship their enemies."

"Why your parents? I thought your family didn't concern the NKVD."

"Father refused to vote and both he and Mother were involved in the politics of President Ulmanis." Valdis invented this story rather than tell her that his parents were arrested for helping hide her.

"How are Mother and Liesma holding up?" Anna asked fearfully.

"Very frightened, but otherwise unharmed. Anyway, your mother was very worried about you. She told me in whispers that the NKVD wanted you because you are considered a dangerous hooligan. She said you were still hiding in Riga. I said I should go back and help you and she thought that would be a good idea, but wondered how I could get off the train without being killed. We were locked in these cattle cars but I said I'd find a way. I worked my way over to one of the sliding doors and was able to reach my hand out through the slats. I found the door latch. They must have forgotten to lock it, as I was able to open the latch and then slide the door open far enough that I could get out. The train was traveling quite fast so I stepped around to the outside using the slats as if they were rungs of a ladder. I heard Mother and Father calling out for me to be careful as I climbed up the side of the car. A few other daring individuals joined me and we climbed out on the roof. A gunshot rang out and one of the others fell off. There was a soldier on the roof guarding the train. A second escapee was also shot as the soldier came near us. As the soldier drew nearer, I sprang up and rushed him, thinking I had nothing to lose. We both toppled off the train into a deep ditch and I landed on top of him. I injured my leg, but soon discovered that he was dead. His neck was broken by the fall. I had to think fast as I knew they would come looking as soon as they discovered we were missing. I dragged his body into the nearby forest then took his rifle and a few rubles he had in his pocket then headed west. I don't think we were more than a hundred kilometres from the Latvian border. The forest was dense and the going difficult with a wounded leg. It is fortunate that the days are long in this northern latitude. I plodded on till dark then collapsed among some fallen logs. I estimated that I had put several kilometres between the point and myself when we had jumped off the train. I had to stop to bandage up my leg and give it a rest.

"The following morning I found a dirt road leading westward and as I started along it I heard the sound of motors running so ducked back into the bush. It was a convoy of army trucks heading west. I wondered if they were going to Latvia. They were moving quite slowly so I considered jumping on board the last one in the convoy. As it passed, I threw aside the rifle, but I detached the bayonet and kept it, slipping it inside my trousers. I then prepared to get on the rear truck, thinking how difficult this might be with an injured leg. The convoy stopped just as the last truck was abreast to me. The driver, who was alone in the truck, got out to talk to the driver in the truck ahead of him. They were concerned as to why the convoy had stopped. Since they were on the opposite side to me, I went quickly to the back of the truck and climbed in. It was full nearly to the top of the canopy with small crates. I worked my way along to the front and found a tiny space where I could roll down to just below the bottom of the rear window of the cab. After a time a group of soldiers came along and I could hear their conversations. They were looking for me, calling me an escaped murderer. I could see them searching the truck ahead of me so I lay as low as possible and managed to find a piece of tarp to pull over myself. One of the soldiers climbed into the back of the truck and crawled over the crates as I had done. I held my breath as he looked over the end. He poked at the tarp that covered me with the bayonet on the end of his rifle and I could feel it prod me in several places and had to bite my lip to keep from crying out. After a few pokes he was satisfied and crawled back out again. Soon we were on our way again. It was suffocating under the tarp that long, hot, afternoon as the truck slowly rumbled down the road, and my leg ached terribly. Being jammed up against the many crates got me curious as to what was inside so I managed to get my bayonet positioned so I could pry the end of one of them open. Inside were tins of army rations. I hadn't eaten for two days so I was starving. With great difficulty due to my cramped position, I managed to pry open the lid of the tin. It contained foul smelling prepared meat, which wasn't suitable for a dog, but I ate it anyway. To a starving person anything tastes good. When I finished that can, I opened another.

"With my hunger satisfied, I dared lift a corner of the tarp and peer out the window ahead. The sun was low in the western sky and soon the truck drove through a gateway in a high barbed wire fence. There were machine-gun towers on either side of the road and soldier posted. I saw the name Latvia spelled in Cyrillic characters. At last I was home.

"We traveled along moving faster now as there were much better roads in Latvia than there were in Russia. As it became dark, I dared to crawl out of my hiding place and back up on top of the boxes, but not however, before I stuffed two more tins of rations in my pockets. Once on top of the boxes, I cut a slit in the canopy and poked my head out. It was a dark moonless night and the myriad of summer stars twinkled above me. The fresh air was invigorating. We traveled for another hour, then in the distance I could see the lights of Riga. I knew it was time to leave lest I end up in the middle of an army base. I climbed down the back of the truck and dropped to the ground trying to land on my good leg. The landing was painful and I rolled into the ditch gasping in excruciating pain. I lay there for a long time before I began to limp toward Riga still over a dozen kilometres away. Dawn was breaking just as I reached the outskirts. Soldiers were patrolling the city perimeter so I would have to steal into the city under the cover of darkness. I was too tired to try to outwit the guards at this point anyway. I crawled under a low road bridge that spanned a dried-up stream. The weeds grew quite high around the edges so it would be easy for me to hide out and hopefully catch some sleep during the day.

"I pried open one of the two tins of army rations I had taken. As I ate, I laughed as I thought how the soldiers would be scratching their heads when they found the last crate they unloaded at the army base had been broken into. During my meal two vehicles drove over the bridge above me, but there was no indication of anyone thinking of getting out and searching under the bridge. I lie down along the cool damp bank of the dried up stream and soon fell asleep. I awoke in the afternoon to the sounds of voices. There were footsteps above me walking in a rhythmic pattern that suggested that they were soldiers. They were talking to each other but I couldn't make out their conversations. I crouched, ready to spring for my life, but the sounds of the soldiers receded so I guessed they weren't looking for me here.

I waited out the long afternoon and evening for darkness to come, then I carefully crept out of my hiding spot and headed for the city. I managed to slip past the guards patrolling the perimeter of the city. Limping painfully, I managed to work my way into the heart of Riga, moving from house to house, from hedge to hedge. I have lived in the streets these last few days."

"Your leg, is it badly hurt?" Anna asked with a knitted brow.

"It'll get better," Valdis grimaced.

"It should be tended to," Anna said.

"How? If I go to a doctor, the Russians will find me. I am probably more wanted than you are right now." Valdis managed a weak laugh.

"I know a place I can take you to." Anna said, getting up. She helped Valdis to his feet.

"Where?"

"In the old part of town there is a Jewish pawnshop owner named Jacob. He let me hide out there one night. He was afraid the NKVD would search his place, so he sent me away. He said I could come back later, and that was two days ago."

"Do you think it is safe?"

"Do we have a choice? If we don't get your leg looked at, you might get gangrene and you'll die for sure."

"Okay, lead the way."

"How did you find me?" Anna asked as they made their way through the back alleys toward Jacob's place.

"I hung around the central part of Riga watching from the alleyways. I thought I saw you once with Taska and Lana."

"That's another story," Anna said, as she helped support Valdis. "The night before last Taska took me in, but someone tipped off the police, as a Black Bertha came for me in the night and I narrowly escaped. We think Lana has become an informer, as she is the only one who knew I was going to stay at Taska's house. I met some other friends but they are very frightened."

They finally reached the backdoor of Jacob's shop. A small light burned in the living quarters from behind a drawn curtain. Both Valdis and Anna looked carefully up and down the alley and with no one in sight Anna knocked carefully on the door. It opened a crack and Jacob peered out fearfully.

"Please let me in," Anna said in a loud whisper. "It's me, Anna."

He opened the door barely enough for Anna to slip in. Valdis stood against the wall outside.

"What are you doing here?" he asked. Golda stood silently by with an anxious look.

"Has NKVD searched your place yet?"

"They were here the day you left and they searched every corner of it, then left."

"Do you think they'll be back?"

"You never know with them."

"Did anyone see you come?" Golda asked. Her eyes looked fearfully around.

"Both Valdis and I looked carefully and there was no one. We're both quite good at evading the patrols."

"Valdis?" Jacob asked carefully.

"He's my friend from school. He was on a deportation train, but he escaped and came back to Riga to be with me."

"I see."

"He hurt his leg," Anna said gravely. "He should have it looked at."

"We're not doctors," Golda said.

"Can he come in?"

"He might as well," Jacob sighed. "We are condemned already if they saw you come in."

Anna opened the door a crack and let Valdis slip in. He stood against the wall by the window so that anyone looking in wouldn't see him.

Anna introduced them, and Jacob said, "Anna says you hurt your leg."

"Yes," Valdis gasped.

Golda slid him a chair and Valdis sat down with a grateful, "thank you."

She knelt before him and had Valdis put his leg on a stool. He drew back his pant leg revealing a bruised and bloodstained leg along which was a long cut in the calf muscle.

"Get me a basin of water," she said, wincing from the ugly sight.

Anna sprang to the task, and Jacob said, "I'll get the salve and some bandages."

Golda washed up the leg, muttering about how Valdis was very fortunate that he didn't get infection. Anna dressed the wound and drew his pant leg back down,

"You should stay off your feet for a few days," Golda said, as she rose to her feet.

"How? I am on the run," Valdis said.

"You could stay upstairs," Jacob said. "But you would have to be still in the daytime, or go down to the cellar."

"Do we take the chance Jacob?" Golda said. "What if someone finds out? You know that some of our neighbours support the Reds, and others will tell to save their own skin."

"Yes, we will have to be very careful, but these people have done nothing except stick up for their country," Jacob replied. "This is what we'll do. Valdis, you go upstairs for the night. First thing in the morning, you will have to go down to the cellar. Anna, you may stay here at night also, but in the daytime you should be out on the street. You can watch for the patrols and the NKVD, and you can do the shopping."

"I will do whatever I can," Anna said confidently.

"As soon as I have healed, we'll leave," Valdis said. "I would not wish to see kind people like you be shot or sent off to Siberia."

"Let's get you upstairs so you can get some sleep," Anna suggested.

"Yes, I haven't had any secure place to sleep since they uprooted my family."

As Anna helped Valdis up the stairs, Jacob cautioned. "Try not to look out the window in the daytime, and you cannot have a light at night, otherwise someone might see this room is being used and will be suspicious."

For the next two days they hid out in the room above the pawnshop. This bought vital time for Valdis's leg to heal. The second day of their hiding was market day and Anna volunteered to go out, as she needed to get out and about. Anna was confident that she could hide in the crowds. Golda gave her some money and a large shopping bag, and Anna slipped out the back door after breakfast. Anna made her way to the Market Square in central Riga. She used to come here often with her mother to shop for fresh vegetables. It was a fascinating place where the farmers from the surrounding countryside came to town to sell their products.

'At least this is one thing the Reds haven't banned. Yet.' Anna thought, as she moved among the stalls. She came to a stall manned by a middle-aged vendor who gave her a friendly smile. She examined his cabbage and selected a head, picked up a dozen carrots, then asked for the price of two kilos of potatoes. He told her the price and then weighed out two kilograms of potatoes on an old beam scale he had at the side of his booth.

"There you go, Miss, uh or should I say Citizen," he smiled.

"It's quite all right sir, I mean Citizen," Anna smiled in turn. Somehow she felt he was an honest sincere man who was not in sympathy with the Reds.

"Have an apple as a bonus," he winked, handing Anna a nice red apple.

"Thank you, Comrade, ah Citizen," Anna replied. Somehow addressing a person as Citizen sounded better than the communist term, Comrade. "Do you have a farm near Riga?"

"Yes, it is about thirty kilometres to the southeast."

"It must be beautiful in the countryside this time of year."

"If you have an opportunity, come out to my farm." He smiled. "You will be most welcome."

"Well, I should be going," Anna smiled, "and thank you for the apple."

As Anna made her way through the market, munching on her apple she heard a familiar voice call her from behind. Anna turned and froze, there beside her, stood Lana.

"Hello, Lana," Anna said through gritted teeth.

"Hello, Anna," Lana smiled as she came along side Anna. "I haven't seen you for a few days."

"I have been busy," Anna said tightly as she resumed walking, although not in the direction of the pawnshop.

"Have you found a secure place to hide?" Lana continued.

"Why does that concern you?" Anna snapped.

"Take it easy, I was just asking," Lana said defensively. "Taska said you never came back to her house."

"Someone tipped them off about me being there," Anna said tersely as she quickened her pace. "What did Evalds offer you to turn me in?" Then with a sneer, she added, "Comrade."

Anna stepped quickly into a nearby clothing store. Lana followed, saying, "Wait you don't understand." As Anna neared the backdoor, she grabbed a rack of clothing and shoved in Lana's path then ran out the door. Anna ran down the alley and made a turn down another alley. Anna came out onto a side street and ducked into the nearest shop. It was a Variety Shop with lots of high racks and benches. Anna got behind one and pretended to browse a while keeping an eye on both the front and back doors.

After two hours had passed, and neither Lana nor the police had shown, Anna safely assumed that she had given Lana the slip. All during this time, the proprietor, a middle-aged woman, would give Anna a polite smile, but never ask her if she needed assistance. She seemed to sense that Anna was hiding in her shop. Finally Anna moved cautiously near the front door, trying to decide whether she should venture out or not.

The proprietor then spoke for the first time, "It is too early to go out. Come and rest in the back room and I'll make you some tea."

"Thank you," Anna breathed. "Is it near the backdoor?"

"Yes, follow me."

As Anna sat in the back room having her tea, Lana came into the shop. As the room was near the till and the door was slightly open Anna could hear the conversation, as she stood ready to bolt. When Lana asked if anyone matching Anna's description and carrying a large bag had entered the shop, the proprietor denied it. Lana asked what was in the back room and the proprietor lost her temper. "None of your business, now get out of my shop!" She began pushing Lana toward the door. "I'm tired of all you young hooligans running around pretending you are spies for the NKVD. If you think I'm hiding something call the police!"

Lana left the shop and Anna chuckled to herself.

The proprietor went out the backdoor to empty some garbage into a large container out back. Upon returning she said to Anna. "There is no one in the back alley. You should be safe to go now."

"Thank you," Anna breathed. "You have been very kind." Anna hugged her briefly then stepped out into the alley.

After a tiring roundabout journey back, it was dark when Anna stumbled through the backdoor of Jacob's shop. Upon seeing Valdis sitting at the table, she said, "We have to get out of Riga. There are spies everywhere."

Chapter Five

"Anna!" Valdis exclaimed, upon seeing her. "I was afraid they might have picked you up."

"Well, I almost was thanks to Lana," Anna said. She then recounted her rather eventful day, then summed it up saying, "We have to get out of Riga. It is not safe here for me or anyone who hides me."

"Do you think they know you are here?" Golda said apprehensively

"I don't think anyone followed me, but sooner or later we'll be found out. How is your leg mending, Valdis?"

"It is healing quite well," he replied. "I can walk on it without too much pain and the cut doesn't need a dressing any more."

"Good. We should leave Riga tonight, and try and find that farmer who was at the market."

"Tonight!" Jacob exclaimed.

"Yes. They could come any time and I don't want you kind people taken away and possibly shot, for hiding me out," Anna said hurriedly.

"Surely we can have some supper first and use those vegetables you brought," Golda said.

"We can run better with a good meal under our belts." Valdis laughed.

As they ate their supper they talked of long-range plans and Anna said, "I once thought of working my way south through Lithuania, to Germany."

"You can forget that idea," Valdis replied. "It is at least a hundred kilometres to the Lithuanian border and it will be watched. Then we have to cross Lithuania, which is also occupied by the Red Army. The border between Lithuania and East Prussia will be guarded from both sides. We'd never make it."

"So what is your long-range plan? Or do you have one?" Anna asked.

"I thought that if we could hole up on a farm for the winter, they might stop looking for us. Then in spring we could sneak back to Riga and try to get on one of the ships that come to the harbour. That is, if we can find one that is going to Sweden or somewhere in Western Europe. Ultimately, I would still like to get to Canada."

"Still have that dream eh?" Anna grinned.

"When one stops having dreams, one might as well lie down and die." Valdis said philosophically

Then after a moment Anna said, "If you want to catch a ship wouldn't you be better going over to Liepaja or Ventspils? They are ocean ports."

"The Russians have turned the main ports into naval bases and they will be watched carefully," Valdis replied. "We'll have to bide our time and wait for an opportunity." Then after a moment he asked, "If you get out where will you go?"

"I don't know," Anna replied. "Maybe I'll go to Canada too."

"I hope so," Valdis said. "But for now we have to get out of Riga."

Shortly after their late supper, Anna and Valdis prepared to leave. Golda gave Valdis a loaf of bread to take on their journey, and he turned to his hosts saying, "Goodbye and thank you for everything."

"I will never forget your kindness," Anna said, hugging both Jacob and Golda.

It took most of the remainder of the night to make their way out of Riga. Valdis chose to leave Riga from the same point he entered it and dawn was breaking when they reached the edge of the city.

They saw a group of soldiers coming along with shouldered rifles and they quickly ducked behind a hedge.

"Are they looking for us?" Anna wondered fearfully.

"They are probably out on morning exercise." Valdis assured her, "We'll wait until they pass. Once we get behind that clump of trees beside the road, we can hide under a bridge, then plan our next move." Then he added. "The creek bed is dry. I hid there when I came back to Riga."

The group of soldiers marched by and the two fugitives sprang for the clump of trees and dove under the bridge.

After they caught their breath, Valdis pulled out the loaf of bread Golda had given him then broke it in half. Handing Anna her half, he said. "This might be the last meal we'll have for some time."

"Yes. Last year we had homes and families and lived in comfort," Anna swallowed. A large lump grew in her stomach as she thought of her father. "Now we are merely hunted animals."

Valdis laughed bitterly. "Sometimes I feel that we are like rats."

"Father told me never to let them take me, so we must do whatever it takes to survive," Anna said. She put her hand over the locket that was beneath her blouse.

"Lets get moving then," Valdis said, rising. "We'll follow the bed of this stream. The banks are fairly high with tall grass and shrubs along them. If we keep low no one will see us."

They followed the creek bed for many kilometres, stopping to rest in cool shaded areas when the creek bed passed through a wooded area. They continued to follow the creek bed until they reached the Daugava River in the midst of a wooded area. Exhausted and desperately thirsty, they threw themselves in the river bathing in and drinking the clear cold water at the same time. It was such a pleasant experience they laughed as they splashed. This was the first time Anna had really laughed since the Reds had destroyed her family.

When they had their fill, they crawled up on shore soaking wet.

"What are we going to do for clothing?" Valdis wondered. The threadbare set of clothes they wore were the only clothing they had.

"We can strip to our underclothing and hang the other clothing on bushes to dry," Anna suggested as she began to undo her trousers.

"I'd better hide behind some bushes so we won't see each other," Valdis said gravely, looking away from Anna.

"As you wish," Anna said, "but being seen in underclothing is no different than being seen in swimming clothing." She hung her trousers over a bush. "But I do appreciate your suggestion."

"What you say is true, but we talked earlier of keeping our dignity," Valdis replied from behind a dense thicket. Anna turned slightly and saw him hang up his trousers also, though all she could see of his body was his arms. Anna removed her blouse, then her socks and shoes, hanging them all out to dry. She could see Valdis doing the same thing as his clothing went up on bushes.

"Thank you Valdis," Anna said. "I appreciate you being a gentleman."

"I always thought you were a lady," he said from behind the bush. "We should both lay down for a nap while our clothing dries. I think it is quite safe here."

"A good idea," Anna yawned as she lay down on the warm mossy ground. With a laugh she added, "I never thought I'd be sun bathing this way."

"Yeah," Valdis replied, yawning also. "It is such a beautiful, warm, late-summer day."

She felt the locket against her chest and she lifted it. *'Oh dear God I hope it's waterproof'* she realized for the first time that she wore the locket while swimming. She opened it with a desperate hope that the photo of her father hadn't been ruined. *'Thank God it is waterproof,'* she thought with pounding heart.

They slept until early afternoon with Valdis waking first. He checked his clothing and found that they were dry.

"Anna, are you awake?" he called as he began to put his clothing on.

Anna came awake with a start. She had been dreaming of her life before and finding that she was semi naked in the middle of a forest was indeed a rude awakening. She swallowed a deep knot in her stomach at the realization that her pleasant dream was only a dream.

"What did you say, Valdis?" she said as she sat up.

"Our clothing is dry and I'm nearly dressed "

"Uh, okay," Anna said, reaching for her own clothing. "Don't come over here until I tell you."

"I won't. Come over here when you're ready. I have my pants on already."

With all but her footwear on, Anna went around the bush carrying her socks and shoes. It occurred to her just how tattered both their clothing had become from wearing them for days on end without changing or washing them

"You know Valdis, this dip in the river is the first bath I've had since leaving home." she remarked.

Valdis, who was kneeling down, putting on his shoes looked up and smiled.

"I like your hair," he laughed. Anna's long tangled hair was still damp.

"If only I had a comb," she lamented. "If I ever get a chance I'll cut it short."

"If I ever get a chance I'll shave," Valdis said, running his hand over the coarse stubble on his face. The stubble was still patchy because of his youth.

"That is not all," Anna said, as she sat down to put her footwear on. "We will have to find some more clothing soon. The couple of changes I had with me when I left home got lost along the way. This stuff we have on is getting worn and it probably reeks of body odour."

"Yeah, " Valdis remarked. "That will be second priority once we find a safe place to hide."

"Well I'm ready to go now," Anna said, reaching up for Valdis to give her a hand.

He clasped her hand and hoisted her to a standing position and they stood with hands clasped for a long moment. Anna felt a warm tingling feeling, then finally said, "Shouldn't we be going."

"Yes, we should," Valdis said in a dreamy voice, then turned to go, still holding her hand. They walked briefly hand-in-hand until the woods got too dense for them to continue walking side-by-side. They came to a forest trail and walked along it, and, had it not been for the gnawing hunger in their stomachs, they might have enjoyed the pleasant walk through the hardwood forest under spreading oaks and stately linden trees. The trill of many birds made the grim reality of what their country had become seem far away.

After walking along for a while, Valdis said. "Too bad we didn't have a cottage in this forest."

"Yes, with a flower garden out back where I could sit and do nothing but listen to the birds," Anna replied as her pace became slow and leisurely.

"We could have a vegetable garden, and maybe a cow or two in the barn."

"And food," Anna said with her stomach growling. "Bread and fruit on the table with a slab of cheese."

"And ham and sausage," Valdis added. "Oh what I'd give for some *speka piragi*."

He reached for her hand again but their fingers had barely touched when they saw a man driving a horse and cart come around a bend in the trail. He was dressed in rough clothes and his cart carried a load of firewood.

Anna was about to bolt but Valdis grabbed her. "He's only a peasant farmer. He may even help us."

As he drew closer, Anna cried out, "He's the vender at the market who gave me the apple."

They stepped in the road and the man stopped his cart. Feeling confident that the tattered-looking couple were harmless he said, "Are you friends or comrades?"

Anna was uncertain how to answer the question, but Valdis dared say, "We are friends. Friends who are in desperate need of food and shelter."

"You look familiar," the man said to the bedraggled-looking Anna.

"You had a stall at the market in Riga the other day," Anna said anxiously. "You gave me an apple."

"Ah yes, the girl who looked like she lost her best friend." he laughed.

"I did. I lost a lot more than a friend. I lost my whole family."

"What are you doing out here?"

"We had to get out of Riga," Valdis said.

"Is the invitation to visit you still open?" Anna dared ask.

"Running from the Reds, are you?"

"Yes. If they catch us we'll both be shot!" Anna exclaimed

"Have they bothered you?" Valdis asked.

"Not too much," the farmer replied. "They came and searched my place once just to see what I owned then gave me a quota of produce that I have to give to the state."

"What about the produce you sell at the market?"

"That's my own to keep. When I have enough to sell."

"Would you like some help on your farm?" Valdis asked. "We only ask to be fed and have a place to sleep."

"We'll even sleep in your barn," Anna added.

"You might as well climb on the cart. I'll see what we can do for you when we get home."

"Thank you kind sir," Valdis said, as he and Anna climbed on board.

A short while later they arrived at a well-appointed farmstead. The house and other buildings were clustered together in a block that resembled a small fortress. The buildings were made of stone with large thatch roofs.

The farmer, who had since introduced himself as Atis Vagris, took them directly into the house.

His wife, however, regarded them with suspicion as they entered the main room. Anna's heart fell as they saw both a small plaster bust of Lenin and a framed photograph of Stalin on the mantle.

Noting Anna's concern, Atis said to his wife. "You can put them away Astra, these people are friends not comrades. Astra quickly put a shroud over the bust and put the picture in a nearby drawer.

"Anytime someone comes," Atis chuckled, "we get them out in case our visitors are Comrades."

Both Anna and Valdis felt greatly at ease for the first time.

"Astra, Anna and Valdis here will be staying with us for a while to help, but no one must know they are here."

"Hiding from the Reds?" Astra asked with a half smile.

"If they catch us they will shoot us," Anna replied.

"They want to shoot everyone it seems," Astra replied. "Either that or take everything you have. I used to own over a hundred hectares. I was told I could only keep thirty hectares. The state took the rest."

"They took my father in the night and I know they murdered him," Anna said with a pained look in her eye. She sobbed as she added, "they took my mother and sister away to Siberia."

Astra put a sympathetic arm around Anna and eased her down to a chair. "Our own daughter Jelena, who is about your age, disappeared when the Russians came," she added with a note of sadness in her eye.

"We have no way of knowing whether she is dead or alive," Atis added in a morose tone.

"I, along with my family, was on a prison train," Valdis said. "But I jumped off and came back to Latvia."

"You are welcome to hide out here," Astra said, "but our house is small."

"We could sleep in the loft of your barn, at least until winter," Anna said. "We don't want to put you in danger by being here."

"They don't bother us much," Atis said. "As long as we give the state its share of our produce and mind our own business. Besides, if you're an enemy of the Reds, you are a friend of ours."

"Yes Astra. Make a place at the supper table for them while I unload the firewood," Atis said.

"I'll help you," Valdis offered.

"We will gladly help you with whatever chores need to be done," Anna added.

Valdis helped unload the firewood and Anna helped with preparing supper. It was a simple meal of roast chicken and fresh vegetables with cake and tea for dessert. It was the first filling meal that either Anna or Valdis had eaten in some time. The meals that Jacob and Golda provided were sparse in comparison.

About the time they rose from the table, an automobile drove into the yard. There was a tiny red flag on the hood.

"Quickly, you must hide," Astra said. "Go to the pantry. There is an access door to the attic there."

Valdis stole a glance out the window and exclaimed, "Evalds! What is he doing out here?"

As Anna and Valdis went to the pantry, Astra quickly pulled the shroud from the bust and got out the photo of Stalin. Atis went outside both to greet them and to stall them. Valdis lifted Anna up so she could push the trapdoor open and pull herself into the attic. Once there, Valdis jumped up grabbing the edge of the opening. He soon pulled himself into the attic with Anna's help, and pushed the trapdoor shut again and waited.

"Welcome Comrades welcome," Atis said as the two men got out of the car. A uniformed man accompanied Evalds. The uniformed man carried a submachine gun "To what to I owe the pleasure."

"Two reasons," Evalds said. "For one, the state is increasing its quota. We need two more litres of milk and a dozen more eggs a week from you and we will take another calf in the fall."

"But Comrade Commissar, what if the chickens quit laying? Or the cow dries up?"

"If you have problems with the livestock, you will have to prove it to us. Now the second reason. We have reason to believe that one or two criminals may have fled into the country. One, a man named Valdis, escaped from a prison train and killed a soldier, and his accomplice is a woman named Anna, who is a dangerous agitator."

"Do you think they might come this way?" Atis asked, feigning concern.

"It is possible. Do you mind if we check your buildings, Citizen Vagris?"

"By all means comrade. I haven't been out to the barn yet this evening and if there are criminals in there, you're better equipped to deal with them than I."

Evalds spoke to his companion in uniform, and the man in uniform then headed for the barn. Evalds also brought a machine-gun out of the car but stood in the middle of the yard. This all gave time for Astra to clean up the table and hide the extra dishes used by their guests lest the Comrades come into the house.

Evalds lit a cigarette as he stood in the middle of the yard and thought about his situation. He was supposed to be an assistant commissar, sitting behind a desk helping to organize Latvia as a Soviet republic.

Instead he was out here chasing after enemies of the state, all because of his superior's strange obsession with capturing Anna. Now that rumour had it Valdis was back, they were probably teamed up and the search had been widened to the area surrounding Riga, just in case they had fled the city. Evalds disliked Valdis and was somewhat jealous of his closeness to Anna. Thus, he felt he'd have little trouble arresting Valdis and seeing to his execution if necessary. He still felt ill at ease about capturing Anna and, when the inevitable occurred, he hoped he would not be part of her interrogation or execution.

A burst of machine-gun fire could be heard from the barn loft. Evalds stood poised with his own machine-gun, while Anna and Valdis cringed in the attic. The uniformed man came to the opening at the end of the loft and said, "Just making sure no one is hiding in the straw."

The uniformed man came back from his search and announced he could see no evidence of anyone having been in the barn.

"What about in your house?" Evalds said, eyeing Atis suspiciously.

"Search it if you wish," Atis said evenly. "If they broke in I think either Astra or I would have known about it."

"We'll look anyway," Evalds said, as he and the uniformed man headed for the house, still carrying their machine-guns.

Astra opened the door for them but remained expressionless as they entered. The two men walked through the house. They even went into the bedroom and poked through a closet. They opened the cellar door and clamored down the stairs with flashlights in hand. When they emerged, Evalds said, "You have plenty of preserves and root crops down there, perhaps the state should up its quota from you."

"We always give all we can," Atis said. They noticed he glanced at the picture on the mantle that Astra had quickly gotten out when they had arrived at the farm. "We know that Comrade Stalin wants everyone to share. Long Live Stalin."

"Yes, our glorious leader is working very hard in creating a new world for us," Evalds said. "Well we will leave you now and come back in a few days. Especially if those two criminals haven't been caught yet."

"Yes, please do," Astra said. "We have no way to protect ourselves except with a pitchfork and garden shovel."

"Use them if you have to," Evalds laughed, "but the NKVD wants them alive. Especially Anna."

It was about a half-hour after the two officials left before Astra tapped on the trapdoor so their guests could come back down.

"So they say you are a murderer," Atis said, as Valdis helped Anna out of the attic.

"The soldier's death was accidental," Valdis insisted. "If I wanted to intentionally kill someone, it would be a traitor like that Evalds who was just here."

"And they say you are a dangerous agitator," he said to Anna.

"I defied the rules," Anna said. "I didn't vote, and I used to write articles in my father's newspaper warning of the dangers of a Soviet takeover of our country."

"They hunt you for that?" Astra questioned.

"Who knows what their reasons are, but they want you alive," Atis said

"They want us alive so they can torture us for information." Valdis said.

"Are you going to turn us in?" Anna asked.

"It's too late now. We are already guilty for not handing you over when they were here." Astra laughed.

"Yes, we'll probably all be at the same firing squad someday." Atis sighed.

"So do you think Comrade Stalin is building a brave new world," Valdis laughed

"If there is anyone left in it after he finishes killing everyone." Atis added dryly.

"So now that they have finished searching the loft, it should be safe for Anna and I to make our living quarters there."

"There is plenty of straw from which you can make yourselves comfortable, and I'll get you a horse blanket for a mattress." Atis said.

That night as they lay side-by-side on the blanket in the barn loft, Anna remarked, "The straw is quite comfortable."

"Yes. It is a lot more comfortable than the warehouse floors and alleyways of Riga." Valdis replied.

" It is almost like a feather bed." Anna said in a dreamy voice.

"One day I'm going to sleep in a real feather bed," Valdis said emphatically. "One day, when I get to Canada, I'm going to be rich. Never again will I go hungry or be hunted by the police."

"Yes, Canada," Anna sighed. "That far away land, where they say everything is peaceful and beautiful."

They were silent for a long moment then Valdis said, "Think of how in a different time and place we could be man and wife."

"Yes, in a different time and place," Anna sighed. "For now we are hunted like animals and cannot afford the luxury of love."

"Even though we are hunted, it cannot hide feelings." Valdis continued.

Anna shifted and looked him in the eye. "I love you as a brother she said firmly, I dare not see it any other way. We must not see it any other way."

"Yes, sister," he said dolefully and withdrew his arm.

"I am sorry Valdis. Fate has thrown us together and if we both survive all of this, maybe there will be a time for us. But I don't want to lose you like I lost Father and the rest of my family."

"You'd feel nothing if they shot me or sent me away to Siberia?" Valdis said anxiously.

"I don't want to think about that," Anna said sharply. "Lets think about how we can survive and help these kind people who gave us their loft. Father said 'don't let them take you.' and that should be your motto too." She rolled over turning her back to him

"Yes Anna," Valdis sighed. "I will say this only once. I love you."

Anna wanted to return the phrase, but knew she must place survival and escape foremost in her mind. "Goodnight Valdis," she replied gently. She reached back and squeezed his hand for a moment.

Chapter Six

Anna and Valdis lived the winter in the loft. They bored tunnels in the straw, shored them with boards, and even made a straw door that worked well enough to fool periodic searches by the patrols. Atis collaborated with many of his neighbours in resisting the food searches, and he was also able to secure extra clothing for Anna and Valdis. The winter was cold and as it wore on the state kept increasing its quota of Atis's produce. By late winter he had barely enough food for the four of them. It was fortunate that they lived in the country so Atis and Valdis were able to snare rabbits to supplement their meat diet. The commissars had calculated how much food was needed to feed two people, and that was all Atis was allowed to keep. They hid some of the vegetables in the straw hideout in the loft, and Atis could argue, with some truth, egg production was down because the hens didn't lay as much during winter. By spring, the commissar suspected that he was holding out and more searches were conducted. The attic was even searched. Valdis and Anna spent a lot of time out in the wood lot outside the building area during the day so as to have a better chance of hiding when the commissars made their visits. In late spring the commissars backed off to allow Atis to use his meagre resources for spring planting, a chore in which Anna and Valdis helped. During the planting, Astra would serve as lookout, lest the Comrades, as Atis called all government officials, show up.

On the morning of June fourteenth a neighbour dropped by. As he was a trusted friend, Anna and Valdis joined them for tea.

"Good morning Rojs," Atis said as his neighbour arrived. "Something is troubling you."

"Yes. As you know my place is beside the main railway line leading to the Soviet Union." Rojs said, wearing a disturbed look.

"Yes," Atis replied.

"Well, when I was outside tending my animals, I saw a train go by and most of the cars were cattle cars. However, the cars were full of people."

"Oh my God," Anna said.

"It is beginning," Rojs said. "There have been rumours of deportations for months. People have been disappearing at an increasing rate. Last week the local school teacher disappeared and the night before last so did the postmaster of the village."

"My mother and sister were deported last summer," Anna added with a pained look.

"My parents were along with them and so was I, but I escaped," Valdis said. "But there were only two cattle cars full of people on that train."

"This is mass deportation," Rojs said gravely. "There have been rumours of lists being drawn up for some time now."

"Our *Glorious* Comrade Stalin wants to destroy Latvia," Atis spat.

"I'm afraid so," Rojs replied.

"Maybe we should get out of here," Valdis said to Anna. "We are a danger to these kind people."

"No, stay." Atis said. "If we are on a list, they will come and get us whether you are here or not."

"Our best hope is that the Germans will invade," Anna said soberly. "They can't possibly be any worse than what we have now. Every day we live in terror of a police raid."

"Yes that would seem our best hope," Atis reiterated. "No one else will help us."

"The Nazis have a peace pact with Stalin though," Valdis added.

"Well we can always hope." Astra added.

The deportation trains continued to roll and by the end of the next week, Rojs had also disappeared. Atis was so enraged upon hearing the news that day that he picked up the plaster bust of Lenin, which Astra had not yet put away and smashed it against the hearthstones. He grabbed the picture of Stalin and was about to do the same, but Astra stopped him.

"We need these things for when the Comrades come around."

"Put it away then," Atis said, handing the picture to her. "Long live Stalin indeed. May he burn in hell."

"I'm sure he will," Valdis added.

As Astra placed it in a drawer, Anna said, "We will have to leave here. Sooner or later an informer will notice our presence here and we've had too many close calls already."

"We would hate to see you get sent to Siberia or get shot for hiding us," Valdis said. "If we go now while they still think you are good comrades, you may survive and survive well."

"Where will you go?" Atis wondered.

"Back to Riga," Anna said.

Valdis gave her a curious look and Astra said worriedly, "Won't that be dangerous? The Reds are probably still looking for you."

"True, but since I haven't been there for nearly a year they might not be looking as hard as before. My hope is to steal on board one of the ships that come to the harbour and get away to Western Europe. Do you remember, we talked of doing this before. If things have cooled down, we can probably hide out with the Jewish couple that helped us before."

"The Nazis control all of Western Europe, except Sweden and Britain."

"Well, if we can find a ship that is going to Sweden, or even Finland where my brother is."

"I wouldn't go to Finland," Valdis said. "They may have beat back the Soviets once, but if our 'Glorious Leader' wants Finland," he said through gritted teeth, "he will eventually take it."

"Well, we can try for Sweden," Anna said hopefully.

"Like the old saying goes, you'll be jumping from the frying pan into the fire," Atis added

"Well, we are running from the comrades, wherever we go, so why not go to Riga at least for the summer." Valdis said. "How far is Riga from here?"

"About thirty kilometres," Atis replied.

"If we leave now, we might get there by late evening," Valdis said.

"It never gets really dark this time of year," Astra said.

"We can wait under the bridge until dusk, then we should be able to slip into the city unnoticed," Valdis said. Then smiling at Anna, he added, "Without assaulting them,"

"The sun barely goes down this time of year though," Anna worried.

"Well, if we have to wait for midnight or later, so-be-it," Valdis said

"Let's go then," Anna said, anxious to get on the road. "Every moment we delay increases the chance that we'll be discovered. Then all of us will go to the firing squad."

"Let me make you an early dinner first," Astra said. "At least have one meal here and I'll make you a lunch to take with you. Who knows when you'll eat again?"

"Since we never really had a chance to celebrate *Jani*[1] properly we can do it tonight, although we are a week late."

"I have some cheese hidden away, and wine," Astra said excitedly.

"I will go out in the woods and gather some oak boughs to make us each a *Janu Vainags*," Valdis added enthusiastically.

"Do we dare light a bonfire?" Anna wondered. "Or would it attract the Comrades?"

"Maybe we should not push our luck," Astra said cautiously.

"After our celebration, we could start out this evening and if we don't get to Riga tonight, we can sleep in the woods," Valdis said. "At least if we are away from here when the Comrades come back, no harm should come to Atis and Astra."

"True," Anna added. "The evenings are warm and sleeping in the woods will be little different from sleeping in the loft."

They rejoiced at the supper table as Astra provided the very best from the resources at hand, as their meal included homemade cheese and wine, while everyone wore their oak wreaths on their heads. They toasted and reminisced their winter of hiding and to the hope of escape. After dinner, Astra made them a large lunch consisting of a loaf of bread, a chunk of cheese, and two hard-boiled eggs for each of them.

As they said their tearful farewells in the yard, they could hear a rumble in the south that sounded like distant thunder.

"Is there a storm coming?" Anna wondered.

"It doesn't look like it," Valdis said. They all looked around and the sky was perfectly clear.

"Maybe the Comrades are having artillery practice," Atis said. "The sounds of cannons in the distance is like thunder."

"We'd better get going," Anna said, "lest some of the Comrades come here."

In early evening, Anna and Valdis were on their way, still wearing their *Janu Vainags*. Valdis joked that the head covering would serve as camouflage. They hiked along country trails, sometimes taking shortcuts across fields and woodlands, angling toward Riga. They made much better time than they did on their journey away from Riga. The

[1] *Jani* – a midsummer festival also known as *ligo svetki*

rumble of thunder in the south seemed to grow louder and since there was still no evidence of clouds, they concluded that it must be artillery practice. As dusk overtook them, Anna and Valdis stopped in a densely wooded area near to where they swam in the river that time to hole up for the night. They decided to rest up and have their full strength the next day before trying to steal back into the city. They were surprised that the rumble in the south continued on during the night.

The thunder was still with them when they awoke the following morning. It was growing louder and spreading to the east as well. There also seemed to be the drone of many aircraft in the distance. "It is strange that the cannons are still firing," Anna said.

"Yes, but maybe it is something else." Valdis wondered. "It sounds like there is also machine gun fire in the distance."

They just finished eating the food that Astra had given them for breakfast when they heard the sounds of approaching airplanes. They quickly put the wreaths on and climbed into a nearby oak tree to hide among the foliage. Two airplanes passed low overhead. The under-side of the wings bore Maltese Crosses, and a swastika could be seen on the tail fin.

"They are German airplanes," Valdis said. "The swastika is a Nazi symbol."

"What are the Germans doing here?" Anna wondered.

"They are invading," Valdis said excitedly. "That sound of thunder in the south must be the sounds of Russian and German cannons firing at each other. I don't think you'll have to worry much about the Comrades looking for us. They will be too busy."

They resumed their hike trying to stay as close as possible to wooded areas. The drone of many airplanes could be heard as they flew over at a much higher level. They watched one airplane go into a steep dive, making a terrifying wailing sound as it did so. It dropped a bomb and climbed back up as steeply as it dove.

"Studkas," Valdis said, as the bomb dropped by the airplane ex-ploded a few kilometres away. "I read about how the *Luftwaffe* has Studka dive-bombers as part of its arsenal." Valdis was growing visibly excited, as a battlefield seemed to be slowly enveloping them. As they came near a roadway, they heard the sound of vehicles and horses coming down the road. They watched from a dense thicket on the side of the road as a large contingent of Red Army troops was moving rapidly to the north.

"Look at that," Valdis cried. The Red Army is running from the Germans. He grabbed Anna and hugged her.

"You seem awfully excited," Anna said laughing.

"So I should be! The Germans are liberating Latvia from the Russians. Let's get going."

"Yes, to live again without looking over my shoulder," Anna said, also becoming excited as the gravity of the situation sunk in.

Their pace was brisk as they headed for Riga. They came across a large open area of farmland. It was alive with military action. Several army tanks bearing the swastika emblem raced across the fields ploughing through fences as if they didn't exist. Soldiers on motorcycles swept along the roads followed by truckloads of soldiers. Some of the trucks were towing cannons. Many soldiers on foot poured over the fields with rifles ready. They wore trim olive-coloured uniforms and coal scuttle-shaped helmets. It was truly fascinating to watch this very professional army move with such precision over the countryside. Several soldiers went by them, apparently unconcerned by the two civilian spectators. One of them spoke to Anna in German, and Anna answered.

"What did he say?" Valdis asked. Unlike Anna, he had virtually no knowledge of German.

"He told us to stay out of the way so we won't get hurt."

"That was considerate of them." Valdis said. "We must be witnessing what they call a *Blitz Krieg*."

"It means lightning war," Anna said.

"They used it to conquer Poland in less than a month, and Western Europe in less than six weeks." Valdis was fascinated with the German army.

Anna and Valdis continued to boldly move toward Riga in the open, following in the wake of the German invasion force. At one point they witnessed a contingent of German soldiers herding a group of weary-looking Red Army troops to the south as prisoners.

"Now there's a pleasant sight to see," Valdis grinned as he watched the procession.

"If only the Germans would had come two years ago," Anna lamented. "Father would still be alive and Mother and Liesma would still be in Riga."

Maybe the Germans will conquer the Soviet Union and my parents and your mother will be found and set free."

"Wouldn't that be wonderful," Anna added, as they walked along the road with a new spring in their step.

Truck load after truck load of German soldiers went by them along with groups of soldiers mounted on motorcycles. Large numbers of airplanes roared overhead and the hair-raising sounds of Studkas in action could be heard everywhere. Other airplanes strafed retreating Red Army troops with machine-gun fire.

By late morning they were within sight of Riga. The city seemed surrounded by German troops with their cannons pointed inward at the city.

"Do we dare get closer," Anna wondered.

"Why not," Valdis said bravely. "The Germans aren't looking for us. They are our liberators. If they stop us you can explain, since you know how to speak German."

As they cautiously approached the German positions, a voice cried out from behind in harsh German, "Halt, put your hands up!"

Anna and Valdis froze and stretched their hands up high.

The soldier, bearing an automatic rifle, came around to face them. "What are you doing here? He demanded. "This is a restricted area."

"We are trying to get to Riga," Anna explained innocently.

"Riga is not secured yet," he said as another soldier came upon them.

"Search them," the first soldiers said.

"We are unarmed," Anna said as the soldier ran his hands quickly over their bodies."

"How do we know you are not working with the Red Army?" the soldiers demanded.

"We hate the Red Army," Anna said. "We welcome you as liberators."

"What about you," the soldiers demanded of Valdis.

Valdis, who didn't understand, nonetheless said out of desperation, "Heil Hitler."

"He can't speak German," Anna explained.

"He knows the right words at least," the soldiers laughed.

"What is going on here?" another voice asked. A man, obviously an officer, with his high peaked cap, tall boots and riding breaches walked up to them.

The two soldiers froze at attention and the first one answered. "Sir, we found these two civilians coming from the rear."

The officer walked up to Anna and Valdis and regarded them with a cold arrogance, then turned to the soldiers. "Were they armed?"

"No sir," the second solider answered smartly. "I searched them myself, sir."

"So, why are you sneaking up behind our army?" the officer demanded.

"We were trying to get to Riga, sir," Anna replied.

"Why do you want to go to Riga?"

"I was hoping to find a way to escape from the Reds by sea."

"Escape is quite impossible."

"There is now no need to escape as you have liberated our country from the Soviets," Anna replied.

"I see. And you?" he said turning to Valdis.

"*Jawohl, Herr...*[2]" Valdis said trying to find the right words with his limited knowledge of German.

"Is that all you can say," the officer said.

"He does not speak German," Anna interjected.

"But you do," the office turned to her.

"Before the war I studied German. I thought of going to Germany for my university training." As Anna's arms grew weary she began to slowly lower them

"Well I don't think that will be possible any time soon," the officer laughed.

"May we be allowed to go into Riga?" Anna persisted. She dared to let her hands slowly drop but no one challenged her. Valdis cautiously followed suit.

"I will let you pass, but it is at your own risk," the officer said. "If you get shot by a Red Army sniper, or get hit with one of our artillery shells don't say we didn't warn you."

Anna and Valdis were allowed through the German lines and made their way into the city. As they cautiously walked through the streets of Riga, the city seemed deserted.

"Everyone must be hiding," Anna mused.

"Yes. Even the patrols are gone, hopefully the Red Army has deserted the place, but we should stick close to the alleyways in case we have to run for it."

As they carefully worked their way through the city, they could

---

[2] *Jawohl Herr* – Yes surely, sir. The correct way to address a superior in the German military

hear the occasional explosion of an artillery shell though none fell near them. Occasionally a low-flying aircraft would pass overhead, no doubt looking for Red Army holdouts. Late afternoon found them in the midst of a residential district footsore and weary.

"Let's stop and rest a while," Anna said. "There doesn't seem to be any patrols around."

"Yes, I've never seen Riga so deserted-looking," Valdis observed. Then, with a laugh he added, "The Reds have probably all run away."

"We should see if we can find some food. I'm starving," Anna said, putting her hand on her stomach.

"Yes, we should get rested and have a full stomach when the Germans arrive, so we can better cope with how they plan to run things."

"Let's try one of these houses." Anna suggested. "If there is anyone at home, perhaps they'll give us something to eat. If the house is empty perhaps we can find some food left behind."

They carefully checked out a nearby house and found it deserted. Inside they found a well-stocked larder that included a few bottles of wine. In the living room they found some Party literature and other paraphernalia including large photos of both Lenin and Stalin.

"This house was used by a Party official," Anna scoffed.

"Then we shouldn't feel guilty about eating any of the food left behind," Valdis laughed.

That evening in the abandoned house they dined on bread cheese and Georgian wine, while they laughed as they burned the Communist Party literature in the fireplace.

"Burn in hell you bastard," Valdis laughed as he tossed the photo of Stalin into the fire.

"You too," Anna added as she tossed the photo of Lenin into the fire beside it. The red flag with the Hammer-and-Sickle that was pinned on the wall followed the photos into the fire, while Anna and Valdis finished the bottle of wine rejoicing at their own private destruction of communism. That night they passed-out, in drunken bliss on a big bed in a nearby room. The following morning, after a hearty breakfast of bread and honey from the larder, they resumed their trek to the city centre, but the streets of Riga were still deathly quiet.

They were nearly at Cathedral Square when several low flying German warplanes passed overhead. Anna and Valdis stepped into an alleyway near the square and watched warily. The roar of motorcycles could be heard as dozens of mounted German troops raced through the streets. Several battle tanks also converged on the square and a phalanx of German soldiers marched down *Bivibas Bulvaris* in tight formation stepping high as the clomp, clomp, clomp of their heavy boots could be heard on the pavement. People suddenly began to pour out of the buildings cheering wildly as the German troops marched by. Some even threw garlands of flowers. Roses were stuffed in pockets and rifle barrels by well-wishers. Anna and Valdis joined the mobs, cheering on their deliverers from harsh Soviet rule. They were surrounding the marching troops and the tanks that rumbled into Cathedral Square. One zealous group of civilians pulled down the giant portrait of Stalin and tore it to shreds often spitting on the pieces. As several hundred troops converged on the square a group of shiny, black, open topped, limousines drove up. They were full of officers. Some army trucks also arrived delivering a large group of uninformed men with round, peaked hats, who then spread out through the crowds. As some of them passed near to Anna, she noticed that they had armbands bearing swastika and had twin lightning bolt insignia on their collars. The officers among them wore black uniforms and a death's-head badges on their caps.

"Don't cross them," Valdis said quietly. "They are the SS. They are auxillary police who specialize in torture."

A group of German officers including two stone-faced SS officers climbed into the back of a large flatbed truck using it as a podium. A Public Address system was set up and a high-ranking officer addressed the crowd in German, while another translated into Latvian.

"Today we liberate your country from the Soviet beast. We liberated Lithuania yesterday and tomorrow we will liberate Estonia." Wild cheering interrupted his speech. "Soon our mighty *Wehrmacht*[3] will destroy the dark armies of communism. Our Fuehrer has declared that the Russian beast is to be destroyed." He raised his right hand in a stiff-armed salute and cried, "*Heil Hitler, Sieg Heil.*"

All of the soldiers and SS men raised their arms in similar salute chanting the phrase *Sieg Hiel* over and over again. Some Latvian civilians also joined in.

"What does *Sieg Heil* mean, Anna?" Valdis asked.

"It means hail victory" Anna replied.

Valdis raised his arm in stiff salute and also cried "*Sieg Heil.*"

[3] *Wehrmacht* – a term for the regular German army.

When the chanting died down, the speaker cried out, *"Achtung."* All of the uniformed men snapped to rigid attention. Two officers took down the red hammer-and-sickle flag of communism from the flagpole in the square and handed it to some civilians nearby where it was promptly torn to shreds. The soldiers remained at rigid attention as a new flag was raised. Anna noted that it was not the flag of free Latvia, but was a rust coloured flag with a circle containing a swastika in its centre.

"We did not get our freedom," Anna said dryly. "We just acquired new conquerors."

The officer then addressed the crowd again. "Because Latvia is such a small country our Fuehrer has taken it into the protective custody of the Third Reich, and you will now be required to serve our Fuehrer and the Reich as subjects. Everyone will have to register at the office to be set up near this square and everyone will have to seek gainful employment. All young men will be asked to join the *Wehrmacht*, or the reconstituted Latvian Army so you can help us crush the Red Army and destroy the Bolshevik monster for all time." Wild cheering erupted from the crowds as his words were translated.

Chapter Seven

Anna and Valdis lingered in the square listening to the new edicts being issued. Valdis remarked, "At least they don't require us to have passports, yet."

"In some way though, I fear they may be just as bad as the Reds," Anna added.

"In many ways I suppose they are," Valdis said. "What do you plan to do?"

"I will lie low and wait to see how the Nazis plan to run things," Anna replied. "I hope there is a way to work with them as I am tired of hiding."

"Since they are fighting the Reds and we are declared enemies of the Reds, that should put us on the same side as the Nazis," Valdis replied.

"If we are stopped by the SS we can tell them we are enemies of the Reds and welcome the Nazis as our liberators," Anna added

"At least that will be an honest answer," Valdis laughed.

. "Meanwhile let us go over to Taska's house." Anna suggested. " I hid there one night from the Reds. Her mother is understanding and will give us shelter and advice."

"Lead the way," Valdis grinned.

When they arrived at Taska's place, they found the house dark and with the front door kicked in. Anna went inside calling Taska's name, disregarding the obvious. The house had been stripped of all furniture. It appeared to have been abandoned for some time.

"They've moved," Anna said limply.

"Or they've been deported." Valdis said gravely.

"The deportation trains Rojs talked about. Oh no. Poor Taska," Anna felt tears well up in her eyes with the realization that this could very well be her friend's fate. Valdis put a consoling arm around her.

"Taska was a dear friend," Anna sobbed, "She and her mother hid me out at great risk to themselves and I nearly was caught because Lana squealed. Oh, I hate Lana."

"Come let's get out of here," Valdis said gently as he guided her out of the house.

"Where will we go?" Anna said weakly.

"Perhaps to our old house, or yours. We can hole up there and gather our wits before going to register with the Nazis."

"Whatever you say," Anna said, "but the memories will be painful."

"To deal with the future, one must face the past," Valdis said with an air of great wisdom as he lead her out the door.

They had gone a few blocks when a female voice called out from behind. They turned and saw Lana running up to them.

Anna, Valdis, wait," she gasped.

"What do you want?" Anna said coldly.

"Wait, you don't understand." Lana had a tone of desperation in her voice.

"Where is Taska?" Anna demanded.

"Her family was deported on the thirteenth of June. The night of the mass deportation to Siberia." Lana said with a frightened voice.

"You turned them in," Anna sneered. "Just like you squealed on my staying there that night."

"You don't understand. They made me be an informer," Lana said, sobbing. "They said they'd kill my mother if I didn't cooperate, but I had nothing to do with Taska's family being selected for deportation."

"So why don't you run to Evalds, since you were his friend before."

"They arrested him just after the Nazis captured Riga. All the senior Party members fled with the Red Army, but Evalds and a few of the lower ranking members got left behind."

"Why didn't they arrest you?" Anna asked coldly.

"I'm not a Party member," Lana said. "I hate the Party, I hate what they made me do. Especially after seeing Taska's family being taken away." Lana began crying with shame and guilt.

"What do you want with us?" Valdis said.

"I'm afraid," Lana sobbed. "I have nowhere to go. They deported my mother and brother also."

"Why don't you go to the Gestapo? They, no doubt, employ informers," Anna said unfeelingly. "After what you have done, I can never trust you as a friend. I never want to see you again. And if I ever suspect you following me, I will tell the SS that you are a communist. Come let's go Valdis." Anna turned her back on the distraught Lana and they walked away.

"You were a bit harsh were you not?" Valdis said as they continued on down the street.

"She betrayed us," Anna said flatly. "Because of her, Taska is somewhere in Siberia suffering, if she is even still alive. She has probably squealled on many people by now. She would turn us in, in a moment and I wouldn't be at all surprised if she does become an informer for the Gestapo."

"We'll have to watch out for her then," Valdis said gravely.

As they continued along their way, the long summer evening enveloped them, it seemed that the Nazis were taking advantage of the long daylight in their ceaseless activities to secure control of Riga. Their vehicles were everywhere going up and down the streets.

A truck carrying SS men stopped at a house down the street and they poured out and entered the house without knocking. Soon a man and woman with two children were brought out of the house at gunpoint. When the man wanted to know why, an SS officer coldly informed him that his family was being relocated, as all Jews were being placed in the same part of the city. As they continued down the street, another Jewish family whom Valdis recognized as the Goldsteins was being rousted out of their house in the next block.

"Are they rounding up Jews?" Anna asked in a concerned tone.

"Yes. The Nazis hate Jews," Valdis added.

Oh my God! Jacob and Golda," Anna started to go pale, "we must get to them and warn them."

"I wouldn't go there," Valdis cautioned.

"After all they've done for us," Anna said firmly. "We owe it to them to try."

Valdis stopped in his tracks, "Anna don't be foolish."

"Well, I am going to help them even if you're not." Anna turned and headed toward the part of the city where Jacob and Golda lived. Reluctantly Valdis followed her.

When they arrived at the street where Jacob had his shop, they found the SS depositing Jews here from all over Riga and non-Jewish families were being moved out. This area was designated as a Jewish ghetto. Regular army troops had cordoned off the area but Anna and Valdis were still able to see what was going on. SS men were going from house to house and shop to shop, smashing windows and kicking in doors. A harsh voice over a loudspeaker was demanding that everyone come out into the main street that ran through the area. A group of SS men smashed in the doors of the Synagogue and herded out, at gunpoint, a group of frightened women, children and old men who had been praying within. Some SS men stayed behind and Anna could hear an orgy of smashing as they desecrated the Jewish temple, while the growing but terrified crowd looked on. Anna let out a gasp of fear as she saw Jacob and Golda among them. Gold chalices and other objects used in worship were confiscated, and sacred Torah and Talmud scrolls were thrown on the street and one SS man bent down with a cigarette lighter to set them ablaze. A trembling Rabbi begged them not to destroy the sacred scrolls and as he bent down to retrieve them, he was kicked in the face with a heavy boot and sent sprawling. The scrolls were set ablaze and the Rabbi started weeping.

"Now!" said the harsh voice of an SS officer over the loudspeaker. "You Jews are the dregs of the Earth and the bloodsuckers of civilization. For that, you will be treated like the parasites that you are. All of you will sew a yellow Star of David on your coats and shirts. If you are caught on the streets without this emblem of your shame, you will be shot on sight. We know who you are. If you should venture out of this area without permission, you will also be shot on sight."

Anna ran to one of the guards and cried, "Why are you doing this? What have these people done?"

"They are Jews," he said coldly. "This should not concern you."

"Some of these people are my friends, they helped me hide from the Reds." Anna continued.

"Anna keep your mouth shut," Valdis cried desperately.

"Jews have no friends except other Jews," the guard said in his cold flat voice.

Two SS men and an officer came upon the scene wearing their usual grim looks.

"What is going on here," the officer demanded.

"This woman says the Jews are her friends."

"Is that so," the officer said, glowering at Anna. "Are you a Jew?"

"No," Anna quivered.

"If you are not a Jew then no Jew is your friend."

"But one Jewish couple there helped me," Anna continued.

Valdis cautioned her to be quiet.

"Jews don't help anyone but themselves," the officer said harshly. "May I see proof of your ethnic background?"

"I-I lost my papers. I am a Latvian hunted by the Reds," Anna stammered.

"Indeed, and you?" he said harshly to Valdis.

"The NKVD confiscated mine sir," he trembled.

"Take them in for interrogation."

They were grabbed firmly by two SS men and put in the back of a truck and one of them climbed in to stand guard with an automatic rifle.

"Now you've done it, Anna," Valdis said morosely. "We might have been able to survive under German rule. Now we'll be lucky if we don't get shot."

"I couldn't bear to watch Jacob and Golda being treated like animals for no reason." Anna replied.

"I know. I felt for them too."

"Why do the Nazis hate the Jews so much?" Anna asked.

"Who knows," Valdis shrugged. "A lot of people hate Jews."

"Silence!" the guard yelled, pointing his rifle at them. It bothered him that he couldn't understand Anna and Valdis as they were speaking in Latvian.

At the SS headquarters, Anna and Valdis were booked and taken away to the basement. They were put in a large cell. It was one of two cells in the basement that contained a large number of terrified people.

After a time Anna heard a hoarse and painful voice call her name from the other cell. She looked across and stopped short at the sight of Evalds. It was evident from the scars and bruises on his face that he had been beaten.

"Anna!" he cried with a painful smile.

"What do you want with me, traitor?" Anna spat, then she turned her head away.

"What does it matter? We are on the same side now."

"We'll never be on the same side as Communist scum like you," Valdis sneered.

"Trying to be friends with Nazis didn't help you either," Evalds continued.

"I'd rather be a Nazi than a Communist any day," Anna interjected. She noticed that the guards were paying close attention to the conversation.

"We have to stick together," Evalds pleaded.

"I don't want to talk to that traitor any more," Anna said as she turned away again. Valdis led her to a far corner of the cell where they could no longer see Evalds.

"Anna, put in a good word for me when they question you?" Evalds begged. "I did let you escape that night they took your mother and sister."

Anna wanted to argue that he was in on the arrest and probably saw to both their deportation and the later deportation of Taska, but she held her tongue and buried her head in Valdis's shoulder.

A while later, a small group of SS men came into the cell-block and unlocked the cell containing Evalds. "All of you Communist swine come with us," he barked

The entire contingent from the other cell was marched upstairs. Shortly thereafter they heard the sound of rapid gunfire. Anna clung to Valdis in fear. Even though Evalds was a traitor in her mind, she had known him all her life and his apparent execution left a painful knot in her stomach.

They were left there overnight and spent it huddled in a corner. Throughout the night the guards would take someone away, probably for interrogation. None returned, although they didn't hear any more gunfire outside the cells.

At dawn two guards came and opened the cell door. Chunks of dark bread were thrown at the prisoners and each got some thin watery soup issued in a tin cup. Anna and Valdis like most prisoners were starving and ate greedily. A short while later two guards came again, pointing at both Valdis and Anna. One of them said, "Come with me."

Anna and Valdis were taken upstairs. Upon approaching the door-way of their apparent interrogation room, one of the guards opened the door and they were literally shoved in, tripped as they were shoved so that they would fall on their faces. The two guards entered and stood on either side of the door like statues, but with rifles ready. As Anna and Valdis looked up in terror from their prone positions an SS officer in shiny black boots that came up to his knees strode over to them and scowled down with contempt. He held a riding crop with both hands the crop was bent around his backside. It appeared that he was ready to strike them with the slightest provocation. He towered over them huge and terrible and his face bore a cold sneer. Anna trembled at the sight of the skull-and-crossbones insignia on the cap of his black uniform.

'Anna, you must not let them take you,' echoed her fathers words. She could feel the locket on her chest but dared not touch it.

"I suppose neither of you can speak German," he said in heavily accented Latvian.

Valdis shook his head and Anna held her tongue.

"The pair of you are very fortunate," he continued in a measured voice. "Normally I would have simply had you taken out and shot. That may well still be your fate in the end, if I am not satisfied with this interrogation. However, for now, I am curious about you and why you seem to sympathetic to the Jews."

Both Anna and Valdis swallowed hard.

He nudged Valdis with his boot and said, "What is your name?"

"Valdemars Zirnis, sir." Valdis replied quickly.

"And you?" The officer said, nudging Anna in a similar manner.

"Anna Lindenbergis, Comrade Officer," Anna blurted.

The riding crop struck her sharply across the buttocks and she cried out in pain.

"You will not address me or any German officer by that communist term again," he cried harshly and struck her several more times as Anna cowered to protect her face.

"I am sorry *Herr Kapitan*," she gasped. Although Anna was uncertain of his rank she felt that calling him Captain would show proper respect. "I was so used to addressing *them* that way."

"Better," he said. He regarded her for a moment and said, "Are you a Jew?"

"No." Anna said rolling over to face him.

"Why do you say you have friends that are Jews?"

"A Jewish family helped me hide from the Reds at great risk to themselves."

"That is unusual. Jews don't help anyone but themselves. There must have been another reason."

"I can think of none, sir."

"Where did you go to school?"

Anna gave the name of her school in Riga

"And church?"

Anna gave the name of the Lutheran church in which she was baptized. For the first time Anna noticed a clerk in the background. The clerk appeared to be going through a file. Anna wondered if the Nazis had collected the files that the NKVD had on her and Valdis.

"The Reds may have destroyed my records, sir" Anna blurted in German.

The officer turned to her with a sharp eye and said in German, "So, you can speak German. Why didn't you say so before?"

"Valdis can't speak German and since you can speak Latvian, I let matters be." Anna answered in German.

"I see." He regarded her coldly for a moment and continued. "Why did you learn to speak German?"

"German is required in school for those of us who wish to go on to university."

"Indeed. What were you planning to study?"

"To be a doctor."

He laughed and continued, "An unusual trade for a woman is it not?"

"Not in Latvia, sir," Anna said. "Although my father…"

"And your father is?" the officer said, cutting her off.

"Was, Andris Lindenbergis. The Reds murdered him, sir."

"And the rest of your family?"

"They took my mother and sister Liesma away to Siberia. And my brother Karlis is in Finland."

"I see." Turning to Valdis he said, again in Latvian "So, Valdemars Zirnus, your dossier, according to the NKVD, says you are a murderer and an escaped criminal." He glanced over at the clerk and the clerk nodded. "Are you a murderer and criminal?"

"Only in their eyes sir, I escaped from a deportation train and in my struggle I accidentally killed a Red Army soldier."

"I see. Are you a Jew?"

"No sir," Valdis said quickly.

"Then prove it," the interrogator demanded.

"P-prove it," Valdis said uncertainly.

"Yes, pull down your pants."

"If you would look away please Anna." Valdis said.

Anna turned her head away as Valdis arched his mid-section and pulled down his trousers. The interrogator chuckled and even the fro-zen-faced clerk cracked a smile. "You have proven you are not a Jew so you can pull your pants back up."

"Thank you sir," Valdis said drawing his trousers back up.

"It's a pity you could not prove that you are not a Jew so easily," the interrogator said, looking at Anna.

"I assure you sir, she is not a Jew," Valdis said.

"And can you prove that?" the interrogator asked, with a smirk on his face.

"I have known Anna all my life. We went to the same school and church together."

"I would need better proof than that," the interrogator said. "Get up."

"Valdis crawled to his feet and stood perfectly still."

Anna also moved to get up but the officer barked, "Not you! I will tell you when to get up."

Anna cowered back down to her prone position.

The SS officer looked Valdis directly in the eye and continued. "Since you have so cleverly proven that you are not a Jew, you must now find a productive life. The Reich does not tolerate slackers. You have two choices. You can volunteer to serve in the *Wehrmacht* and get your chance to have revenge on your communist oppressors, or you can go to work in the mines or factories in the Fatherland so one of our young men can do the job for you."

"Where might I sign up to join the *Wehrmacht*, sir," Valdis said smartly.

The SS officer chuckled and said, "I will write you an identity card and you can take it to the office at the front of the building. They will show you where to sign up. Oh, because of your record, you will be under suspicion until you prove your loyalty. If there is any suspicion of disobedience or defiance, you will be shot."

"There will be no defiance from me sir. I will gladly help your army destroy the Reds, sir."

The officer went over to the desk where the clerk sat and wrote on a small card, then brought it to Valdis. "Take this to the clerk at the front desk and he will give you further instructions."

Valdis clicked his heels together in true German fashion and said, "Thank you sir. Then to Anna's astonishment his right arm shot up and he said, "Heil Hitler."

"Heil Hitler," the officer replied. "I can see you have a proper attitude. You are dismissed."

When Valdis reached the door, he turned and said, "Will Anna be detained long."

"She is not your concern," the SS officer said curtly. "Be on your way before I change my mind." One of the guards opened the door and Valdis stepped through, though he gave Anna one last longing look before the guard closed the door again.

As Anna lay on the floor, she felt very disturbed. First, Evalds joined the Communists to become one of their slaves. Now, Valdis apparently threw in his lot with the Nazis and volunteered to serve in their army. Again her father's words echoed, *'Anna don't let them take you.'* She put her hand over her blouse, above where the locket was concealed The officer strode over to her. Towering over her from her prone position, he looked like a terrible giant.

"Get up," he finally said.

Anna crawled to her feet, watching the officer like a cornered animal. He paced slowly around her with riding crop in one hand and striking the palm of the other with it. Anna stood frozen in her tracks, just like the two guards at the door.

"So Anna Lindenbergis," he finally said, speaking German. "You say you are not a Jew."

"No sir."

"Were any of your grandparents a Jew?"

"No sir, I can trace my family back four generations. My paternal grandfather was actually German."

"Silence!" he shouted. "You will supply information only as I ask for it."

"Yes sir."

"Your German grandfather, what was his name?"

"Hans Lindenberger, sir. "He came from East Prussia sir."

"You are talking out of turn again."

"I am sorry sir."

"Better. Was your grandmother German also?"

"No, she was Latvian, sir."

"Mongrel," he muttered as he paced around her. He the turned sharply on his heel and continued. "Your father, what did he do?"

"He ran a newspaper, sir."

"And the Reds shot him?"

"Yes sir."

ANNA

"I presume his paper was critical of the Communists. Tell me, was it also critical of us Nazis and our Fuehrer?"

"Father was not concerned as to what went on in Germany, sir. He feared, quite correctly, that the Russians wanted to reclaim Latvia."

"Your dossier says you are a dangerous agitator. One who does not vote but prints lies about the state."

"I - I was protesting the Soviet conquest of our country, sir," Anna replied.

"Do you plan to protest the German conquest of your country?"

"No, I welcome you as our liberators. I will gladly serve the Reich if you will let me, sir."

"Indeed."

The interrogator stopped in mid pace and drew a cigarette out of silver container. He lit it and inhaled.

"Do you smoke?" he finally asked, offering her one.

"No sir."

"This young man, Valdis. Is he your lover?"

"No. He would like to be but . . ."

"But what?"

"I do not want to fall in love. Not during this time when I don't know whether either of us will live to see tomorrow."

"An interesting perception and entirely correct." The officer smiled sardonically.

He looked at Anna for a moment then continued, "There was a man in the cells downstairs who knew you?"

"Evalds Ivakovs," Anna replied flatly. "A Communist traitor."

"You not only have friends that are Jews, but you also associate with Communists. I might have guessed since they are one in the same."

"I did not associate with him sir," Anna stated. "I went to school with him. He helped destroy my family and hunted me using the NKVD."

"I see. Do you know his fate?"

"I suspect you shot him sir."

"Our Fuehrer has issued a general order declaring that all Communist Party members and their commissars are to be executed upon capture."

Anna swallowed at this confirmation of Evalds's fate and wondered if Lana might meet the same end, but she made no further comment.

84

The officer came close and blew smoke in Anna's face. He walked around her and then grabbed her firmly by the jaw. Forcing her mouth open, he looked her over as one might look over a horse or dog that one was considering purchasing. It was a terrible feeling standing in the presence of a man who held the power of life or death over her on a whim.

Releasing her jaw he finally said, "No, I don't think you are a Jew. There is definitely strong Aryan blood in you. However, the Fuehrer says that Baltic people are inferior to true Aryans. You may serve the Reich freely. However, if you persist in showing any concern for the welfare of the Jews, including any you may have known personally, or complain in any way about the way Latvia is being governed by us, you will meet a very harsh fate. Do I make myself clear?"

"Yes sir," Anna replied.

The officer went over to his desk again and wrote on another card. "I am giving you a conditional identity card on the assumption that you are not tainted with Jewish blood. However, do not attempt to leave Riga without permission. You will take this card and report to the Work Kommisariat office down the street. They will determine how you may best serve the Reich. If it is discovered that you have been lying to me about your ancestral bloodlines you will not have the benefit of another interrogation. Dismissed."

"Thank you sir," Anna said turning to go.

"Aren't you forgetting something," he said curtly

Anna snapped to attention raised her right-arm and said, "Heil Hitler." Although she said it with much less enthusiasm than had Valdis.

Chapter Eight

As Anna stepped from the SS headquarters, Valdis was there to meet her. She regarded him with a cold expressionless look and walked briskly down the street to report to the work assignment headquarters. Valdis struggled to keep pace. Her earlier joy at the arrival of the Germans was now rapidly evaporating as she now felt they were little better than the Communists and that Hitler was no better than Stalin.

"I presume they have determined you are not a Jew," Valdis said, trying to make conversation.

"Lucky for me," Anna said coldly. "Otherwise you could use me for target practice once you join the *Wehrmacht*."

"The *Wehrmacht* is the army. It fights the Russians. The SS kills the Jews."

"How do you know they won't order you to kill Jews?"

"All I know is that I was given a choice. Go work as a virtual slave labourer in some factory or mine in Germany, or help defeat the Russians. I chose the latter, because the Russians have my family, and yours."

"I suppose you have a point," Anna said without expression. "But it looked like you sold your soul to them."

Valdis stopped Anna and faced her. "You and I talked many times of doing whatever it takes to survive. Your father told you to survive at all costs. That is what I am doing. It is also what you are doing, since you are now on the street rather than lying somewhere with a bullet in your head, or taken away in chains to some slave pit."

Anna looked at him without blinking.

Valdis continued, "The Reds never gave us a chance. They simply shot your father and rounded up our families. Then they hunted us like animals. The Nazis at least give us a chance, if we cooperate."

"If we cooperate," Anna scoffed. "If we are not Jews." She turned and resumed walking.

"You must forget about the Jews," Valdis said. "For some terrible reason that no one can fathom, they have been singled out. If you go along with the Nazis, you may survive. If not, I fear the Gestapo is much more efficient and thorough than the NKVD."

Anna walked along in silence then she finally asked in a matter-of-fact way. "How were you able to prove that you were not a Jew?"

"All Jewish males are circumcised. I am not," Valdis replied.

"Oh." Anna said, her face flushing with embarrassment. "That's very convenient."

"Yes, at times like this it certainly is," Valdis replied. "So can we be friends again?" Valdis asked as they approached the registry office.

"I'll think about it," Anna said flatly as she climbed the steps of the Kommisarriat

"Remember your father's words," Valdis said as Anna turned her back to him to open the door. She made no comment but merely walked in. Valdis turned and headed for the recruiting office.

Inside was a large crowded room presided over by two *Wehrmacht* guards. This was a small relief for Anna as she felt that Army personnel seemed less formidable than SS personnel did. They neither wore swastikas on their arms or deaths-head insignia on their lapels. She handed her identity card to a uniformed woman at the desk. The woman looked it over and replied coldly, "Conditional, citizenship eh? Go and wait until we call you."

As there were far more people than seats, Anna stood for as long as she could tolerate then slid down to the floor as so many before her had done.

After a long time a man dressed in army officer's uniform came out through the doorway by the desk to speak to the receptionist. He noticed Anna and looked directly at her. His eyes lit up for a moment as if he had known her from before, then just as abruptly his expression turned to one of pain. He spoke briefly to the receptionist then returned to the area behind.

Finally, after a time, the matron at the desk said, "Anna Lindenbergis."

Anna immediately sprang to her feet and came to the desk, "Yes Madam."

"Our employment kommissar will see you now," she motioned for Anna to go into the next room. '*So the Nazis have commissars too. I should not be surprised?*' Anna thought as she followed the receptionist. They passed several cubicles where people were being interviewed finally arriving at an office at the end of the hall.

"You must have something special on your file," the receptionist said with her flat voice. "The Kommissar only does interviews in special cases."

The receptionist opened the office door and announced Anna, addressing him as Colonel Brandt before Anna stepped in. It was a simple office consisting of a desk. Behind it, on the wall was a large photo of Adolph Hitler scowling out at the world. The man at the desk was the same one who had come into the front a while back. He was a middle-aged man evident by the lines on his face and his graying hair. He glanced at the file and spoke in German, "Anna Lindenbergis"

"Yes sir," Anna replied.

"The Gestapo has just handed me this file," the officer said. "It clears you of having any Jewish blood, but does suggest you have potential as a troublemaker. Are you a troublemaker?"

"I hope not sir," Anna replied. "I am not suicidal."

The officer smiled and Anna observed that he had a warm smile. "You are outspoken though."

"Yes sir. I'll try to control myself sir."

He chuckled again. "So Anna Lindenbergis, do you have any special skills besides writing articles about Russian bears?"

"I had hoped to study to become a doctor, sir."

"Indeed. However, our universities are reserved for our own people and anyone else hoping to go there has to have special permission and take up a career that will help the war effort."

"Soldiers must need doctors, sir." Anna said.

"Our medical staff is capable of handling any emergencies," the officer replied. "And I doubt that our medical chief wants any foreigners on his staff."

"Am I not a citizen of the Reich now, sir?" Anna said innocently.

"You are a subject of the Reich, but not a citizen. Citizenship is reserved for true *Reichdeutsche[1]*. Now do you still want to be involved in medical matters?"

"Yes sir, I would like that," Anna replied.

"I will assign you to our medical department as a general worker. This means you will do everything from scrubbing hospital wards, to folding bandages, to running errands."

"Yes, sir."

"You will work diligently during the hours that you are required to work at the job you are given and for the pay we give you. If you complain about your working conditions, I am sure we can find less pleasant things for you to do. Do I make myself clear?"

Reichdeutsche – German citizens living inside Germany proper.

"Extremely clear sir," Anna replied.

"Good. I will get you proper papers. The NKVD files say you didn't vote and branded you a dangerous agitator, but I presume you've changed your mind now."

"Oh yes sir," Anna replied. "I'm tired of hiding and I don't want to be on your Gestapo's wanted list."

The colonel chuckled and wrote on a slip of paper. "This will be your temporary ID until proper papers are made out. Do not lose them as you did your other papers."

Oh, thank you sir," Anna beamed. She was so glad to pass this first major hurdle, she turned to the portrait of Hitler raised her arm and said, "Heil Hitler."

The officer laughed and said, "I admire your spunk. Don't let it get you into trouble."

"Oh no sir, it won't."

"Now, go report for work. If you have nowhere to stay the hospital will assign you a place to sleep and supply you with meals."

When Anna came out into the reception area she spotted Lana. Lana smiled at her, but Anna ignored her. As she left the room, Anna heard Lana being called by the receptionist.

As she left the building, Anna thought of Valdis and how enthusiastically he had apparently embraced Nazism. Had she not just done the same thing in the name of survival. She was disappointed that he was not outside waiting, as she wanted to apologize for giving him the cold shoulder earlier. She had to walk several blocks to the hospital and fully expected him to pop up any time but he failed to show. She was struck with the terrible thought that he could have been whisked away to the battlefields in Russia and she might never see him again.

Anna reported to work at one of the main hospitals of Riga. It had been expropriated by the Germans and used both to receive battle casualties and to attend to other ailments or injuries that the German occupation force in Latvia might sustain. Some of the staff remained Latvian, but the members of the controlling board were all German army medical officers. Anna was placed as a general hospital worker. She sometimes helped receive and file medical supplies that came in, other times she helped wash the floors. The closest she came to learning about anything medical however, was counting and folding bandages.

Since Anna had nowhere to stay, she was placed in a dormitory near the hospital and was given a cot in a barracks-like room by the store-room. Several other workers shared the room, and she was given regular meals, though they were plain skimpy meals. The supervisor, who was a middle-aged German matron, presided over the dormitory and strict curfew laws were observed.

Toward the end of summer, after earning a certain amount of trust by her employers, Anna was given a new job. She was issued a bicycle and sent delivering errands to various points around Riga. This might include trips to the *Wehrmacht* and SS headquarters, or the dockyards along the river.

During those times when she was dispatched with her bicycle, Anna got a good view of Riga under German occupation. Riga was a bustling place with both on and off duty army personnel walking the streets. There seemed to be a constant stream of military vehicles, including tanks, unloading at the dockyards and moving through the city and eastward heading for the front, deep inside Russia, along with thousands of marching troops. Nearly all motor vehicles on the streets belonged to the Germans. In addition to the army trucks were the black limousines carrying either Army officers or SS personnel. The SS seemed to be everywhere, and they occasionally stopped her to ask her business. Anna was glad that her purpose for being on the streets was legitimate in their eyes.

One day Anna rode her bicycle through her old neighborhood past the house where she was raised. She found that there were several black limousines parked along the block. Anna was shocked to find that a short flagpole bearing a Nazi flag projected from just above her old bedroom window. She stopped and stared at her old house for a long moment. There were fleeting memories of happy days gone by, but the stark reality of the present kept them from the surface.

"What are you doing here?" cried a harsh voice.

Anna turned to find an SS man, bearing an automatic rifle standing beside her although he wasn't pointing the gun directly at her.

"I ... ah, used to live in that house."

"It is now the home of the major who is my commander," the man said flatly. "May I see your identity papers?"

Anna handed over her papers, a procedure that was now second nature to her.

The SS guard glanced at it and said, "You are a little off your route are you not?"

"As I said sir," Anna said innocently, "I grew up in that house and this is the first time I have seen it since the Reds kicked us out. I will not come by here again unless directed to do so."

"If that is a promise you intend to keep, I will let you go this time," the SS guard replied.

Anna quickly headed down the street and back to her work headquarters. As she pulled up to the gate leading into the compound at the back of the hospital a soldier dressed in off-duty uniform wearing a wedge cap stepped in front of her. It was Valdis.

"Hello Anna," he laughed as Anna slammed on the brake to keep from hitting him.

"Valdis! What are you doing here?" Anna gasped as she swung off the bicycle.

"I have finished training and they granted me a few hours leave before I go to the front."

"The front?" Anna gasped in horror at the thought that Valdis was actually going into battle where he might get killed.

Valdis, who seemed enthusiastic about that very prospect, replied cheerfully. "Yes, they are sending me to the Finland front to attack Leningrad from the north."

"You are going to Finland?"

"Yes. Our ship sails for Helsinki tonight. Finland is an ally of Germany you know and the Finns are most anxious to get back at the Russians."

"If you get a chance to find Karlis, tell him of the fate of our family and that I'll try to get to him someday."

"Yes, on one condition," Valdis said with a lopsided grin.

"What condition?" Anna demanded.

"You spend some time with me as it may be the last time we ever have together."

"I am off in two hours," Anna said. "Come back here then and I will come out."

"I'll be here," Valdis smiled.

"Goodbye, Valdis. I really must report for work." Anna climbed back on her bicycle and rode into the compound.

Anna's supervisor was there to greet her when she entered the building. "You were late getting back," she said in her dour manner.

"I was stopped by the SS," Anna said quickly.

"Why would the SS stop you?"

"Who knows," Anna shrugged. "They stop people all the time to make sure their purpose on the streets is legitimate. Could you not put a name-tag on my bicycle so that they know that I am out on business serving the Reich?"

"It could be arranged. And who was that soldier you were talking to at the gate?"

"An acquaintance of mine. He asked me if I could spend some time with him after work, as he is leaving for the front tonight. Do I have your permission madam?"

"Yes you may," the supervisor said. "It is the duty of Latvian girls to please our boys before they go into battle."

Anna was shocked at the remark, but said nothing. Being a whore for the soldiers was the last thing she ever intended to do. If she were ever forced into such a position, she would go into hiding again.

Shortly after coming off duty, Anna found Valdis waiting by the gate and he grinned as she came out to meet him.

"So where are we going?" Anna asked as they walked along.

"We can just walk along. Or we can go to a pub. There are plenty of pubs in Riga."

"Maybe just walk along for now," Anna said. "It has been a long time since we could just walk along the streets of Riga without looking over our shoulders."

"True, we could walk along by the river like we used to do. Or I could treat you to a meal at a café."

"Do they pay you enough to go out for a meal?"

"We don't get the same pay as regular soldiers, but we get some pocket money, which I have been saving just so I could treat you."

"You're luckier than me," Anna said. "What little they give me, goes mainly for lodgings. I'd be lucky if I could go out once a month."

"Well, I guess it is better than being hunted."

"Yeah," Anna sighed.

They stepped into a café that was filled with a noisy crowd of off-duty soldiers of the enlisted ranks. Some were Latvians and some were German. The soldiers of Latvian units had little Latvian flags as shoulder badges as did Valdis. They were supposedly part of the re-stored Latvian Army but they were really just an extension of the *Wehrmacht*.

"Would you like a beer," Valdis said as a waiter came to their table.

"Sure," Anna replied. When the waiter returned with their beer, they ordered a simple meal from a sparse menu.

Anna sipped at her beer and said, "I meant to apologize for that day after we were interviewed by the SS. You were right. We are both doing whatever it takes to survive."

"Maybe I did sound a little enthusiastic," Valdis said, looking around for prying ears. "I was just so glad to see the Russians chased out of our country, but we are still slaves."

"Yes. I am just fortunate that Father saved all the venom in his paper for the Russians. Had he been critical of the Nazis, I may not be here to enjoy this meal."

"Well you are here so enjoy it. If you don't run afoul the SS, maybe you can find a way out of this."

"What about you? You'll be on a far off battlefield."

"Well, if I live to see the Soviet Union conquered, I will try my best to learn the fate of my family, and yours."

"Try to find my brother anyway."

"I will certainly keep an eye out for him when I am in Finland."

The waiter came and set down their meal. It consisted of a thin slice of bread and an even smaller slice of meat along with a few vegetables and some watery coffee. Wartime rationing had even affected most restaurants.

"You know. I went by our old house today," Anna said, as they began to eat.

"And?" Valdis replied, as he took a bite of bread.

"Some SS officer has expropriated it and it has a Nazi flag hanging above the window."

"Did the house bring back painful memories?"

"No. I think because of all that has happened, and the fact the SS now have it, seems to make it seem like it wasn't our house at all. Anyway I was questioned for being there."

"Did they run you in for interrogation?"

"No. After I explained I was let off with a warning."

"You like living dangerously don't you."

"I am what I am, but I will survive." Anna instinctively touched the part of her blouse covering the locket.

"I have no doubt of that." Valdis replied. "Why do you touch your chest when we talk about either surviving or your father?"

Anna undid the top button of her blouse and pulled up the locket just enough for him to see it. "This is my mother's special locket. It contains a photo of Father. She gave it to me just before they took her away. Whenever I am in danger or am ready to give up I touch it, or if safe to do so, I take out the locket. It reminds me of my promise to father to survive."

"Interesting," Valdis replied. "Keep it hidden. If anyone, especially the SS, knows you have a gold locket they'll confiscate it."

"Yes, I know," Anna said, looking warily around.

After their meal, Anna and Valdis strolled down *Bivibas Bulvaris* past the Freedom monument. Valdis looked up at the monument, a stylized female figure holding three stars, and remarked. "It is kind of ironic that our country has been conquered twice in the last two years and *Milda* still survives." Valdis used the folksy name given to this precious monument.

"Maybe *Milda* is meant to survive as a hope for Latvia's future," Anna replied.

They walked along in silence, clasping hands as they entered the nearby Espanade Park. It was already dusk and at one point they turned and watched the setting of the late summer sun in the west over Courland[2].

"Remember that last Midsummer Festival before our world turned upside down," Anna said wistfully.

"Yes," Valdis sighed. "We stayed out all night with all the bonfires and singing."

"We had so much fun that night," Anna laughed.

"Yes. We had a future to look forward to," Valdis said quietly.

"Even then I had a sense of foreboding," Anna said. "When we watched the sun set that evening, I felt as if the sun was setting on Latvia."

"It will rise again," Valdis said confidently. "One day it will rise again."

"I hope so, Valdis I hope so."

They watched the dusk turn into twilight and turned to walk back into Riga as it was drawing near the time for Valdis to catch his ship.

"If I write to you Anna, will you answer?" Valdis said as they neared the dormitory where she stayed.

[2] Courland – a historic region comprising western Latvia

"Yes," Anna replied as she let her hand slip into his. "I will miss you while you're away. If I get in trouble with the Germans I'll have no one to hide with me."

"Just stay out of trouble with the Germans," Valdis said firmly. "I want you alive when the war is over."

As they reached the gate of the compound, they turned to face each other.

"Promise to wait for me Anna," Valdis said tearfully. "I love you."

"I promise," Anna said. Although she could not bring herself to repeat his phrase, they hugged and kissed each other tenderly for a long moment.

Chapter Nine

Anna was alone again. Valdis had shipped-out to the Finnish front, and while she could hope, she did not fully expect to ever see him again. Thus, she buried herself in her work. She still ran frequent errands with her bicycle, and still had a tendency to drift off her route from time to time. One day in mid autumn, she chanced to ride close to the Jewish ghetto wondering if there might be a way to visit Jacob and Golda. However, the ghetto was enclosed in a board and barbed wire fence and helmeted SS sentries with automatic weapons seemed to be every-where. She had often seen Jewish work gangs in the streets. Men and women with heads bowed, wearing their yellow stars and being herded by scowling SS men. They were brought daily into the city for menial tasks such as collecting garbage, cleaning sewers, and other unpleasant toil. Some were put to work at the docks or in the factories at drudge jobs. They were beaten if they faltered in their work and if any col-lapsed from exhaustion they were simply executed on the spot as one might dispose of a floundering draft animal.

That afternoon as Anna rested on her bicycle near the ghetto she saw several Army-trucks drive up. A large contingent of SS men went into the ghetto and soon herded out a large group of people composed of the elderly, infirm and children. Many were weeping as they were being ordered into the back of the trucks. Mothers of the children being taken were crying and begging for them to be spared, only to be or-dered back at gun-point by unfeeling SS men. When the trucks were all loaded with people packed together with standing room only they started up and drove away. The older people in the trucks began a ritual wailing that left Anna gaping in horror. Although she had no expla-nation as to what was going on, she was certain these people were being taken to their death. Sickened at the sight, Anna turned and rode away, wondering what the Jews had done to earn the special wrath of the Nazis. Anna thought she saw a shadowy figure watching her from about two blocks away. As she headed toward it, the individual van-ished into a side street. She thought of Lana, and wondered if the Nazis had indeed recruited her as an informer.

Later, when Anna had reached the gate of her compound a car drove up beside her. She turned and recognized the driver as Colonel Brandt, the same officer who had interviewed her at the Kommissariat. He smiled and said, "Hello, Anna, Lindenbergis is it?"

"Yes sir," Anna said flatly, wondering if she was going to get called-in for venturing too near the ghetto.

"Would you like to come for a drive with me?" he said pleasantly.

"Am I under arrest, sir?"

He laughed and said, "If you were under arrest, you would have two black uniformed men throwing you into the back of the car by now."

"Then why should I go with you if I have a choice?"

"I would like the pleasure of your company," he said smoothly, "and there are some things we need to talk about. I assure you no harm will come to you."

Anna put her bicycle away and returned. She was not comfortable about going with Colonel Brandt, but feared that an outright refusal would weigh against her. Anna climbed into the car and clung to the passenger door, ready to spring at a moment's notice. After her supervisor's earlier comments, she couldn't help wonder if the officer was going to demand sexual favours, or outright rape her if she refused.

As they drove along the streets of Riga, the colonel lit a cigarette and told her to relax. "I can sense that you are afraid of me."

"Well, sir it is unusual that a German officer would offer to take a lowly Latvian girl for a drive unless . . ."

"Unless he had designs upon her," the colonel laughed. "I assure you I have no designs. You see, I used to be a combat officer, but I received a severe abdominal wound during the French campaign. It made other things and me unfit for combat duty, so they gave me this pencil-pushers job. Besides that, I am old enough to be your father."

"I'm sorry," Anna replied, relaxing her grip on the door handle somewhat.

"Don't be," he laughed. "I am an officer in an army that has just conquered your country."

"You mean liberated it from the Russians," Anna replied.

The staff car was waved through the checkpoint at the edge of the city and they drove until they reached a high point from which they could see the Gulf of Riga in the distance. He turned and drove off the road, stopping at a viewpoint.

"Now then Anna," he said turning to face her and lighting another cigarette at the same time. Anna's hand was on the door handle again and she was ready to spring. "I was impressed by our interview that day, and even more impressed by the dossier that our *friends* in the Gestapo have prepared on you from the NKVD files they confiscated. It seems you are a very intelligent and curious individual who likes to speak her mind."

"I can't help what I am sir," Anna replied.

"Kurt. You may call me Kurt when we are not in the company of others. And when we are in the company of others you will call me Colonel Brandt."

Anna was silent and Kurt finally said. "Tell me what is uppermost on your mind? That is, besides your continuing fear that I may assault you."

"Two things," Anna replied.

"Yes, I am listening."

"Are you winning the war against the Soviets?"

Kurt laughed heartily and replied. "Winning the war! Our *Wehrmacht* is at the gates of Moscow as we speak and Leningrad is surrounded. We've taken over a million prisoners of war, occupy millions of hectares of Soviet territory, and you ask if we are winning." He laughed again and then said abruptly, "What is the other question?"

"Why do you hate the Jews?"

This triggered a brief monologue about the Jews being bloodsuckers and parasites, and then he abruptly stopped and looked firmly at her. "Why does this concern you so much?"

"I just can't see why a collection of small shopkeepers, most of whom don't even live in the rich part of the city, are such a threat to civilization."

This brought another monologue about how all Jews were part of a secret collective planning to destroy the Aryan race and that because a Jew founded communism, it was also part of this conspiracy. Anna couldn't see the logic in his rants so chose not to argue lest she jeopardize her own precarious position with the Nazis. Anna also sensed that his rants were a well-rehearsed line developed to impress the ever-watchful Gestapo rather than a reflection of his personal beliefs.

Finally Kurt said. "Why are you so concerned about the Jews? No one else seems to be."

"You read my file, sir. It probably states that I have friends that are Jews."

"You are very daring. Yes, I read in the file about your claim that a Jewish couple helped hide you from the Reds. So you found two compassionate Jews. Consider yourself lucky." Kurt started the car and headed back to Riga. Anna breathed a sigh of relief.

"One more thing?" Anna asked as they drove along. "What did they do with the Jews that were taken from the ghetto today?" Although afraid of what the answer might be, she still felt compelled to ask.

"How should I know," he answered quickly. "Handling Jews is the business of the SS, I am a *Wehrmacht* officer assigned to administration of army personnel and free citizens of the Riga area. I do not concern myself with Jews. This is an attitude that I strongly urge you to adopt also."

Although many thoughts and questions raced through her mind, Anna remained silent.

"So Anna," Kurt said as they drove along. "I said earlier that you are a very curious person. Do Latvians also have the saying that curiosity killed the cat?"

Anna looked at him curiously.

"I know you often wander off your route when you are on bicycle errands. I knew also that you passed near the ghetto today even before you asked that question."

Anna swallowed and said, "Did the SS tell you?"

"If the SS would have reported you there, you would now be in a torture chamber rather than in the car with me. Let us just say I have been keeping an eye on you."

"So it would seem," Anna said quietly. She then thought, *If the SS isn't watching me for Kurt, who is?* She thought of the shadowy figure and of Lana. "Why? Wouldn't it be simpler just to complain to the SS about my behavior?" she asked abruptly.

"As I said Anna, you are a bright intelligent girl, and you remind me very much of my daughter. In fact your resemblance to her is uncanny."

Anna remembered his momentary look of joy that faded to one of sadness, the time he first set eyes upon her. "What happened to her, sir? If I may ask?" Anna finally asked.

"She was killed in an auto accident along with my wife," Kurt replied with a painful look. Then changing the subject said, "Now, so that curiosity doesn't kill you, I am changing your job."

Anna looked anxiously at Kurt.

"How would you like to be a van driver?"

"A van driver sir?"

"We will train you how to drive. You will make both in-city deliveries, and later long distance deliveries. You will both haul mail for the soldiers and medical supplies to transfer points. None of your routes will go anywhere near any ghettos. Do you understand me."

"Yes sir, Kurt, uh Colonel Brandt sir," Anna replied. "Perfectly clear."

"Excellent," Kurt smiled. "You begin your new job tomorrow morning."

As they drove up to the compound and stopped Kurt said to her. "It would please me if I could take you to dinner some time."

"I will have to check my new schedule, sir."

"It was a pleasure talking with you," Kurt said as she stepped from the car.

Upon entering the compound, Anna found her supervisor waiting for her. She was wearing her usual frown.

"Out joy riding, when you should be working," the supervisor said firmly.

"I could not refuse that man who is an officer of some stature. Colonel Brandt, no less." Anna smiled sweetly.

"Colonel Brandt!" the supervisor said with surprise. "You are very fortunate to have caught his favour."

"You did say it was the duty of Latvian girls to please the German soldiers did you not," Anna added with a crooked grin.

"Yes. Well if someone with the power and influence of Colonel Brandt wishes you for a consort, then by all means attend to his desires."

Anna was taken aback but said nothing, The supervisor was again talking as if she were the Madam of a brothel, and Anna one of the girls.

Anna was trained to drive a van. At first she drove within the confines of Riga. Although she carefully avoided the ghetto, Anna could not help but wonder how Jacob and Golda were holding up under the severe restrictions forced upon them or whether they were still alive. By now word had got out that those Jews she saw being loaded onto the trucks that day, and others like them, deemed unfit for labour, had indeed been massacred in the forest outside of Riga.

As winter approached Anna was making an occasional run to other cities within Latvia. Sometimes she traveled as part of a convoy and sometimes alone. She noticed that the main roadways of Latvia were still busy with trucks and tanks moving eastward to the front in Russia. However, things appeared not to be going as well as hoped on the Russian front. Although news bulletins on the loudspeakers and in the papers still described glorious victories, there were also guarded reports of stubborn Russian resistance and inclement weather slowing the advance. The weather did turn frightfully cold in Latvia that winter and the Gulf of Riga showed a few ice patches, although ships still kept coming in. Anna's sleeping quarters never seemed quite warm enough as fuel was rationed due to the war demands.

That winter, Kurt frequently took Anna to dinner. They went to special restaurants reserved for German officers, which offered much better menus than the café where she dined with Valdis that time. He even once took her to the Riga opera house where she endured a four-hour sitting of Wagner's *Taunhauser*. Almost all of the attendants at the opera were German officers and officials. Precious few Latvians could afford to go to an opera these days. She also endured a monologue from Kurt explaining how Wagner glorified the German race with his operas.

After one such monologue on the way home from the opera, she asked innocently. "Why haven't the Russians been defeated yet?"

Fortunately street traffic was light as Kurt slammed on the brakes and looked sourly at her. "Why do you ask such things?"

"You assured me that Moscow would be taken by Christmas and it's now February. Even the Fuehrer said that Russia would never rise again,"

"So it won't. Because the Russian beast is a bear, it is difficult to kill," Kurt said sharply. "Have you ever gone bear hunting?"

"No," Anna replied in a small voice.

101

Kurt sighed and continued, "The Russians have two great natural allies that make them difficult to bring down. They have geography. Moscow alone is thousands of kilometres from the border, and its God-forsaken weather. Do you know it is forty below at the front? Do you have any idea how cold that is? Both men and machines quit working at that temperature. Only those Mongol savages from Siberia can stand those temperatures."

"You will defeat them in the spring then?" Anna asked.

"Certainly we will," Kurt assured her as he started up again. "Or are you hoping for our defeat."

"Oh, no," Anna said quickly. "The last thing I want is to have the Russians in Latvia again. I mean if I had to choose . . ."

"We are the lesser of two evils," Kurt chuckled.

A fleeting grin swept across Anna's face but she said nothing.

Kurt invited Anna to his apartment for a quiet cup of coffee. She was quite apprehensive even though Kurt had behaved like a gentleman thus far. As he opened the door she said, "If I am seen going to your apartment, people will think . . ."

"Let them think," Kurt chuckled, as he closed the door behind her. "If they, especially the SS, think you are my consort, they will give you more leeway."

"Is it common for German officers to have Latvian women for mistresses?" Anna asked pointedly.

"Well . . . er . . . we have certain prerogatives in occupied countries."

"To make the women your whores'?" Anna put her hand on the doorknob.

"Don't get me wrong," Kurt said gently. "I told you I am not interested in you, in that way. If, however, they assume such, it will help you survive. If anyone implies to you that you are Colonel Brandt's mistress, don't give them reason to think otherwise. It could mean the difference for your long-term survival. Now sit down and have some coffee. It is much stronger that what they serve you in a restaurant."

Anna sat uneasily on a chair while Kurt made a small pot of coffee. She was repelled by the idea that people might think her to be Kurt's mistress, then she heard her father's words echo in her mind, *'Anna you must survive.'* If Kurt were truly the gentleman he appeared to be, then idle gossip would not matter. She relaxed as she watched Kurt go over to a small portable gramophone. He wound it up and placed the stylus on the record. The smash wartime hit in Germany, *Lili Marlene*, began playing. As Anna listed to the lonely words of a soldier leaving his sweetheart behind by the lamplight, she thought of herself as Lili Marlene and Valdis as the soldier.

"This song is so popular, even the Englishmen are singing it," Kurt laughed.

When the song was over, Kurt put on another record. It was a pleasant tune that caught Anna's ear.

"What kind of music is that?" she asked.

"Glen Miller. It's swing music. The tune is *Moonlight Serenade*."

"Swing music?"

"It's from America. Although it is not forbidden, the Party frowns upon people indulging in it."

Anna smiled. She sensed that there was indeed a decent person behind that trim uniform.

"There is one thing you can do for me while you are here," Kurt said as he rose from his seat. He began unbuttoning his tunic and Anna rose, ready to flee from his apartment "I need a shoulder massage," Kurt said as he dropped his tunic over a chair "Have you ever massaged anyone's sore shoulder muscles?"

"Yes," Anna replied in a small voice, wondering to where this might lead.

Kurt sat in a chair with his back to her and Anna came cautiously over to him. She began to carefully knead his shoddier muscles amid soft cries of relief. With his tunic and cap removed and along with it the most obvious signs of his military rank, Kurt seemed like a harmless middle-aged man. One who was lonely and who genuinely sought pleasant company for its own sake.

One day the following spring, as Anna was making her deliveries, she took a shortcut down a country road near Riga on her return trip. The countryside looked very familiar and she was sure she was quite near to the farm where she and Valdis hid out from the Reds. As she looked around she drove off the track and her van slid into a small ditch where she become immobilized in the mire. After several tries at trying to get out, she gave up. It was unthinkable for her to abandon the van and seek help with the valuable cargo of mail and military documents so she decided to sit and wait. Surely someone would come looking for her if she was late.

After about an hour, a familiar figure driving a cart pulled by two horses came along. Upon recognition, Anna jumped from the van and cried, "Atis!"

He regarded her for a moment and smiled, "Anna?"

"Oh it's so good to see you Atis," Anna beamed.

Atis looked over the van with a swastika emblem on the door and said, "Do you work for the Nazis now?"

"Yes," Anna said, looking down. "It is better to work for them than to be hunted by them."

"True. Does your friend Valdis work for them too?"

"He's in the Army, somewhere on the Finnish front."

"I see," Atis said gravely.

"And you?" Anna asked. "How are the Nazis treating you?"

"About the same as the Comrades. They also searched my place made an assessment as to what I could produce and left me a quota to fulfill."

"Do they come by often?"

"No. Since I've been able to fulfill my quota so far, they haven't bothered me. If I fall behind, I expect they'll come around and demand to know why."

"Did they at least let you keep your land?"

"They said I could keep it as long as I meet my quotas."

Looking at Anna's predicament, he said, " So, I see you're stuck in the mud."

"Yes, I slid off the road. Could you pull me out with the horses?"

"I think so."

Atis unhooked the horses from the cart and they found a long piece of chain in the van. A couple of mighty heaves from the horses and the van was back on the road.

"Thank you Atis," Anna cried from the van.

"Come and see us again if you are allowed," Atis said. "You know the way."

"Yes, I was looking down that trail when I drove off the road. If I come, may I bring my officer friend?"

"You have a new boyfriend?"

"Well, he seems more like a father figure as he is much older than me. He says he is looking after my welfare because I remind him of his daughter who was killed in a car accident. He has a very powerful position in the Nazi administration of Latvia. He was wounded in battle so they gave him a desk job."

"You could bring him along. I try not to do things to make the Germans suspicious."

"If I do bring him. Don't offer him your best lunch. Make it sparse and maybe he'll persuade the administration to back off on its demands. He has a lot of influence you know."

"Then you'd better bring him along and I'll have Astra put on the poorest meal we can manage."

"Thanks again," Anna said as she started the van and headed back down the road.

Anna had scarcely gone two kilometres when she met a truckload of SS people. They blocked the road and stopped her.

"What is the problem?" Anna asked innocently as an officer came to her window.

"You are over two hours late. Get out of the van." the officer, said harshly. To his men he said, "search the van."

"I slid into the ditch and got stuck," Anna said as two SS men climbed into the back of the van, "You can see the mud on the fenders . . ."

"Silence!" he shouted. "I will ask the questions." Then after a moment he asked, "How did you get out?"

"A farmer came along with his horses and pulled me out, and I can show you the spot."

"Silence! Don't answer questions before they are asked."

"All is in order back there sir," one of the SS men said upon returning from the back of the van. "All the military documents and mail are still there."

"What are you looking for, sir?" Anna asked in a concerned voice.

"It does not concern you. If you are not hiding anything, then you have nothing to fear."

Finally Anna was allowed back into the van and the SS truck followed her all the way back to Riga.

When she arrived at the mail depot, she found Kurt there waiting, standing beside his car. Upon backing her van into the loading dock, she climbed out and headed for him.

"I am glad you are here Colonel Brandt," she breathed.

Two SS officers came up to them saluted and one said to Kurt. "We found her along the road, sir. She said she was stuck in the mud."

"Was she?"

"There is mud on the van, sir. She said a farmer pulled her out with his horses."

Anna tried to interject, but Kurt ignored her and said, "I trust the mail was still all there and not tampered with."

"We could find no evidence of such, but we will check again inside the depot."

"Carry on then," Kurt said. Then turning to Anna he said gently. "Get in the car."

As they drove down the street, Anna said, "Are you so important that SS men listen to you?"

"Sometimes," he replied. "If it is a really big issue, I can be overruled. Don't become a big issue Anna, or I won't be able to save you."

"I am innocent," Anna declared. "I really was stuck. My story is true. If the mail was tampered with, it was unknown to me, and I stayed with the van as per orders until Atis came along."

Anna realized her blunder and cut herself short. As they reached an intersection, Kurt stopped and lit a cigarette. He exhaled and said, "Atis?"

"All right," Anna confessed. "Atis is a farmer who along with his wife Astra, live on a farm near there. Valdis and I hid at their farm from the Reds. I was daydreaming, thinking of how it would be nice to visit them sometime if I could ever get the opportunity. I wasn't watching and I slid off the road. As per orders, I stayed with the van expecting that someone would come looking for me because of my cargo. However, Atis happened by with his horses and cart about a half hour ahead of the SS and he pulled me out."

Kurt exhaled a large volume of cigarette smoke and said, "That is quite a story, but incredibly, I think you are telling the truth."

"Would you like to meet Atis and Astra?"

"Me? Why would I want to meet them?"

"I would like to visit them, since they helped me so much. Since I don't have authority to take a vehicle on my own time, I thought maybe you could drive me out there. It would satisfy your concern that I was up to something by being late."

"You really do talk a lot," Kurt laughed. Then more seriously he added, "That could one day be your downfall."

"So could you take me out to their farm sometime?" Anna persisted.

"For peace and quiet, more than to satisfy any suspicion, I will take you out there on Sunday."

"Thank you sir. Uh Kurt," Anna grinned.

"That is, if you stop by the apartment for coffee and give me a massage."

"It's a deal," Anna smiled. By now she had become a frequent visitor to Kurt's apartment. Sometimes she gave him a neck or back massage and sometimes they just sat and talked over glasses of wine or cups of coffee while they listened to his large collection of records ranging from swing music, to German folk music, to the great classics. Sometimes her visits would go past the midnight curfew and Anna would have to spend the night sleeping on Kurt's sofa. As a result, it soon became common gossip around Riga that she was his mistress.

The following Sunday, Kurt made good his word and took Anna for a drive out to the farm. Anna gave a long spiel about how poor Atis was, and that the quotas were really squeezing him. Kurt could only say that everyone had to contribute to the Reich war effort.

Anna showed him the spot where she got stuck and there was still clear evidence of vehicle tracks in the ditch. As she chattered away about it Kurt said with a heavy sigh. "I am sure the SS have several photographs of that spot. They probably interviewed every farmer in the area also."

"They don't miss anything do they?" Anna said gravely.

"No, they do not. I hope, for your sake, that you are not on their list of suspicious people, because then I'll be on it and they'll watch us both like hawks."

"After spending a year hiding from the Comrades, I don't want to be on anyone's list."

"The what?"

"Comrades, that is what Atis calls the Reds because they always address everyone as comrade."

As they drove into the farmyard a small flock of chickens scattered in front of the approaching car. A sow lying in a pen by the barn nursing a litter grunted, and a sheep bleated from beyond the fence. Astra looked anxiously out the kitchen window and Atis came out of the barn. He set down a pitchfork he had been holding.

"The farm looks very prosperous," Kurt said. "I though you said we were squeezing them."

"You are. What you see is deceiving. Let's get out and look for ourselves."

Kurt gave her a quizzical look. Anna was getting very presumptuous lately. As they came from the car Anna introduced Atis to Kurt, though she had to translate as neither Atis or Astra could speak German and Kurt couldn't speak Latvian.

"Now I know why you brought me here. You have the upper hand as an interpreter. Very clever."

"All you have to do is sit back and observe." Anna smiled innocently.

Anna turned to Atis and said, "Kurt is uncomfortable as he cannot understand us."

"Tell him to come on in. He is welcome," Atis said. Then more seriously he added. We had a visit from your friends in the black uniforms the other day."

"Oh the SS," Anna said with a concerned look. She then explained to Kurt.

"They wanted to know all about me pulling you out of the mud hole and just to show me how much they are in control, they searched my place again."

Anna laughed and translated to Kurt, just as Astra came out of the house.

"Astra!" Anna cried as she rushed to embrace the woman.

As they hugged, Astra said, "You are looking good, the Nazis must be treating you well."

"Well, better than the Reds did. No more hiding," Anna grinned.

"And your friend. I hope he didn't come here to search," Astra said more seriously. "Our farm has been searched so many times a mouse couldn't hide here."

"No search," Anna laughed. "I befriended this gentleman and persuaded him to take me out here for a visit. Maybe if he sees first hand, they'll stop squeezing you so hard for produce."

"Yes, they want most of my vegetables and all of the pigs. I don't know what we'll eat this winter."

Anna translated to Kurt with a bit of sarcasm about his earlier remark about a prosperous farm. Astra invited them in for tea.

When they entered the main room of the house Anna scanned for photos on the mantle. The same frame that once held a picture of Stalin now held one of Hitler. A small Nazi flag on a stick was held up behind the photo.

"You keep up with the times," Anna laughed.

Neither Astra nor Atis made comment while Kurt asked Anna what she had said.

"I commended them for being respectful of our new rulers," Anna answered glibly.

"Yes, well I'll note that in my report."

They were served a simple snack of locally grown herbal tea, coarse dark bread made from home ground rye flour and a few thin slices of fatty pork. Atis grumbled that soon they would be without the pork and Astra complained that real tea or coffee was no longer available to them. Kurt asked for details about the quota levied on them and made note as they explained. After the snack, Atis offered to give Kurt a tour of his farmstead. Anna translated with a bit of sarcasm, "Atis would like to show you his place, since you are the first governing official who hasn't demanded a search, he feels disappointed."

"Tell him I'd be honoured. The more evidence I can actually see of his poverty, the more I might feel like getting them to ease up on his quota."

Anna translated.

While Kurt could see evidence of crops growing and animals fattening in the pasture, it was explained that virtually none of this would go toward Atis's enrichment. It was all going for the war effort.

As they drove home that day, Anna asked Kurt. "Are you really going to get them to ease up on Atis' quota?"

"I will look into it, but I have to tread carefully or they'll start asking *me* questions. Why are you always so concerned with other peoples problems?"

"They helped me hide from the Reds for a whole winter so now it is my turn to help them." Anna said in a matter-of-fact way.

"I see. I hope they are not Jews," Kurt replied.

"Humph," Anna replied, "How many Jews do you know take up farming?"

Kurt chuckled. "You have a point there. I can see that you'll make a fine Nazi yet."

Anna made no comment. Although she prided herself in finding the right things to say to the captors of her nation, and found her blunt talkative way to be effective, it would be a cold day in hell before she would ever become a Nazi.

l

Chapter Ten

Kurt was good to his word, and the quota on produce from Atis and some of the neighbouring farms was eased slightly on the grounds that they showed a correct attitude toward the Reich. In this pivotal year of 1942, the Germans resumed their offensive against Russia by attacking further south. Kurt explained to Anna that this "brilliant new strategy by the Fuehrer" of attacking Stalingrad rather than Moscow would be sure to bring the Bolshevik monsters down. It was also the year of an insidious new program by the Nazis in their ongoing persecution of the Jews, the introduction of the Final Solution.

Anna heard of it at first from rumors among off-duty personnel in the cafes and on street corners. SS personnel in particular talked excitedly about finally getting rid of the Jews. More Jews were being taken out of the ghetto never to return. They were usually the sick and injured as the strong and healthy were left behind for continued forced labour duties. Other Jews from elsewhere in Europe were brought in, again only the young and strong, and deposited in a second ghetto set up beside the first one. As virtually all Latvian men suitable for millitary service had been drafted by the *Wehrmacht* the manual labour required in the local industries and at the dockyards was performed by Jewish slave labour gangs.

One morning Anna's duties took her to the main laundry depot for military officers stationed in Riga. She had to go around back for a pick up of dress-uniforms for some high-ranking officers. There, among the Jews bent in toil lugging heavy laundry bags, she saw Jacob. Anna almost cried out to him, but bit her lip. Then she saw Golda come out of a steamy back room for another bag of dirty laundry. Golda studied her for a moment and the word Anna was on her lips, then she quickly turned away.

Anna's heart leapt. *'They're still alive! Jacob and Golda are still alive. I must try to save them before they are also sent to their deaths.'*

Tomorrow she had a run to an outpost on the Russian border. If she could get them out of the ghetto and into the back of her van she could drop them in the forest near Atis's farm. Even if he didn't take them in, they would have at least a chance for survival. Today, after delivering the uniforms, she was going to Valmera up in the northern part of Latvia. It was about a hundred-kilometre trip so she should easily make it back before dark.

On the way back, as Anna was passing through a heavily forested region about forty kilometres east of Riga she was intercepted by a band of armed men and women. They wore no uniforms, but wore an armband of the colours of the Latvian flag.

"What is going on?" Anna asked in Latvian, when one of them came to the window. She sensed they were some sort of partisans.

"Get out of the van," the man ordered. "What is in the back?"

"Mail and empty cartons."

"Mail?"

"Mail for the Army. The soldiers personal mail."

As Anna climbed out of the van one of the band was about to climb in the back. "Don't disturb it, its only mail."

"What's in it?" demanded the man who ordered her from the van.

"Just mail. If they find that it has been disturbed. They will want to know why."

"We could just shoot you and take the van and the mail."

"You could," Anna said evenly, "but if I am late, the SS will come looking for me and if they know there are bandits in the area, they'll hunt you down."

"We're not bandits. We are the Green freedom fighters. Who are you? Your spoken Latvian is good for a German."

"I'm Anna Lindenbergis and I am Latvian."

"Why are you working for them? Are you a Nazi sympathizer?"

"No. I hid from the Russians for a year after they shot my father and took my mother and sister away. When the Germans came, I first saw them as liberators. Now they are just another conqueror. They gave me a job and I was so tired of hiding that I went along with them, but the SS doesn't completely trust me, so that's why I ask you not to disturb the mail."

"Climb out of the back," the man said to the two that had just climbed into the back of the van. As they climbed out, the leader said to Anna, "How do we know you won't tell them about us?"

"How would they find you if I did?"

"Like you say, they'd scour the area and probably torture some of the farmers for information."

"Do you know Atis and Astra Vagris?" Anna dared ask.

"How do you know them?" the leader demanded.

"They hid me from the Russians one winter. Do you know them?"

There was an awkward silence, then Anna added. "If you see them soon, ask them about Anna Lindenbergis."

"If we let you go, will you help us?"

"If I can, and if you can help me?"

"What do you want?"

"They are shipping all the Jews out of Riga. I hear they are exterminating them."

"You've heard correctly, the murdering bustards. In the forest north of here, several hundred of them were shot in cold blood and buried in a mass grave. It was a most terrible sight to see, this long column of Jews who knew they were on a death march wailing as they trudged along."

"I saw them being hauled away from the ghetto by the truck load and they were also wailing." Anna said. Then after a moment she added. "There is a Jewish couple who also helped me hide from the Russians, at great risk to themselves. I discovered this morning, that they are still alive I'm going to try to get them out tonight."

"You play a dangerous game. The SS will torture you to death if you're caught."

"So? The Reds would have done it to Jacob and Golda if they had been caught hiding me."

"I see. So what are you going to do with this Jewish couple then?"

"Bring them out here. I have a run to an outpost on the Russian border tomorrow. So I will be able to drop them off."

One of the others said, "If she is willing to do this for a couple of Jews, she could be valuable to us."

After a brief discussion among them the leader said. "You may go now. We will be watching tomorrow. You will hear from us again one way or the other to return the favour."

Anna climbed back into the van and headed back to Riga. While she was sympathetic to the partisans she was not anxious to do their bidding. She was walking a thin enough tightrope as it was.

Anna made it back early that day and persuaded her coworkers to load her van that day so she could have an early start for the long journey to the Russian border. She lay waiting until the summer twilight had descended over Riga, then slipped out of her quarters making her way toward the ghetto. Though she had lifted a flashlight from the office, she used it only as a last resort so as not to attract attention. There were few people on the streets and patrols were cut to a minimum as the war was placing a heavy drain on German resources. The SS ruled with such terror that to get caught doing some misdemeanor was unthinkable. Thus, a handful of their men could keep order in Riga. The streets were also dark as most streetlights were turned off to save electricity. When she approached the area around the ghetto however, it was brightly illuminated around the perimeter. There were several SS men with guard dogs to make sure no one either entered or left the ghetto. While this seemed to present an insurmountable problem, it also offered hope. If the ghetto was still being guarded, there must be people still within its walls. Hopefully Jacob and Golda were among them.

As Anna stood in the shadows assessing what to do, she spied a manhole cover. There had to be storm drains and sewers running through the ghetto since Jacob and Golda had plumbing in their home. The manhole was about a metre from where she stood at the end of the alley. The nearby streetlights were turned off and a quick glance told her that there were no patrols in sight. The summer twilight provided her only lighting.

Anna managed to lift the lid and found the rungs that led down. She shone down her flashlight and saw a horizontal tunnel at the bottom lead toward the ghetto. She crawled in, pulled the lid over the hole from below and was soon on her way. The sewer pipe was less than two metres in diameter and she had to crouch to walk through. As the pipe was dry and carried no foul odor, Anna assumed it was a storm sewer. At the first manhole she came to, shafts of bright light streamed down through the holes suggesting it was at the floodlit edge of the ghetto. The next manhole she came to was dark. Assuming it was inside the ghetto, she went out.

The streets were dark, as there was no electricity at all in the ghetto during the night. At regular intervals a searchlight would sweep over the streets, but Anna could easily dodge the sweeps. The sweeps also helped her locate Jacob's shop. She made her way around the back and knocked on the door.

"Who is it?" asked a frightened voice within.

"Anna."

The door opened a small amount and a gaunt, frightened-looking Jacob peered out. He held a candle in his hand.

"What is it you want?" he asked.

"To help you. Please let me in."

Jacob let her in, and in the dim candlelight Anna could also see a fearful looking Golda.

"What are you doing here?" she asked. "We heard that you work for *them*. We saw you at the laundry this morning."

"I do, sort of. After the Germans came, Valdis and I came out of hiding. I saw what they were doing to you people, but could do nothing about it. As it is, the SS is suspicious of me."

"And you took a chance to come here?" Jacob asked

"You hid me from the Reds at great risk to yourselves. Now that you are the persecuted, the least I can do is help you."

"What can you do? We are being shipped out tomorrow to a re-settlement camp," Golda said.

"You mean a death camp," Anna said gravely. "I have heard what happens to the Jews who are shipped out. Some don't even get as far as any camp."

Jacob swallowed and said, "I know, they massacred all the children and old people but what can you do?"

"I can smuggle you out of the ghetto the same way I came in, through the storm sewers. My job with the Nazis is a courier. I am scheduled to go on a run to the Russian border tomorrow, and I can drop you off in the forest along the way. I met some partisans who will take care of you."

"But what if we get caught?" Golda said.

"We'll all be shot," Anna replied. "You are doomed anyway so you have nothing to loose."

"But you do." Jacob said with a concerned look "The Nazis gave you a chance."

"A chance to spend my life as one of their slaves. I was told I would never be allowed to go to university, because I am not a German, and I may not change my job without special permission," Anna said bitterly. "It is the same situation you faced with the Reds. They let you live in your ghetto, but I was the hunted one. The chance you took is no different from the chance I take now. Come, we must hurry."

Golda looked at Jacob for a decision, and Jacob said, "Anna is right, we have nothing to lose."

"Tear that horrid Star of David from your clothes," Anna said, looking at the yellow star on their shirts.

"But if we are caught without it . . ." Golda worried.

"You'll be shot anyway," Anna said quickly. "Without the star, they won't know you are Jews."

Jacob grabbed the star on his shirt and after a moment of hesitation, he tore it off. Golda followed suit. "You don't know how long I've been waiting to do that," she said bitterly. They also tore the star off their coats.

They headed out into the darkness, again easily dodging the searchlight as they made their way to the manhole. When they passed under the manhole by the floodlights one of the guard dogs came up to the lid and began barking furiously.

"Quickly, we must get to the next exit," Anna said desperately. "The guards will surely investigate."

They ran, nearly doubled over, to the next exit where Anna had originally entered the sewer. Anna scrambled up to the lid, followed by Golda, and Jacob. One of the guards had opened the other manhole and climbed down. Jacob had just pulled his leg up out of the horizontal shaft as the guard shone his flashlight down the length. Anna carefully lifted the lid and slid it aside. Crawling out into the darkness, she glanced around to make sure all was clear before motioning Jacob and Golda to follow. They slid the manhole cover back into place and quickly slipped into a nearby alley. The guard who had entered the drainage tunnel came back to surface chalking it up to rats.

Meanwhile Anna and her companions were creeping toward her van. Anna had a key to the compound. She carefully opened the gate grateful that there were not sentries about at this late hour. Anna quickly led them to the back of the van. As she opened the back door, she told them to crawl under the mailbags. Anna quietly closed the back door. She was going to sneak back to her quarters, but then out of instinct for survival, she went instead to Kurt's place.

Kurt was already in bed, when she knocked on his door. He came to the door dressed in a wrap around and slippers. He smiled as he let her in then after closing the door asked. "What are you doing here this time of night?"

"I was out with some friends." Anna said quickly. "It was past curfew and rather than argue with the matron I came here." Then with wry grin she added, "Everyone knows I stay here overnight sometimes."

"True, they do," Kurt chuckled. "I'll get an extra blanket and you can use the sofa as always."

"Thank you Kurt, you are a real friend. I will have to be up early as I have a run to the Russian border."

"I am an early riser also. Will you be too tired to come to the opera with me tomorrow evening?"

"I would be delighted," Anna smiled. The perfect alibi had just been established.

Anna left early the following morning without a hitch. The rollcall of the remaining people in the ghetto did not begin yet and probably wouldn't start for a few hours, so she should be able to get safely out of the city. As she left Riga, the SS guards at the exit points gave their usual nod.

In a heavily forested region near to where she had encountered the partisans, Anna stopped the van. "Quickly, you must get out," she called in as she opened the back door of the van. Jacob and Golda crawled to the back opening where Anna helped them out.

"What are we going to do now, Jacob?" a bewildered Golda asked.

"Live in the forest I suppose," an equally bewildered Jacob said.

"There are partisans around here," Anna said as she climbed in the back and adjusted the mailbags and other items so as to make it look as if they hadn't been disturbed. "I encountered a band yesterday. They said they'd take care of you, and that they'd be here this morning."

"How will we eat way out here in the forest?" Golda wondered.

"I have a loaf of bread stashed on the seat. I brought it for you," Anna replied.

Jacob retrieved the loaf as Anna closed the back doors.

"Hurry into the woods and hide. When the SS discovers you missing this morning, they will start searching and my van will be suspect," Anna said hurriedly. "Watch the roads and watch the farms. If you go to a farm for food don't tell them you are Jewish if it can be avoided. Think up a convincing story while you are trekking through the forest."

"Thank you for your kindness. It will never be forgotten," Jacob said.

Anna hugged them both then climbed back into her van. In the mirror she could see Jacob and Golda stepping into the forest. It felt good to help someone who had helped her and while their fate was uncertain, they, at least, had a far better chance here than being sent to a death camp. After travelling a few hundred metres, two partisans appeared at the edge of the road and waved at her. Anna smiled and waved back knowing all was in hand.

Anna travelled for perhaps another twenty kilometres when she came to an SS roadblock. Though this was not unexpected, she braced herself for an interrogation. Upon stopping the officer in charge demanded she get out of the van. Several SS men poured over the van even checking behind the seat, under the body and under the hood.

"What is going on?" Anna asked with a trembling voice.

"Two Jews escaped last night." said the iron voice of the lieutenant in command. " You are under suspicion."

"Me! Why would I want to help Jews escape?"

"Silence!" the lieutenant barked.

"We can find nothing, sir," the head of the search team said.

"She could have let them out already. We will have to search the surrounding forest."

The lieutenant called for Anna to put her hands behind her back. Then she was handcuffed.

"But I have my run," she protested.

"Your run will not concern you. You are under arrest."

"For what?" Anna demanded.

"You will answer all questions to the interrogator."

Anna was pushed into the back of a truck and an SS man climbed in beside her. Her heart was pounding and her stomach was filled with knots, as she knew that her next stop would be an SS torture chamber. Although she could not touch the locket with her hands bound behind her back, she thought of it and her father's last words, *'Anna don't let them take you.'* "I'm sorry Father," Anna sobbed quietly.

Kurt was barely settled in his office, when two SS officers approached him. He was immediately on the defensive, as the SS did not usually visit him unless he called for them. He had also heard of a rumour that morning of some trouble in the ghetto. He thought of Anna.

"*Guten Morgen Herr Hauptmann,[1]* " the senior officer, who was a major, said politely.

Kurt stood and saluted, "Heil Hitler."

They both repeated the Nazi greeting, the major said "This mistress of yours, Anna."

"Yes, what about Anna?" Kurt said frankly.

"Do you know of her whereabouts last night?"

"Why does that concern you?" Kurt said brusquely. He was indignant that men of a lower rank, even if they were SS, should ask about his private life.

"Two Jews have escaped from the ghetto," the major continued. "She is known to be sympathetic to Jews."

'*So they suspect Anna was involved and are probably torturing her at the moment,*' Kurt thought. '*Is this why she came to me last night in such an anxious state. Nonetheless I must try to save her.*'

"She may have been at one time," Kurt said with a chuckle. "Since I have become *involved* with her, she has seen the greater purpose in our efforts to purge the Earth of this vermin."

"Are you sure she is sincere in her claims?"

"I will not answer your questions any further. I am going over to *Schulzstaffel[2]* headquarters and talk to Colonel Schaeffer. We will discuss this matter like officers and gentlemen."

"As you wish Colonel Brandt. We were about to suggest that you come to headquarters."

"I will be there within the hour. You go on back and report to him. I do not want people to think that I am under arrest," Kurt said bluntly.

Anna was taken to a bare room and made to stand in the centre. Two floodlights, each shining on her from a forty-five-degree angle, were switched on. They were of such intensity that room around them seemed an inky void. A rope dropped in front of her and she was uncuffed. Her hand was tied together at the end of the rope and it was

[1] *Guten Morgen, Herr Hauptmann* – Good Morning, Colonel sir
[2] Schulzstaffel – full name for the SS

pulled up, hoisting her by her arms until her feet barely touched the floor. The pain was excruciating and she could already feel the intense heat of the floodlights. The two men who secured her left the room and she was left alone for a time. Many thoughts raced through her head. The pain she was feeling now would only be the beginning, as the SS would do everything they could to force a confession out of her. Once that was accomplished, the pain would then end with a simple bullet in her brain. She must hold out. If she confessed to helping Jacob and Golda, Kurt could also be in danger. Could she hold out? She must hold out.

A door opened and an officer walked in. She could not see his face as his body had the outline of a black silhouette. Anna could see the outline of an officer's cap in that silhouette.

"So, Anna Lindenbergis, you have come back to me," said a sneering voice.

Anna recognized the voice of the person who interrogated her and Valdis when the Nazis first came to Latvia. "*Herr Kapitan*," she gasped. "Heil Hitler."

The riding crop he was carrying struck her hard across the midsection. "Do not use the name of our Fuehrer, Jew lover."

Anna cried out in pain. The interrogator walked around her, slapping his crop against his other hand.

"Now then, I warned you to cease having concern for the Jews, or face harsh consequence."

"I have done nothing," Anna gasped.

"Did you help some Jews escape from the ghetto last night." he demanded.

"How could any Jews escape? The ghetto is watched by the patrols with floodlights."

The crop struck out again, this time across the calves of her legs. Anna again cried out.

"Answer my question," he cried harshly.

"No sir," Anna gasped.

"No sir, what?" he demanded again.

"No sir, I didn't help any Jews escape."

"Why did you leave so early this morning?"

"It is a long drive sir. I wanted to get back early.

"Where were you last night?"

Anna was silent and again the crop lashed out.

"I will ask you again," he said. "If you do not answer, I will have your clothing removed. My crop is more effective on bare skin."

Anna's thoughts raced wildly. The thought of being strung up naked in front of her interrogator was unbearable. She must find an alibi.

He was about to strike again but Anna cried out suddenly, "He doesn't like me to talk about it."

"Who is he and what are you talking about?" The crop struck across her buttocks.

"Colonel Brandt," Anna gasped.

"What, that you are his whore? Everyone knows that." The interrogator walked directly up to Anna and breathing in her face he said contemptuously. "Because that is all you are, is a whore. Maybe when this session is over, we will let you live and keep you in the basement for the pleasure of the whole Riga detachment."

Anna shuddered at the thought. Her interrogator stepped back and lit a cigarette. After a long moment of listening to her gasping in pain, he said. "I will leave you now and when I come back we will discuss how the same two Jews whom you say helped you hide from the Reds are the same two who escaped last night." He said as he turned and walked out the door.

"What is the meaning of detaining my mistress, Anna Lindenbergis," Kurt demanded as he addressed the SS Security Chief, Heinz Schaeffer. As Kurt was a full colonel and Schaeffer was only a lieutenant colonel, he still held rank.

"It seems that your mistress may have been involved in the escape of two Jews from the ghetto last night." Schaeffer replied.

"Why do you say that?"

"The two Jews who escaped are the same ones that she once said were her friends."

"They were friends of convenience and offered to hide her from the Reds."

"Nonetheless she showed sympathy for the Jews at the time of our arrival."

"And since that time?"

"She was seen near the ghetto once."

"Once," Kurt snorted. "She was curious. She told me about it and I told her to stay away from there."

"Her whereabouts last night are under suspicion," the chief continued.

"Last night, she was with me."

"You can prove this?"

"I don't have to prove anything. Do you honestly think that I would protect someone who is helping Jews? I demand that you release her."

Just then the interrogator stepped into the office. "I need to confirm her whereabouts last night," he said quickly, then he noticed Kurt. "Colonel Brandt," he said smartly. "Heil Hitler."

Kurt repeated the Nazi greeting then continued, "I overheard you say something about Anna's whereabouts last night."

"Yes sir."

"She was with me all night. Now if you will release her."

"I am still convinced she knows something about the escape of these particular Jews. It is a coincidence that they were the ones who escaped, and that she left so early this morning."

"She left early because we planned to go to the opera tonight. She has taken quite a liking to Wagner," Kurt said quickly. "Now I demand that you let her go."

The chief stood up and looked directly at Kurt. "You may outrank me technically, but in matters of security, the SS outranks the *Wehrmacht*."

"I have a suggestion, *Herr* Chief." Kurt said puffing himself up and looking directly at Schaeffer. "If you ever have the opportunity to check the personal staff of *Reichsfuehrer* Himmler you will find a person by name of Monika Schultz employed there. She is my sister."

The Chief swallowed hard. The very mention of Heinrich Himmler struck terror to his heart. Himmler was the most feared man in all of Nazi occupied Europe. He was forsworn only to Hitler and controlled both the SS and the Gestapo. Even leading Nazis such as Goebbels and Goering trod carefully around him. It was said that this almost inhuman, *man from Mars*, as other Nazis called him, had files on everyone. Such lowlife as the mere head of the Riga SS detachment, who lived in terror of crossing their superiors, would not even dare to check if Kurt was telling the truth.

"I think you know that *Reichsfuehrer* Himmler views incompetence in the lower ranks of the SS with as much contempt as he does the enemies of the Reich." Kurt said with a measured but contemptuous voice.

"Yes sir," the Chief said weakly.

"I will have Anna back if you please," Kurt said quietly.

When the door opened Anna braced herself for probably even more intense torture. Her interrogator instead, let down the rope and Anna collapsed on the floor.

Get up," he said.

Anna struggled to her feet but her arms felt limp and useless. He told her to hold out her arms and as he undone the binding he said, "You are one lucky whore. Come with me."

"C-Colonel Brandt," Anna gasped, when she entered the main office.

"Have they treated you well?" he asked calmly.

Anna made neither comment nor eye contact with anyone.

"You may take the wench home with you," Colonel Schaeffer said. "It will be wise to remember though, that in matters of security regarding the Reich, the SS prevails. We will continue our investigations and if we find your mistress guilty of helping Jews, your connections in the office of the *Reichsfuehrer* will be of little use to you."

"Yes, Colonel," Kurt replied evenly, as he motioned for Anna to follow. Outside the building, presided over by two stone-faced guards, Kurt beckoned Anna to climb into his staff car.

They had gone about two blocks when Anna spotted a woman on the sidewalk. The woman turned away into the crowd as they approached. Anna wasn't certain but she suspected that the woman was Lana. If Lana was still working as an informer and saw her last night, she was doomed and so was Kurt. Kurt glanced over and noticed that Anna was very pale.

"You look like you've seen a ghost."

"Worse than a ghost," Anna said in a tiny voice. "That woman back there?"

"What woman?" Kurt asked.

Anna said no more, she was too weary to try to explain and if Lana were still an informer, it wouldn't matter anyway.

As they drove along down a street along the river, Kurt said after a time, "I don't know if you helped those Jews and I don't want to know. All I know is that I was barely able to save you from being tortured to death. I risked my career and possibly my life for you, and I don't want to have to do it again."

"Yes Kurt," Anna replied meekly. "I'll never forget your kindness."

"Kindness indeed," Kurt snorted. "I am a fool. Why should I be so concerned about some Latvian wench?"

"You are a kind person," Anna replied.

"I will do just one more act of kindness," Kurt said gruffly. "I am assigning you to the hospital as extra nursing staff, since you want to be a doctor anyway. A room will be provided for you there and it will be wise for you to stay inside the hospital even when off duty. Also it will be wise for me not to see you again, at least for a long time. They will be watching both of us very carefully."

"Yes, Colonel Brandt," Anna replied in a downcast tone. "When do I start?"

"Tomorrow morning you will report, though I will tell them to give you an extra day off to recover from your experience with the SS."

Chapter Eleven

Anna was again assigned as a hospital worker. This time she was actually in the hospital. She did everything from scrubbing floors to folding bandages. Sometimes she was a stretcher-bearer and other times she wheeled the dead to the mortuary. She seldom left her quarters even on days off, and Kurt seldom called. If he did his visits were quite brief. Anna lived in terror for the first while, fearful that Lana might have seen her with Jacob and Golda, but as time passed and she was not arrested, Anna began to breathe more easily.

As the years moved through 1943 and on into 1944 it became increasingly evident that something was very wrong with the campaign on the Russian front. The arrival of wounded from the front moved from a steady trickle to a torrent. Wounded soldiers sometimes talked in wide-eyed terror of being attacked by vast hordes of Russian troops who fought with an uncommon ferocity. News bulletins while still sounding optimistic, talked more of strategic retreats including the withdrawal from the siege of Leningrad. To all but the most naive ears, the war was clearly turning against Germany. This was the worst possible news for Anna - defeat of Germany would mean the return of the Soviets and she may be still on their wanted list.

The summer of 1944 was a beautiful summer. The weather was warm and sunny and the land was bountiful with flourishing crops, while the flowers were in bloom with great profusion. However, this was just the calm before the storm. Soviet bombers appeared in the skies launching strikes against Riga. Refugees arriving from eastern Latvia told of the approaching Red Army. Anna listened to news bulletins with grave concern. They stated that the Estonian capital of Tallinn had fallen to the Red Army. To the south the Soviets had advanced into central Poland and they had also broken through into Eastern Latvia. Anna was driven to desperation, terrified that the Red Army would soon be at the gates of Riga. *'I must go to Kurt,'* she thought. *'I have to get out of Latvia before the Soviets return.'*

Kurt answered the frantic pounding on his door to find an anxious looking Anna on the other side.

"Come in," he smiled as he opened the door. "*Guten Abend*, Anna. *Wass ist loss[1].*"

"Aren't you afraid to let me in?" Anna asked as she cautiously entered his flat.

"Did you see a guard at the door?" he smiled.

"No."

"The manpower situation is so critical, that even many of the SS have been withdrawn and sent to the front." Kurt explained. "Oh they still patrol the streets, but their main concern is watching for deserters. The SS have standing orders to shoot any deserters on sight. Since I have kept my nose clean these past two years and stayed away from any outspoken Latvian women, I have probably ceased to be a concern to either the SS or the Gestapo."

"Then you are sure your flat isn't bugged?"

"Positive. I doubt that it ever was. Were you followed?"

"I took every precaution," Anna replied, though her eyes darted around fearfully.

"Then we should be safe. Now, what's on your mind?"

"Are we losing the war?" Anna asked in a quiet voice as she looked fearfully around.

Kurt chuckled as Anna was using the word we again. "Yes I'm afraid we are," Kurt said gravely. "It is only a matter of time before the Red Army overruns Latvia again as they have already crossed the border."

"I heard they captured Tallinn and are also in Poland," Anna swallowed.

"Yes, and in the Balkans as well. The Americans have taken most of France and Italy and the British are in Belgium."

"Oh my God," Anna said. She wanted to be sarcastic in view of Kurt's earlier overconfidence in the *Wehrmacht,* but now she felt empathy for him and the German war effort in the face of this grave new threat. "What about the Finnish front?"

"Finland is suing for peace."

"Oh," Anna said in a small voice, as both Valdis and Karlis were in that area, though she hadn't got a letter from Valdis for several months.

"You came here for other reasons besides discussing the war news did you not?" Kurt asked directly.

[1] *Guten Abend* – Good Evening. *Wass ist loss* – German colloquial, what's up, literally what is loose.

"Yes. I must get out of Latvia," Anna said in a desperate tone.

"How do you propose to do that?"

"Help me," she pleaded. "I cannot be here when the Russians return. I may still be on their wanted list, and I don't want to live under communism again."

"Yes, and if they found out you worked for us . . ."

"Please help me! Can't you put me on a ship?"

Kurt looked at her gravely and said, "I don't see how that is possible. The dockyards are one place that the SS and Gestapo do watch carefully, in case deserters try to slip out. Only the severely wounded and their medical attendants are allowed on the hospital ships."

"Please, I must get out," Anna cried. "At least some of my ancestors were German."

"There are some other ships taking refugees back to the Fatherland. They mostly leave from Liepaja"

"What do they do with them there?" Anna asked gravely. She had heard that even some non-Jewish Latvians had been taken away to Germany for slave labour during the course of the Nazi occupation.

"They go to refugee camps." Kurt replied.

"And work as slaves." Anna scoffed.

"Your alternative is to stay here and take your chances with the Soviets."

"Please isn't there some way I can sneak into Germany and pass as a citizen. I don't want to go to any camps. My spoken German is almost flawless."

Kurt looked carefully around then picked up a notepad and paper, even though he had said his flat wasn't bugged, he could never be absolutely certain. As he wrote he spoke. "My first duty is to the Reich. Asking me to issue you false papers is something I cannot do."

As a look of horror swept over Anna's face he handed her a note. She read:

'I'll see what I can do. I'll move you to patient care. Please destroy this note.'

She smiled wryly for a moment then feigned a sobbing voice; "You were my last hope. The Russians will surely kill me."

"I am sorry Anna," Kurt said gravely as he saw her to the door. "If I could help you I would."

The Baltic division to which Valdis had been assigned, had been sent to help the Finnish army retake their stolen territory and in some cases push into the parts of Karelia,[2] legally belonging to the Soviets. They fought through terrain consisting of deep snow and dense coniferous forest in winter, and muskeg bogs in summer. The auxillary units also enlisted some Karelians from the territory stolen from Finland during the Winter War. Valdis made friends with a Karelian named Jari Makki and through their friendship he gained a passable fluency in Finnish. He thought of how he could boast to Anna that he could now speak three languages. It was necessary for him to learn enough German to obey orders, as a soldier in the *Wehrmacht*.

As the war moved into 1944 the Red Army intensified its efforts to reclaim lost territory. After the siege of Leningrad was broken the Red Army advanced toward Finland with such intensity that even the fierce-fighting Finns could not stop them. After the retreat from East Karelia there was talk of Finland suing for peace. Among the demands of the Soviets were that the Finns turn on their erstwhile German allies and that all Baltic troops be handed over. As rumour of this got out, Valdis and Jari became very concerned.

"We have to get out of here," Valdis said to Jari one day while on patrol. "If we are captured by Russians we'll either be shot or die horribly in the camps."

"Are you thinking of deserting?" Jari asked.

"Is there another way out? You speak Finnish and know the land and you could help us get through into Finland proper."

"I am still legally a Finnish citizen since I was born and raised in Vipuri. I could be tried for desertion."

"Maybe not. After all it is not the Finnish army you re deserting from. We were both drafted into the German Army. If the German Army is being destroyed or ordered out of Finland as part of the surrender terms, then no one will care. You are just a refugee escaping from the Soviets."

"If we could sneak past the SS patrols, we could get into civilian clothes and flee with the other refugees leaving Karelia ," Jari said, with growing interest in the idea.

"Let's do it. We have nothing to lose. You know this country and

---

[2] Karelia   a region in eastern Finland and northwest Russia inhabited by Finnish speaking people.

we could slip through the forests to a nearby town and get rid of these uniforms. If worst comes to worse, I'd rather be shot by the SS than get captured by the Russians."

"And die a slow death in their camps," Jari added dryly.

As their patrol area took them through a dense coniferous forest, Jari and Valdis simply faded into the forest and headed for a nearby town instead of returning to their army post. It was dusk when they reached the town and they found it crowded with refugees waiting to get into Finland proper.

"Let's ditch this stuff," Valdis said, removing his helmet and other combat gear.

"When we get into the village we will have to find some civilian clothing," Jari added. "Then we can pass as refugees."

They managed to each steal a set of ill-fitting civilian clothes, then as Jari tucked his too-large shirt into his trousers, he said, "I can smell something cooking."

"Yes, there is a soup line down the street. We should go there; for who knows when we will eat again," Valdis replied.

Later as they sat and ate a meager meal of watery soup and black bread, Jari said as he looked cautiously around. "We will have to slip into the forest as soon as we have eaten, for sooner or later our unit will report us missing."

"Yes, and the SS patrols will be on the lookout for us," Valdis added "We'll stay near our weapons in case we have to defend ourselves."

"You would kill SS men?" Jari asked.

"Why not. They would shoot us without hesitation. Besides, I will do almost anything, even die, before I will go back under Soviet rule."

Jari and Valdis spent the night in the forest under a spruce bough shelter. The next day they stole back toward the village and observed a large column of refugees moving westward.

"Let's get into the crowd. All those people are heading for Finland, as no self-respecting Finn wants to live under Soviet rule either."

"We should get into the middle of the crowd and keep our heads down, lest an SS patrol comes by." Valdis added.

The column moved steadily all day until it reached the next town. "Look, we're home, that's the Finnish flag!" Jari exclaimed. He pointed to the white flag with the blue horizontal cross. The soldiers and police that were about were all wearing Finnish uniforms and there was no evidence of SS personnel. Nonetheless Jari and Valdis stayed as far away from uniformed people as possible. Then, as they heard a train whistle blow, Valdis said, "There is a railway here, perhaps we can get on a train going west."

"Yes maybe we can get to Helsinki," Jari said excitedly. "I was at our capital once. It's a pretty little city."

"Yes, the deeper we get inside Finland, the less likely it is that we will encounter our friends in black," Valdis added.

That night they, along with several other refugees, stole on board a westbound freight train composed mainly of empty boxcars.

The following morning Jari and Valdis arrived at Helsinki penniless and starving. As they made their way through the Finnish capital, they found much of the core in ruins. It had just sustained a heavy raid by Soviet bombers as a way of persuading the Finns to sue for peace. Though the bombing had taken place several days before, there was still much cleanup to do, so Jari and Valdis pitched in. As they had hoped, their efforts earned them a place in the midday soup line set up on a nearby street to feed the workers. As they queued up for their bowl of soup and chunk of dark bread, Valdis sensed a certain familiarity about one of the organizers, a tall lanky man with craggy features. Upon getting his ration, Valdis was close enough to recognize the person supervising the noon day meal.

"Karlis Lindenbergis," he cried.

The man turned and studied Valdis and a slow smile crossed his face, "Valdemars Zirnis," he replied.

"I was hoping I might find you," Valdis said in Latvian, "but I didn't expect to as Finland is a big country."

"Come and see me after your lunch and we can talk," Karlis replied also in Latvian. "We'll go to a small public sauna down the street. It's a good place to talk."

Jari looked perplexed and Valdis explained in his broken-Finnish. He introduced Jari as his friend and confidant. Karlis spoke to him in Finnish with much better fluency than Valdis. Jari was pleased to hear that they were going to a sauna. He hadn't enjoyed one in some time.

"So how did you come to be in Finland?" Karlis asked in Latvian, once they were sitting in the steamy room wearing nothing but their towels. As they talked, Jari was busy savouring this favourite Finnish pastime.

"When the Germans took Latvia, I volunteered to join the German Army," Valdis explained. "Anna and I had been hiding from the Russians for a year and welcomed the arrival of the Nazis."

"Anna! You were with Anna?" Karlis exclaimed. "How is she, and what about the rest of my family?"

"They shot your father you know." Valdis said sadly. "The NKVD took him in the night, but it was quite certain that he was executed."

"The swine," Karlis said, with tears in the corners of his eyes.

"That's not all Karlis. They took your mother and Liesma away to Siberia. They took my family too but I escaped and came back to Latvia."

"What about Anna?" Karlis choked.

"She was alive and well, and working for the Germans when I left Latvia. We've written a few letters but the mail has not been very effective lately."

"I hope she can get out before the Russians return," Karlis said, wiping tears from his eyes.

"Yes, I do too, but I think Anna will be all right. She's a survivor." Valdis smiled weakly. "But I do wish there was a way to go back and get her."

"We can forget about that," Karlis said with a pained look. "We can forget about ever returning to Latvia."

Valdis swallowed at the prospect that he would probably never see Anna again. "I know," he said in a low voice. Resolving to face the future, he said to Karlis. "So, are you planning to stay the rest of your life in Finland?"

"No, I am getting out of here. Maybe tonight. I fear that this time the Soviets may succeed in conquering Finland, or at least subjugating it. If so, there is no future here for you or me."

"Where are you going?"

"To Sweden for now, and when the war is over, as I expect Germany will be defeated within a year or so, I plan to go to Canada and see if I can find my Uncle Janis."

"I had thoughts of going to Canada," Valdis laughed. "But the

Soviets came before I had enough money to leave the country."

"Come with me then. I have managed to make a deal with the captain of a freighter bound for Stockholm. If I can find a way to get on board his ship, he'll not report me as a stowaway. You can squeeze in with me. Sweden is neutral and even Jews find safety there, so you will be safe from the SS for deserting."

"I'll go. It is time to think of the future and to get far away from this crazy European continent," Valdis said. "There is no hope of finding either of our families and we can only hope that Anna can find a way out." He swallowed again at the thought that his chances of ever seeing Anna again were slim to nonexistent, even if she did escape.

As the conversation between them was in Latvian, Jari hung back, feeling awkward.

"What about your friend here?" Karlis asked.

"Jari, he is a Karelian from Vipuri and also joined the Army, to get back at the Russians for taking his land," Valdis said in Finnish. "We deserted together, when we heard that Finland was about to surrender to the Russians."

"So, do you want to come with us to Sweden?" Karlis asked Jari.

"No, I am a Finn at heart. I will stay and fight for my country. I'll lie low and when the Germans have left, I'll join the Finnish army."

"That is commendable," Karlis said. "If you Finns fight hard enough, the Russians might just let you keep your independence. If there is one person a bully will respect, it is someone who fights back. Our country is small and is already lost so we have nothing to fight for. All we can do is take a little piece of Latvia with us and remind the world of the enslavement of our country."

After dark that night, Karlis and Valdis made their way to the dockyards. Jari came along to serve as a lookout. He and Valdis hugged each other goodbye at the water's edge and he watched Valdis and Karlis steal on board the ship. Karlis and Valdis remained hidden in the hold of the ship even after it slipped out of port and moved down the Gulf of Finland into the Baltic Sea. They came out on deck the next day as the ship drew into the harbour at Stockholm. Keeping true to his word the captain did not treat them as stowaways. Once safely on Swedish soil, they filed as Latvian refugees and were granted asylum. For the first time in nearly five years, Valdis felt a great sense of freedom, safe from both the Gestapo and the NKVD.

Meanwhile, Anna was made an assistant nurse and spent a lot of time caring for the wounded. However as the weeks passed, she grew increasingly anxious. There were reports of Red Army troops within a few dozen kilometres of Riga. Then one day, Kurt appeared at the hospital. He first spoke to the head nurse, explaining that Anna would go on the hospital ship back to Germany. The nurse, a prim and proper German woman, who believed in following regulations to the letter, objected because Anna was a Latvian.

"This will all have to be cleared through the SS," she said frankly. "Anna should go with the other refugees if she wishes to go to Germany."

"Nurse, I have come into some evidence as of late that your grandmother was a Jew," Kurt said with his quiet measured voice.

"Impossible! There is not a drop of Jewish blood in me," the head nurse said indignantly.

"This evidence is contained in my files," Kurt continued, ignoring her. "And if you bring this matter about Anna to the SS, the Gestapo will go over my files and find this evidence. Then . . . well then, I'm afraid that you and I will be sitting side-by-side in the torture chamber trying to explain things to them. Do I make myself clear, Nurse?"

"Very clear sir," the head nurse swallowed. Although she was innocent, the sheer terror of an interrogation by the Gestapo bought her cooperation.

"I will speak to Anna now, if you please," Kurt said calmly.

"*Jawohl Herr Hauptmann*![3]" the nurse replied directly.

After taking Anna into a side room, Kurt said. "I will tell you this once. There is a hospital ship scheduled to leave Riga tonight taking the severely wounded back to Germany, where they are to go to a veteran's hospital in Berlin. Some of the nursing staff will go with them. You will be among that staff. I have signed exit papers for you, except that your name will be Anna Lemberg, a German national living in Latvia. You must assume this identity to avoid the camps and find your freedom."

"Will the SS accept these papers?" Anna asked, as Kurt handed her the documents.

"They should. Their main concern is deserters from the army. Since I signed these papers, they will probably accept them as such. Just answer their questions directly and give them no reason for suspi-

[3] *Jawohl Herr Hauptmann* – Yes surely, Colonel sir!

cion. Their personnel have changed so much over the last couple of years, it is unlikely anyone will recognize you."

"If I am found out?"

"Then we'll both be shot."

Anna swallowed and Kurt added. "I have every confidence you can pull this off."

"Thank you Kurt, er Colonel Brandt," Anna smiled with glistening eyes. "You have been a real friend and I will never forget your kindness."

"I will miss your charming outspoken company," Kurt replied, swallowing. "And especially your back rubs."

"I guess I was your massage mistress," Anna laughed weakly.

"Yes, well *Auf Wedersehen*. May life do you well," Kurt replied. He turned and walked out of the room. Anna tucked the papers into her dress.

That night when time came to evacuate the wounded, Anna was appointed to go with them. Her first duty was stretcher-bearer, carrying the wounded on board the ship. When the medical personnel and patients were delivered to the dockyard, the SS checked both. Some SS officers looked over the wounds and medical reports of the patients to make sure their condition was genuine. Others checked the papers of the personnel assigned to go on the ship.

Anna presented her exit papers without waiting to be asked. The SS officer looked both the papers and Anna over, then said. "Anna Lemberg."

"Yes sir." Anna replied without inflection.

"So your parents were German nationals living in Latvia."

"Yes sir.

"Why are you still here? All German nationals left the Baltic countries in 1939."

"My father wanted to stay behind. He liked living in Latvia."

"Indeed. And where is your father now?"

"The Reds shot him sir. They took my mother and sister away to Siberia."

"I see. How then did you escape?"

"I hid in the streets and in the country until our liberation. Then, I freely volunteered to serve the Reich."

"Yes, according to your papers you served quite well. Although you should stay behind to help with more of the boys coming back from the front, we will let you go. *Heil Hitler.*"

Anna clicked her heels together and raised her arm repeating the phrase. The SS officer stamped her exit papers.

As the ship headed to the northwest through the Gulf of Riga Anna came out on deck. She looked out at the Eastern Shore in the distance and could see the flashes of artillery duels between the Red Army and the *Wehrmacht* lighting the overcast skies like grotesque lightning. Soon the Red Army would be in Riga again. She thought of Kurt and swallowed. Would he survive the Red Army onslaught? She laughed weakly at the thought of how the entire German garrison in Riga had thought that she had a torrid affair with Kurt when in reality he was just a lonely man in want of pleasant company. Anna wiped a tear from her eye as she said goodbye to Latvia, the beloved land to which she could never return.

PART 2

FREEDOM

Chapter Twelve

When Anna emerged on deck the following morning, she could see a city in the distance, that the ship was heading for.

"Are we at Lubeck already?" Anna asked a seaman who came by. She was surprised at how quickly they had arrived at this port on the southwest corner of the Baltic Sea.

"No we are disembarking at Danzig," the seaman replied.

"Danzig? That's quite a ways from Berlin."

"The dockyards at Lubeck were bombed pretty heavily last night so we have to unload here and the casualties will be transferred from here by train to Berlin."

Anna stood on deck a while longer watching the ship approach the city located at the mouth of the Vistula River, before going below to help with the patients. As they drew close to the city, there was evidence that it had also sustained some bomb damage as a number of shattered buildings were visible.

The patients were quickly transferred from the ship to a special hospital train. The roofs of the coaches were painted with large red crosses. This was to hopefully discourage enemy bombers from attacking as per the Geneva Convention. The ever-attendant SS officers only briefly glanced at Anna's papers before giving the nod.

Soon the train was on its way, speeding westward across the German countryside toward Berlin. Sometimes their train was shunted to a siding to allow priority trains such as those carrying military equipment and supplies to the front. On these, Anna would see flatcars bearing tanks and cannons. Other times they were side tracked to allow for trains of a different type of cargo. These trains were made up of cattle cars and through the slats in the cars she could see human faces bearing forlorn looks of quiet terror.

'Oh My God,' Anna thought. 'This is a trainload of Jews on its way to the death camps. I wonder if Jacob and Golda were able to elude the Nazis?' A porter quickly came by and asked everyone to draw the blinds so that they couldn't see the train that was transporting human cargo.

Anna was glad that she had risked her own life to give Jacob and Golda a chance at life and freedom. If they were able to survive until the return of the Red Army, they might live to old age.

It was evening when the train pulled into the bomb-scarred German capital. Even the railway yard had a deep crater, rimmed by mangled rails and cars, in its midst.

The patients were quickly transferred to the hospital. During the transit, Anna could hear sirens wailing and searchlights scanning the skies. This soon followed by streams of red tracer bullets fired by antiaircraft guns. Overhead were the drones of many aircraft that were soon followed by the explosions of falling bombs. Although none were dropped near the hospital, it was somewhat unnerving for Anna as she witnessed her first air raid. There were loud cheers from everyone as an explosion overhead indicated that one of the bombers was hit.

Everyone was hustled inside the hospital as the head nurse said, "We will be safe here. It is against the Geneva Convention to bomb hospitals."

"Don't count on it," one patient moaned. "The British and Americans will bomb anything. They destroyed the whole city of Hamburg with fire-bombs."

When the patients were settled in, the Surgeon General approached Anna.

"Your accent is different. Where are you from?"

"I am Anna Lemberg," Anna said quickly. She wondered if the Surgeon General was a Gestapo agent. "I was raised in Latvia. I have approved papers to be here."

"It is all right, don't bother to get them out," the Surgeon said as Anna fumbled for her papers. "Save them for the police if they should stop you."

"Yes sir," Anna replied.

"We are short staffed at the hospital. Would you like to stay on as a nurses assistant?"

"Yes sir," Anna grinned. "Before the war broke out, I planned to study medicine."

"Well, you'll have plenty of first-hand experience here," the surgeon said. "You will need to have a place to stay and I will write you up a paper requesting that you be allowed to stay in Berlin."

"Oh thank you sir. Can you tell me where I might stay?"

"There is a list on the bulletin board of people who will billet hospital staff."

"Thank you."

As Anna scanned down the list, she stopped at the name Klaus and Erna Schmidt.

'I wonder if it is them,' she thought. *'Would they turn me in?'*

Anna took the chance, in this time when the curtain was about to come down on the Third Reich, she felt she had little to lose.

Anna knocked on the door of the residence at the address given. It was a stately house located several blocks to the west of the hospital. Erna answered the door, she looked much older and grayer, than when Anna had seen her last.

Anna smiled and said "*Frau* Schmidt. Do you recognize me."

Erna squinted and said, uncertainly, "Anna?"

"It is me."

"Come in child come in," Erna beckoned.

Anna stepped into the house. After closing the door, Erna turned and they hugged for a long moment.

"What are you doing here?" Erna finally asked.

"I came with the wounded soldiers and the Surgeon General is going to write me a permit to stay in Berlin. I was given this address as a place to stay."

"Certainly you may stay here," Erna smiled. "Come in. I am afraid we don't have much to eat, but I can spare a cup of tea for you."

"If you have little tea I can do without," Anna replied.

"Nonsense, I will make you a cup of tea and you can tell us all about how you survived to get here."

As they came through the house, Erna called out, "Klaus, oh Klaus we have a guest."

When they entered the drawing room, Klaus came toward them, pushing himself in a wheelchair.

"*Herr* Schmidt," Anna said respectfully.

"Anna?" he said with a puzzled look.

"It is me," Anna smiled.

"But how?"

"I will make a cup of tea and Anna will tell us how she came to be here," Erna said as she turned to go to the kitchen.

"Sit down," Klaus beckoned.

As Anna eased herself into a chair, she asked. "Did you have an accident *Herr* Schmidt?"

"War wound," Klaus grunted. "I was at the front in France."

"Imagine them drafting a man his age into the army," Erna said from the kitchen.

"We lost our son," Klaus said with sadness in his eyes.

Anna's eyes drifted over to a photograph of their son Ernst, handsome in his *Luftwaffe* officer's uniform.

"He was shot down during an air raid over England back in 1941."

"And Gerda?" Anna asked, as Erna brought through some tea and cakes.

"Gerda was in Hamburg last we heard," Erna replied, as she set down the tray. "She is an army nurse."

"Yes, in the last letter she wrote us, she told us how the Americans and British had set fire to the whole city with incineratory bombs," Klaus spat. "They massacred thousands of civilians."

"But that's war," Anna sighed. "I will probably never see any of my family again."

"Do tell us about your family," Klaus said.

Anna related the whole sad story of her family and her personal history from the day the Soviets seized Latvia until the present. While she didn't mention Kurt by name, she told them how she had been allowed to slip into Germany with false papers to avoid being sent to the refugee camps. Finally she added, "Please don't tell the SS, I don't want to be in any camps and I can't go back to Latvia and live under the Russians."

"Who is there to tell," Klaus shrugged. "The SS is busy chasing deserters and our nation will soon be defeated. The Red Army is in East Prussia and ready to cross the Vistula, the Americans are approaching the Rhine and the British are in Belgium."

"And to think, we believed in Hitler," Erna said bitterly. "He has led our country to ruin, cost us our son, and made a cripple out of Klaus. Heil Hitler indeed, I wished they would have succeeded when those officers tried to kill him last summer."

"Aren't you afraid that the Gestapo might hear you?" Anna said fearfully.

"Who cares?" she threw up her hands. "The world is coming to an end anyway and if they shoot me they put me out of my misery."

"My wife can get very emotional at times," Klaus chuckled. "We are a family in good standing and I am sure the Gestapo have better things to do than watch us. What's left of them that is. "You will be safe here, and if you can help us find enough to eat, you are more than welcome to stay."

"Thank you very much," Anna smiled. "I have had to hunt for enough to eat ever since the Bolsheviks destroyed my family, so I should be good at finding food."

Anna endured that terrible winter in Berlin as the great city sustained daily bombing raids, frequent cuts in electricity, and chronic food shortages. Every day she saw the flower of German youth, children barely past puberty, carrying rifles and heading for the front, while a torrent of casualties poured in. The front was getting closer and closer as Anna shuddered with every news report. First the Red Army had captured Warsaw, then crossed the Oder right into the heart of Germany. In the south the Red Army was advancing up the Danube, and was now at the gates of Vienna. In the west, the Americans had crossed the Rhine and were sweeping into central Germany. Anna prayed that they would reach Berlin before the Russians. News bulletins from the loudspeakers still talked of strategic retreats, but often spoke optimistically, of the western powers joining up with Germany to stop the Russian hordes from overrunning Europe. Refugees streaming in from the east spoke horrifically of barbaric atrocities committed by Red Army soldiers, pillaging and raping their way across Germany. This compounded Anna's panic as the Red Army drew ever nearer to Berlin. At one point she considered fleeing Berlin to the west, but was forewarned that the SS would shoot anyone attempting to leave the city, particularly if they had a vital job like hers.

Then came the news that spring. The Red Army had now surrounded Berlin. As Anna walked the several blocks to the hospital one morning she saw them coming. The streets were rubble-strewn with bombed out buildings everywhere while evil-smelling smoke filled the air. The sounds of cannons firing and constant machine-gun fire seemed all around her. Every so often she would hear the awful sound of an incoming artillery shell and would duck for cover hoping it wouldn't hit her. Red Army soldiers were everywhere coming down every street. Anna ducked behind the wall of a bombed out building and cowered in terror. Soldiers, some wearing helmets, some wearing fur caps, swarmed around and past her, scurrying over the rubble like ants from a disturbed hill. They seemed to show little interest in her as they had their guns poised shooting at German snipers offering resistance. A tank, with the red star of communism painted on the side of the turret, ploughed through a wall next to her and Anna barely sprang out of the way in time to avoid being buried by falling masonry. Anna did not go to work that day. Instead, she crawled into the cellar of a house that was still reasonably in tact, cringing in terror as the Red Army went by her. She thought of Klaus and Erna. Would the Red Army take their house? Concern for them eventually overrode her fear, and Anna crept out of the cellar and picked her way through the streets amid the rubble and dead bodies. Among the dead were Russian soldiers, German boys in early youth still clutching their rifles, and civilians of all ages. Other civilians were staggering around the streets totally disillusioned.

When Anna reached the Schmidt house, she found that the door had been stowed in.

"Erna!" she cried desperately as she ran into the house. She screamed in horror at what she found. Klaus lay beside his wheelchair in a pool of blood and Erna lay nearby, her clothing torn to shreds. Her sightless eyes stared upward and a look of utter terror was on her face.

"Erna, oh Erna," Anna cried. She picked Erna up and cradled her as she cried abundantly, but the woman was stiff from being dead for several hours. Slowly Anna lowered Erna to the floor. She went to the nearest bedroom and pulled a sheet off the bed and wrapped Erna up in it. As she looked around the house, Anna could see that it was trashed, gold and silver ornaments of value were missing. Pottery and earthenware lay smashed and all of the food from the kitchen was taken. Amid this were pieces of broken furniture, and various ornaments deliberately smashed. The framed picture of their son Ernst, had been thrown on the floor and ground by a boot heel.

"Animals!" Anna cried in anguish. "Savage, bloody animals!"

She dragged both bodies into a side room and closed the door, then went upstairs to her own room. The vanity and closets had all been torn apart in a search for valuables, but the bed was still in tact. Anna dropped down on it and cried for a long while before falling into a tortured sleep. Daylight faded into darkness then back into daylight again as Anna lost all track of time. She just lay in her room in a torpid state of shock as the world had crumbled down around her. Her father being shot and her mother and sister being taken away, she thought to be the ultimate horror. This act of utter barbarity vented on two help-less late middle-aged people was beyond comprehension.

Then one morning she awakened from her state to an eerie silence. There were no more bombs exploding and no more constant rattle of machine-gun fire.

'The war must be over', she thought. *'I must get out of here.'*

Slowly Anna struggled to her feet and crept downstairs not daring to look toward the room where Klaus and Erna lay, nor did she look at the large patch of dried blood on the sitting room carpet. She slipped out the backdoor and headed down the back alley, trying to think of a way to get past the Red Army into the western part of Germany pre-sumably occupied by the British and Americans.

She had gone several blocks, then she saw two Russian soldiers studying a bicycle in fascination. She ducked out of sight behind a wall, but could still see and hear them.

"How does it work, Yuri?" one soldier said to the other. "It has only two wheels."

"They are called bicycles, I have seen pictures of them, Ivan," Yuri said. "People sit on them and pedal them."

"You show me then."

Yuri climbed on the bicycle and started to pedal it but had gone less than a metre before it toppled over.

Ivan laughed and said, "I think there must be a wheel missing. How can a machine stand up on two wheels?"

"I tell you I saw pictures of people riding them," Yuri insisted.

Anna was totally amazed. Where did these people come from? It was incredible that they did not understand what a bicycle was or how it worked. She then noticed, that while they spoke perfect Russian and had Russian names, they were Asiatic in appearance with their wide cheek-bones, flat noses and small eyes that peered through slit-like lids.

'They're Siberian Shock Troops,' Anna shuddered. She had heard of them being used by the Red Army to terrorize civilians.

Anna turned to go when a lusty voice behind her said, "Come here little girl."

It was another Russian soldier and as she sprang to go past him, he grabbed her wrist with an iron grip. His uniform was dirty and bloodstained, while his sheepskin hat looked moth-eaten. A rifle was slung across his shoulders with the muzzle pointing downward. He grinned wickedly at her.

"*Nein, nein!*" Anna cried in terror as the Russian soldier leered at her with his broad lustful grin. Then switching to Russian she cried, "*Nyet, nyet.*" She clawed at him and tried mightily to pull free of his vise-like grip. She kicked him in the shins. He winced and backhanded her with a force that would have knocked her down, had not he such a firm grip on her arm. Anna spat blood and tooth-enamel at him and the soldier laughed.

"What have you got there Alexi?" Yuri said as he and Ivan came to join them.

"I got a wench so we can have some fun." Alexi grinned lustfully.

"Ah, she's a pretty one," Ivan said as he reached to stroke her chin.

"No, no, please don't hurt me," Anna begged in Russian, as she recoiled away from his hand.

"You speak Russian?" Alexi said with surprise. "Where did you learn to speak Russian?"

"My brother taught me," Anna said in a small voice.

"Let's take her to that building of many houses over there," Yuri said, motioning to an apartment block. "We'll have fun there."

"No, no!" Anna cried again. She struggled to break free and attempted to kick Alexi in the groin.

He slapped her so hard across the face that she nearly passed out. "I like a girl with fight, we have lots of fun." The others both laughed.

"Oh God, no." Anna murmured. "Oh dear God save me from this."

As they approached the apartment house another soldier came out the front door. He was grinning broadly and held a kitchen faucet in his hands. Water was still dripping from it."

"Look!" he said excitedly. "Magic water taps."

"What are you talking about, Oleg," Ivan said. "Magic water taps indeed."

"They fit in the wall and make water come out," Oleg said, with wonder in his voice. "I'm taking them back to my home in Siberia."

"Magic water taps," Yuri snorted, "I think you are crazy." Everyone laughed and even Anna was astonished. She found it incredulous that these people thought that taps magically produced water.

"Come inside and see," he beckoned.

"We were going there anyway to have fun with the woman," Alexi said. He tugged at Anna and she tried to shrink away.

They entered the kitchen and water was gushing out of the wall where the taps had been removed. They all looked at it for a while. Then Oleg said, "come into this room." They all crowded into the bathroom and Oleg demonstrated his discovery by working the taps at the washing sink. The others stared in amazement, and Ivan had to try the taps.

"What's this?" Ivan said as he turned and looked at the flush-toilet. They all looked curiously at the fixture and Ivan turned the handle. They were utterly astonished to watch the water swirl down through the bowl.

"Maybe they use this to wash potatoes," Yuri ventured.

"Yes, it could be used for this," Ivan added.

"And this big trough?" Alexi said, pointing at the bathtub. "Do they bring animals in here to water?"

Anna couldn't believe that anyone could be so totally ignorant of such basic elements of civilization as plumbing. These soldiers must indeed come from a far corner of Siberia. Alexi became so curious that he too, had to try the taps of the bathroom sink. He was so fascinated, he relaxed his iron grip on Anna's wrist. Seizing the opportunity for escape, Anna pulled her hand free and bolted.

"Come back here," Alexi cried as he ran after her.

Anna slammed the door in his face as she ran out through it. She grabbed the bicycle that so fascinated then, mounted it and rode away. They were so transfixed to see her ride that they didn't even try to stop her. As Anna rode westward through the streets of Berlin as fast as she could pedal, many Russian soldiers she passed also stopped and stared. Others tried to grab at her, but she was moving too fast.

She saw the Brandenburg Gate ahead of her, as she rode for her life down bomb-shattered *Unter Den Linden*[1] , and aimed for it. She didn't know what was on the other side, but it was a gateway. A stout female Russian soldier who was directing traffic, stepped in her path just as Anna reached the gate and Anna collided headlong into her with a sickening thud. Anna was knocked from the bicycle but crawled toward the gate just as a group of Russian soldiers were closing in on her, shouting for her to stop.

[1] *Unter Den Linden* – Under the Lindens, a fashionable street in Berlin lined with linden trees

147

As she scrambled past the pillars, she noticed that the Russians did not follow though they still yelled at her to come back. Anna heard footsteps in the other directions and turned to see more soldiers. They were different. They had baggy uniforms and wore round helmets. Some of them were shouting at the Russians, while others regarded her curiously as she looked up at them with a pleading fear in her eyes. The soldiers spoke to each other in a strange language that sounded vaguely similar to German. Anna noticed that several of them seemed to be chewing something.

"*Englanders*?" Anna asked, as she was sure they were speaking English.

One of them laughed and replied, "No, we're Americans."

"*Amerikaners ja?,*" Anna said with a hopeful smile.

"Can you speak English?" one of them asked.

"*Nein,*" Anna said apprehensively. She was sure they were asking her if she could speak English. She asked, "*Sprechen Sie Deutsche?*"

They spoke to each other and she heard the word *Kraut* in the midst of their conversation. There was still a heated exchange going on with the Russians, and these soldiers appeared ready to shoot if the Russians came through the gate.

Presently, another soldier, apparently an officer, drove up in a jeep. He addressed the Russians in their own language. The Russians insisted Anna had escaped custody and they wanted her back.

"No, no," Anna begged. "Don't send me back. I didn't do anything wrong. The Russians do things with women. Please don't send me back." Anna started sobbing. She spoke in Russian.

"*Vy govorite po Russky*[2]?" the American officer asked Anna in Russian, with a book-learned accent.

"My older brother, who travels a lot, taught it to me," Anna replied. "I am German." She would have liked to tell him she was a Latvian, but the uncertainty of her situation and fear of the Soviets, dictated that she keep her alias.

"They say you are a spy," the officer said gravely.

"No, I'm not a spy," Anna pleaded. "They assaulted me, and they want to . . . Oh please don't send me back."

"Come with me," he said with a smile. "I will take you to the military police and we'll decide what to do with you."

[2] *Vy govorite po Russky* – Do you speak Russian

He offered her a hand and Anna accepted. The Russian soldiers shouted curses as Anna climbed into the jeep and they drove away.

"Why are you here? I thought the Russians controlled Berlin." Anna asked as they drove through the rubble-strewn streets.

He laughed and said, "Not all of it. You are in the American sector of Berlin."

"That's good. I was afraid that the Russians had all of Berlin," Anna said.

"That's what they hoped," he replied. "They have a sector, we have a sector, the British have a sector, and the French have a sector."

He drew a small flat piece of something from his pocket and placed it in his mouth and began to chew.

"What is it, that you have in your mouth?" Anna asked.

"Chewing gum." he laughed. "Do you want some?"

Anna shrugged and he handed her a stick Anna placed it in her mouth and began to chew. It had a mild fruity taste at first and in a short while it had no flavour at all. When they reached their destination, Anna spat it out.

The officer took her inside to an office where another man sat behind the desk. The Stars and Stripes flag hung on a mast at his side. Anna wondered if this was going to be an SS style interrogation all over again. She stood at rigid attention, as they spoke to each other in English. Finally the man at the desk spoke to her in German, his German was more articulate that the Russian of the other officer. The other officer left and a guard with a round helmet with the letters MP stamped on it stood silently at the door.

"So what is your name *Fraulein*?" The man at the desk asked.

"Anna Lemberg sir, I have approved papers to be in Berlin."

"Approved by whom?"

"The SS,"

He laughed and said, "The SS no longer exists. So, why were you running from the Russians?"

"They were going to rape me," Anna said sobbing. "Please don't send me back."

"The Red Army has a bad reputation for raping every woman they can lay their hands on. So I can understand your plight." He studied Anna's face. It was beginning to swell from being slapped by Alexi. "Did they beat you?"

"Yes, they slapped me for trying to resist them," Anna sobbed.

"Animals," the officer muttered.

"So you won't send me back then?" Anna said hopefully.

"This city is crawling with refugees running from the Russians. What's one more? We will let you stay if you stay out of trouble."

"Oh thank you sir, thank you," Anna said gratefully.

"You will need new papers," the officer said. "The old ones mean nothing."

He called for a secretary and instructed her to make up a resident permit for Anna Lemberg.

"These papers I am making up will allow you to travel freely in the American, British or French sector. There you will be protected by law. If you wander back into the Soviet sector, we can't help you."

"How will I know to avoid that sector sir."

"Watch for signs and flags. You do know what the Soviet flag looks like?"

"Yes, the red flag with the hammer-and-sickle. You may be sure I will stay far away from there," Anna replied. "Tell me sir, is the whole of Germany divided up like Berlin?"

"Yes, we all have a sector, but Berlin is inside the Soviet sector."

"How could I get over to one of the other sectors of Germany proper."

He laughed and said, "There is a very long waiting list for that. Everyone wants to get out of Berlin."

The secretary returned with the documents and the officer signed them and handed them to her. "Good luck Anna and stay away from the Russians."

"To be sure I will," Anna replied as she got up. The man at the door opened it for her without a word. Anna thought how this was a much easier interrogation than the one she had with the SS back in Riga that time. The thought of Riga reminded her of her lost family and Valdis and she felt a sharp pain in her stomach. The past life and people were lost to her forever.

Anna wandered down the street alone and hungry, clutching her new identity papers. She stopped beside a trash can and tore up her old papers. No one need ever know that she came from Latvia.

After walking several blocks she came to a bread line and queued up with the hope of getting a meal. When her turn came, she was issued a bowl of thick soup loaded with beans, and chunk of bread. A cup of weak coffee was also available. As they were eating, the matron in charge of the bread line began to lecture them. She said that food and lodgings would be provided for anyone willing to sign up for a work gang to help clear the rubble and rebuild Berlin. As there was virtually no recourse, Anna signed up and was assigned a flop. She was to start work in the morning.

Chapter Thirteen

One evening, several weeks after she had settled into her new life, Anna got wanderlust and went for a walk down the streets near to where she was staying. She watched for flags and signs to make sure that she didn't stray into the Soviet zone. The streets were filled mainly with off-duty American soldiers and military vehicles. Occasionally jeeps full of soldiers would pass by and issue catcalls that made Anna uncomfortable. As she walked along, Anna happened by a tavern. She stood in the doorway and looked in. It was full of a noisy crowd of American soldiers swilling beer while a piano player played German folk songs in the background.

'*It must be nice to be a victor,*' Anna thought. '*You drink and celebrate then go home to a comfortable home somewhere across the ocean far from the Nazis and Communists.*'

"Hey babe come on in and I'll buy you a drink," said a soldier who came alongside her.

Anna didn't know what he said but he smiled and winked and gestured for her to come inside with him.

Even though Anna didn't understand, she sensed he was being friendly and she smiled fleetingly but was hesitant to accept an invitation from a strange soldier speaking a foreign tongue.

"Come on *mein Fraulein*" he beckoned. " I won't hurt you. I think you're cute."

"*Amerikaner ja,*" Anna said noticing the initials USA imbedded on his collar.

"Ya American," he laughed. "We won this war against you people. Come on babe, just one drink." He nudged her to come with him.

It had been a long time since Anna had enjoyed a carefree situation, so she accepted the invitation.

Once inside the tavern, the soldier called for a beer and asked Anna if she wanted one. She shook her head in the negative. She also refused an offer of a cigarette.

Another soldier came by stumbling as he walked and slopping his large mug of beer. "Well now Andy what y'all got there?" he said with a southern accent.

"She was looking in through the door so I invited her in," Andy replied.

The southerner put his hand lightly under Anna's chin and said, "Y'all look like a pretty li'l wench."

Anna recoiled away from him with a frightened look.

"You're scaring her," Andy said.

"Ain't no need to be scared a us, we're Americans," the southerner slurred. "We kin show you Kraut women a real good time." He stumbled as he slurred his speech and nearly slopped beer on Anna. "Hey, cat got yer tongue?" he laughed. "Sprecken see English." he slurred in a clumsy attempt to speak German..

"*Nein. Ich verstehe nicht Englisch,*[1]" Anna said in a small frightened voice

"Well I don't speak Kraut either," the southerner said with a sneer. "But you Kraut broads should be good to us Americans for savin' y'all from them commie Russians. How's about a little kiss."

"Lay off Joe," Andy said to the southerner. "She's frightened."

"Like I said, there ain't no need to be frightened of us. We're Americans. Now, about that kiss."

As Joe leaned to kiss Anna she turned away and Andy grabbed him by the collar. Joe wheeled and drove his fist into Andy's face knocking him to the floor.

"What's going on here?" asked another soldier.

"I'm just having a little fun with this l'il ole Kraut wench. She was gonna give me a kiss till Andy got jealous."

"Leave her alone," Andy said springing to his feet. Joe knocked him down again saying. "Ain't no need to get riled, she's just a li'l ole Kraut woman lookin' for some fun." Turning to Anna he added, "Right wench?"

Joe reached for Anna and grabbed her in a similar way that Alexi had done that time. She thought, *'Maybe these Americans are no better than the Russians after all.'*

She wrenched herself free and turned to go but Joe grabbed her again and this time pressed his sodden face against hers much to the amusement of his comrades. Anna slapped him hard making sure that her long fingernails clawed a set of parallel lines across his face. The other soldiers laughed uproariously as blood oozed down Joe's face.

---

[1] *Nein. Ich versteh nicht Englisch* – No, I don't understand English (app. Translation)

"Why you ungrateful l'le wench," he shouted, reaching for her again. Anna kicked him in the shins and bolted.

"This Kraut broad needs to be taught some manners," Joe shouted, as he gave chase. One of his buddies joined in the chase, more with the idea of controlling Joe than to molest the terrified Anna.

They ran down the street with Joe shouting curses at her. They ran for several blocks until Anna virtually stumbled into another soldier. As she fell at his feet in exhaustion she looked up. He wore a different type of uniform with a helmet that looked like an inverted soup plate. He must have been on duty as he was armed with a sten gun[2].

"Whoa there Miss. Where are you going in such a hurry?" he smiled, helping her up. Although Anna was frightened and by now was terrified of all soldiers, she could see he had kind eyes and a disarming smile.

"*Kanadier, ja,*" she said noticing the flashing on his shoulders.

"Yes, I am Canadian," he said in a friendly tone as he reached to help Anna up. Anna moved away from him and pulled herself up.

Joe and his buddy caught up to them. "Give her back to me she's mine," he demanded.

"*Nein, nein, Amerikaner nein,*" Anna said with terror in her eyes.

"She's afraid of you," the Canadian said with a gentle firmness.

"After what she's done. Get out of the way Canuck."
The Canadian soldier swung his sten gun into position and stepped firmly between Anna and Joe.

"Hey now, don't y'all get threatening with me," Joe said belligerently. "I am an American and we won this war."

The Canadian snorted and drew back the bolt of his sten gun. "I never met an American soldier yet who could fight his way out of a wet paper bag."

"Them's fightin' words, now give me that wench or I'll bring my buddies over and whoop yer ass."

"Go on back to your booze, Yank," the Canadian said. "You touch this woman and I'll shoot."

"Y'all wouldn't go shoot an American would you. We're on the same side in this war, and besides, the whole American army'll be over her to whoop yer ass," he took a step further.

"Hey, Joe," his buddy said. "Don't go pick a fight with a Canadian They got a battlefield reputation."

[2]sten-gun - a small, hand-held machine-gun

The Canadian backed up and Anna stayed behind him, "One more step, I'm warning you. You're in the British sector now."

"I don't give a hoot. That woman clawed and kicked me and I want my due."

Joe moved to take a step and the Canadian fired a short burst from his sten gun at the ground in front to his feet. Joe jumped back saying, "Wait til I tell my CO."

"Go ahead tell him. I'm sure this lady and I will have a story of our own to tell," the Canadian said calmly.

"Let's go, Joe," his buddy said. "She will holler rape and we'll be in trouble."

Joe turned and walked away. The Canadian turned to her and uncocked his sten. "Now Miss, do you speak English?"

"*Nein. Ich verstehe nicht Englisch.*"

"Please understand, I will not harm you," he said gently with a smile. "Come along with me to my CO. He can speak German."

He reached to take Anna by the sleeve, but she shrank away crying, "*Nein, nein.*"

"I'm sorry," the soldier said. "Someone must have really hurt you." He smiled and nodded for her to follow.

Somehow Anna felt she could trust him. After all, he came from that wonderful land called Canada that had acted as a magnet for so many Latvians. She followed his gentle lead as they came to his headquarters building. They entered an office where once again there was a man with officer's decal on his uniform sitting behind a desk. He looked up at the soldier and they had a conversation in rapid English.

The officer dismissed the soldier and turned to Anna.

Anna smiled at the soldier and said, "*Danke schon.*"

"You're welcome, I think," the soldier said as he left the room

"Now then miss," the officer said in German. "What is your name?"

"Anna, Anna Lemberg, sir" Anna said directly.

"Do you have any identification?"

"Yes, I have a permit to be in this part of Berlin," Anna replied quickly as she pulled the papers from her dress pocket.

The officer looked them over. "So you were in the American zone. Why were you running away?"

"The American soldier, he was going to . . . He tried to kiss me so I slapped him and ran."

"I see. Sometimes those Americans can be so crude."

"They're almost as bad as the Russians," Anna said tremulously.

"You've had encounters with them too?"

"Four of them were going to…" Anna said with terror in her eyes. "It was a miracle that I got away." Then abruptly changing the subject she said, "Do you know that the Russians don't know anything about plumbing?"

"I'm not surprised. Tell me about it?"

"They think a toilet is for washing potatoes and that faucets can magically draw water from the wall. They became so fascinated with the plumbing that they let their guard down and I was able to escape."

The officer laughed and said, "I've heard a lot of stories about Red Army soldiers. None of them are very good."

"Can I stay in the Canadian zone?' Anna asked with a pleading voice. "I don't trust Americans."

"Actually we're in the British zone. As part of the Commonwealth, a few Canadians have been assigned as part of the British occupation force in Berlin. By right I should report you to the British military police."

"What will they do?"

"Probably send you back. Maybe all the way back to the Russians. We have a huge problem with refugees. Everyone is trying to escape from the Russians. We even have Poles flooding in here."

"No, no, not the Russians," Anna begged as she dropped to her knees.

"Well, if you walk out that door now, you can stay in the British zone and I will forget this interview took place."

"Thank you sir, thank you," Anna said as she rose to her feet.

"Do Canadian soldiers hurt women?" Anna asked

"No," the officer said. "The standing rule is if any Canadian soldier is found guilty of rape he will be shot by a firing squad. You're pretty safe among our boys. Now go before someone finds out you've been here."

"Thank you again," Anna said as she left the room.

As Anna walked down the street wondering where she might sleep or find her next meal, she resolved not to go back to the job in the American zone. She would stay here, safely among the Canadians.

The following day Anna found a job in the British sector similar to the one offered in the American sector. It was work in exchange for a flop and two meals a day at a soup kitchen. She joined a large number of other displaced women working on rubble clean up known "as the women of the bricks." It seemed little different to the gentle slavery she endured under the Nazis in Latvia. The only thing missing was the SS. The military police of the British and especially Canadians seemed much less ominous, and their presence was almost invisible.

Anna had heard stories of how some people such as former prisoners-of-war, were being returned to the Soviets, so Anna remained ever tightlipped about her origins, fearful that she too could be returned to Latvia. When asked about her accent, Anna merely said she was from the east and it was assumed she meant East Prussia, a part of Germany not only annexed to Poland, but from which, the entire German population was being expelled. She also heard of camps with squalid living conditions, where refugees from Eastern Europe were often housed. Having no desire to live there, Anna was determined to continue passing herself off as a German citizen.

Since Anna was living in the British sector, she overheard the English language being used a lot, she soon picked up a few words and expressions of the English language. This was crucial if she was to ultimately go to Canada.

One day in August as Anna was returning from her job, she met a Canadian soldier coming down the street. He was in his off-duty uniform and was wearing a beret. There was a certain familiarity about him. He must have sensed the same as he stopped and looked directly at her. Finally he said, "You are the woman who was running from the Americans, are you not?"

Anna looked puzzled for a moment then said, "You soldier vis gun, stop *Amerikaner*?" Her accent was a mixture of German and Latvian.

He smiled and replied, "That's right. I see they allowed you to stay in the British sector."

"Ya stay, I got chob," Anna smiled.

"Would you like to walk with me? I will buy you dinner at a café that has recently opened."

"Valk? Get din-ner?" Anna was puzzled.

"You know eat," the soldier made a gesture like he was eating.

"Ya, eat dinner, I come ya?"

"Ya, you come," the soldier said. He offered her his arm and Anna reluctantly took it. They smiled at each other as the soldier led her to a nearby café. She thought of the last time she saw Valdis, he was also a soldier who took her to a café. She swallowed with this reminder of the past. Was he still alive? Would he ever find her?"

As they settled in chairs facing each other, they smiled awkwardly and finally Anna said. "Vhat name you?"

"Larry," he laughed. "Actually, my first name is Yrjo."

"Yrjo?"

"Yes It is a Finnish name. My father is Finnish and he named me after a good friend of his. My mother however, is Swedish. She said Yrjo is too hard of a name to spell or say properly, so she gave me the name Clarence for a middle name. Naming me after Uncle Clarence, her brother. So they call me Larry which is short for Clarence."

Anna laughed but looked perplexed.

"You didn't understand a word I said did you," Larry laughed. "What is your name?"

"Name Anna."

"Anna, that's a nice name."

Presently a waiter came with menus. Larry looked at them puzzled, as they were printed in German. "You read them," he said to Anna. "I can't read German."

Anna was not familiar with the dishes offered as she had seldom been to a restaurant. In Riga, when Kurt would occasionally take her to dinner, he did the ordering. She recognized Vienna Schnitzel as a dish she once tasted at the Schmidt's back in Riga. Finally she said, "You eat schnitzel."

"Yes, schnitzel sound good, whatever it is." Larry replied.

Anna placed the order and included beer for Larry.

"So where do you come from?" Larry asked.

"Come from?" Anna asked. She was almost tempted to tell him that she was a Latvian, but instead replied. "I run avay from ze Russians."

"Yes, a lot of people run away from the Russians."

"Zhey stupid, zey zhink, toilet for vashink potatoes. Zhey don't know vhat bicycle is."

Larry laughed. "Yes, I heard all about them."

"Vhere you from inside Canada?" Anna asked, wishing to turn the topic away from both her origins and the Russians.

"Inside Canada, I am from Alberta. I grew up in a village called Morning Glory."

"Mornink Glory, sound like nice name, ya," Anna replied.

"It's a nice place. There are lots of nice people there."

"Canada so far from vars. Ya. Is zhere Latvians in Mornink Glory?" Anna blurted.

Larry studied her and asked, "Latvians? Latvia, is that one of those little countries that the Soviets took over?"

"Ya, Soviet Russians stole zhem."

"Ya," Larry laughed. "Are you per chance from Latvia? Your accent doesn't sound like that of a typical German."

Anna swallowed and replied quickly, "I come from east."

"It doesn't matter," Larry said assuredly. "I won't hand you over to the Russians."

"Not hand over?" Anna asked uncertainly.

"No," Larry said shaking his head. "You are far too beautiful to give to the Russians."

Anna smiled and the waiter brought their schnitzel.

"Say this is good," Larry said as he tucked into his meal.

"*Ist gut ja*?" Anna replied as she took another fork full.

"It is good to see some of the basic services so quickly restored to Berlin," Larry remarked.

Anna looked puzzled.

"I am sorry," Larry said. "I keep forgetting that you don't understand English."

"Learn *Englisch*, ya," Anna replied. "Go Canada soon."

"You want to go to Canada?"

"Ya, go avay from vars, Communists und Nazis."

"You have a point there. Well, at least you won't have to worry about Nazis any more." Larry laughed. " Where in Canada do you want to go?"

"Don't know. Maybe goink Alberta too," Anna replied. "Got how you say fazzer's brozzer, zhere."

"You mean uncle?"

"Ya Uncle Janis. He not live near you?"

"No, never heard of anyone named Janis. I'll watch for that name when I get home though."

"You go home soon?"

"Yes, later in the fall my stint in the Army runs out and I'll go back to Canada, back to Morning Glory.

Anna was disappointed. In the short time she had known Larry she was beginning to like him.

Throughout the remainder of the summer and autumn Anna and Larry continued to see each other when opportunity permitted. On each of their dates they were able to observe that more services were being restored to Berlin as the streets were cleared, most of the bomb-damaged buildings were rebuilt and the unexploded bombs were removed. With Larry at her side, Anna even ventured into the American sector again.

One day on an outing, in late autumn that took them near the Soviet zone, Larry noticed the terror in her eyes at the mere sight of the red flag with the hammer and sickle, he remarked, "The Soviets must have done something terrible to you."

"Zhey shoot Fazzer, take Mozzer und Liesma avay. I hide for year until . . ." Anna stopped before giving herself away.

"Oh my God," Larry said. "You are from Russia aren't you?"

Anna gave him a fearful look.

"It doesn't matter. You are here now and they can't hurt you any more. Do you have any other brothers and sisters?"

"Have brozzer someplace, up norz, in Finland."

"Finland?" Larry said

"Ya, Finland. Valdis go zhere fight Russians."

"Valdis?"

Anna blushed and said, "How you say good friend."

Larry's face dropped, as he feared that Valdis might have been her lover.

"Maybe zhey kill him. Not hear for long time, but he not know I comink to Chermany."

"Not come to Germany?" Larry said. "Are you from one of those Baltic countries, such as Latvia?"

Anna sighed and replied, "Ya come from Latvia. Please not tell."

"My lips are sealed, but you should file as a refugee."

"Refugee?" Anna was unfamiliar with the word.

"You know, people fleeing from the Soviets. The part of Germany controlled by the western allies is full of them."

"Not send back," Anna was still concerned.

"No, they never sent back any civilians."

"I zhink I leave as is," Anna said. "Not vant to live in camps. Zhey put all ze people from East in camps. I goink to Canada, sometime."

"I hope you do," Larry said. "I hope you come to Alberta, to Morning Glory. My outfit is moving back to the British zone of Germany proper tomorrow. Within the month I should be shipped back to Canada and be discharged from the army."

"You leavink for Canada?" Anna said apprehensively

Larry was silent for a moment and said, "There is one way for you to come to Canada quickly."

"How zhat so?"

"As my wife. If you marry me, you could come with me when I return to Canada." Larry looked at her hopefully. "I love you Anna," he said.

Anna guessed at what he was saying, "You vant me for vife?"

"Yes," Larry said.

Anna's heart was pounding. While she was quite fond of Larry she wasn't sure that she loved him. She had a flashback of the day that Valdis asked her to wait for him. What if Valdis is looking for her, and what if he found her? It was very tempting to accept Larry's proposal as a sure way of getting to Canada, but she liked him too much to use him for her own ends.

"You not know much in my past," Anna said. "I not know much in your past."

"What's our past got to do with it," Larry persisted.

"You nice man Larry. Vhat your last name?"

"Kekkonin," Larry replied

"You nice man Larry Kekkonin, but my heart for anozzerr. I promise I vait for him ya."

"Valdis," Larry choked.

"Ya Valdis, he find me someday, I know."

"So you will spend your whole life waiting for him then?" Larry said in a dejected tone.

"I also vant to be doctor. Have to study many years."

"I see," Larry swallowed. "You are a brave and determined woman. I wish you well."

"You nice man Larry Kekkonin. You find good vife someday."

"Yeah," Larry sighed.

He extended his hand to her, but Anna grabbed him and hugged him tightly for a moment. Then she kissed him on the cheek before letting go. "I not forget you, Larry Kekkonin."

"You know I never did get your last name," Larry laughed, putting on a brave face.

Anna relented and said, "Anna Lindenbergis."

"I won't forget you either, Anna Lindenbergis," Larry said with a teary smile.

He reached for her to hug her again and Anna briefly kissed him on the lips. He turned and walked away. Anna was very tempted to run after him, but her life was in too much disorder right now to think about love.

Chapter Fourteen

For the next three years Anna remained in Berlin, helping rebuild the city shattered by war. She soon graduated from a labourer picking up rubble, to an administrative person sitting in an office behind a typewriter. As a new banking system was being installed, she was now working for wages rather than just for her keep. She even had money in the bank. Anna had applied to get out of Berlin and into one of the western occupation zones. She hoped to get to either to Cologne or Hamburg as these cities had world-famous medical colleges. The waiting list for those seeking to leave Berlin, however, was still quite long. Then one day in June of 1948 came shattering news over the radio:

'All overland corridors between West Berlin and the outside world have been closed by the Soviets with a claim that major repairs are needed. The Allied Control Commission is protesting this high-handed action by the Soviets, but so far there has been no comment from Moscow. American President Truman has warned Soviet Premier Stalin that West Berlin will be defended by force if necessary.'

"Can nothing stop the Soviets," Anna complained to Eva Gruber, her friend and roommate, one morning. "We'll all starve to death before long if food can't be brought to the city."

"I hear that the Americans and British are going to organize an airlift," Eva assured her.

"Just as things settle down and I think my life is in order, the Soviets are at it again." Anna continued. "Will those Reds stop at nothing to get me?"

"You ran from the Reds?"

"Yes, I fled into West Berlin a few days after the war. Four of those bastards were going to rape me."

"Tell me about it," Eva said. "I followed the advice of a friend and pretended I was stark-raving mad whenever any Red Army soldiers came near to me. As a result they kept their distance. Believe me, with the terror I felt I had no trouble acting the part."

"Do you think the Americans will stop the Soviets from taking West Berlin?" Anna asked.

"I surely hope so," Eva replied.

"Well, I'm going to keep trying to get to the west part of Germany," Anna said adamantly. "I'll spend every *pfennig[1]* I've saved thus far to buy air passage if that's what it takes."

"I was born and raised in Berlin," Eva said. "I survived both the Nazis and the first Soviet conquest, so I'll keep on surviving."

The following day, Anna went to several outlets to seek a way out of Berlin and came home frustrated as she complained to Eva. "Everywhere I go there are big lineups. Everyone wants to get out. I think they're all as afraid as I am of the Soviets."

"I don't think they'll take West Berlin," Eva tried to assure here. "The Americans and British have soldiers and tanks everywhere. They say Berlin won't be taken without a fight."

"It's just what we need, another war," Anna grumbled.

"Panic is just what the Russians want," Eva said. "We are urged to stay calm."

Just then a huge cargo plane roared low over their apartment. As it descended to the airport, Anna complained. "The planes sure are loud. Every time one goes over, it rattles the windows, and they come so often."

"It's better than bombers," Eva said.

"That's for sure," Anna replied. "I guess we should be grateful. Those transport planes are what is keeping us alive and free."

"Yes, for that I think we can put up with the noise." Eva sighed.

"Still I find all these tanks and troops on the streets somewhat unnerving, even though they are here to protect us." Anna said.

"It's the food rationing and fuel rationing that I find so hard," Eva said. "It's the siege of Berlin all over again."

"Well I'm getting out of here at the first opportunity," Anna reiterated

By spring Anna had enough. The line-ups for people applying to leave Berlin were as long as ever, and the refusal to the applicants as blunt as before and airline tickets were jacked-up to astronomical prices to further discourage the anxious applicants.

The common excuse was, "If everyone leaves Berlin, then we might

[1] Pfennig – a small German coin equivalent to a penny.

as well give it to the Soviets. We must stay here and stand up to communism."

In Anna's mind however, her father's words still echoed, *'Anna you must not let them take you.'* The surest way to stop them from ever taking her was to get out of Berlin, then get out of Europe to the "promised-land" of Canada. She already had a feeling that Karlis, and probably Valdis were already there. She pulled out her locket and held it for a moment. "I will keep my promise Father. I won't let the Reds take me." She kissed the locket and put it back.

She thought of Larry. *'I was a fool not to have accepted his proposal. I would now be safe in Canada instead of being trapped in Berlin, surrounded by the Red Army. He is safe and probably happily married with children. Would that have been such a bad life?'*

Anna shook her head. She must not think of Larry. She threw that chance away. Nor should she think of Valdis, as she would probably never see him again. *'If only I could have brought myself to say, 'I love you,' to him. Now he will never know how much I really do care for him and how much I need him. Together we would have found a way out of West Berlin.'* Anna smiled at the thought for a moment, *'Escape - that's it!'* She had heard rumors of people stealing on board the big cargo airplanes and escaping to the west. Perhaps she should try her hand at it.

When the time of her planned escape drew near she told Eva

"You're crazy!" Eva exclaimed. "Steal aboard a transport. If you get caught they'll probably throw you in jail."

"I have been watching the airport for several days, studying how I might get on board an airplane," Anna said confidently. "I'm sure I can do it."

"I will get on board a British transport. They fly to an airfield near Bremen, well within the British zone of Germany proper."

"I still think you're crazy," Eva said. "I don't think I could even ride in a passenger airplane let alone a transport."

"I have no choice. I'll die before I'll live under the Soviets again, and I may still be on their wanted list."

"You're not from Germany arc you?" Eva asked, she had noticed that Anna's dialect of German was not of the Berlin area for some time but had not commented previously. "Your accent, are you *Volksdeutsche?*"

"Yeah," Anna sighed. "I was in Latvia when the Reds came." She wanted to say that she was an ethnic Latvian, but the sheer terror of the Reds and the barest possibility that she could be returned to her homeland, made her silent. She would tell no one of her true ethnic background until she was far away from the Soviets, perhaps not until she could get to Canada.

"Oh my God," Eva said. "So you were on their wanted list. A so-called enemy of the state."

"Yes. They shot my father and took my mother and sister to Siberia. They'll shoot me too if they catch me."

"I can understand your dread," Eva said sympathetically. "But I'm enough of an optimist to believe that they will not let the Soviets take West Berlin and the Soviets know it or they'd have done it by now."

Anna wanted to believe her friend, but the terror of that horrible year of the Soviet occupation of her homeland made her want to flee as far away from their sphere of influence as possible. "I am leaving tonight," she said. "I have transferred all my money to a bank in Bremen. As soon as it is dark, I'm going to the airport and see how I can get onboard a transport, a British transport."

"How can you tell a British one from an American one?" Eva asked.

"British planes have marking like targets, the Americans have the star and bar," Anna explained.

"You have this well planned," Eva remarked.

"I've been on the run since 1940."

As Anna looked out the window and observed the gathering dusk, she turned to her roommate and friend of these past three years and said goodbye. Eva hugged her and wished her well.

"May you find peace of mind and security in the west," were her final words.

"Every day I will pray that the Soviets will call off the blockade," Anna replied tearfully. "You have been a wonderful friend and I will miss you greatly."

"Goodbye Anna. You must go now and find your destiny."

It was after dark when Anna arrived at the airport. The gates into the grounds were closed and guarded by soldiers. A large cargo plane had just came in for a landing and the roar of its mighty engines was almost deafening. A column of army trucks, with canvass covered boxes was arriving at the gate, probably there to gather the cargo from the airplane. Anna remembered the story that Valdis told her about how he returned to Latvia via a Red Army truck convoy. Perhaps his method of escape would work again. Anna stole her way along to the last truck and climbed in the back. It was full of large empty cartons placed on pallets, she crawled along the top of them and lifted the lid on one near the cab and slipped inside. There was a large sheet of cardboard in the bottom and she pulled it over herself as she rolled up in a fetal position. When that truck reached the gate, one of the soldiers climbed up on the back bumper and shone his flashlight around inside, no doubt looking for stowaway's like her. He lifted the lids of several cartons including the one in which Anna was hiding. Anna held her breath and clutched her locket as he shone his light in. Apparently he was satisfied and climbed back down. The truck moved forward moving through the airport grounds to an area near the great cargo plane.

After a time, the trucks were unloaded. A forklift picked up the pallet containing the carton in which Anna hid and moved it into the cargo hold of the airplane. There were many voices as men moved around securing the empty containers being loaded into the airplane, and she cringed every time some of them came near, but no one looked inside her crate again. She heard the great door at the back of the aircraft close. She stayed cramped in the carton for a long time not daring to move lest there be someone in the cargo hold. Then she heard the plane engines start with a deafening roar. There was a feeling of a forward motion of the aircraft as it moved into position and taxied down the airstrip. The engines revved up in a manner that shook the whole airplane then the sense of motion seemed to fade away. Anna peered cautiously out from the top of the carton but could see only darkness save for the small windows along the side of the aircraft. They seemed illuminated with an eerie orange light from outside. The roar of the engines was so intense that she found herself putting her hands over her ears as much as possible. Seeing that there was no one about in the cargo hold, Anna crawled out of the box and stretched her cramped body. She went over to the windows and saw that the orange light was caused from the exhaust of the motors, there were two on each wing. She could occasionally see lights on the ground far below suggesting they were passing over some town. It was a strange new feeling to be airborne.

After about an hour of air travel, they came to a massive bank of lights below suggesting a major city and the airplane appeared to be descending.

'*We must be arriving at Bremen,*' she thought. '*I'd better hide again.*'

Anna crawled back into her crate and waited. She felt the bounce and the return of the sense of motion as the airplane touched down on the runway. She was at last in the British sector of Germany. If she could get out of her present predicament undetected, she would at last have her freedom

Again her crate was handled via forklift and placed in some holding area. Anna waited until she could no longer tolerate her cramped position then carefully climbed out of the large crate. She was inside a large warehouse and there appeared to be no one around. She stole to the main door and peered out. There were several trucks parked outside and a closed gate ahead of her. She crept in among the trucks aiming for the gate area. There were people about tending to their various tasks concerning the shipping business, but she didn't see any police. As she stole among the vehicles suddenly a voice called out. "You there halt!"

Anna froze, then looked cautiously around. A soldier came up to her. Although he was carrying a rifle he didn't have it pointed directly at her. He wore a khaki uniform with a "soup plate" helmet and as he drew closer she saw that his uniform showed no badge to say that he was Canadian.

Nonetheless she said in her faltering English, "Canada ya."

"No Miss I'm British."

"*Englander?*"

"Yeah. I say, what are you doing here?" the soldier demanded.

"I uh. . . vas lookink for vay out," Anna replied innocently.

"How did you get here?"

"It long story."

"You can tell it to the CO then," the soldier said. "Let's go."

He motioned her forward to a building that had a jeep parked out front. Anna's heart was pounding. With only a chain-link fence between her and freedom, was she doomed to be sent back to the Soviets. Inside the office she stood facing the commanding officer.

"So, who are you and what are you doing inside the airport compound?" He spoke in German with an accent that suggested that he had been taught the language from a book.

"My is name is Anna. I uh. . . and after a long pause said quickly. "I want to file as a refugee."

"Indeed," the officer said. "Did you steal a ride on one of the air transports out of Berlin?"

Anna was silent, uncertain how to answer the question then said, "Will you send back me to the Soviets?"

The officer studied her for a moment and said. "I can assume you fled from the Soviet zone of Berlin and somehow got past airport security to get on board a transport."

"Something like that," Anna replied. "Please don't send me back."

"We have refugees pouring in from behind the Iron Curtain all the time, and you aren't the first to sneak on board an aircraft."

"Iron Curtain?" Anna was puzzled at the term.

"It's a new term describing the border between the communist and non-communist countries."

"Yes, that's a good term. The border is like a wall of iron."

"So, why didn't you stay in West Berlin? It is free there."

"West Berlin is blockaded and I was afraid that the Soviets might take over so I fled. It will be much safer here I think."

"True, but you should know that the blockade is failing. Our airlift is keeping the city supplied, and the Soviets are showing signs of backing off."

"I need to get out of Berlin anyway and the waiting list is long. I want to go to Canada one day."

"I see, but sneaking on board an aircraft is not the way to do things. You could have been killed."

"Sometimes I wonder if I am not better off dead, sir."

"You know, by rights I should send you back to West Berlin so you can wait your turn."

"Oh please sir don't do that," Anna begged. "I am a refugee."

"You can be a refugee in West Berlin also."

"Oh please sir no," Anna dropped to her knees sobbing. "Let me live in the British zone of Germany. I am afraid to live in Berlin."

The officer looked down at the desperate woman with tears in her eyes. This person who had no doubt witnessed the true horrors of communism and who had even dared to steal aboard a transport to get here should not be denied her freedom when she was this close to it. He had seen refugees beg for their freedom before, but somehow she touched his heart.

"I say, you are very fortunate that we are lenient toward people fleeing from communism," he frowned, hiding his sympathy for her. "So get off your knees. I am a British officer not an SS commander."

Anna smiled as she rose to her knees. After groveling before the Soviets and the SS, it was a great relief to be treated like a human being by a military officer

"All right," he said. He drew out an application form which, among other things, required Anna to fill out her full name and place of birth. Even though Anna had been assured on more than one occasion that people fleeing from communist countries would not be returned, she stuck to her alias, Anna Lemberg, and stated that she was born in East Prussia. She hoped to one day tell the world that she was born and raised in Latvia and proud to be an ethnic Latvian, but this was not the time or place.

.   "Now then," he stated in his ever-gruff manner. "I will escort you to the gate and give you the address of the refugee processing centre. When it opens in the morning, go there and file. That should allow you to be securely established in the British zone of Germany. Once you have proper papers, you can then apply to emigrate to Canada if you wish. Come let's go then."

"Thank you sir, thank you."

"Once you are out the gate I don't want to hear from you again. If you are a troublemaker we'll both be in trouble," he said firmly.

"I want no trouble sir," Anna said humbly. "I only want my freedom."

As they walked along, Anna asked out of curiosity, "Do all officers from the West learn how to speak German?"

"No. I learned it because I am posted in a administrative position and it is quite useful when I go into Bremen. I haven't met too many Germans who can speak English."

"Interesting."

As they approached the gate, the officer said in a grumpy tone, "I suppose you don't have any money to catch a bus."

"Yes, I have ten marks in my pocket. Is that enough?"

"You can probably get a ruddy taxi for that," he laughed.

They reached the gate and the guard snapped to attention and saluted. The officer returned the salute and said. "Let this woman through. She needs to catch a bus into Bremen."

"Another stowaway from the transport sir?" the guard said flatly.

"I doesn't matter where she came from," the officer said curtly. "You didn't see her and you let no one out."

"Yes sir," the guard replied.

Anna caught a late bus and spent the rest of the night in a hostel in downtown Bremen. The following morning she made her way to the refugee processing centre. She observed that the city core was bustling with a modest amount of automobile traffic, a few military vehicles and lots of bicycles. There was scant evidence of bomb damage as most of the damaged buildings had been either demolished or repaired.

At the refugee centre, there were a large number of people in the waiting room. Most of them spoke German, but a few were speaking a language similar to Russian. As she sat beside one of these people, a middled-aged man, she asked him in Russian if he was indeed Russian.

"He recoiled away from her and said, "No, I'm Polish!"

"I am sorry," Anna said in Russian. "I hate the Russians too."

"Are you from the east?' he asked."

"Yes," Anna replied. "East Prussia."

"Yes, the Russians gave it to Poland to help compensate for all the land they stole from our country."

Anna wanted to tell him that the Russians stole her whole country, but held her tongue.

Finally Anna was called in for an interview. The woman who led her into a cubicle for the interview looked strangely familiar and Anna wracked her brain to trying to think where she had seen the woman before. As the woman sat down she also scrutinized Anna. She glanced down at the application form and said questioningly. "From East Prussia?"

"Yes."

"From Konigsberg?"

"North of there ma'am," Anna said uncomfortably.

"Much north of there I suspect," the woman said flatly. Then she grinned and spoke in Latvian saying, "*Ka Jums kla jas,*[2] Anna Lindenbergis?"

[2] *Ka Jums kla jas* – how are you

Anna's heart skipped a beat, *'she knows who I am.'* Then in sudden recognition she exclaimed, "Gerda Schmidt!"

"Gerda Brandt now," Gerda smiled. "You are a long way from Latvia."

"Yes, it was a long journey. Please don't turn me in."

"Turn you in to whom," Gerda laughed. "We certainly won't give you back to the Russians, if that's what you are worried about."

"Thank you," Anna breathed.

"Now, are you going to carry on with your alias, or go by your real name and origin?"

"I would like to keep my alias," Anna replied. "Things are still too unsettled."

"I can see that you are still terrified that the Soviets will get you. We would prefer that you state your true name and origin, but since this country is overrun with refugees from the east and East Prussia is now in their hands, no one will ever know the difference. So, I will put you down as Anna Lemberg from East Prussia, born in Konigsberg. That way you can avoid being sent to the refugee camps."

"Camps!" Anna exclaimed. "I don't want to go to any camps!"

"I didn't think so, they say that living conditions aren't very good in the camps."

"Thank you ma'am," Anna replied.

"No need to call me ma'am. We grew up together in Riga," Gerda laughed. "Come by this office at five P.M. I am off work then. I'll take you home for supper and help you find your bearings here in Bremen."

"Thank you Gerda," Anna said rising.

Gerda saw her to the door and called for the next claimant.

Chapter Fifteen

Anna was there to meet Gerda after her working day was done. They climbed into a tiny, odd-shaped automobile and headed down the street.

"This is an unusual automobile," Anna said. "The motor is in the back."

"It's called a Volkswagen," Gerda laughed. "They also call them a Beetle because of their shape. Hitler had promised them to the German people before the war but then decided to build tanks instead. Now that the factories in the Rhineland are running again they are making them for the people as was originally intended."

"Interesting," Anna replied.

"So Anna, how did you get from Latvia to Bremen? It couldn't have been an easy journey."

"It wasn't," Anna said carefully.

"Still afraid I'll turn you over to the Soviets," Gerda said, realizing Anna's reluctance to speak of her past. "If that was the intent, I would have done it at the office. However Anna, you must understand, no one here will ever force you to go back to Latvia and probably not even West Berlin."

"They shot my father you know," Anna said. "They took my father in the night just after they held those phony elections.. I suspect they shot him. Then they took my mother and sister Liesma away to Siberia or somewhere. I ran away and hid. You remember Valdis Zirnis?"

"Yes," Gerda replied.

"His family was deported too, but he escaped from the train and came back to Latvia. We hid out together for a year until the Germans came. We welcomed their arrival as liberators. Valdis joined the Army and was sent to the Finnish front. He used to write to me but I haven't heard from him since late 1944. I was employed by the Nazis, first as a courier, then as a hospital worker."

"You always wanted to be a doctor."

"Yes, well, I saw plenty of blood from all the wounded German soldiers. A German Army officer, who was an important administrator in Riga, watched out for me. He looked out for me and helped me keep away from the SS."

"Yes, you wouldn't have wanted to fall into the hands of those swine," Gerda spat.

"When it was apparent that the Soviets would retake Latvia, I persuaded my protector to get me out of Latvia. He arranged papers so I could go out with a shipload of wounded soldiers to Berlin. I was there when the war ended."

"When the Red Army took Berlin?" Gerda said apprehensively.

"Yes, when they were running around looting, and raping every woman they could find. Four of them were going to rape me."

"Oh my God," Gerda said, as she stopped at a traffic light.

"You wouldn't believe this, but those people were so ignorant they had no concept of plumbing. One of them took the taps out of the kitchen sink, thinking that they magically extracted water from the wall. They thought the bathtub was for watering animals, and that the toilet was for washing vegetables."

"You're joking," Gerda said incredulously.

"They were so fascinated about the plumbing that they momentarily forgot about me so I bolted. I jumped on a bicycle that was lying outside and rode for my life until I reached the American sector of Berlin. The Russians didn't know anything about bicycles either. They were amazed to watch me ride it."

"So you were living in the American sector then?" Gerda continued.

"Not exactly," Anna said carefully. "I went into a tavern with some American soldiers one night and one of them who was quite intoxicated, started making advances at me, so I slapped his face and fled."

"Two of them chased me because I clawed one of them while defending myself. I ran until a Canadian soldier came to my rescue. He shot at them to make them back off."

"I've heard about Canadian soldiers." Gerda said. "They are terrors on the battlefield, but gallant with civilians," Gerda added.

"The officer that interviewed me and gave me permission to live in the British sector assured me that any Canadian soldier found guilty of rape is shot at a firing squad."

"I believe it," Gerda said. "So you jumped on board a transport plane from the British sector?"

"I couldn't bear the thought of West Berlin being taken by the Russians, so I left."

"Well, I don't think they'll take Berlin. The Americans and British won't let them and the Americans have the atomic bomb."

"I still don't like living in a place surrounded by the Red Army."

"I don't blame you. Well, you're here now, living in freedom."

"It will take a while to get used to it. I haven't lived in freedom since the spring of 1940."

They pulled up to an apartment block and climbed three flights of stairs to Gerda's apartment. When they entered the flat, her husband was home.

"Hello dear," Gerda said to him. "We have a guest."

He looked at the bedraggled-looking Anna and smiled. "How do you do."

"Anna this is my husband Erwin. Erwin this is Anna Lindenbergis. I've known her from the days when we lived in Latvia. "

"Her parents gave me lessons in conversational German," Anna said quickly.

"I can see they have done an excellent job," Erwin smiled in reply. "Welcome to our humble flat."

"Anna has an interesting story to tell about how she got from Latvia to Bremen," Gerda said. "I'll tell you about it later."

"I am sure it is," Erwin smiled. "During this time of fluid populations, fleeing war and tyranny, I've heard some real horror stories."

As Anna studied Erwin's features and listened to the tone of his voice, something about it was very familiar. Then she saw a photograph of an officer in uniform on a nearby shelf. It was Kurt.

"Is he your brother?" Anna asked in amazement.

"My father," Erwin said going over to the photograph. "Wait a minute, he served in Latvia as an administrator."

"His name was Kurt?"

"Yes, Kurt Brandt. Did you know him?"

"Yes, he was my protector. More than once he saved me from the clutches of the SS, and most importantly, he gave me exit papers so I could leave Latvia before the Russians returned."

"Incredible," Erwin replied.

"Did he escape?" Anna asked.

"No," Erwin replied in a downcast tone. "He was killed when the Russians recaptured Riga. That idiot of a Hitler would not evacuate the Army from the Baltic countries until it was too late."

"I am sorry to hear that," Anna said. "I probably owe him my life."

"It's a small world," Gerda said. "You found me, and now you discover that my husband's father was your protector in Latvia."

"Yes, a very small world," Anna smiled. She thought that if she could find these people from her past in this post war jumble, perhaps there was hope that she could one-day find Valdis.

As Gerda prepared some supper, Erwin shared with Anna some of his own stories of serving in the army as a youth and being captured by the Canadians who treated him well.

Gerda came through as supper was cooking and said to Anna. "Since you were in Berlin at the close of the war. Did you ever see Mom and Dad?"

"I did," Anna said in a small voice. The horrific vision of finding them lying dead flashed before her. "I stayed with them for a time."

"Are they still alive? I can't find out anything about them."

"No," Anna replied. Then looking sorrowfully at Gerda said, "The Russians killed them."

"Those *schweinhund!*[1] They didn't. . ?" Gerda said horrifically, not really wanting to hear how they died.

Erwin glanced at his wife as she used the strong expletive.

"I found them dead," Anna said flatly. She did not want to reveal that terrible vision of Erna lying in the middle of the floor with her clothing in shreds. "The house was ransacked."

"Oh my God," Gerda said.

Erwin put his arm around her in comfort.

"Please don't ask any more questions about them." Anna said. Her eyes were watery.

"I don't want to hear any details," Gerda replied. Then abruptly changing the subject said. "You had a brother named Karlis who travelled a lot. What became of him?"

"Last I heard he was in Finland. Hopefully he's safe, since the Soviets spared that country."

"I think they found the Finns a little too feisty to handle," Erwin chuckled.

"Hopefully Valdis got out too," Anna added.

"You were quite fond of him weren't you," Gerda grinned.

[1] *Schweinhund* – pig dog, a German obscenity

"He was a good friend," Anna said quickly. "We went through a lot together."

"Well, you found us, so maybe one day you'll find him."

"I hope so. He planned to go to Canada, but the Russians came before he could save enough money for passage. Maybe he got there after the war."

"Maybe."

"Did you ever think of going to Canada?" Anna asked.

"The idea has crossed our minds," Gerda replied.

"However, things in Germany are improving," Erwin added. "The economy is starting to work again, we have new money, and they are going to create a republic out of the American, British and French sectors called the Federal Republic of Germany. Dr. Konrad Adenauer is organizing a democratic government and will probably be our first Chancellor. If this all happens we will stay and help build a new Germany. One that won't be a Reich."

"If we ever did emigrate," Gerda added. "Canada would be our first choice."

"I can see things are happening in Germany," Anna said, "but Germany isn't my homeland, Latvia is. It remains enslaved by the Soviets, so Canada seems like the hope of the future."

"You were going to be a doctor once," Gerda said. "Is that still your dream?"

"Yes, I may stay in Germany long enough to study in one of the universities. That was forbidden to me during the Nazi era."

"No doubt it was," Gerda said. "There wasn't much going on at the universities then. Everything was for the war."

"We all believed in Hitler then," Erwin added. "But because of him, our country is in ruins, divided among its conquerors with the Soviets pillaging half of it."

"So do you have a place to stay here in Bremen?" Gerda asked.

"No," Anna replied, "but I have some money transferred to a bank here. I'll find an apartment then look for a job."

"You may stay here and sleep on our sofa," Gerda offered. "That is, until you get on your feet."

"Yes, you are welcome to stay here. We have no children," Erwin added.

So Anna stayed with the Brandts until she was able to rent an apartment of her own. She found a clerical job with an importing company, one of many operating in the great river port of Bremen. As time passed and it appeared that Germany was the eye of the Cold War, Anna found it was an increasingly unsettling place to live. One evening she vented her feelings to Gerda and Erwin.

"I've got to get out of Germany. This constant threat of war is grating on my nerves."

"It's all noise," Erwin said. "The Americans and Soviets like making noises at each other."

"I think things are getting better," Gerda added. "The blockade of Berlin has ended."

"But communism is still advancing," Anna said anxiously. "Just recently Czechoslovakia has been forced to accept communism. The Soviets have set up a puppet government in their part of Germany, and even in far-off China the communist rebels have won."

"They won't come any further west though," Erwin insisted. "Most Western European nations have joined with the Americans and Canada to form the NATO alliance, to resist communism."

"They say the Soviets now have the atomic bomb too. If another war starts Germany will become a radioactive wasteland."

"Because both sides have the bomb, I don't think there'll be another war," Gerda tried to assure her.

"Well the Soviets are too close for me," Anna said. "Their army is poised less than a hundred kilometres from here. Besides, every day when I go to work I see army trucks and soldiers."

"Some of the soldiers are Canadian," Gerda said with a wink.

Anna smiled as this reminded her of her brief affair with Larry. It gave her even more reason to want to get to Canada. "No, I'm leaving at the first opportunity. I commend you for wanting to stay and help rebuild what is left of your country, but like I said, mine is already lost to those Soviet swine."

"What about your plans for medical college in Germany?" Gerda asked.

"I'll study medicine when I get to Canada," Anna replied.

"You'll have to learn English and they say it is very difficult language to master," Gerda pointed out. "And the English way of measuring things is a complicated jumble that doesn't make any sense at all."

"Miles and feet, pounds and ounces, and quarts and gallons," Erwin mocked. "You have to be a mathematician to convert from one thing to another."

"I will learn it," Anna said confidently. "I can already speak three languages and read in two alphabets, actually three alphabets as our Latvian alphabet has some extra characters."

"Well, I can see your point about wanting to leave, and I wish you luck," Erwin said.

Again as Anna applied for an exit visa, she found that the waiting list was long. There were not only German nationals wishing to get out, but also large numbers of refugees from all over Eastern Europe.

During one visit to the emigration office a few months later, she encountered a small group of people speaking in Latvian. Feeling comfortable among fellow countrymen, Anna dared to introduce herself in Latvian as Anna Lindenbergis from Riga. She met with polite smiles and hellos.

"Has anyone heard of my father, Andris Lindenbergis? He used to run a newspaper." Anna asked hopefully.

"I'm not from Riga," one of the others replied.

Another replied, "Ah yes, I used to read his paper. He warned us all about the Russians."

"How long have you been away from Latvia?"

"We were rescued from a resettlement camp in East Karelia when the Finns and Germans came during the war."

"Did you meet a woman named Lita with a daughter named Liesma?" Anna asked, hopefully, even though Valdis had said they were bound for Siberia.

"I don't recall them. We were all in that camp," he said indicating the group around him. "We were all deported together."

"My mother and sister were deported also," Anna said. "That is of whom I speak. Also with them went the Zirnis family. Have you heard of them."

"Most deported Latvians went to Siberia. We were an exception." Then after a moment he said, "What is your name again?"

"Anna Lindenbergis, daughter of Andris Lindenbergis." Anna replied.

He asked around among the others whether they had heard of the people of whom Anna had inquired. It appeared no one had seen either her family or Valdis's.

"I am sorry," he replied.

"It is all right. I really don't expect to ever see my mother or sister again," Anna replied soberly.

"What about your father?"

"They shot him."

"The swine. They killed thousands of Latvians outright and of those sent to the camps, only the strong survived."

"So where are you all going?" Anna asked.

"We are going to America."

"I want to go to Canada," Anna replied.

An elderly man came forward and said to Anna, "Did you say your name is Lindenbergis?"

"Yes," Anna replied hopefully.

"When I was in Sweden right after the war I met a fellow named Karlis Lindenbergis."

"Karlis! That's my brother," Anna cried. "Was he all right?"

"He seemed pretty healthy. He had a young man with him."

"Was his name Valdis Zirnis?" Anna asked anxiously.

"I don't recall. He was a handsome lad with curly hair."

"Valdis had curly hair. Did they say where they were going?"

"I think it was either America or Canada. They were going to try to book passage to the New World."

Anna was buoyant, as she thought, *'Karlis and Valdis are safe and alive, probably somewhere in Canada by now. I must get to Canada.'*

"Why don't you come with us." the first man said, "Once you are in America, they say it is easy to get to Canada."

"They say I am at the back of a long line of German nationals waiting to get out."

"German? I thought you were Latvian."

"I've been using a German alias since the Nazis let me leave Latvia during the war. It has kept me out of the refugee camps."

"You might have a problem then. Since we never denied that we were Latvian refugees, the Germans will gladly help us leave and the Americans seem willing to take us in."

"Well now that I know my brother is alive and somewhere in the New World, I will try even harder to get to Canada."

When Anna was interviewed for an exit visa, she was turned down, told that she was far down on a long list of applicants.

"I met some Latvian refugees today," Anna persisted. "They said they had only a short while to wait before they got their exit papers."

"They are foreign refugees and Germany is overrun with refugees. So if another country will take them we help them on their way."

"I came from the east also," Anna said. "Am I not a refugee?"

"You were, but now you have a job and place to live so your situation is not so urgent. I am sorry but you will just have to wait your turn."

Anna left the office despondent. It could be years before she could get to Canada. She should have filed as a Latvian refugee and went to the camps, perhaps she'd be on her way to the New World by now. Lost in thought, Anna went for a long walk along the banks of the Weser River. As she walked Anna saw several large barges and a small ship coming up the river. Many of the barges went past Bremen for destinations deeper inside Germany while other barges and the ships stopped at Bremen to unload their cargo. Anna had learned that the big ships could not go up the Weser and always docked at the port of Bremerhaven near the mouth of the river. *'There must be ships that go to and from Canada that come to Bremerhaven.'*

She went quickly over to a nearby newsstand and asked the vender, "How far is it to Bremerhaven from here?"

"About thirty kilometres," he replied.

"How could I get there quickly?"

"Trains and buses go there all the time."

"Thank you sir," Anna said. As she turned away, she thought. *'Tomorrow is my day off. I'll take either a train or bus to Bremerhaven and see if there was any way for to me to steal on board a ship bound for Canada. If I could sneak on board an airplane to get out of Berlin, I should be able to get on board a ship.'*

The following day, after Anna arrived in Bremerhaven, she went to the dockyards and walked among gangs of burly sailors and stevedores busy at their tasks, undeterred by the occasional catcall. She saw a posting advertising for crews for Tramp Steamers. Anna learned through inquiries that Tramp Steamers were ships that would hire extra hands that could work their way across the Atlantic. She saw the Captain of one such ship come down the gangplank. It was a medium sized freighter. She approached him out of curiosity.

"*Herr Kapitan*," Anna said humbly.

"Yes, young lady," the old salt replied in perfect German.

"Is your ship bound for Canada?"

"Eventually it is," he replied gruffly. "We have a few stops along the way. Why?"

"Do you take passengers sir?" Anna asked with hopeful eyes.

"My ship is a freighter, not a liner," he snorted.

"I can pay. I have over five hundred new deutschemarks in the bank." Anna continued, walking backwards in front of the Captain.

"Why are you so anxious to get out of Germany? Are you a criminal?"

"No, a refugee. Please sir, I will work my way across the Atlantic as a crewman. "

"But you're a woman."

"After what I've been through, I can do anything a man can do," Anna persisted. "I'll swab your decks or clean your galley. Whatever you want."

The Captain stopped walking and looked carefully at her. "You really want to get out of Germany badly, don't you?"

"It's not that I want to get out of Germany. I want to get to Canada, I have some family there."

"Your accent, you are not from this part of Germany are you?" the Captain asked.

"No. I am from the east."

"You escaped from the Soviets then."

"Yes."

"So you want passage across the Atlantic, then you plan to jump ship when we get to Canada."

"Yes sir."

"I see. You'll be entering the country illegally."

"It seems that everywhere I want to go I have to do it illegally," Anna said. "All I want is a safe place to live and prosper in freedom, far away from this crazy war-torn continent."

"I see." The Captain was silent for a long moment as he thought over the predicament of this pretty but desperate woman. Finally he said, "Well, bring me those five hundred marks in cash by tomorrow night and be ready to board ship. We are leaving the following morning. I will assign you a work detail and give you a bunk. As far as I am concerned you are a crewman who signed up. When you jump ship in Canada, I will no longer be responsible for you."

"Yes sir, I'll be here tomorrow night."

"You're mad," Gerda said, when Anna told her of her plans. "He is taking advantage of you. Once he gets your money, he might dump you off at the next port or worse throw you overboard in the middle of the Atlantic Ocean."

"You are certainly taking a chance," Erwin added.

"I have to get out of here. It is too close to the Russians. If another war comes Germany will be the battleground, and another war could come as one has already started in Korea."

"There won't be another war," Erwin assured her. "The NATO alliance has scared the Soviets into line."

"There are other reasons too," Anna added. "I met some Latvians yesterday at the emigration office. One of them thinks he saw Karlis and Valdis in Sweden right after the war. He said they were going to the New World. I have to get over there and find them. That's all the family I have left."

"But are you sure you can trust this Captain?" Erwin worried.

"I think so. His ship is what they call a Tramp Steamer. Part of the crew of any Tramp Steamer is made up of people working their way across the ocean. He wants my money, because I am a woman and he thinks I can't put in a day's work like a man."

"He's still taking advantage of you," Gerda said.

"You'll be entering Canada illegally. The authorities there might deport you once you are discovered."

"I left Latvia under false pretenses and stole out of Berlin in an aircraft, so I'm used to moving from one place to another illegally. When I get there and learn the ways of Canada, I'll claim refugee status and reveal my true origin." Then after a pause she asked. "They wouldn't hand me over to the Soviets would they?"

"Probably not, but I will say you are a brave and foolish woman."

"A woman who has nothing to lose. I'm leaving tomorrow night, so I'd better go home and get everything in order."

Erwin and Gerda shook their heads at this brave and determined woman and Erwin finally said. "We'll drive you over to Bremerhaven tomorrow evening."

"Thank you," Anna replied, as she turned to leave. "Come as early as you can."

The following evening the three of them and Anna's duffel bag containing all her worldly belongings were loaded into the Volkswagen and they drove to Bremerhaven. They stopped near the dockyards to say their fairwells.

"Since there is no stopping you, we can only wish you Godspeed and good luck," Erwin grinned.

"Thank you, Erwin and Gerda. Thank you for all you have done. I will never forget you."

She reached for Gerda and the two women hugged for a long moment.

"I hope you find your brother and your young man," Gerda said with a teary smile.

"I hope so too."

"I hope you find the happiness and security that you so desire and so richly deserve," Erwin said as they also hugged.

Chapter Sixteen

As she approached the ship, Anna walked up the gangplank as if she had always been a crew-mate. Her duffel bag was slung over her shoulder and a sailor's toque was pulled over her hair. Anna felt pretty confident in her bold new adventure.

"Where are you going?" called a hard voice. Two sailors stepped out of the shadows to confront her.

"I signed on as a mate," Anna said quickly.

"Indeed. Since when does the Captain hire women as mates?"

"Take me to him please," Anna persisted. "He will explain."

"I hope so little lady," the sailor said. "If you're lying, I'll throw you overboard." The other sailor laughed heartily.

The Captain admitted Anna to his office then dismissed the two sailors. He studied the anxious-looking woman who stood in front of him clutching her duffel bag containing all her worldly belongings. "So you are really going to sign on as a mate for the crossing?"

"Yes sir," Anna said. "I even have the money you need."

"That's good," the Captain said. "By the way, the term among seamen is, Aye, aye sir, not yes sir."

"Aye, aye sir," Anna repeated.

"Good. I guess I'll have to set up a special bunk for you," the Captain said, ever gruffly. "I don't imagine you'll want to sleep among all those men, especially after a few days at sea."

"No sir."

"First I'll introduce you to the crew."

Anna was taken to a large room below decks used as a common area for the sailors. They were sitting around smoking and playing cards. All stood up when the Captain arrived with Anna and his officers.

"I would like to introduce you to Anna," the Captain said. "She will be joining us as a hand at least until we reach Canada. My First Officer will assign her specific duties as required."

A murmur rippled through the assembled crew and several of the crewmen grinned lustfully at the prospect of a woman on board. One big man among them however, gave her a sincere friendly smile.

"I want to make one thing clear," the Captain continued in his rasping voice. "Anna has signed on as a hand, she is not the ships whore. She will be assigned her own quarters and anyone who says inappropriate things or makes inappropriate gestures will be dealt with harshly. Do I make myself clear?"

A murmur of the affirmative rippled through the crew and the Captain dismissed them. It so happened that the ship had a spare cabin, a tiny room barely large enough for a bunk, near the Captain's quarters.

"As a seaman, you will keep this room spotlessly clean at all times," the Captain said as he showed her the room.

"Yes, I mean Aye-aye sir," Anna replied.

"Here, keep this with you in bed," he handed her a long truncheon. "If any sailor should come here in the night with amorous intentions use it freely. Incidentally, that comment about not being the ship's whore also applies in reverse."

"Absolutely sir," Anna said indignantly.

The ship left Bremerhaven early the following morning, sliding easily down the estuary of the lower Weser to the North Sea. As Anna watched the North German countryside slip by, she thought of the night she left Latvia, but she was leaving this time with little regrets even though she would miss the friendship of Gerda and Erwin. Although she had lived in Germany these past six years, the country was in turmoil and she never really considered it her home.

The freighter did not directly set sail across the Atlantic, but made two ports-of-call along the way. It went first to Oslo in Norway, then threaded its way through the rocky Scottish archipelagoes, down the West Coast of Britain to Liverpool. Anna's duties during the course of their voyage consisted of primarily being the cook's helper and one responsible for keeping both the mess and the galley in the impeccable tidiness demanded by the Captain. The crew was made up of primarily German sailors, but there were sailors of other nationalities including Nick the cook, who was a Greek.

As she looked out over the great port of Liverpool, one of the seamen, the big sailor who had given her the friendly smile the night she came onboard, came up along side her.

"Hi Jan," she smiled. Anna had since learned that he was called Big Jan.

186

"This is not as pretty as Oslo." he remarked.

"It's so grimy-looking," Anna replied. "Is this England's main port?"

"Yes, most of the cargo shipped to England comes here," he replied.

"So have you been a sailor for a long time, Jan?"

"No, I just signed on so I could get across to Canada."

"Me too. I don't know what I'll do when I get there. I have no papers and no money," Anna replied.

"Me too," Big Jan laughed.

"Your way of speaking," Anna said. "You are not German, yes?"

"No, I'm Hungarian," he replied. "I left Hungary when the Reds came."

"I left my homeland for the same reason." Anna replied.

"I didn't think you were German." Big Jan grinned wryly. "Your accent is also different."

"No, I'm Latvian," Anna said cautiously. "Don't tell anyone, in case they send me back."

"They won't send anyone back to a communist country." Big Jan assured her. In spite of many assurances over the past few years, the terror the Reds had instilled in Anna was so great; she dared not take the smallest risk. Perhaps once she was firmly established in Canada, she could dare talk about her origins to the authorities.

The Captain called out on the bullhorn for everyone to make ready for exchanging cargo when they docked. He also said no one would be going ashore, as the stop here would be brief.

As they set sail across the Atlantic Anna found that the crew treated her generally with great respect and courtesy, sometimes treating her almost as if she were a child on board. She had made friends with Big Jan, who watched over her almost like a bodyguard. If another sailor made suggestive comments, Big Jan would come and sit beside her and glower at the other sailor. Because of his size and formidable scowl, no one challenged him. Once, another sailor made the mistake of accusing Big Jan of keeping Anna as his private whore. He soon found himself in the sick bay where the doctor had to extract his broken front teeth.

Nonetheless there was one incident on the second night out from Liverpool. Anna woke with a start as she felt a presence in her cabin. She clutched the truncheon and said, "Who's there?"

"Shhh," said a voice and she felt a hand close over her thigh, though through the blankets.

Anna swung wildly with the truncheon, heard a crack and a yelp of pain. "Get out of here!" she cried. She swung again and felt contact with more cries of pain. Her door swung open and a shadowy figure limped out, but not before she struck him again across the shoulder blades.

As he limped out of sight, the Captain appeared in his doorway holding a lantern. He was dressed in his wraparound, but had his Captain's hat on.

"What is going on?" he demanded.

Anna turned to him with truncheon in hand almost as if she was going to strike him. "There was a man in my bunk," she replied.

"It looks like you got the better of him," the Captain chuckled.

"I want to thank you sir for giving me this club," Anna said with a grin. "I seems to work."

"I thought it would," the Captain chuckled. "I'll have that man found out and punished."

"You don't think he's punished enough," Anna grinned as she slapped the club against the open palm of her other hand.

"Perhaps, but your privacy must not be violated."

The following morning when Anna was left to clean up the mess and galley, the Captain had a crew line-up for questioning. All but one sailor was present. He was found still in his bunk, so badly battered and bruised that he could hardly move. He admitted to having stolen into Anna's cabin. Even though the Captain suspected that the sailor had been beaten by someone other than the truncheon-wielding Anna, he would admit nothing. The Captain did not punish him further, save for a verbal dressing-down. In another crew line-up the Captain probed everyone, especially Big Jan his number one suspect, about the beating.

Big Jan only said, "Nobody will hurt Anna. Captain sir."

"Well, I can't prove who gave the sailor that beating, but I want you to know that I will not tolerate others taking matters into their own hands. I am the Captain, and I will mete out any punishment due. Do I make myself clear?"

"Aye, aye sir" was the response.

One the fourth day at sea, a storm overtook them. The ship tossed and heaved amid a torrential downpour, with swells so large that they nearly capsized the ship on several occasions. Everyone was kept busy manning the pumps to keep the ship from being inundated both from the rain and the great waves that swept over the decks. Even Anna had to don her oilskins and come out on deck in the face of blinding rain to help with setting up extra pumps. Anna, who had been mildly seasick ever since they reached open sea, now completely forgot all about her queasy stomach in the face of the grave peril engulfing them. Everyone working on the decks was tethered with a lifeline lest they be swept overboard.

Anna was working on the bow with Big Jan helping set up another pump, when a huge wave smashed over the deck.

"Anna!" Jan cried desperately as he heard her scream as the wave swept her over the railing.

Anna was left dangling in midair and her body felt like it had been pulled apart as the rope that encircled her waist was now around her chest just below her shoulders. She clung desperately to the rope both to relieve the pressure and to keep from slipping out of the rope altogether as great waves inundated her, slamming her against the hull of the ship. She was only dimly aware that she was being slowly hauled upward by the powerful hands of Big Jan on the other end of the rope and was semiconscious when he and the Captain hauled her over the railing.

"Take her below," the Captain called through the howling tempest.

Anna was carried to her berth by Big Jan. He removed her oilskins and a blanket was placed over her. The Captain and the ship's doctor removed her wet outer clothes from under the blanket, so as not to violate her privacy. Then, after an examination for broken bones and other injuries, the doctor tucked Anna into her bed. A side-rail was put up to keep her from rolling out. She lay there for a long time in a torpid state, as the world seemed to spin out of control. She had vague flashes of the Captain, the doctor, and Big Jan looking in on her from time-to-time.

After a time she came fully awake and aware that the ship was no longer tossing and heaving. *'The storm must be over,'* Anna thought as she tried to look around the dark room. The first thing she did was check to see if the locket was still with her. She drew it up to her face and kissed it saying softly. "Thank you for looking after me Father."

Carefully, with wobbly legs and throbbing pain from her wrenched shoulders, she climbed out of her berth, dressed and made her way to the door. It was dark as she came out on deck, a half-moon was trying to shine through a broken cloud cover that overlaid a calm sea. As she stood clutching the handrail looking over the sea, the Captain came along side her. "Feeling better are you?"

"Yes. What happened to the storm?"

"We survived it." Looking at Anna, the Captain added. " In your case, just barely. If it wasn't for the lifeline, you would have been a goner."

"I thought I was going to die when I was swept overboard. As it is, I feel like my arms have been ripped from their shoulder sockets." Then after a moment, she added, "It was worse than being strung up by the SS."

"The SS?" the Captain asked curiously.

"Yes, I got on their bad side once and they strung me up by my arms to torture me for information."

"And you lived to tell about it?" the Captain replied incredulously.

"Fortunately, I had a benefactor who saved me. Otherwise I would have died in agony."

"Indeed," the Captain replied. "You are a very interesting person and now I can understand why you are so desperate to get to Canada."

"Are we far from Canada?" Anna asked.

"No. We are in the Gulf of St. Lawrence, bound for the river by the same name."

"Where in Canada are we going?"

"Montreal. It's a river port something like Bremen, however the St. Lawrence River is much bigger and deeper than the Weser." Then changing the subject he said. "You must be hungry. You haven't eaten in two days."

"I'll bet the galley is in a mess because I haven't been doing my chores."

"You can tend to that tomorrow. Come, I'm sure Nick will have a bowl of soup for you."

When they entered the mess, there were still some of the sailors lingering and sipping coffee, among them, Big Jan. He smiled broadly at the sight of Anna.

"Feeling better I see," he said coming over to her.

"I want to thank you Jan, for saving my life."

"Luckily you were tied to a good strong rope."

"Would you like a bowl of soup," Nick called from the galley.

"I'd love one Nick. Maybe after I finish it I'll help you clean up the galley."

"Don't worry about the galley I'll clean it up today. Tomorrow you help."

After her morning duties of cleaning both the galley and mess room, Anna came out on deck. Her arms and shoulders still ached unbearably, but the doctor had given her some strong painkillers so she could carry on with her duties. The ship was in the midst of a wide river and it must have been at least a kilometre to either shore. The shoreline seemed to slope gently upward from the edge of the river and it abounded in an endless array of long narrow farms. She could see a train go by along a railway on one of the shores. Anna was beside herself with joy as the land she saw along the banks of the river were the golden shores of Canada.

"So have you finished your morning duties?" said a voice behind her.

She turned to face the Captain. "Aye, aye sir. Galley ready for inspection."

"That is good. Nick will serve one more meal before we reach Montreal."

"It has been an interesting voyage," Anna said.

"For you, a little too interesting."

Anna laughed.

"I didn't put either you or Big Jan officially on my crew roster," he said in a gentle voice.

"Why is that?" Anna asked.

"When we get to Montreal the authorities will want to see my crew roster," he said gravely. "Everyone has to be accounted for before I leave, and if I report you and Jan missing they will look for you."

"If I am caught I'll say I was a stowaway."

"If you are caught I will deny knowing you and also say you were a stowaway. However, if you ever want to become a citizen of Canada, or get yourself registered in their system, you'll have to explain your origins."

"I will cross that bridge later," Anna said. "I can claim, with all honesty, that I am a refugee from Soviet oppression."

"You are a remarkable woman, Anna," the Captain replied. "I admire your bravery and I almost wish you would stay on board as a permanent hand."

"I don't know how many more storms I could endure," Anna laughed. "I think I knew what they were talking about when they said they used to keelhaul sailors for punishment."

"Yeah," the Captain laughed. He reached in his pocket and gave her a handful of bills saying, "You've been a good hand and have endured a lot, so I can't keep all your money. This is fifty Canadians dollars. It will keep you from starving for a few days."

"Canadian money!' Anna exclaimed. She looked at a bill with the image of King George VI on the front. "Where did you get it?"

"My ship goes all over the world so I keep money from several different countries on board."

"Thank you Captain," Anna grinned. "I will never forget your kindness."

A voice came over the bullhorn calling him to the bridge. Anna lingered on deck a while longer, then Big Jan came along.

"So Anna, we will soon be in Canada."

"What are your plans when we get there?"

"I'm going to jump ship and see if there are any other Hungarians in Montreal. From there I'll get a job and learn how to live in my new home. And you?"

"The same. I will get a job and learn how to speak English properly. It will be my fourth language."

"If I learn English, it will be my third language." Jan replied.

"Your German is good. Did you learn it in school?"

"Yes, German is a second language in Hungary. And you?"

"It is in Latvia also, but I did extra study in the language, as it was important for higher education. I planned to become a doctor."

"What changed your mind?"

"The war and running from the Reds."

"I know the feeling," Jan said gravely. "When the Red Army came to Hungary, they forced communism on us, so I left."

"Are you going to apply as a refugee?" Anna asked.

"If I do, they might send me back to Germany because I didn't wait my turn."

"My feelings too. I'll just stay low until I learn the laws of the land, then maybe, one day, I can tell them I fled from Latvia. But I do have an uncle living somewhere in Canada and maybe my brother and friend Valdis are here."

"Canada is a big country," Jan said. "I saw it on a map. It's bigger than all of Europe."

"Yes, well learning to speak English will have to be the first thing that I undertake Once we get ashore," Anna said. "Then everything will follow that."

The bell rang for the midday meal to be served. During the meal the Captain reviewed the duty of the crewmen once they docked. After fulfilling their duties they would all be granted a few hours of shore leave.

When her list duties as mess and galley cleaner were complete, Anna went back out on deck. They were approaching Canada's great metropolis of Montreal, a city that appeared to be as big as Bremen. As she and Jan stood on deck with their bags in hand the Captain said to them. "You'll have to steal past the customs patrols because I can't issue you a pass if you are to be considered stowaway's."

"We'll manage," Anna said. "We both spent our lives sneaking past guards with orders to shoot."

"I don't think the Canadian customs people will shoot, but they could detain and deport you if you are caught."

"We'll be careful," Jan assured him. "I'll look out for Anna."

"I somehow don't think that Anna needs much looking out for," the Captain chuckled.

"Thank you Captain," Anna said extending her hand. "My friends back in Germany said you would take my money and throw me overboard, but I proved them wrong."

"Well you did go overboard but there was a rope tied to you," he laughed. Big Jan laughed too.

"Good luck both of you," The Captain said as he turned to go back to the bridge to help navigate the ship into port.

Anna and Jan blended in with dozens of other sailors milling about the dockyard area. However, one had to get through customs to get out of the area. This task for experienced escapees like Anna and Jan was quite simple. They hid themselves, each in a separate load of cargo being taken from the dockyards.

Once out of the dockyard area, Anna and Jan met up again and made their way into the heart of Montreal. To Anna's dismay she found that everyone was speaking an unfamiliar language, and it seemed that no one knew how to speak English. Attempts to hail them in Latvian, German or Russian brought blank looks. Likewise, Jan could find no one who could speak Hungarian.

"I thought English was the language of Canada," Anna grumbled. "I don't know what these people are saying."

"I think they are speaking French," Jan replied. "I was in the part of Germany where the French Army is stationed and their speech is like this."

"Oh, great," Anna said. "I can speak fluently in three languages and am trying to learn a fourth. I spent time trying to learn English when I should have spent it learning French."

Chapter Seventeen

With some effort, after wandering the streets for hours, Anna and Jan managed to find rooms in a rooming house that catered to destitute foreigners. It was in a rundown part of town and the cockroach-infested rooms carried a sour odour. Anna had slept in worse places and it was at least shelter and it was next door to a soup kitchen, so they would be assured at least two meals a day.

"So this is the land of milk and honey," Anna scoffed as the two of them sat together in the soup kitchen eating a bowl of pea soup and a thick slice of brown bread. "I tried to learn some English so I could get along in Canada only to come to a place where everyone speaks French."

"Perhaps there is a paradise waiting," Jan replied. "We are strangers in a strange land and we didn't really get here through due process you know."

"Shhh," Anna said, looking around. "We could be overheard."

"As for French, I know nothing of this language either, but I suppose I'll have to learn it if I'm going to live in this part of Canada." Jan said.

"My head is full of languages. I am fluent in German and Russian and have some knowledge of English, but I don't know if I can learn to speak both proper English and French at the same time. Even though my teachers say I have a gift for picking up a foreign language." Anna replied

Just then a handsome dark-haired young man came along with his tray and asked them in English. "Mind if I join you?"

"You speak *Englisch*!" Anna exclaimed. "Ya sit, you first person we find who talk *Englisch*."

"Yeah, I should have known better than to get off here," the man said. "This is the French speaking part of Canada, La Belle province, as they say."

Anna noticed that Jan, who couldn't speak English, was perplexed with their conversation. She said, "Jan not speak *Englisch*. *Sprechen Sie Deutsche?"*

"Oh a couple of ruddy Gerries. No, I'm afraid I can only speak English."

"Ve not Cherman, I Latvian, Jan from Hungary. Ve boze learn Cherman. I know only few vords *Englisch*" Anna explained in her thick accent that was a curious mixture of Latvian and German.

"I see. My name is Edward Smith. I'm from Doncaster England."

"Pleased to meet you *Edvard Schmidt*. My name Anna. He Jan."

"Pleased to meet you Anna and Jan," Edward said, shaking both their hands, but my last name is Smith not Schmidt, though they probably mean the same thing."

"Ya, you talk English, I try understand und tell Jan vhat you say. Ve need know some zhings like how to find chobs."

"I'm afraid I don't know any more about this ruddy city than you do and I can't speak a word of French," Edward laughed. "But maybe we can pull together and muddle through."

"Ya muddle zru," Anna laughed.

The following day, Edward found a job for himself and Anna handling crates in a warehouse, while Big Jan struck out on his own. The foreman who could speak both English and French addressed them. "So you people want a job?"

"Yes," Edward said. "We're new to the city and to Canada."

"Ya, chust comink to Canada," Anna said.

"What's your name?" He looked at Edward.

"Edward Smith."

"English eh, I can tell from the accent."

"From Doncaster to be exact sir."

"And you?" the foreman said, facing Anna.

"Anna Lemberg, from Europe."

"Another DP," he scoffed.

"DP?" Anna said.

"Yeah, since the war this country is overrun with them." the foreman scoffed.

"I vork very hard," Anna said.

"I'm sure you will. Most of you DP's are hard workers. Be glad you're in a country like Canada."

"It vas dream to be here."

That evening, Jan returned in a buoyant mood, "I got a job," he said to Anna in German.

196

"So have we," Anna replied "In a warehouse."

"I got a job in a restaurant," Jan said. "While wandering downtown, I came across a Hungarian restaurant. As the owner could speak Hungarian, I was able to explain my predicament so he took me on as an assistant cook."

"You had restaurant experience in the Old Country?"

"Yes. We had a family restaurant in Budapest, so my experience helped me get the job. He also offered me board and lodgings so I'll be able to leave this bug-infested hostel."

"I looks like I'll ruddy well have to learn German," Edward said, feeling frustrated that he was left out of the conversation.

Anna turned and explained, "Jan got chob, in restaurant. He movink out from zis smelly place."

"I say, that's jolly good for you," Edward said, smiling at Jan. "I'm moving away from this hole at the first opportunity also."

Jan gathered his few belongings from his room and returned to the others. He shook hands with Edward then turned to Anna, speaking German.

"Well good luck Anna. May you find a way to become a doctor. Maybe our paths will cross again."

"Thank you, Jan," Anna replied in German with a teary smile as she hugged him tightly for a moment. "You have been a real friend, you protected me and saved my life. In another time and place. . . Well, may you be successful. Give me the name of your restaurant, and one day when I have some money I'll come there for dinner."

"God bless you Anna." Jan smiled weakly as they let go of each other. "You are a wonderful person."

Turning back to Edward he spoke, "Vatch out Anna no hurt her."

Edward knitted his brow, then replied, "I'll keep an eye on her for you," he slapped Jan on the shoulder. Jan turned back to Anna and they again hugged for a long moment and she kissed his cheek.

Anna noticed, in the course of her work, the foreman and other Canadians working there often referred to her as a DP, as they did other Eastern Europeans.

"Is DP vord for foreigner in Canada?" Anna asked Edward as they ate their lunch one-day.

"It's a derogatory term for a foreigner from Eastern Europe. It means displaced person."

"You not DP?"

Edward laughed and replied, "No, I guess Englishmen are the exception."

"Vhat zhat vord, de-rogat. . .?" Anna faltered

"Derogatory?"

"Ya, vhat it mean?"

"It's a bad name. Have you ever heard of a black person being called a *nigger*, or a Polish person being called a *polack*?"

"Boss think I nigger-polack?" Anna wondered.

"Probably, but don't let that worry you." Edward laughed. "He's probably afraid that you're smarter than he and will take his job one day."

"Take chob? Vhat you mean?"

"Forget it. When you can speak English a little better, I'll explain."

"You teach me more English, ya?"

"I can try, but I'm not much of a teacher."

Anna worked at the job until early in 1951. She and Edward were constant companions spending much of their leisure time together enjoying each other's company in spite of the language barrier. Her English improved somewhat but was still very broken. Edward had taught her many words and phrases, but was not skilled at teaching her proper grammar. She complained to Edward one lunch break after struggling to learn a few more phrases. "Zis English language, it so how you say complicated, all zese little vords, und ze spellink izt very confusink. All zese vords zat look ze same but meanink somezink different." Anna threw up her hands.

Edward laughed and replied, "They say that proper English is the second most difficult language to Chinese for an outsider to learn."

"I zink zat Chinese vould be easier. Zhen I need to know French, it very confusink," Anna scoffed. "Und zis vay of measurink, all zis pounds und feet, it not fit togezzer."

"Ah yes, you continentals use the metric system," Edward laughed. "When I hear people talking about grams and centimetres, I think they sound like a ruddy a doctor or scientist."

"Vell if I am goink to live in zis country, I vill have to learn all zese zings," Anna sighed.

"Speaking of which," Edward said eagerly. "I am planning to go to Toronto, they say there are better job opportunities there."

"Go to Toronto?" Anna replied anxiously.

"Yes, I am handing in my notice this afternoon. I've received word from a friend living there. He said I could stay with him until I got established."

"You are only second person I know in Canada und you are goink avay too?" Anna said in a concerned tone.

"It will be good to get out of that bloody hell-hole in which we stay. I say, why don't you come with me? Down in Toronto, everyone speaks English and you wouldn't be stuck having to learn French at the same time."

"I don't know. Vhere vould I stay? Vhat I goink to do zhere?"

"I don't know. We could probably work something out until you find a job."

"I don't know," Anna replied. "I got chust about enough money saved to find better place to live. My own rooms."

"I'll be leaving on the train tonight. If you change your mind you're welcome to come along."

"I vill give it some. . . I zink about it."

"I'd love you to come a long," Edward said, "I've grown to like you, Anna."

"I like you too Edvard," Anna smiled as the whistle blew telling them to return to work.

When they returned to the rooming-house that evening Edward asked Anna again but she declined. Part of her wanted to go with Edward as she had became quite attracted to him, however, when she felt herself weaken she would suddenly think of Valdis - of their fond fairwell and the promise. This scene with Edward was remarkably similar to the situation with Larry in Berlin. Anna walked Edward to the railway station that was only a few blocks away.

As he was about to board the train, Edward turned to face her. "Since there seems to be no way to convince you to come along, I will drop you a note when I get there. When I get established I will send for you."

"I zink zhat vonce you get to zis Toronto, you vill forget about DP voman you met here."

"Oh no, I won't forget someone as beautiful and charming as you. You are one of a kind Anna. I just wished I could have persuaded you to come along.

"It vould be not good for me," Anna said, "My heart is somevhere else. Ve have our lives to live und you vill find good voman in Toronto."

"But Anna I. . ."

"Goodbye Edvard," Anna said somberly as she turned to go.

Edward grabbed her by the arm and as she turned he kissed her firmly on the lips, "Goodbye Anna, I'll never forget you." They held each other for a long moment before Anna let go saying, "Goodbye Edvard, may you find much happiness."

Edward smiled weakly as he stepped onto the train.

As the train pulled away, Anna wondered, *'Why do I keep letting men slip through my life, clinging to a foolish dream that I might find Valdis again.'*

One day, about a week after Edward had left, Anna started looking at job postings on a wall in the lunchroom. Although she could not truly read English she did recognize some words. She noticed an ad:

Wanted. Part Time Maid. Applicant Must be Fluent in English.

"Vhat fluent mean?" Anna asked a co-worker beside her who was also studying the job postings.

"It means you must be able to speak English clearly."

"Oh, I speak English good, ya" Anna said.

"That's a matter of opinion," the other person said.

Anna looked at the other person uncertain what he had said, but she took down the ad as it contained the address of the person doing the posting. This crate stacking warehouse job was getting quite monotonous, especially since Edward had left. Anna thought that if she could get into a household, she might have a better chance to learn English. Anna had already started to learn English and it seemed easier than French, given her prior knowledge of German. Anna decided that she would learn proper English first before tackling French. She traced the word fluently.

That afternoon, Anna booked time off and hired a taxi to take her to the address on the posting.

"Are you sure you want to go dere madam," the cabby said with a French-Canadian accent.

"I goink zhere to find chob," Anna held up the ad.

"Dat makes more sense for sure," he replied.

As they drove into an upscale neighborhood, the cabby said to her. "Dis is Westmount. De part of Montreal where all de rich Englishmen live, dat own everyting." Then as they pulled up to a stately house, he turned and said. "I wish you luck eh."

"Zhank you much," Anna said as she stepped from the taxi. "How much money?"

"You better go see. Mebe dey don't want you. I wait here mebe take you back eh."

"Zhank you much. I von't keep you vaitink."

"I turn de meter off eh, while you see about de job."

Anna walked directly up to the large front door and rang the bell. A long moment passed and she was about to ring again, when the door opened. A strikingly attractive woman with a tall slender build smiled pleasantly at her and said, "May I help you?"

"I come to see about chob," Anna smiled holding up the ad.

The woman looked at it and smiled. "Where did you get this?"

"It vas on vall in lunchroom at varehouse."

"I see. You must work for my husband then."

"Your husband own varehouse?"

"He owns several," the woman said. "He is a partner in a shipping company."

"Oh," Anna said, amazed at the revelation. "Zis vhat you say coincident?"

The woman laughed and said, "Yes I guess you would say it is a coincidence. Come in and I will interview you."

"I got taxi cab vaitink. I pay driver first."

"Yes, pay him. I can call another cab for you later."

Anna quickly went back to the taxi and paid the cabby.

"Did she give you de job?" the cabby asked.

"She goink to give me interview," Anna said excitedly.

"Well, I wish you luck again and hope you get de job. Don't let dem pull de wool over your eyes eh."

Anna looked perplexed and the cabby drove away.

The woman was at the door and led Anna into the big house. They stepped through a foyer into a side room. One wall was lined with books and there were side cupboards and tables. The most prominent feature however, was a great oak desk located near the centre of the room. The woman sat in a broad armchair behind it and beckoned Anna to sit in a chair facing her.

"Let us begin with your name," the woman said ever pleasantly.

"Name, Anna Lemberg," Anna wanted to say Lindenbergis but held her tongue for the present.

"Well Anna," the woman smiled, "what made you decide to want to be a house maid?"

"Vell, chob at varehouse is, how you say, borink. I vant to vork in house, maybe get better learn English. Out on street everybody speak French. I learn too many languages already."

"I see," the woman smiled. "Well Quebec is the French speaking part of Canada, save for this little island of Westmount. I trust by your accent that you haven't been in Canada long."

"Chust about year. I chust DP voman from East Europe. I vant to live in Canada avay from var und troubles."

"You're not a DP," the woman laughed. "Don't let anyone ever call you a DP. If you are from Eastern Europe, you are probably a refugee."

"Ya, refugee. Zhat's it."

"Well," the woman sighed. "I had hoped for someone who could speak English more clearly, and I am only looking for a part time maid. My last part-time maid, Chantel, quit to get married."

"I villink to vork part time," Anna said, looking downcast. "I vork part time and learn to talk English part time ya."

"I can see that you are a very determined person," the woman said. "Were you a house maid in the Old Country?"

"No, I vant to be doctor, but Russians und var got in ze vay. I used to do house vork for Cherman family. Zhey teach me Cherman."

"A doctor. That's interesting," the woman smiled. "So, once you get established in Canada and learn at least one of our languages, do you still plan to be a doctor?"

"Zhat is dream, when I learnink how to talk und read English very good."

The woman thought about how much trouble she had finding a replacement for Chantel. Finally she said, "Do you like children Anna?"

"Ya, I like children. Someday maybe have children."

"I have a daughter who is nearly seven years old who should be home from school soon. If you are to work for me, you will have to take care of her when my husband and I are out."

"Zhat not problem, I take care of daughter. Vhat her name?"

"Patricia, but we call her Trish."

"Treesh, zhat good name ya."

"Tell you what, Anna," the woman said. "You sound like a very interesting person so I will try you out. I will show you around the house. You give it a good dusting and cook a supper for two adults and our daughter, plus enough for yourself and I will discuss with my husband about employing you. I think it would be an interesting challenge to teach you how to speak English."

"*Danke schon*, I mean zhank you," Anna said humbly as she also rose.

"When in the presence of my husband or guests in the house, you should address me as Madam," the woman said, "but when we are alone you may call me Mandy."

Chapter Eighteen

After Mandy had shown Anna around the house, she informed her that supper would be expected at six o'clock sharp."

"Vhat you vant cooked for supper?" Anna asked.

"Just make us something simple from the stuff in the refrigerator. Since you are new to this house and the kitchen, we won't expect anything fancy," Mandy smiled. "I'll be working in the study where I interviewed you if you have any questions."

"Zhank you Madam Mandy. I be very busy."

Mandy smiled and went back to the study.

Anna scoured through the well-stocked larder. She found some ham and vegetables to make a simple supper. With supper organized, she went through the main rooms with a duster and furniture wax working almost like a whirlwind, being especially attentive to the main sitting room and the dining room. She then went through the upstairs bed-rooms and gathered dirty laundry and organized it to be sent out. Though there were five, only two of the bedrooms were currently in use. By the time Trish came home from school, Anna was back in the kitchen tending to the supper.

Little Trish came bounding into the house calling for her mother. As Mandy was on the telephone in the study, she didn't immediately answer, so Anna came out to greet her. Trish stopped short at sight the strange person in the house.

"Hello Treesh," Anna smiled.

Noticing her apron, Trish said to Anna in an innocent voice. "Are you our new maid?"

"Vell I hope so, your mozzer vill hire me. Anna smiled pleasantly. "Vould you like milk und treat."

"Yes please," Trish, said. "But where is Mummy?"

"Mummy busy in study," Anna replied. "You come to kitchen I give you snack."

Trish bounded after Anna and climbed up on a kitchen stool while Anna poured a glass of milk then gave her a cookie from the nearby jar.

"Thank you, these are good," Trish said in her innocent manner. What is your name?"

"Anna, name is Anna."

"You talk funny. Are you from another country?"

Anna laughed and said, "Ya I come from Old Country, chust learnink to speak English."

"Now Trish," Mandy interjected, as she entered the kitchen, "it is not polite to ask such questions."

"Girl is curious, ya," Anna laughed. "She vant to know who I am."

"You should have waited until I explained," Mandy said to Trish with an understanding smile.

"It okay to give snack to Treesh?" Anna asked.

"Oh yes, a snack after school doesn't hurt, but I wouldn't give her more than one or two of those cookies,"

"You hear mozzer," Anna smiled, with a wink. "Von more cookie and zhat's it."

Just then another person entered the house and a male voice called for Mandy.

"Excuse me Anna, that's my husband. I must go and tell him all about you."

Trish bolted from the kitchen calling, "Daddy, Daddy."

Anna watched from the kitchen as the others greeted the man of the house in a touching family scene with the father scooping up Trish and turning his head to kiss Mandy. She had not seen a family scene like this in twelve years. It reminded her of home. As she turned back to her duties, Anna thought, *'I hope this beautiful woman with her darling child will hire me, I have never felt so much at home since my own family was destroyed.'* She could hear the excited conversation and was sure her name came up, but the words were indistinguishable through the walls. She must put extra effort into making this supper a success to impress Mandy's husband of her worth to the household. Although lacking in formal training as a domestic, she had learned enough etiquette from time spent with the Schmidt family to set a dining room table properly. With everything in order she went to the study, where Mandy and her husband were discussing Anna's future in the household, to inform them that dinner was ready. When she knocked on the study door, Mandy answered.

"Dinner is ready Madam," Anna said.

"Come in," Mandy smiled. "I would like you to meet my husband."

A tall, dark, handsome man rose from behind the desk and smiled and said, "How do you do Anna. My wife has been telling me about you."

Anna looked apprehensively at them. He continued. "It sounds like you've had an interesting life story. And we are impressed at how you have tidied up the house this afternoon."

"Zhank you much, sir," Anna blushed. "I vork hard, try my best, sir"

"No need to call me, sir," he laughed. "My house is not an army barracks. My name is John but you may call me Mr. Gerrick."

"Zhank you *Herr*, I mean Mr. Gerrick. I hope you enchoy supper."

"I am looking forward to it."

Anna went to fetch Trish from her playroom and found the child sitting watching television. Anna had heard of television but had never actually watched it. She stood and watched it with fascination as she informed Trish that dinner was ready.

"*Howdy Doody* will be over in a moment," Trish said. "Mummy always lets me watch *Howdy Doody*."

"Chust von moment zhen," Anna said. "You don't vant Mom and Dad vaitink."

The closing credits to the program came on and Trish switched off the set. "Do you have TV where you come from?" Trish asked.

"I never vatch, how you say, TV before."

"Never watched TV?" Trish said incredulously, as the walked toward the dining room.

"Ve don't have it in Old Country."

As Trish took her place at the table she said to her parents, Mummy, Daddy, guess what? Anna has never seen TV before."

John looked at Trish and replied, "Television is a new thing, I suppose a lot of European countries don't have it yet. As it is, the TV sets are quite expensive."

"Ya I heard about it, und zhey vere talkink about it in Chermany." Anna replied as she set out the steaming meal before them.

"Um, smells good," Mandy said as Anna retreated to the kitchen.

Anna periodically popped into the dining room to check on the progress of the meal. The main course had ham as a main feature. Side dishes abounded in greens with sliced cucumber dominating.

When Anna came through with the coffee and desert, John smiled and wiped his face with a napkin saying, "This meal is very delicious."

"Zhank you," Anna smiled, pleased that they enjoyed her cooking. *'Thank God I spent a lot of time with Mother in the kitchen when I was a youth.'* "Vhen I know kitchen better, I make for you good supper, ya."

"Like my husband said, the meal you put on was excellent," Mandy said, "So did you learn how to cook in Germany?"

"No. In Latvia, mozzer teach me," Anna blurted.

John noticed that she checked herself and he asked. "Are you from Latvia?"

Anna's eyes darted about for a moment wondering whether or not she should reveal her origin, and thus lead to an explanation as to how she got to Canada. Somehow she felt she could trust these people, and that honesty would be the best way to maintain that trust.

"Ya," she replied in a small voice, looking down.

"Latvia? Where in Europe is that?" Mandy asked, smiling. "I'm afraid geography was not my best subject in school."

"Over by Baltic Sea," Anna replied.

"That's right," John said. "It's one of those three little countries the Soviets stole. The other two are Estonia and Lithuania are they not?"

"Ya, zhat's it," Anna replied, as she began removing plates from the table.

"So, you escaped from communism then?" Mandy said.

"Ya, I run avay from Russians. I come to Canada to get avay from vars."

"No doubt," John replied. "You're safe over here now."

"Ya," Anna said avoiding eye contact as she loaded the last dishes onto the trolley. "I bring coffee now."

"Bring it to the study," John said. "Bring a cup for yourself and we will discuss your future there. Trish you may go and do your homework. It has to be done before watching any more television."

"Yes, Daddy," Trish said, rising from the table. "Would you like to watch TV with me after, Miss Anna?"

"I don't know," Anna replied. "I havink lot a vork to do in kitchen first."

Anna wheeled the trolley into the kitchen with a heavy knot in her stomach. Were they going to grill her about her past? Would they dismiss her if they found out she had entered Canada illegally? She should have waited her turn and immigrated through the proper channels. She drew her locket from beneath her blouse and clutched it thinking, *'Father I have found sanctuary here, please dear God let me keep this sanctuary.'*

Anna brought three cups of coffee through on a tray. John was behind the desk and Mandy sat on a chair in front of it. Anna was invited to sit on a third chair, beside Mandy's.

"Now then, Anna," John said pleasantly, as he took his cup of coffee. "We are impressed with both your housekeeping and culinary skills, and our daughter seems to like you. However, we had only planned for a part-time maid who could be here in the afternoons for when Trish comes from school, and to prepare supper as both Mandy and I have busy schedules."

"Part time okay," Anna said. "I like family und little girl. I vorkink in house part-time and study how to talk and read English part-time. It vork good for me."

"Having you part time was our original intent, however, Mandy and I have discussed the situation and Mandy will explain our proposal."

"We have decided to hire you full-time," Mandy smiled, She took a sip of her coffee and continued. "We have plenty of rooms in this house and we will give you a bedroom so you can live here, and look after our house all day. I will give you your full list of duties later this evening. While you are here, I will give you English lessons in the evenings, and during your spare time the following day you can study what you've learned thus far. You appear to be a very bright person and will catch on fast I am sure."

"You very kind to me," Anna blushed. "Vhy you so kind?"

"You remind me of a story my mother once told." Mandy smiled. "She was born into a wealthy family in Toronto. Then one day when they needed a maid, an Italian girl, who like you could barely speak English, applied. My mother took a liking to her and convinced her parents to hire this girl. Mom taught her English and they became good friends which they are to this day."

"I vould like to be your friend von day," Anna said.

"I'd like to be your friend too," Mandy said.

"My wife is a very compassionate person," John said.

"Very kind in heart." Anna added

"Since you came with just the clothes on your back, do you have other belongings somewhere?" Mandy asked.

Anna looked puzzled.

"Other clothes. Where did you stay?" John asked.

"I stay in rooms down by varehouse beside soup kitchen."

"I think I know where she stayed," John said. "There are a couple of run-down hostels in the area. I'll arrange to pick up your belongings tomorrow."

"You very kind," Anna replied. Then with an anxious downcast look she said, "But I must make confession. Maybe you kick me out und not vant for friend."

"Oh what is it?" John asked gravely.

"I not, how-you-say, come here properly to Canada."

"You came here illegally?"

"Ya," Anna said meekly. "I, how-you-say, jump ship. I convince Captain to bring me to Canada und he charge me money und make me vork to get across ocean."

"Oh, Anna, why didn't you apply for emigration from Latvia or wherever you came from?" Mandy asked.

"I run from Latvia to get avay from Russians. Cherman officer help me escape. I come to Berlin but Russians come zhere too. I run from Berlin vhen blockade on. Always, wherever I go, Russian follow. Some say zhey make var vis Russians, so I left Chermany. Big lineup to come right vay, so I make shortcut. Jump ship."

"I see," John said. "Quite an interesting story."

"I leavink now. You not vant illegal DP in house. Please don't tell police, I don't vant to go back to Chermany." Anna rose to leave.

"Sit down please," Mandy said, putting a hand on Anna's arm. "Surely we can work this out. John, will they deport her if she is found out to have come here illegally?"

"They won't be happy, but there is a lot of this going on since the war. Especially with the communists taking over Eastern Europe." Turning to Anna he said, "They could send you back to West Germany but that is not your country of origin and I know they won't send you back to Latvia. Your best bet would be to claim refugee status and they'll probably allow you to stay."

"Do you have family back in Latvia?" Mandy asked.

"No, ze police take my fazzer, shoot Fazzer and take Mozzer und little seester avay to Siberia." Anna began to cry. For twelve years she had carried the horror of seeing her family destroyed, pent up in her mind and now in the presence of these beautiful, sympathetic people she released her emotions and cried abundantly. Mandy reached over and cradled Anna in her arms. "Zhey took Fazzer in zee night, ve never see him again, I know zhey shoot him. Mozzer und Liesma probably die in camps." Anna sobbed. "Zis all I have left." Anna pulled out her necklace with the locket on it. "Mozzer gave it to me, last time I saw her." Anna opened it and continued tearfully, "Zis all zhere is of my fazzer."

"Incredible," John said, trying to fathom what Anna had experienced in life.

"Do you have any other family?" Mandy asked gently.

"I zhink Uncle Janis somevhere in Canada, Maybe brozzer Karlis too und Valdis." Anna choked.

"Valdis. Is he your brother too?"

"Chust special friend," Anna said as she started to regain her composure. "He vas in Cherman army up by Finland. Karlis vas in Finland and I zhink zhey boze escape to Sveden, zhen to New Vorld. I must find zhem. Zhey all ze family I got."

"Can't we help her?" Mandy said to John. "Isn't there a way we can keep this poor woman in Canada so she can have a chance at life?"

"I will consult with my lawyer tomorrow," John said. Then to Anna he said, "I am sure that if you file as a refugee, especially one who has a home and job to go to, they will allow you to stay here and become a citizen. Meanwhile, you are welcome to stay in our house until your life is all sorted out."

"Zhank you much Mr. Gerrick," Anna said tearfully. "I never forget kindness."

"Come I will show you where you can have a nice hot bath and a bed to sleep in," Mandy said as she rose and put her hand on Anna's shoulder.

"Zhank you Mandy, Madam," Anna said. "You beautiful voman."

"I'll agree with that one," John laughed.

"Later as Mandy was about to show Anna her room, they passed by the sitting room where Trish was watching television.

"Arc you going to watch TV with me, Anna?" Trish asked

"You should be more respectful and call Anna, Miss . . . What is your last name?"

"Lindenbergis," Anna smiled. "But Treesh can call me Anna."

Nonetheless, Mandy said to Trish, "It will be more respectful if you call her Miss Lindenbergis."

"Are you going to watch TV with me, Miss Linberg?" Trish asked.

"Lindenbergis," Mandy corrected her.

"Linberg-is," Trish repeated.

Anna laughed and said, "Maybe better to call me Anna."

Anna and Mandy lingered in the doorway. Noticing that Anna was transfixed with the television, Mandy said, "Why don't you sit and watch the show with Trish? She has to go to bed when it is over, then we'll all go upstairs."

"Zhank you Madam," Anna said. She really wanted to see this wonder of television.

Mandy turned and left while Anna accepted Trish's invitation to sit beside her on the sofa. The program on the black and white screen featured a fair-haired woman with large eyes and very mobile facial features moving from one ridiculous situation to another. Both Trish and an unseen audience laughed uproariously at the antics. Soon Anna was even laughing, although she was startled at the abruptness of the commercial breaks that kept interrupting the program.

"Vhat name of show?" Anna asked, during one of the breaks.

"*I Love Lucy*," Trish replied, "it's my most favourite show on TV."

After the program Mandy reappeared and they all went upstairs. As Trish was about to go in her bedroom she turned and said to Anna, "Would you tell me a bedtime story Anna, I mean Miss Lindenbergis?"

"Sure I tell you story." Anna smiled.

"Why don't you get your pajamas on and brush your teeth while I show Miss Lindenbergis her room," Mandy suggested. "Then she can tell you a story."

"You do vhat Momma say," Anna added. "I be right zhere."

Trish bounded away to attend to the tasks as Mandy showed Anna her bedroom and the bathroom. Anna remarked, "You don't have servant room." She was surprised that she would be given a room in the same part of the house at her employer.

"Please," Mandy laughed. "I prefer to think of you as a guest or employee, but never a servant. Besides, this house is large enough for us to have guests and still have room for you."

"Zhings sure different in Canada," Anna said. Mandy only smiled.

Later when Anna sat at Trish's bedside, Mandy passed by the bedroom and she could hear Anna trying to explain to Trish in her broken English that Latvia was a country in Europe beside the Baltic Sea. Mandy was glad that John agreed to hire Anna in spite of reservations about the language barrier. Anna seemed like a sincere honest person who had gone through hell and was in desperate need of a home. She looked forward to the challenge of teaching Anna English.

Chapter Nineteen

Anna did go to the immigration centre and declare herself a refugee. With Mandy at her side she explained the circumstances that led her to enter Canada illegally. Since John and Mandy agreed to sponsor her, Anna was granted landed immigrant status under her proper name of Anna Lindenbergis.

Anna exceeded John and Mandy's expectations as the housemaid and proved a good companion and chaperone for Trish. She became like an aunt to Trish, taking her to the playground and other amusements such as the local movie theatre. Going to the movies was also a novelty for Anna. John and Mandy's lives were busy with commitments - John with his shipping business and Mandy with her school for the handicapped. Nonetheless Mandy found a couple of hours on most evenings to give Anna lessons in spoken English and very basic literacy in the written form. Anna found the written form of English even more confusing than the spoken form with its multitude of words spelled much differently than they were pronounced and words that were spelled the same but meant something completely different. Although Anna learned to use the articles and minor prepositions, she still spoke with an accent. To help improve her literacy, she read the daily newspaper thoroughly in spite of the depressing news of the cold war in Europe and the hot war in Korea. Trish also helped in her own small child's way and often got Anna to read her bedtime stories, helping Anna when she stumbled over a word. By the end of that summer of 1951, Anna was fluent enough in English that Mandy enrolled her in an advanced English class so that she could truly master the language well enough to meet the requirements of university entrance.

Then one evening in early fall after John came home from work he called both Anna and Mandy into his study. "I made an interesting discovery today which could be significant to Anna."

"Oh, what is it?" both Anna and Mandy asked.

"Do you know that several western countries, including Canada, have never recognized the Soviet takeover of these countries and have allowed the diplomats, from before the Soviet time, to continue to function."

"There is still a Latvian embassy in Canada?" Anna asked incredulously, with her much improved English.

"No, but there are still some diplomats in New York and London."

"That is a long ways away and the Soviets probably won't tell us anything of what goes on back home."

"True, but I also found out that our External Affairs department will help people like you try to find lost relatives. So, they may help you find your brother if he lives here in Canada, or even in the States. It may be worth a trip to Ottawa to find out"

"How far away is Ottawa?" Anna ventured.

"Just a few hours by car or train," John shrugged.

"I will have to go there and talk to this External Affairs department," Anna said

"I have to go to Ottawa on business next week anyway," John said, " so why don't we all go. It will be an educational experience for Trish so I'm sure her teachers won't mind her missing a few days of school."

"True, since my role is mostly administrative now, I could leave my school too," Mandy added. "Besides I've never been to our nation's capital."

"Then it is settled. I'll make the necessary train and hotel reservations," John said excitedly.

Anna was beside herself with joy. Thanks to the incredible kindness of these people, she was finally going to begin to try to find her brother, Uncle Janis and Valdis. She couldn't wait to get to Ottawa.

The train trip to Ottawa, which took only a couple of hours was as exciting for Anna as it was Trish. The two of them had a grand time pointing out various features along the way. Once in Ottawa, while John was on business, Mandy took Anna and Trish on a tour of the sights of the nation's capital. They visited the House of Parliament, the National Art Gallery, museum and other cultural features. In a break between business meetings, John accompanied his family when they took Anna to the External Affairs department. They were then directed to the office dealing with the tracking of lost relatives.

"May I help you?" the woman behind the reception desk asked.

"Yes, I am Anna Lindenbergis a Latvian ex-patriot who has come to Canada as a refugee. I need to contact the Latvian community to search for my brother Karlis and a friend named Valdemars Zirnis."

"I will get someone to help you" The receptionist said, as she rose to go into another room and came back several minutes later with a pleasant-looking middle-aged man.

"Hello, my name is Egils." he smiled. Then looking at the anxious looking woman in front of him, he continued "And you are Anna I presume?"

"Yes, I am," Anna replied. "I am Anna Lindenbergis, daughter of Andris and Lita, Lindenbergis, and I was born and raised in Riga." Anna then added, speaking Latvian "Your name Egils, are you Latvian also?"

"Yes, my parents came here after the First World War." He replied in Latvian. "I was hired by External Affairs to help process the many Latvians who came here after the Second World War. Are these people with you Latvian also?"

"No. They are friends whom I work for in Montreal." Anna replied again in English.

"Friends who are helping Anna find her way." Mandy replied.

"I see," Egils replied.

"They are John and Mandy Gerrick, with their daughter, Trish." Anna said, introducing them.

"Pleased to meet you," Egils smiled. "Would you like to come to my office?"

"I'll take Trish for a walk," John offered, getting up. "You may go with Anna if you wish, Mandy."

"Perhaps this is a private affair," Mandy said looking at Anna.

"No, do come," Anna said. "Perhaps I will need you."

As they settled in Egils' office, he asked Anna how she came to be in Canada.

Anna gave a synopsis of her life including the part about how she came to Canada illegally.

"An interesting story," Egils said. "You have learned to speak English very well in such a short time."

"She's an excellent student," Mandy laughed.

"She has been so kind," Anna smiled. Then changing the subject she said, "Do you have any contact with Latvia?"

"Not directly. The Soviet embassy speaks for Latvia. Of course you can get very little information out of them."

"I am not surprised," Anna replied. "So do you keep records of Latvians who come to Canada?"

"Somewhat," Egils replied. "A lot of Latvians like to keep our culture alive so the Latvian Society is very active in both Canada and the USA. I presume you are looking for family over here?"

"Yes, my brother Karlis was in Finland when the Soviets seized Latvia and I have reason to believe he went to Sweden with the intent of coming to the New World, presumably Canada. Also a very dear friend of mine, Valdis Zirnis, may be with him. He had planned to immigrate to Canada before but the Soviets took our country before he could get out. He hid out with me, when I was hiding from the Reds and after the Germans came he joined the *Wehrmacht* and was sent to the Finnish front."

"We could find out if your people entered Canada legally, and through the Bureau of Vital Statistics, we may be able to find out where they live but it will be a time-consuming search that could take years. If, however, they have chosen to be involved with the Latvian community of either Canada or the U.S., the search should be shortened somewhat. If they are looking for you, you should be registered with us."

"Then register me," Anna said eagerly. "I'll give you my address in Montreal and if either of these two people inquire of me, they will know where to find me. Also I have an Uncle Janis Lindenbergis who came to Canada in 1939 with his family."

Egils took down Anna's name and address and instructed a secretary to check and see if either a Karlis Lindenbergis or Valdemers Zirnis immigrated to Canada since the Second World War, and also to run a check on a Janis Lindenbergis.

"If any of these people are on our lists, we will know if they are in Canada or at least have been here. Follow up traces could take months or years however," Egils said. "As there are lots of other Latvian refugees also looking for relatives and friends."

They waited for about an hour as records were scanned. The secretary said after her search, "I have a Carl Lindenbergis entering Canada in 1946 from the U.S. with a Swedish passport."

"That's him!" Anna exclaimed. "Karlis was in Sweden."

"But the name is Carl not Karlis," Mandy said quietly.

"It could have been changed," Egils said, "Carl is the Swedish version of Karlis"

"What about Valdis and Uncle Janis?" Anna pressed.

"There is no record of a Valdis Zirnis, but a Walter Sirnis came about the same time as Carl Lindenbergis."

"Walter Sirnis," Anna said. "That's close to Valdis Zirnis. I wonder. . . Now that you have those names will it take long to find them?"

"Depends where they are and how clearly they left any trails as to where they have been."

"What about Uncle Janis?"

"I will contact the Bureau of Vital Statistics, and have you sent any information they have, If your Uncle has been in Canada that long they should know something about him."

"So you will be able to find her family then?" Mandy interjected.

"In time we should be able to find them if they still live in either Canada or the U.S.," Egils assured her.

Although Anna left Ottawa with less that what she had hoped to discover, she was buoyed by the thought that Karlis for sure seemed to be in Canada, and probably Valdis as well. She would have to be patient.

Anna applied herself to her studies and by late November, when the course had ended, she passed with flying colours. Anna proudly announced that night when she served supper, that she was now fluent in four languages and two alphabets.

"Two alphabets?" Mandy said with a puzzled look.

"Yes, I also learned to speak and read Russian and it has a different alphabet." Anna replied.

"That's that funny alphabet in which R's look like P's and S's like C's," John laughed. "CCCP means USSR."

"Does the C stand for a U too?" Trish asked. She was puzzled at the triple C.

Anna laughed and replied. "No. The Russian word for union is *soyuz*. Thus, if they used our alphabet it would read SSSR."

"What is the name of their alphabet again?" John asked

"The Cyrillic script."

"That's it. Sometimes I get shipping documents printed in Russian. Maybe I'll get you to translate them."

"I would be glad to read any documents written in Russian for you Mr. Gerrick," Anna replied. After seeing that the family had been served, she served herself a dish and sat at the table with them. It had been established some time earlier that Anna could eat with the family when they weren't entertaining guests.

217

"I have some other news," Mandy said. "I received a letter from Mom today, Mom, Dad and Martha have agreed to come down for Christmas."

"Excellent," John said, "it will be good to see them again. Did you hear that Trish? Grandma, Grandpa Polsen and Auntie Martha are coming down for Christmas?"

"Oh goody!" Trish exclaimed.

"Your parents, do they live far away?" Anna asked.

"They live on a farm out at Morning Glory, Alberta," Mandy replied.[1]

"Morning Glory," Anna puzzled. "I've heard that name before."

"In conversation around here?" John wondered.

"No, no, somewhere else." Anna wracked her brain. "Wait a minute. Yes. It was in Germany. A Canadian soldier. . ."

"Was his name Paul?" Mandy asked. "My brother Paul was in the war."

"No. I think his name was Larry, his last name. . . it was a Finnish name. He said his father was Finnish and his mother Swedish."

"Larry Kekkonin," Mandy said. "His parents are Astrid and Esa. They're really nice people."

"That's it. You know him, yes?"

"I grew up with him," Mandy said. "We were in the same grade in school. His mother's sister, Ingrid, and Mom are the best of friends."

"Small world," John chuckled.

"Very small world." Anna added. "He saved me from some American soldiers. He used to take me places and I guess you would say court me. He wanted to marry me, but I didn't think I loved him because I was waiting for Valdis."

"It *is* a small world," Mandy laughed. "Imagine meeting Larry Kekkonin a way over in Germany."

Anna gave the house a thorough cleaning in preparation for receiving their Christmas guests. John bought a large Christmas tree, which was put up near the fireplace in the main sitting room. Anna and Trish had a delightful time decorating it. Anna was beside herself in anticipation of meeting Mandy's parents. John had told her that Mandy had inherited both her good looks and warm personality from her mother.

---

[1] The story of Mandy's family is told in, *Ginny – A Canadian Story of Love and Friendship*

The Polsen family arrived on the morning of Christmas Eve. They had flown from Edmonton to Montreal and all of the family went to the airport to meet them. Anna stayed home to fuss about the house to make sure everything was immaculate. After a seemingly interminable wait Anna heard voices outside the front door. She rushed to the door to open it at the same time, as John was about to turn the handle. She held the door open wide beckoning with her arm for all to enter. Trish bounded in and began undoing her outer wear while John retrieved their luggage setting it aside with Anna helping. As Mandy's family members removed their coats, Anna grabbed them and put them in the closet.

"Now then Anna," Mandy finally said, when everyone had their outerwear put away. "I would like you to meet my mother, father and sister Martha."

Her mother was clearly an older version of Mandy with the same warm smile, though her carefully kept ginger-coloured hair displayed flecks of gray. Her father, whose receding hair was almost snow-white, also radiated a warm smile. Martha, a short, stout, woman also with ginger-coloured hair, likewise smiled pleasantly at Anna.

"Pleased to meet you," Anna beamed. "I have heard so much about you."

"And we about you," her mother smiled. "Mandy has told us in her letters all about your rather interesting life story."

"Yes, well come in to the sitting room. I will make you coffee and a treat, yes."

"Come Grandpa," Trish said, clasping and tugging at her grandfather's hand. "I'll show you the Christmas tree." He followed her to the sitting room with a laugh.

"Trish sure has her Grandpa wrapped around her little finger," John laughed.

"Marty just adores his grandchildren," her mother replied.

As Anna wheeled in a tray containing Christmas snacks, a pot of tea and a decanter of coffee she smiled at sight of the family gathering. The Christmas snacks included a platter of *speka piragi*. Trish was bounding from one grandparent to another and from them to her Aunt Martha. All made a big fuss over her. Anna had not seen such a warm family scene since the sun had set on Latvia. She then turned to begin the laborious task of carting their luggage up to their respective bedrooms.

"We can carry our own luggage," Marty said as he noticed her heading for the stairs lugging a large suitcase. He, along with Martha and John, came along each taking some of the luggage.

Although grateful for the assistance, Anna said. "It is my job as a maid to take care of these things."

"Nonsense, you are much more than a maid," John chided as they went up the stairs.

"Well now that you are up here, I can show all of you where your rooms are," Anna replied.

When they came back down, John said to Anna. "Why don't you join us for a while? There is nothing pressing in the kitchen is there?"

"No, nothing pressing. But I'll be sitting in a private family gathering."

"As far as I am concerned, you are practically family," Mandy called from the sitting room. "My family is dying to know all about you."

Anna came reluctantly into the sitting room and was going to sit on a chair to one side but Mandy's mother said. "There is room on the sofa beside me. Come and sit here." She patted the vacant spot on the couch. Marty sat down on the other side of her next to the chair where John sat.

"Are you sure Mrs. Polsen?" Anna said. "I'll be right in the middle of the family."

"Come please sit beside me," she smiled warmly. "I prefer to be called Ginny. Only children call me Mrs. Polsen."

"Thank you Mrs. Polsen," Anna said as she reluctantly came over to sit beside Mandy's mother. As she sat beside Ginny, she said. "You and your daughter are a lot alike."

"Thank you," Mandy said. "To be compared with my mother is a great honour."

"This relationship you have with Mandy reminds me of my own past," Ginny smiled. "When I was a teenager, Mom hired a maid. An Italian girl named Gina, who like you was new to Canada and could barely speak English. She and I became good friends and we still are."

"Yes, she followed you out west, didn't she Mother," Mandy said.

"Yes, she married one of our good neighbours. It's hard to believe that she was once a maid."

"I keep telling Anna, that she is not a servant. Just a guest and employee." Mandy said.

"In the Old Country there was always the upper and lower class," Anna said.

"In Canada things are different," Ginny said. "Oh there are households where domestic staff are treated like servants, but no one is bound by that lifestyle. When my friend Gina came out west she was behaving like a good servant concerned about her mistress. I had to convince her that she was my equal in every way."

"Anna wants to study to become a doctor," John said.

"Really," Ginny smiled. "That's excellent. There are not many female doctors in Canada. I wish you every success."

"Thank you," Anna blushed.

"You will have accomplished more than any of us," Marty added.

"I only got as far as secretarial school," Martha added.

"It doesn't matter who you are or how much education you have," Ginny said with an aura of wisdom. "You are what you are, and no one is better that you, *ever*."

"Mom ran away from a rich household," Mandy laughed, "to join Father on a homestead."

"I guess true love is the key to any success in life," Marty added, squeezing Ginny's hand.

"Did you know that Anna knows Larry Kekkonin?" Mandy said.

"Really! How did you meet him?" Martha asked with surprise.

"I met him in Berlin, just at the close of the war. Does he still live in Morning Glory?"

"No, he and his father have a lumber and hardware business in Kasper Beach." Marty replied.

"Kasper Beach!" Anna exclaimed. "That was the place where Uncle Janis had lived. Do you know many people there?"

"No, it's at the other end of the lake from us. About twenty-six miles away." Marty said.

Anna who still thought in terms of the metric system did a mental calculation to compare miles with kilometres. "That is forty kilometres. Have you ever heard the name Janis Lindenbergis, from around there."

"Janis Lindenbergis," Marty mused. "The name is vaguely familiar. Is that a Latvian name?"

"Yes, my name is Anna Lindenbergis."

"There are a lot of Latvians around Kasper Beach."

"Anna is looking for her brother Karlis and a friend named Valdis," Mandy said.

"Well, next time I happen to be at Kasper Beach. I'll inquire of the Lindenbergis family." Marty said.

"Uncle Janis is dead though," Anna said sadly. "According to the records at the Bureau."

"I'm sorry to hear that," Ginny said, touching her arm.

"What are these buns?" Martha gasped as she sampled the *speka p255pitcRBG.* "They're absolutely delicious."

"Speka piragi," Mandy replied, looking at Anna to make sure the pronunciation was correct. "She treats us to them all the time."

"It's just a common Latvian dish," Anna blushed modestly.

"Oh they are good," Marty said as he also sampled one. "They taste like they have bacon in them."

"They do," Anna replied.

"I must try one," Ginny added.

Anna got up and passed her the platter, then she asked to be excused. She had to check on dinner cooking in the kitchen. When supper was served that evening, Anna declined an offer to sit at the table insisting this was a family affair.

The following morning as gifts were opened Anna was astonished to find that she not only received gifts from John, Mandy and Trish, but she also received them from Marty and Ginny, and Martha.

"You shouldn't have," Anna gasped as she was given a gift from Marty and Ginny together. It was a picture book about Alberta. "I don't know what to say, I never thought." She felt embarrassed that they had given her gifts but she had not thought to get any for them.

"Don't let it bother you," Marty said.

"You didn't know us, so you wouldn't know what to get," Martha added.

"But. . ."

"An oversight on my part," Mandy said apologetically, placing a hand on Anna's arm. "I should have known that Mom, Dad and Martha would give you gifts."

"Thank you Anna, Miss Lindenbergis" Trish said running to hug Anna. She was clutching a doll dressed in the Latvian national costume. John and Mandy likewise discovered that their presents from Anna had a Latvian flavour. Anna had earlier discovered that the great cosmopolitan city of Montreal had many European boutiques including stores that sold products from the Baltic nations.

Christmas dinner was set out in the dining room with flair. Anna resisted offers by all three women in the house when they offered to help. Although the cuisine was Canadian, and included a large turkey, the table was laid out in the Latvian manner. This brought compliments from all around. In the final preparations however, she did relent and allow John to carve the turkey.

As everyone came to the table, Anna stood back like the dutiful servant. Mandy looked around the table and said, "There's one plate missing."

Flushed with embarrassment, Anna counted both the places and number of people while John and Mandy both wore mirthful looks.

"I don't understand Madam," Anna said humbly. "There is a plate for everyone."

"You forgot a plate for yourself," Mandy said.

"This is a family Christmas dinner, I'll eat in the kitchen again."

"You'll do no such thing," John said adamantly. "You weaseled out of sitting with us last night but this is Christmas dinner. You must sit with us."

"Yes, please sit with us," Ginny added. "Dinner would not be complete without you."

"I forbid anyone to sit down at the table until Anna brings herself a plate," John said firmly.

"Here, here," Marty added.

Anna wiped a tear from her eye and went to the kitchen to fetch the necessary tableware for herself. She was so nervous when she returned, she nearly dropped her plate on which was balanced the cutlery and a wineglass. Martha and Trish, who sat at the side opposite Marty and Ginny, quickly moved their plates over to make room for Anna. John poured wine for everyone and Anna fussed about making sure all the food dishes were in order.

When everyone was properly seated, John rose with glass in hand. "I would like to propose a toast to Anna, for laying this succulent feast before us. To Anna." The others raised their glasses.

"I would like to welcome Anna to her first Christmas in Canada. May it be the first of many, many happy Christmas s to come." Mandy added, raising her glass.

By now Anna's eyes were glistening from being the centre of attention. She rose with her glass and said in a choking voice that augmented her accent. "To all you kind, vonderful peoples who make me feel so velcome in Canada. God bless all of you."

Anna turned and fled from the room in tears and Mandy went after her. Anna slumped down in a kitchen chair and cried abundantly. Mandy came over and put a reassuring arm on her shoulder. "Vhy you so kind to me. Vhat I do to deserve zis" Anna said reverting to speaking broken English.

"You are a special person Anna," Mandy said gently. "Anyone who has lived through the things you've lived through, seen the terrible things you've seen, and are able to tell about it must be special. Someone is looking out for you Anna, and that *Someone* sent you to us to help you get started in your new life here in Canada."

Anna sniffled and looked up at Mandy with watery eyes.

"Come, your dinner will get cold," Mandy beckoned with a smile.

Anna stood up and the two women hugged for a long moment. "God bless you Mandy, you are a wonderful person," Anna finally said. She wiped the tears from her eyes and they went back to the dining room.

Chapter Twenty

The following autumn, after passing aptitude tests to prove that her Latvian education met university entrance standards, Anna enrolled in the prestigious McGill University in Montreal to begin taking her pre-med. John and Mandy both paid for her tuition and sponsored her admission, while she in turn continued to work as their domestic. Since her classes ended before Trish arrived home from school and she was allowed plenty of time to prepare dinner, everything worked out well for her. Anna wrote to the Latvian consulate several times asking for progress reports in the search for either Karlis or Valdis. All she was able to find so far was that her Uncle Janis was deceased and Aunt Katrina was in a senior's lodge in Edmonton and that one of their children was in Calgary and the other in Vancouver. As for inquiries about Karlis and Valdis, the Latvian consulate told Anna that they were trying their best but had to honour similar inquiries by other Latvian refugees looking for relatives. The only satisfaction she got during the first year of inquiries was from the world news in March of 1953. This was the announcement over the news media that Stalin had finally died. While she dared not hope that things would get better over in Latvia, she was sure they couldn't get worse.

Anna passed her exams with high marks and went on to ultimately graduate from the Faculty of Medicine. in the spring of 1957. John, Mandy and Trish all came to the graduation ceremonies with an aura of pride, that made them feel as if it was one of the family who had graduated. As a treat they took her to a posh restaurant in downtown Montreal.

When they entered the foyer to await seating, a waiter came to attend to them. As he was about to speak, a big man in a white jacket stepped up beside him, scrutinizing Anna. Anna thought he looked familiar and it induced her to ask Mandy, "What type of cuisine is offered in this restaurant?"

"Hungarian." John replied. "I thought we'd try something exotic tonight."

"Anna?" the big man said. "Anna Lindenbergis."

"Jan!" she cried. "It's Big Jan."

She opened her arms and the two of them hugged tightly for a moment. Jan finally said with a laugh and a distinct accent, "So do you speak English yet?"

"Oh yes, I'm going to college and studying to be a doctor," Anna smiled. "And you?"

"I'm the assistant manager of this restaurant. I learned both English and French."

"Excellent," Anna replied. She turned and introduced John and Mandy as her dear friends. "They took me in, taught me English and helped put me through university."

"I couldn't turn down this poor destitute woman who came to my doorstep looking for a job," Mandy laughed.

"She is just like one of the family," John added.

"Yes, I know," Jan laughed. "I looked after her on the ship when we crossed the ocean."

"And he saved me from drowning," Anna laughed.

"Yes, well come with me," Jan said. "I will set you at the finest table in the restaurant."

Jan led them through the large darkened room lighted primarily by candlelight at the various tables and they could hear enchanting Gypsy music in the background.

When they were seated, Jan presented them with menus and told them their meal was on the house.

"That is more than generous of you," John said.

"Anna and I are old friends. We went through many trials together," Jan insisted.

"We even jumped ship together," Anna laughed. "Oh, I trust you are a Canadian citizen by now?" she asked Jan in a sober note.

"Yes, I got my citizenship last year. I filed as a refugee."

"So did I," Anna said. Then with a laugh, she added, "We did all right for a couple of DP's"

Everyone laughed. Jan lit the candles for their table and suggested a selection of Hungarian wines from which they might choose. They dined on exotic spicy food that included *tizai balazle*, a fish based soup, and they had stuffed cabbage and noodles with cottage cheese for a main course. Dessert was a delicious walnut roll. Jan sent them a bottle of expensive Hungarian red wine, and a Gypsy violinist to serenade them while they dined. They admired the Hungarian decor of the restaurant, which included a giant mural of the Danube flowing through the heart of Budapest. Later as they enjoyed their coffee and apricot brandy, Big Jan joined them so that he and Anna might reminisce old times. They left the restaurant that evening full and content, while Jan still refused payment for the meal. John, however, managed to leave a substantial tip at the table.

One day in early June, a letter came from the consulate stating that there was a Carl Lindenbergis who was living in Edmonton, Alberta. He had been born in Riga and his father's name was Andris.

"It has to be him!" Anna exclaimed to Mandy. "Since they gave me his address, I'll write him a letter."

Dear Carl/Karlis,
IF your first name is truly Karlis, your parents were Andris and Lita Lindenbergis, and that you have sisters by name of Anna and Liesma, you must be my long lost brother. I am Anna Lindenbergis and I am alive and well, living in Montreal. I have been desperately trying to find either you or Valdis since arriving in Canada in 1950. I am doing well here in Montreal studying to be a doctor. A wonderful family has taken me in as one of their own, helped me learn English and even helped pay my way through university.
Please answer this letter and confirm that you are indeed my brother. If so, I will come to Edmonton to meet you. I have just graduated from Medicine so am at a turning point in my life.

Your Loving Sister
Anna

Anna posted the letter with great hope in her heart. She received a reply about two weeks later. She tore open the envelope and read with pounding heart. Mandy stood by with anticipation as Anna read.

Dear Anna,

Words cannot explain the joy I feel in finally finding you. I have searched all over for you and had nearly given up hope. This is indeed a great day, Anna. Liesma is coming to Canada this summer also. The new Soviet regime under Khrushchev is a bit more lenient and has allowed many exiled Latvians to come back to Latvia. In finding that out, I inquired through the Soviet embassy and discovered that Liesma had returned to Latvia, but Mother is dead. After going through much red tape I managed to make arrangements to get her out of Latvia so she could join me in Canada. Now we are all here. Liesma has already arrived in Sweden so is clear of the Soviets and she should be in Edmonton in a few days. When we all get together we'll have a grand Latvian celebration. We will hold it at my summer home on the lake by Kasper Beach. There are a large number of Latvians settled in this area. As you may know, Uncle Janis has passed on and I bought a sizable chunk of his lakeside property to build a summer retreat.

I do not know the fate of Valdis as we got separated shortly after we both arrived in Canada. He does not keep contact with the Latvian community as I do. However, in view of the wonderful news of contacting you, I will put out a bulletin in the newspapers to try to track him down and invite him to the celebration. He goes by the name Walter Sirnis now. We both changed our names somewhat when we were in Sweden. If you cannot afford to pay the fare to get here let me know and I will pay it for you. Life in Canada has been good to me. Until we meet again:

Love From Your Brother
Carl/Karlis

"It's him, it's him!" Anna exclaimed. She grabbed Mandy and hugged her fiercely. "At last I've found my brother." Tears were streaming down her face.

"Oh Anna, that is so wonderful," Mandy said. Her eyes were also becoming misty.

"That's not all. He somehow got our sister Liesma out of Latvia.

She's in Sweden now and expected to arrive in Edmonton soon. Oh I can't believe it."

"Oh Anna, I'm so happy for you," Mandy said. Then on a more sober note she added. "So I expect that you'll be leaving us."

"For now anyway," Anna said with a teary smile. "I have to go out there and meet them. Then I'll decide my fate from there."

"You know that a degree from McGill is recognized anywhere in Canada. If you choose to stay out there, you could always intern in a hospital in Edmonton." Mandy assured her.

"True, but I'd be leaving you and your family behind," Anna sniffed.

"You must follow your destiny," Mandy said. "Your real family is waiting in Alberta. You must go to them and stay with them if need be."

"I will miss you people so much," Anna said tearfully. "You are my real family."

"We will miss you too, but we'll manage," Mandy said. "Trish is nearly eleven years old now and doesn't need so much close supervision."

"Maybe there will be another DP woman looking for a job if you still need a maid," Anna laughed.

"Maybe, but no one can replace you," Mandy smiled.

A week later the Gerrick family took Anna to the railway station in Montreal. She had thought of taking an airplane, as it would have gotten her there more quickly. Anna decided, however, that she wanted to see the breadth of Canada. Besides, the train would deliver her directly to Kasper Beach.

"Well Anna, it has been a real pleasure having you in our house," John said, as he was first to say goodbye. "It will be very empty without you." He shook hands with her then Anna reached for him and they hugged briefly.

"Goodbye Anna," Trish said tearfully. Anna bent down and Trish ran into her arms and they hugged tightly for a long moment. "Be a good girl and mind your mother and father. They are very precious you know." Anna said.

"I will," Trish replied tearfully. "You will come back to see us?"

"Absolutely. I'll come back as quickly as I can." Anna straightened up to face Mandy.

"Well I guess this is it," Mandy said with a teary smile. "I hope you find your friend Valdis as well as your family."

"I will never forget your kindness to a DP foreigner," Anna laughed weakly.

"We're all DP's or at least our ancestors were," Mandy laughed. "Don't ever let anyone ever call you by that name."

"God bless you again," Anna said as she and Mandy hugged tightly for a long moment.

"Write to us when you get settled," Mandy said. "Don't forget that Mom and Dad live near the next town past Kasper Beach and Martha lives in Edmonton. Say hello to them as they will all be glad to see you."

"I will." Anna sniffed as the call came to board the train.

It was early afternoon when Anna arrived at Kasper Beach. Although the rail trip across Canada was interesting, it was quite long. Anna thought that when she went back to Montreal again, she would travel by airplane. She got off at a plain wooden station and her two suitcases were taken from the baggage car and set on a hand truck. She looked absently up at the semaphore signal attached to the station. Both arms were down displaying stop as the train pulled away. She went into the waiting room to find it empty, then went to the wicket.

"Has there been a Karlis Lindenbergis here today, looking for an Anna?" Anna asked the station agent.

"There was a Carl Lindenbergis here this morning about the time the train should have arrived," the agent replied. "I told him that the train was several hours late and he left again. Have a seat. If he's expecting you I'm sure he'll be back."

Anna settled on the hard wooden bench staring at the ticking pendulum clock on the wall, wishing she had brought along a book to read. As the seat was uncomfortable, she got up and walked about. It was a nice day so she strolled out on the platform and looked around the corner of the station at the sprawling village. About two blocks down Main Street she saw a large building with a sign that read KEKKONIN LUMBER AND HARDWARE. *'Kekkonin,'* she thought. *'Larry Kekkonin? Mandy's mother said he lived at Kasper Beach. I wonder. . ?'*

Anna found herself walking quickly down the street toward the big building. She entered the building into a large room containing shelves full of hardware while the air bore the aroma of newly cut lumber. She looked uncertainly around as she walked down the main aisle.

"Can I help you with something?" said a pleasant-looking, middle-aged woman who came along side her.

"Uh, yes, does a Larry Kekkonin own this store?"

"Yes, he and his father owned this store, until his father passed on a couple of years ago."

Anna noticed a twinge of sadness in the woman's eyes. "You are his mother, yes?"

"Yes, my name is Astrid. Do you know my son?"

"Yes, I met him in Germany at the close of the war," Anna replied. "We uh . . . Well he, what you would say, stuck up for me."

"I see, and you are."

"Anna Lindenbergis."

"Lindenbergis is that . . .?"

"A Latvian name," Anna said cutting her off. "I ran away from Latvia to get away from the Russians."

"Was Janis Lindenbergis related to you?"

"Yes, he was my uncle."

"You don't say."

"Did you know him?"

"Oh yes, he and his wife were one of many Latvian families that live around Kasper Beach. Astrid replied. "You must be related to Carl Lindenbergis."

"He's my brother and the reason I came out here," Anna replied. "I haven't seen him since just before the war."

"He built a big fancy place by the lake on Janis' old farm," Astrid said.

Just then a customer came in.

With an eye on the customer, Astrid said quickly, "Larry is in Edmonton on business today, but I'll certainly tell him that you called."

"Thank you. It was nice meeting you," Anna said as Astrid moved to serve the customer. "Best I get back to the station."

When Anna climbed back on to the station platform she saw a man and a woman standing there. The man looked very familiar with his craggy features and the woman vaguely so.

"Anna?" the man said.

"Karlis!" Anna cried with sudden recognition. She threw herself into his arms sobbing. "Oh Karlis, I thought I'd never see you again."

"Anna, oh Anna," Karlis sobbed, holding her tightly. "I searched and searched, never guessing you were in Montreal. But look who's beside me."

Anna and Karlis let go of each other and Anna turned to the woman and said, "Liesma?"

"Hello, Anna," Liesma said in Latvian. Her voice had a certain hollowness and her face bore hard lines around the eyes. Although she was five years younger than Anna, she looked older. "I thought I'd never see you again. Never thought I'd get out of the camps."

"Oh Liesma," Anna said also in Latvian. "We are safe in Canada now, the Russians can't hurt us any more." She reached for Liesma and they hugged although Liesma's hug was limp."

"Mother did not survive the camps?" Anna asked.

"No," Liesma said flatly. "They were too much for her. Her heart was broken from seeing her family destroyed."

"But you survived," Anna said.

"Yes, I survived. It was like a terrible nightmare." Liesma said with her hollow voice.

"Liesma is still in shock," Karlis said. "Come let's go home."

They climbed into Karlis's big limousine-like car and Anna remarked, "You must be rich, to be able to drive a Lincoln."

"I got involved in the oil business when I came to Alberta and have done well by it," Karlis replied. "But I'd give it up tomorrow if it meant keeping us all together. Are you going back to Montreal?"

"I don't know. Mandy, the woman with whom I stayed, says I can start my interning in an Edmonton hospital if I wish."

"I'm sure you can." He laughed and said, "My sister the doctor."

"That is what you've always wanted," Liesma added.

"And what do you want to be?" Anna smiled at Liesma.

"I want to be free. Free to come and go as it was when I was a child."

"So Anna, how did you come through all of this?" Karlis asked "Valdis told me about the time when you and he spent a year hiding from the Reds and how you both cooperated with the Nazis."

"Father told me to survive at all costs and never let them take me. Actually a German officer who was one of the administrators in Riga was my benefactor. He helped keep the SS off my back and looked after me. Most importantly, he got me out of Latvia as the Soviets were returning. I was in Berlin when the Red Army captured the city and I nearly got raped by four of those animals. However, I managed to get to West Berlin and when the blockade was on I sneaked on board a transport plane to Bremen. Later I got on a Tramp Steamer that brought me to Canada and I jumped ship."

"You came here illegally?" Karlis asked.

"Yes, but the people I was staying with helped me get straightened out with the authorities and I am now a Canadian citizen."

"It sounds like I've had an easy life compared to my siblings," Karlis laughed as they pulled up to a large sprawling cottage with several high-peaked roofs, large windows and wide verandas on all but the north side. "Well this is my summer cottage," he laughed as he stopped the car.

"Some cottage," Anna said. She surveyed the sprawling building that faced the lake across a large sloping lawn with several shade trees growing on it and a number of well-tended flower beds. A sandy beach separated the lower end of the lawn from the lake. A boathouse was at the water edge and a small pier projected into the water.

As they walked up on to the veranda a woman came out of the house. "Anna I'd like you to meet my wife, Jelena. Jelena, my sister Anna," Karlis spoke in Latvian.

"Pleased to meet you," Anna said, also in Latvian. "So, since you know the language, I presume you are Latvian."

"I was born and raised there, on a farm just outside Riga." Jelena said.

Jelena, the name rattled around in Anna's head as they went into the house. *Jelena raised on a farm near Riga.* Something was very familiar about all this.

Anna settled on a large couch facing a huge bay window that looked southward over the lake. From her vantage, Anna could both hear and see motorboats racing around the lake. Some were towing water skiers.

"What a beautiful view," she gasped.

"Yes, I like it," Karlis said as he settled into an easy chair near Anna. "I just can't get over you being here."

"Yes, it is so good to have a conversation in Latvian again," Anna said. "It's been years since I've been able to use my native language."

"Do you want a cold drink?" Jelena asked from the kitchen. Both Anna and Karlis said yes. Liesma wandered outside and sat on the veranda staring out at the lake.

"It's like being in a dream," Anna said. "Poor Liesma, she seems so lost."

"She's been to hell and back," Karlis said gravely. "It will take a lot of loving on our part to bring her around."

"I'm glad I decided to stay here for a week or two before planning my future. Maybe I can try to reach out to Liesma."

"Did Liesma want anything?" Jelena said, as she brought a pitcher of lemon-aid and some glasses.

"She didn't say." Karlis shrugged.

"So, when did you escape from Latvia?" Anna asked Jelena, as she sat down to join them.

"In 1940. The day the Soviets took over in those so-called elections. A group of us students stole on board a ship bound for Sweden. I stayed there over the war. I met Karlis when he and another Latvian fellow . . ."

"Valdis Zirnis," Anna interrupted.

"Yes, Valdis," Jelena continued. "Anyway, a group of us had enough money to get passage to New York after the war. Karlis and I were married there. Valdis came with us when we decided to immigrate to Canada, but we lost track of him in Toronto. He seemed fascinated at how one, even with humble beginnings, could get rich over here. I presume you know Valdis."

"We grew up together, and we hid out from the Soviets together. We have a special bond."

"Were you lovers?"

"No, though he wanted to marry me," Anna said. "I said that hiding from the Russians like hunted animals was not a time for love. He told me he loved me, but I could never say that I loved him."

"Did you?"

"Yes, I think I did. I wish I could see him again."

"Maybe he'll show up." Karlis said.

"Valdis Zirnis," Liesma said plainly. She had quietly re-entered the room while they were talking.

"Ycs," Anna smiled.

"Would you like a drink of lemon-aid, Liesma?" Jelena asked pleasantly.

"I like Coca-Cola," Liesma said in her near monotone.

"I'll get you one," Karlis said, rising.

"Beautiful home you have here Jelena," Liesma said abruptly.

"Thank you," Jelena smiled.

When Karlis handed Liesma the bottle of pop she said, "Thank you brother Karlis." She took the soft drink and returned to the veranda.

"So you were raised on a farm near Riga?" Anna asked Jelena. Her suspicions about the familiarity of Jelena were beginning to focus. "Was it southeast of Riga?"

"Yes."

"What was your maiden name?"

"Vagris. Why?"

"Your parents, were their names Astra and Atis?"

"Yes. Did you know them?" Jelena was astonished.

"Yes. Valdis and I hid out from the Reds, or the Comrades as your father called them, on their farm all one winter. They were wonderful people."

"Well this is incredible," Jelena said.

"So I suppose the Reds killed them by now," Anna said soberly.

"No they're still alive. After Stalin died and we were allowed some contact with Latvia, I discovered that they were still alive."

"They thought the Reds killed you though." Anna said. Then with a laugh she added. "Your father was quite a survivor. I remember he had a photo of Stalin and a bust of Lenin. He kept them hidden, taking them out only when one of the Comrades came by. Not only that, but when the Nazis took over Latvia, he made sure he had a photo of Hitler to display for the right people."

Both Karlis and Jelena chuckled at the story and Anna added. "I'd love to see them again. Too bad they couldn't get over here."

"We thought of it, but they both said they were too old to move and would stay put in Latvia," Jelena said. "At least we can write to them, although the KGB probably reads all the mail."

"The KGB?" Anna said.

"Yes, that's the new name for the secret police."

As they talked they noticed that Liesma had left the veranda and was walking along the lawn, looking listlessly at the flowers. She walked with a slow dream-like walk down to the lake shore and sat on the pier. Her feet were dangling over the edge nearly touching the water.

"We really do need to find a way to reach Liesma," Karlis said gravely. "The horror of what she has gone through is still locked up inside her."

"Was it hard to convince her to come to Canada?"

"No. When I made contact through the letters, she was readily agreeable. I had friends, who were going over to the Old Country, deliver her the airline tickets and travelling money. They escorted her to Sweden. It seems that her condition got worse since she arrived here."

"The shock of what she has gone through, the loss of family and life in the camps, finally caught up to her once she was over here, free of the Soviets." Jelena observed.

"Something like war veterans," Anna added. "We had a psychology class about them. The ones who couldn't cope with the horrors of war usually didn't break down until they were safely back home. Liesma was only twelve years old when they shot Father and took her and Mother away to the camps."

"At least she is safe over here and has most of her family to help." Karlis added.

"If you'll excuse me," Anna said. "I'd like to go speak to Liesma. Maybe I can reassure her as a big sister."

"A good idea," Karlis said. "I have to go pick up my children anyway. They are over at a friend's house."

"And I'll start supper," Jelena added.

Liesma, who sat on the end of the pier with her back to the house, didn't acknowledge Anna's approach even though Anna's shoes made a clomping noise on the boards. As Anna came up alongside her, Liesma turned slightly and wore a trace of a smile on her face. Anna sat down beside her. The toes of her shoes were touching the water.

"I can't describe how wonderful it is to see you Liesma," Anna said warmly.

"It's good to see you too," Liesma replied somberly. "I never thought I'd see you again."

"Neither the Reds nor the Nazis were smart enough to get me," Anna laughed. "Though it seems the Reds followed me everywhere I went. That's why I came to Canada. I hope the Atlantic Ocean is wide enough to stop them."

"I hope so," Liesma said flatly. "This all seems like a dream. When

I was in the camps, I dreamed dreams like this, of a golden country, of Canada. I never thought I'd live to get here."

"Well you are here now and you have Karlis and me. Those swine may have killed Mother and Father, but we are free. I wish Mother and Father could see us now here in a land of plenty, free from fear." Anna put her arms gently around Liesma. "I have seen some terrible things my dear sister, gone hungry for days on end, lived in fear of getting caught by either the NKVD or the Gestapo, I was nearly raped by four Russian soldiers, but I survived. It seems like a terrible nightmare now and every day it gets further away."

"It was so horrible," Liesma sobbed on Anna's shoulder. "They beat Mom. They beat me. We had to work from dawn till dusk. We were always cold and hungry. They did horrible things." By now Liesma was crying.

"That's it Liesma get it all out," Anna said gently holding her sister. "Remember when we were children and I was the big sister who always picked you up?"

Liesma nodded with tear sodden eyes. "They did things . . ."

"I don't want to hear the details," Anna said with an anxious tone. "Seeing you and Mother getting taken away was enough for me. Those Reds were such animals."

"Valdis was so glad to see the Germans come, he joined the *Wehrmacht* to fight the Russians. He hoped the German army would liberate the part of Russia that held his family."

"They shot his parents you know," Liesma said flatly. "After he jumped off the train that time, they took his parents off the train at the next station and executed them right there on the platform as an example and made us all watch."

"Oh my God."

"Oh Anna, those Communist swine are such animals. They do things . . ." Liesma started crying again. "Two of them were going to rape Mother but we fought them off then they grabbed me. They thought I'd be better because I was young. She begged them to let me be, offering to be their whore if they'd leave me alone. When she tried to save me, one of them beat her so badly that she ended up in the infirmary. It was after that, when she found out what they did to me, she lost the will to live."

"Oh no Liesma," Anna started crying.

"I was like a robot," Liesma said, regaining her composure some-what. "I did what they wanted and they made my workload easier and gave me better food. Then one day they told all of us in camp who were still alive that we were going back to Latvia. Riga was a strange and empty place. Strangers had lived in our old house. Then one day the local commissar informed me that my brother in Canada was trying to contact me. So here I am."

"Well we are safe now in Canada. Karlis and I are at your side. The Reds will never hurt you again"

"Oh Anna, God bless you," Liesma sobbed. "Just to be here with you, knowing you are alive and safe."

"Think of the future. Here in Canada you can be what you want to be. Once you learn how to speak and read English, the world is yours. You will always have Karlis and me at your side."

"So, are you still really going to be a doctor?" Liesma smiled weakly.

"Yes, I just have to do my internship, then I'll be Dr. Lindenbergis."

Liesma laughed and then said with an anxious tone "Are you going back to, Montreal, is it?"

"I haven't decided."

"Please stay near us," Liesma begged. "Karlis says that Montreal is over four thousand kilometres away."

"Over here you have to say miles," Anna laughed. "The way they measure things is completely different. As for my future, I will wait until after this celebration Karlis is planning is over."

"I remember that terrible day when we left you behind, hiding in the house," Liesma said. "I don't ever want to see you out of my sight again."

Anna reached under her neckline and pulled out the locket saying, "Remember this?"

"The locket," Liesma gasped. "I remember Mother saying that she gave it to you the night the Reds came for us."

Anna opened it and the two of them looked at the photo of their father.

"You know Liesma, this is only the third time I opened the locket since Mother gave it to me. I didn't want to be reminded of Father and the life that we had lost. I touched it lots though, especially when I was faced with a major crisis. It seemed like his way of communicating with me from beyond the grave, urging me to be brave."

"Yes, I think we had a guiding light," Liesma said. "Something kept me going, giving me the will to live when there was nothing to live for."

"I know," Anna said. "Someone has been watching over us and if Mother and Father could look down upon us today, they would be happy knowing that the three of us found each other and are living in freedom." Anna looked up and cried out, "Can you see us Mother and Father, we're alive, free and far from the Soviets."

Liesma looked up and smiled also. Then the two sisters hugged for a long moment. Then Anna said softly, "Come. Let's go back to the house. Jelena will have supper on soon."

Anna and Liesma walked arm-in-arm back to the house while Karlis observed them from the step. When they drew near, he came to join them in a three-way hug. When they entered the house Karlis introduced Anna to his children Andrew and Ann. He said it was the Anglicized version of Andris and Anna.

Three days later Karlis held his celebration to welcome the reunion with his sisters. Several dozen Latvian families, from both around Kasper Beach and in Edmonton came. Janis's two children came, bringing their mother Katrina. All had a tearful reunion with Anna and Liesma. Liesma was more open now, but still hung in the background compared to the others.

Karlis had erected two flagpoles. One carried the Canadian Red Ensign and the other the dark-red flag, with the white band, of free Latvia. In respect for their new country, the Canadian flag was on a higher pole. Before the celebration got underway, they sang the Latvian anthem and the pastor of the local Lutheran Church led a prayer for all the Latvian people who died by the hand of oppression and to pray for the return of freedom to their homeland. A prayer of thanks that they got to live in their new land of Canada followed this. He also gave thanks that Karlis was able to find his lost sisters. Everyone then sang O' Canada

A great feast of traditional Latvian dishes was laid out, and those so inclined sang and played Latvian folk songs. A singing troupe from the Latvian Society entertained them at one point, wearing traditional costumes. Anna was nearly overwhelmed at the festivities, and Liesma was so taken by event that she was beginning to learn how to smile and laugh again.

Anna noticed a large white Cadillac drive up. When the driver stepped out, she sensed an air of familiarity about him. The familiarity was so strong that she started walking toward him. He recognized her also, "Anna!" he cried, speaking English. "Is that you?"

"Valdis!" Anna cried as she rushed into his arms.

Chapter Twenty-One

"Oh Valdis, I can't believe I've found you," Anna gasped. She spoke in Latvian "Now my life is complete."

"Oh Anna, I thought I'd never see you again." Valdis said as they embraced tightly and kissed with nibbling kisses. "But I did know that you would survive, because you had the will to survive." He continued to speak in English.

"So did you, apparently," Anna said, as she relaxed her hug and looked Valdis in the eyes. This time she used English "Karlis told me all about how you and he met up in Finland."

"That was so long ago," Valdis frowned. "I'm trying to forget about that life. I even changed my name somewhat."

"I know," Anna laughed. "It's Walter Sirnis."

"Wally if you please."

Anna released her hug, but still held onto his hand and said, "So where did you go, Wally, when Karlis lost track of you?"

"I taught myself English and learned about the world of finance. North America is definitely the place to be if you want to make money and I've made lots of it."

"You definitely drive a fancy car," Anna laughed as they walked along, hand-in-hand. "Do you know that Karlis got Liesma out of Latvia?"

"Is that so," Wally said. "I don't expect I'll ever find any of my family."

Anna didn't have the heart to tell him what Liesma told her, about the fate of his parents.

"I've put that all behind me, Anna" Wally continued. "My life in Latvia was a different time and place, and I don't ever want to think about it again. I don't even want to speak in Latvian if I can avoid it."

"Am I of a different time and place?" Anna asked letting go of his hand.

"No, you are the one thing that is unchanged. When Carl put out the bulletin in the papers and mentioned your name, I came."

"Karlis put on a grand celebration to welcome Liesma and myself. We have Latvian food, Latvian music . . ."

"I don't care about any of that," Wally said. "I'm an American now."

"I thought you wanted to be a Canadian?"

"No, America is the place to be if you want to make money."

"Money, is that all you ever think of?" Anna asked. She was beginning to wonder if Wally really was the same person as the Valdis that she knew before.

"Money is what counts. I don't ever want to be where I'm starving and hiding again. Europe is full of small nations getting trampled on by big nations. Look at America. No one will ever tramp on it."

Anna had a flash vision of those American soldiers in Berlin boasting of their victory.

"But I did think a lot about you though," Wally added.

"Did you try to find me?" Anna asked.

"I made some inquiries, in Germany and in Canada." Wally replied. "When did you get to Canada, Anna?"

"In late 1950. I jumped ship to get here."

"Still the same Anna," Wally laughed. "There is nothing that can stop you once you set your mind to it. Are you still going to be a doctor?"

"Yes, I've graduated from the Faculty of Medicine. and will be seeking an interning position, possibly in a hospital in Edmonton."

"Edmonton! Why would you want to live in Edmonton? Go back to Montreal or to Toronto, or some big place."

"What's wrong with Edmonton?"

"It's such a small insignificant city."

"It is near to my family."

Just then Karlis appeared and made loud greetings to Wally. They shook hands and hugged briefly then Karlis took Wally around to introduce him to everyone. Wally carried a flamboyant air and let everyone know of his great wealth. When he spoke to Liesma it was with a condescending politeness. As Anna listened to Wally boast of his great achievements in the world of finance, the less and less she felt she knew him. She thought of the youth who used to wait for her outside her father's office, the youth who jumped off a train bound for Siberia to get back to Riga to be with her, and the young man who asked her to wait for him when he joined the army. Had she waited for an illusion?

As Anna made her way around the large gathering, a voice called out to her and she turned to see who had called. A woman of her age who was strangely familiar said again, "Anna? Anna Lindenbergis?"

"Yes, you are?" Then with a heavy voice added, "Lana."

"Yes," Lana smiled.

"What are you doing here?" Anna asked in a hostile tone.

"I was invited. My husband and I have known Carl for years, or perhaps I should say Karlis for the occasion." Lana spoke in Latvian.

"I see. So you also survived the war and made it to Canada." Anna replied, also in Latvian

"I've been here since 1945," Lana continued. "Could we go down to the lakeside and talk?"

"What's there to talk about?" Anna said flatly. "Will talking bring back Taska?"

"Taska lives," Lana said in her ever-friendly manner, in spite of Anna's continued hostility.

"What do you mean lives?" Anna said, as she turned to follow Lana as she walked toward the dock to where Karlis's boat was moored.

"I have kept in contact with the Old Country, in the post Stalin era when we were given more freedom of communication. Taska and her mother were returned to Latvia just like Liesma."

"And your mother?"

"The Reds killed her," Lana said in a downcast tone.

"So, being a snitch for them didn't help."

"No," Lana said in a small voice. "That was the worst part of my life."

"Did you snitch for the Gestapo as well?"

"Well, er, sort of, but more for Colonel Brandt."

"Kurt?"

"Yes, he found out from the captured NKVD documents about my role as an informer and hired me to watch over you."

"Over me? Then he did not trust me," Anna's face fell.

"It was not that he didn't trust you. He was afraid for you. You see, this time I was informing in a positive way."

"That's why he knew I stopped by the ghetto that time," Anna said flatly, looking away from Lana.

"I also saw you hide those two Jews in your van that night."

"You . . . and you never snitched to the Gestapo?"

"They questioned me very intently, as they were aware I was an informer for Colonel Brandt. They used to question me periodically before that, and because of it, I helped spread the rumour that you were the Colonel's mistress."

"You?"

"I had to tell them something. The Gestapo was just as merciless as the NKVD."

"I suppose it was better than telling them that I helped Jews. But why the change of heart?"

"I felt badly that I had betrayed both you and Taska. And that day when the Nazis came and you and Valdis walked away from me, I knew I had done a terrible wrong. Not only that, I learned from the Gestapo when they were recruiting me, that I was on the next NKVD compiled deportation list because I had failed them."

"How did you get over here?"

"Well, Colonel Brandt got me out of Latvia also. He got me on a refugee ship bound for Denmark and I remained there for the duration of the war. Shortly after the war I met up with a number of other Latvian refugees and joined in with them and we all emigrated to Canada."

"Legally?" Anna asked.

"Yes. Why? Did you sneak over here?"

"Yes I did, but I'm a Canadian citizen now. Where did you meet Karlis?"

"I met him and his wife in Toronto. There is a large Latvian community there you know. Later, after marrying another Latvian émigré, Maris Ozols, we came out west also. My husband and I escorted Liesma out of Latvia."

Anna stood with mouth agape. This school friend who had betrayed her during the Red terror, had striven, ever since that time, to atone for her sins. *'Lana's failure to report that she saw me smuggle out Jacob and Golda no doubt saved both my life and Kurt's, not to mention theirs. She also risked everything by withholding this information from the Gestapo. Now she helped get my sister out of Latvia. It is a strange world indeed.'*

"I know that once a person is betrayed, they can never trust the one who betrays. I will turn and walk away out of your life and that of Karlis and Liesma," Lana said sorrowfully. "They do not know about my betrayal, but I'll not blame you if you tell them."

Curiously, Anna thought of the words of a long forgotten prayer, *'Forgive us our trespasses as we forgive those who trespass against us.'* She was about to speak, when Karlis came up to them. "I see you two have finally found each other. Lana has told me that you were good school friends. I would have told you about her earlier but I wanted her to be a special surprise for you."

"Yes. It was quite a surprise." Anna smiled. "We were just renewing our old friendship after many years of separation," She noticed that Lana was positively beaming with her remark. Turning to Lana, she said, "That which we just shared will be forever between us." Again Lana smiled radiantly. Then Anna said, "I would like to meet your husband."

The celebration lasted well into the night and for a while Anna thought she had been transported back to the Latvia of her youth. *'What a curious country Canada is. It allows people to keep their ethnic identity. It also allows people of different backgrounds, of nations that were enemies in Europe, to live and work side-by-side as Canadians under that great banner of freedom.'*

Liesma was enjoying herself too. Karlis and Anna had even seen her laugh on several occasions. Only Wally seemed more interested in talking about business opportunities than partaking in the revelry honouring the land of his birth. As it was purely a Latvian celebration, there was a tendency among many guests to speak in Latvian. Wally made it plain that he preferred to speak English and whenever someone spoke to him in Latvian he always answered in English. When he was introduced to Lana, he didn't recognize her and neither Anna nor Lana attempted to refresh his memory. When all was settled down Wally was invited to spend the night in the sprawling summerhouse with the Lindenbergis family.

The following morning Anna was sitting on the south veranda enjoying the view of the lake with the sounds of birds chirping in the background. She had a notepad in her hand and was starting a letter to Taska, as Lana had given her the address. Wally came up along side here.

"Good morning Wally," she smiled.

"Good morning," he replied hastily as he drew up a wicker chair to face her. "Anna, I have to leave this morning on business. I'll be flying to Toronto for a week, then I'm coming back for you."

"For me?" Anna said with surprise.

"I need you Anna," Wally continued. "I need you at my side. Come with me and I will show you riches beyond your wildest dreams. You will never be cold or hungry again. We can live in New York or maybe California. Marry me Anna and we'll honeymoon in Hawaii. Have you ever been on a tropical island?"

"No," Anna replied. "Have you?"

"I've been to Hawaii and I've been to the Caribbean."

"You've done quite well for yourself Wally," Anna replied flatly.

"Yes, very well," Wally replied. "Remember that winter we spent hiding out in a hayloft with barely enough to eat and in constant fear of being shot?"

"Yes, I remember it well," Anna replied.

"I vowed that if I ever got out of that seemingly hopeless situation, I'd make sure I'd never be there again. Now I've found the means. I want to share this with you. All of it. Be my wife and I'll build you the biggest mansion money can buy. We'll staff it with servants to cater to your every whim."

"I've worked as servant, you know," Anna replied. "A wonderful family in Montreal took me in. In exchange for working as their domestic, they paid my way through university."

Wally was taken aback for a moment, then continued. "I love you Anna. Please say you'll marry me."

"What about my plans to become a doctor?"

"You won't need to be a doctor any more, but if you insist it could be arranged."

"What about my family? I promised Liesma I'd stay near to her."

"When you get that mansion, you can invite all of your family to come and visit. Liesma can come and stay as long as she wishes."

"I don't know Wally. You know, the dream of seeing you again was one thing that kept me going all these years. When I saw you step from that car yesterday, my heart nearly stopped. I couldn't believe my dream had come true. Now you've bombarded me with so much in the way of offerings, I don't know what to think."

"I know, my darling Anna." Wally said tenderly. "That is why I am giving you time. I would dearly love to take you with me today, but I know that would be too much to ask."

"Yes, there is much to think about," Anna smiled. "When you return, I will have my answer."

"Please say it will be yes. You've always kept me dangling on a string. You would never say 'I love you', to me."

"I know. When you went away to the army, I wished that I had said it to you. I longed for a chance to see you again so I could say, 'I love you'."

"Now is your opportunity," Wally said, rising. Anna rose too and Wally took her gently by the shoulders and looked her in the eye, "You were going to tell me something?"

"I . . .uh. I'll tell you when I get back."

"You will be here when I come back?"

"That much I will promise you, Wally. I plan to stay a week or two with Karlis and help Liesma adjust to her new life. If I go away it would only be as far as Edmonton."

"I will come here a week from today, with hope in my heart, but now I must go."

"Goodbye Wally," Anna leaned forward and kissed him and he grabbed her and kissed her for a long moment before turning to go.

As Wally drove away, Karlis stepped into the veranda. "Renewing an old affair are you?" he laughed.

"Yeah," Anna sighed heavily as she turned to her brother. "He proposed to me and wants me come with him to live a high-flying life of luxury."

"That's a pretty big offer. And a hard one to refuse."

"Yes, it is very tempting."

"You don't sound enthusiastic."

"Just when everything seemed to be falling into place my life is in an upheaval again. Oh Karlis what am I to do?"

"Only you can decide that. When is he coming back?"

"In a week's time."

It was a hot Sunday afternoon and as most of the other guests of the celebration had gone home, Anna decided to go for a long walk. There was much to think about regarding Wally's offer of a gilded paradise on Earth. What would it be like to be married to a business tycoon travelling all over like a glorified Gypsy? It was true she would not have to again be cold and hungry, living in fear, or haunted by the smell of death, but she would in effect have this anyway even without Wally. While it was wonderful to see Wally again, a dream she had nurtured most of her adult life, something about him had changed and she was not sure that she liked it.

Anna walked along the beach past private cottages, past people gathered along the beach for swimming or sunbathing, toward the village of Kasper Beach about a mile away. The heads of many young men turned at the sight of this attractive woman in her flowing print sun dress that still betrayed a trim curvaceous figure and slim, shapely, bare legs, while her wavy brown hair was windblown in the gentle breeze. Although Anna was nearly thirty-six years old she held the appearance of a much younger woman. Anna was too lost in thought to notice that she attracted so much attention. Finally she strode across the broad sandy public beach at the edge of the village itself. Her throat parched from the exercise, Anna stopped at an ice-cream stand and purchased a cone of vanilla ice cream.

As she received the cone she heard a familiar voice say with some uncertainty, "Anna?"

She turned and behind her stood a familiar-looking man. Then in sudden recognition she exclaimed, "Larry!"

"How are you Anna?" Larry smiled. "I couldn't believe it when Mom said you were in town."

"Yes, I stopped at your store the other day and met your mother. She's a very pleasant woman."

"Anna Lindenbergis," he grinned again. "You look even more beautiful than you did in Berlin."

"And you look just as handsome, even without your uniform," Anna grinned.

"I suppose you're happily married with kids," he laughed.

"I've had no time," Anna laughed. "I had to spend all my time scheming how to get to Canada and then learn how to survive once I got here."

"Well you definitely speak English a lot better now," Larry laughed. "Excuse me, I'll grab a pop and we can sit in the shade and talk."

After getting his soft drink, Larry took Anna over to a shaded bench facing the beach, and Anna continued her story.

"Shortly after I came to Canada, I was taken in by this wonderful family in Montreal. The woman of the house knows you."

"Oh who?" Larry couldn't imagine anyone in far away Montreal knowing him.

"Mandy. Her maiden name was Polsen. She said you and she went to school together."

"Ah yes, Mandy Polsen. Now I remember. Her brother Paul, who is a friend of mine, said she was living in Montreal and quite well-to-do."

"Yes. She was wealthy enough to hire me as a maid and pay my way through college."

"Yes. She always was warm-hearted, but very determined like someone else I know."

Anna smiled wryly and continued. "Yes, I've met her parents. Wonderful people they are." Changing the subject she asked, " So Larry, are you married?"

"I almost was," he said uncomfortably.

"I'm sorry, I shouldn't have . . ."

"It's all right. You asked a legitimate question. I was engaged to a girl from River Bend shortly after the war. She jilted me about a month before the planned wedding."

"Oh, my God," Anna replied. "It's hard to imagine any woman wanting to jilt you."

"Yeah, well those things happen," he sighed. "As a result I haven't really looked for another woman."

"I suppose a shock like that would cause you not to trust women."

"I wouldn't say that entirely," he laughed, "but I will be very selective who I choose to get involved with." Then changing the subject he said, "So what are you doing here?"

"I came to be reunited with my brother whom I haven't seen since before the war. As a bonus, I found out that he had managed to spring my sister out of Latvia."

"That's wonderful Anna. So now your family is whole."

"Save for Mother and Father. They're dead."

"I know the feeling, I lost my father last year. After my failed marriage attempt, he and I set up this lumber business over here in Kasper Beach. We've done quite well actually. As everyone from Edmonton wants a cottage at the lake nowadays, we set up this business at the right time. So, are you still going to be a doctor?"

"Yes, I've completed my medical training so I'll be looking to do my internship."

Back in Montreal or. . ?"

"Probably here in Edmonton, close to my family," Anna said somewhat vaguely. She was still thinking of Wally's offer.

"That's great, Anna," Larry smiled. "Dr. Lindenbergis. Next time I have a sore finger I'll go see Dr. Lindenbergis for a Band-Aid."

Anna laughed. Larry looked at her and laughed also.

"Say Anna," he smiled. "Are you in any great hurry to be anywhere?"

"No. Why?" She teased.

"Allow me to show you the sights of Kasper Beach." Larry said, rising from his seat. "It isn't Montreal, but it does look better than bombed-out Berlin did."

"I think Kasper Beach is a beautiful little place." Anna laughed, rising also. He offered her the crook of his arm and she clasped it. As they walked toward his car, she remarked, "Still the gallant Canadian soldier I see. I'll never forget the night you saved me from the Americans."

"I'll never forget the bedraggled-looking but still beautiful young woman, living in terror of the Russians."

"You don't know what I went through," Anna said.

"No, I suppose not, coming from a sheltered country like Canada." Larry said as he opened the car door for her.

"That is why so many Europeans want to come here. Canada is a sanctuary."

They had a most enjoyable time as they drove up and down the streets of Kasper Beach and along the road on the south shore. From here, she could point to the sprawling summerhouse of Karlis across the bay. Larry, who was acquainted with Karlis, referred to him as Carl. They came back to the village and stopped at a modest house beside the lake where they had late afternoon tea with Larry's mother, Astrid. Again Anna found Astrid a very pleasant host. As they sat in the screened-in sun porch Astrid cast eyes from one to the other in matchmaking calculation.

Later as they drove up to the summerhouse, Larry asked. "May I see you again?"

After a moment's hesitation Anna replied. "Sure, come by tomorrow afternoon and have coffee with us. You can meet Liesma."

"I'll come in my motorboat," Larry laughed as he noticed a small dock in front of the summerhouse where Karlis's large boat was moored. "Have you ever been in a motorboat?"

"No, but I'd be delighted to go for a ride in one," Anna smiled. "Is it a big boat?"

"No, just a small red and white motor boat that I use for fishing."

"So, I'll be watching for a little red and white boat then," Anna smiled.

Anna was in a buoyant mood when she walked into the house. Noticing this, Karlis said, "I see you caught a ride back from town."

"Yes, I ran into an old friend, Larry Kekkonin."

"Larry Kekkonin?" Karlis said with surprise. "How did you know him?"

"We met in Berlin at the close of the war. He saved me from some American soldiers who wanted to torment me."

"Amazing!" Karlis exclaimed. "I've known Larry for years. I knew he was in the war, but I never knew in all these years that he saw you at the end of the war."

"He wanted to marry me."

"It would have been an easy way for you to get into Canada."

"Yes, but I didn't know if I loved him and I didn't want to use him."

"He never married you know," Karlis said.

"Yes, he told me all about how he was jilted."

"Wally was married," Jelena added.

"He was!" Anna exclaimed.

"Twice. I overheard him talking to one of the others at the party."

'So he did not really wait for me,' Anna thought. *'I suppose I can't fault him for it, as the chances of him finding me again were very slim. Still I passed up a chance for love with Larry or Edward and to a lesser extent Jan, with the hope that I would again find Valdis.'*

Anna spent a lot of time on the veranda the following afternoon watching for the red and white motorboat. Liesma came along and sat quietly beside her.

"Are you going away with Valdis?" she finally said.

"I don't know," Anna said dreamily. "If I go with Valdis I will never need worry about going hungry again."

"I would miss you terribly," Liesma replied.

"I know. I would miss you and Karlis too. I finally found my family and now I would be going away, though he did say you could come and stay once he got my mansion."

"Stay in a big house?"

"Yes, he could afford to hire you a tutor so you could learn to speak and read English perfectly."

"We'd be away from Karlis."

"True but we could always visit him, or he us."

"I think I'd like to stay here with Karlis," Liesma said emphatically. "There has been so much turmoil in my life. I just want to stay here where it is safe."

"I know the feeling," Anna smiled quietly.

They heard the sound of a motorboat coming from the direction of Kasper Beach. It was traveling quite fast with its bow nearly out of the water as it skipped over the waves. As it approached they could see the red and white colours.

"It's Larry," Anna said excitedly as she rose from her seat. "Do you want to come for a ride in a motorboat Liesma?"

"I don't know."

"Come along it will be fun," Anna said, tugging her arm.

Reluctantly Liesma came along as they headed for the dock as the motorboat pulled up.

"Hi, Larry," Anna called from above the sound of the idling motor. "Do you mind if my sister Liesma comes with us?"

"Not at all," Larry grinned.

Anna made introductions and explained that Liesma couldn't speak English. Liesma went on board first and settled into the back seat, while Anna climbed in the front beside Larry. Soon they were racing down the length of the lake. Both Kasper Beach and Karlis's place were left far behind. They could see the vague outline of the western shore and the rolling blue hills behind it along with the blue outline of the power generating plant. There were several other boats on the lake including a few sailboats with their single triangular sails.

"How do you like it?" Larry asked above the roar of the motor.

"It's kind of exhilarating with the wind rushing through my hair," Anna smiled. She looked back at Liesma, who sat staring around in wonder as they cruised along the lake.

Larry turned a sharp U-turn to head back. Anna cried out as she was on the downward side of the steeply banked boat. "Larry!" she cried. "Don't turn so sharp."

"Did I scare you?" he laughed.

"Did I scare you," she scoffed. "Have you ever been swept overboard in the middle of the Atlantic Ocean?"

"No. Have you?"

"Yes, and it's not a pleasant experience. If I had not been tied to a lifeline, I would not be here to talk about it. As it was, I nearly drowned."

"You sure had some interesting experiences," Larry laughed.

"Yes, I've had a few close calls and some lucky escapes," Anna replied. She again glanced back a Liesma who was smiling quietly, not understanding a word they were saying.

"I'm sorry Liesma," Anna said in Latvian. "I forget that you don't understand English. I was telling Larry about my experience in the North Atlantic, that I told you about."

"Oh, that's all right," Liesma replied. Then with a knowing smile, she added. "Maybe you should keep speaking English. Your man, Larry, doesn't speak Latvian. You two can pretend I'm not here, because I won't know what you're talking about."

Anna turned to face forward again.

"What did she say to you, Anna?" Larry laughed as he noticed her flushed face.

"Nothing. It's a private matter."

"Oh, I see," he chuckled.

When they arrived back at the dock, Anna invited Larry to come to the house. At the house Larry was greeted warmly by both Karlis and Jelena and he accepted Karlis' offer of a bottle of beer.

"So, how is the lumber and hardware business?" Karlis asked.

"Very good. I've just been offered a job."

"Oh, you didn't say anything to me," Anna said.

"Never had the opportunity," Larry laughed. "Edward McDonald of McDonald Lumber in Edmonton called me to his office last week and offered me the job of being his field man. He is the supplier of hardware and exotic woods for most of these small towns around including my business and that of Uncle Clarence over in Morning Glory."

"That's wonderful Larry," Anna smiled. "So, does that mean moving to Edmonton?"

"Probably. I would be travelling a lot to service all these lumber-yards."

"McDonald Lumber eh," Karlis said. "They're a pretty big outfit."

"They've been associated with our family ever since Grandpa set up his first sawmill back in 1910," Larry said.[1]

"That's right, your father was also in the business." Karlis said.

"Yes, he was both Grandpa's and Uncle Clarence's right-hand-man for many years."

"What will you do with your business here?" Karlis asked.

"Mom said she could look after it for now. She does the books anyway and my Uncle James expressed an interest in buying it."

"James, that's your mother's younger brother isn't it?" Jelena said.

"Yes, the lumbering business runs strong in the Erlander family," Larry laughed, in reference to the maternal side of his family.

"So when are you making the big move?" Anna asked, with a touch of anxiety in her voice.

"Possibly as soon as next week. I have to tidy a few things up yet," Larry glanced at his watch and said. "Which reminds me, I should get back and tend to business." He finished his beer and excused himself.

As he left, he smiled at Liesma who had been sitting in the background, left out of the conversation. "It was really nice to meet you Liesma."

"Pleasure to meetink vis you, Larry Kekkonin," she faltered in broken English.

Anna saw Larry to his boat and accepted an offer to go to Edmonton with him next Thursday so she might inquire about an internship in an Edmonton hospital.

Liesma watched them from the veranda. She was wearing a satisfied smile.

---

[1] The background on Larry's family is found in, *Ingrid – An Immigrant's Tale*

Chapter Twenty-Two

Liesma was still smiling as Anna stepped up onto the veranda and this prompted Anna to say, "What are you smiling at?"

"Your friend Larry is a nice man." Liesma replied.

"Yes he is a very nice person," Anna replied nonchalantly.

"You are quite fond of him, yes?" Liesma continued.

"He's a good friend," Anna replied quickly.

"He's not rich enough for you then?"

"Being rich isn't everything," Anna said. "It's the person that counts."

"He is a nicer person than Valdis, yes?" Liesma probed.

"Why are you asking me all this?" Anna asked uneasily.

"I just hope my sister makes the right choice from the two men courting her."

"The choice is mine to make," Anna said sharply as she went into the house.

On that Thursday, Anna went to Edmonton with Larry in his automobile. It was another interesting experience for Anna, as she had never travelled any great distance in Canada via automobile before. Anna applied for internship at the University Hospital to intern for a General Practitioner with the ultimate aim of becoming a Pediatrician. Since she did not know her way around Edmonton, Larry had to drive her around and still find time for his own appointment with McDonald Lumber. When they arrived at the lumberyard, she was invited into the office. Larry introduced her as a friend, but she received *knowing looks,* implying that they suspected that there was more to the relationship. One of the women working in the office, who had not been introduced to her, addressed her as Mrs. Kekkonin. All of this left Anna with a peculiar feeling inside.

It was late afternoon by the time they got out of Edmonton, so they decided to stop at a roadside café, in one of the little towns along the way, for some supper. This was another experience for Anna. The café was noisy and her nostrils were assailed by the tantalizing smell of frying onions. They sat in a booth by the window and a waitress came with a menu.

"I'm not terribly hungry," Anna said. "I'd like something light."

"How about a hamburger and a milkshake," Larry suggested. "I find that quick and filling."

"I'll have a cheeseburger and a strawberry milkshake," Anna smiled. "I enjoy having fast food occasionally."

"It's not as good as Schnitzel," Larry laughed.

"That was really good Schnitzel we had that time." Anna smiled at the recollection of their first dinner together in Berlin.

Anna began to aimlessly flip through a small jukebox consul mounted on the wall below the window trimmed in chrome. To Anna it seemed that nearly everything in the café seemed to be trimmed in chrome.

"Why don't you put in a dime and choose a song." Larry laughed.

"I wouldn't know what to select," Anna replied.

Just then a couple of youths with long greasy hair slicked back in duck tail style came in and sat at the next booth. One of them began flipping through the jukebox selector and put in some money. Music began blaring out of the machine in the corner.

"What is that noise," Anna said as the so-called music in which the singer was screaming and the emphasis was on the beat.

Larry laughed and said, "That's Elvis Presley, he's a rock and roll superstar who just came on the scene recently."

"Rock and Roll?"

"That's a new kind of music from the States. That tune he's playing is called *Hound Dog*. Actually I find Rock and Roll irritating to listen to also. Although Elvis can sound nice when he sings a slow tune."

"I might have guessed that only Americans could put out noise like that and call it music," Anna scoffed.

The waitress brought their orders.

"So, what kind of music do you like?" Larry asked.

"Opera or symphony. What about you?"

"I like the swing music or pleasant singers like Bing Crosby. He has a nice song out just now; I'll play it for you. Larry flipped through the selector and put in a dime

"That's a little better," Anna said when the song came on. She listened to his crooning voice sing out a pleasant tune called *True Love*. "It's from a movie called *High Society*," Larry said." How do you like your hamburger?"

"It's a little salty but tasty, but I do like the milkshake."

"All this, food and so-called music, is this what they call pop culture?" Anna asked.

"Yes, I guess you could say that.

The rest of the drive home was in relative silence as Ann had many thoughts churning in her mind and the song *True Love* played over and over in her mind. She had enjoyed her day with Larry. He was so considerate and helpful. She also enjoyed the day they toured the lake in his motorboat. He was so sincere, attentive and supportive of her goals in life. Then she thought of Valdis, he was so brash and boastful, as his mind seemed to revolve around money. He had disavowed his roots and become so American in his outlook on life. She thought of the Valdis she knew in her youth, the lad who used to wait on her and talk of his plans to go to Canada. She thought of those tender moments when they were hiding out together from the Reds and the day he said goodbye as he went away to war. Were they really the same person?

As they reached Kasper Beach Larry said, "You've been unusually quiet."

"Uh . . . oh I'm just tired from the long day," Anna said.

"Have you ever been to a dance?" Larry asked carefully.

"A dance?"

"Yes, a band plays and you can waltz or polka."

"Oh yes, a dance. I used to dance in the Old Country. We had our folk dances, but we also learned to waltz and polka. They don't play music like that we heard in the café do they?"

"Oh, no," Larry laughed. "This is nice music. Usually someone plays the fiddle."

"Sounds interesting," Anna replied, as they drove toward Karlis's place.

"There is a dance in Kasper Beach on Friday night," Larry said carefully. "Would you like to go with me to it?"

"Sure, why not. Since coming out here I began to learn a different aspect of Canadian life. I have already learned the big city way and worked as a servant for the wealthy. Now I'm learning the Alberta way. Everything out here is so open, so friendly. Yes I would like to go to that dance with you."

They pulled up to the driveway and Anna stepped out saying, "I will see you Friday evening then."

"Yes, about eight o'clock," Larry grinned as she closed the car door.

Anna entered the house in a lighthearted mood humming the strains of *True Love*, until Karlis said. "Valdis telephoned this afternoon. He will be here on Saturday"

"On Saturday?" Anna said, her voice rising. She felt as if she were a balloon that had just been pricked.

"He was disappointed that he couldn't speak to you personally."

"Did you tell him where I was and what I was doing?" Anna asked anxiously

"I told him you went to see the sights of Edmonton with an old friend."

"You didn't tell him I was inquiring about internships?"

"No, that is for you to tell," Karlis replied

"So what did you find out?" Jelena asked.

"Find out?" Anna asked absentmindedly. "Oh the University Hospital is very interested especially after finding out I graduated from McGill."

"And you have decided?"

"I don't know what to decide," Anna said. "I need to go out on the veranda and think."

As Anna went out on to the veranda she saw Liesma sitting on a bench under a large spreading willow playing the kokle and was softly singing a Latvian lullaby. She smiled as she remembered when Liesma used to play and sing when she was a child. It was great that Liesma was starting to come out of her post traumatic and cultural shock. The announcement that Valdis was coming out however, was unsettling. Although he had said he was coming back to take her away to a life of luxury, her recent outings with Larry had pushed this inevitability to the back of her mind. She would have to tell Larry about Valdis, then be forced to make a choice.

That night she had a troubled sleep mulling over what each man had said to her in their most tender moments and what they each had to offer. In the morning she was still confused as she let a little of her dilemma out to the others Karlis and Jelena were strictly neutral and Liesma favoured Larry. Although Larry was a fine man and would make a good husband, her long association with Valdis and their special closeness during the time of hiding weighed heavily in her mind.

Anna honored her date with Larry and they had an enjoyable time dancing. She already knew how to waltz and polka, and Larry showed her how to fox-trot and to schottische. Although the musical strains were more crude than what she was accustomed to hearing, they were much preferable to rock and roll. She had such an enjoyable time that she almost forgot that her time of reckoning was fast approaching.

As they drove home from the dance Anna struggled to drum up the courage to speak to Larry on the matter. Instead of going home however, he took her to a viewpoint overlooking both the East End of the lake and the village of Kasper Beach. When she inquired as to where they were going, Larry smiled and said he just wanted to show her a beautiful view. For a moment she thought of the time when Kurt took her for a drive along the Gulf of Riga.

He stopped the car and they both expressed their awe at the view, then Larry abruptly turned to her. "Anna, this last week with you has been wonderful."

"Yes, I thought so too, Larry, but . . ."

Larry cut her off and continued, "It fully revived the memory of that time we spent together in Berlin."

"Yes it did . . ."

"This time I won't take no for an answer." Larry caught his breath and continued. "I love you Anna and I want to marry you. There is no longer anything standing between us."

"There is sort of," Anna faltered.

"There is?"

"At the party my brother put on." Then Anna continued with great effort, "Valdis showed up."

"I see." Larry said heavily as his heart sank. " You never told me."

"I . . . I wasn't certain how to react to his reappearance. My mind was in a confusion and that is why I walked to Kasper Beach that day."

"You still love him then?"

"Well . . .uh, he wants me to marry him. He is very wealthy and holds out to me a life of luxury."

"Well, I can't compete with that," Larry said glumly. "You'd be a fool to turn him down."

"Is luxury the begin all and end all?" Anna said. "What about happiness. I have my own plans in life."

"Do you love him?"

"I thought I did. I lived half my life hoping I would see him again, and when I did he had changed so much, I wasn't sure it was the same person any more."

"Do you love me?"

"You are a very wonderful person Larry."

"You don't love me," he said glumly. He turned to start the car.

"I do, I do," Anna said putting her hand on his.

"Do what?"

"I - Love -You," Anna said slowly. She was surprised how easily she said the words that she could never say to Valdis.

Larry reached for her, but she stopped him and said with a twisted grin, "Do you object to my carrying through to be a doctor?"

"On the contrary, I'd be disappointed if you didn't go through with it. That is your dream and you must follow it, and when you get to be Dr. Lindenbergis I hope you won't forget about your lowly lumber salesman, husband."

"Dr. Lindenbergis?" Anna laughed. "If I marry you wouldn't it be Dr. Kekkonin."

"Dr. Lindenbergis sounds better. Since you are a proud Latvian you wouldn't want people to think that you are a Finn, would you?"

"You have a point, but we can decide that later."

"So, are you going to marry me this time?"

"Yes, Larry I will marry you this time."

This time when Larry reached for her she accepted his embrace and they kissed for a long moment.

When they drove up to Karlis's house, the white Cadillac was parked in the driveway and the living room lights in the house were still on.

"Oh my God, Valdis has arrived early." Anna gasped. "I do not want a confrontation with him in the middle of the night. Larry, what am I going to do?"

"Confront him. You have to anyway. Do you want me to come in?"

"No, I'd better do this alone. Come by with your boat tomorrow, about noon," Anna said quickly. "I'll come down to the dock and meet you. Everything will be settled by then."

"Noon tomorrow," Larry said nervously. He still had a gnawing uncertainty, even though Anna had confessed love and accepted his proposal. Anna squeezed his hand and kissed him lightly before stepping from the car.

When Anna entered the house, she found Valdis sitting in the living room alone. The others had apparently gone to bed. He rose to greet her.

"Hello Anna darling," he smiled. "Did you have a nice time at the dance?"

"Valdis, I mean Wally, I thought you weren't coming until tomorrow," Anna said breathlessly.

"I was so anxious to see you that I couldn't wait another day." he continued to smile. "It seems I missed you the other day on the phone."

"Yes, I was in Edmonton. An old friend gave me a tour of the city."

"I see. Did the same old friend take you to the dance?"

"Yes he did. Look I'm very tired and I don't need to be interrogated at this time of night," Anna said sharply.

"I'm still waiting to hear those three magic words," Wally continued, as he came closer.

"Look Wally, I'm really glad you came back to get me, but I'm afraid I'm too tired to be romantic tonight." Anna turned to go to her room.

"Why can't you ever come clean with me? Both those times in the loft and on the night I went away, you always came short on those magic words. Or did you save them for your old friend?"

The vision of those tender moments flashed through her mind in spite of what had transpired between her and Larry that evening. She felt like she was being cornered. Then she said suddenly, "Look Wally, there is much to think about. You come abruptly back into my life last week and again tonight. Did you ever think that things might change?"

"For us nothing can change," Wally said. "We were meant to be together. Now I'm not taking no for an answer."

Anna felt like saying that this was the second time she had heard that. Instead she said, "It's over Wally. What we shared was then, and what's now is now. Goodnight Wally." Anna turned and walked to her room and ignored his call.

When Anna emerged for breakfast she discovered, not surprisingly, that Wally had left. Jelena observed, "It looks like your jilted lover has gone. He left in the night."

"Yeah," Anna sighed.

"It was a shame he came all this way for a broken heart," Karlis added.

In conversations with Karlis and Jelena, before Anna had arrived home from the dance, Valdis had learned that her escort was Larry Kekkonin owner of the local lumberyard. After a sleepless night in the hotel as his mind reeled with her apparent rejection, he decided to visit Larry Kekkonin. He simply could not believe that Anna could reject him for someone she barely knew, especially with all that he had to offer her in comparison to Larry.

Larry answered the knock on the door of his mother's house, to find a well-dressed stranger on the doorstep. "Yes, may I help you?" he said pleasantly.

"You are Larry Kekkonin?" the stranger said.

"Yes, I am."

"I am Wally Sirnis, Anna calls me Valdis."

"Pleased to meet you Wally," Larry swallowed as he stepped onto the sun porch and closed the door behind him. "How can I help you?"

"Perhaps we could go over to my car and talk," Wally said.

"We can talk here. Mom can't hear through the door."

"Anna, are you quite fond of her?"

"Why does that concern you?"

"Anna and I have grown up together. We have gone through many trials together. We have a special bond. You come along and complicate things for her."

"Yes, she has told me," Larry said uncomfortably.

"I love Anna, and I am offering her a life free from want. A life she so richly deserves after what she has been through. What can you, a mere owner of a small town lumber yard offer her?"

"Love. I can offer her love as nothing else matters."

"I see. What if I was to offer you a handsome sum for your lumberyard? You could move away or do anything you like as long as you got out of Anna's life.

"Have you got enough money to buy love? Has anyone? Now if you'll excuse me . . ." Larry turned to go back into the house.

"I'm going to see Anna," Wally said harshly as he turned away. "Perhaps she will see things more clearly in the morning light."

After breakfast, Anna sat on the south veranda enjoying her coffee. Liesma joined her.

"So are you going to marry Larry?" Liesma asked abruptly.

"You like him don't you," Anna smiled.

"Yes, he is very nice. He doesn't talk so much about money."

Anna smiled with this oblique reference to Wally.

After a moment of silence, Liesma continued, "Did you tell Valdis goodbye?"

"You seem very concerned about my life?" Anna said sharply.

"I want you to stay close beside Karlis and me," Liesma said. "I don't want you to be in a big lonely mansion."

"I don't think I want to be far away from you and Karlis either." Anna said. "We have been separated too long."

"Will Larry come for you today?" Liesma said.

"Yes, I told him to come over in his boat. If things were settled between Valdis and myself, I would come down to the dock to meet him."

Just then Wally's Cadillac drove up. "Oh no!" Anna gasped. "He didn't believe me last night."

"Why don't you run away and hide?" Liesma said.

"I've been hiding all my life," Anna said. "This time I have the freedom to stand up."

As Wally approached the veranda Anna did stand up and Liesma ducked inside. She went to the telephone and looked through the phone list. Although she couldn't read English she could recognize names. She dialed and a man answered.

"Larry Kekkonin, come soon in boat, get Anna." Liesma hung up the phone.

"Hello Valdis," Anna said evenly, as he stepped up into the veranda.

"Hi darling," he smiled. "Did you sleep well?"

"Yes, very well," Anna said without expression. "I thought you went away."

"Not without you," Wally smiled. "Look I know you were tired last night and probably had a good time with your friend . . ."

"Larry," Anna added.

"But now it is time to be serious Anna. I need you."

"I was serious," Anna said with resolve. "The Valdis I once knew, the Valdis I dreamed of reuniting with all these years, no longer exists. Instead he has become Walter Sirnis."

"What has the name change got to do with anything?"

"Walter Sirnis is interested only in money. It's not me you love, it is the golden calf."

"That's not true. I've waited for you for many years."

"Is that why you got married? Twice!"

Wally was taken aback. "So you know?"

A motorboat was coming along the lake. Anna noticed that it was red and white, but it was going past Karlis's place heading out into the lake. *'If it's Larry, he is early, but his timing is perfect.'* Anna thought.

Anna turned back to Wally. "Yes I know. Did you know that I passed up a chance for love on three occasions, including a previous chance with Larry, because of the dream and the promise."

"I didn't think I'd ever see you again," Wally said limply.

"I didn't think I'd see you either. What if you were still married, or had found wife number three when you saw Karlis's ad? Would you dump her to come for me?"

"I - I'd,"

"Or if I go with you and you find I do not live up to your high-flying standards will you dump me too?"

"I'd never dump you. I love you."

"Larry loves me too. He asked me to marry him and I accepted."

"Him! You'd spend your life as a housewife for a small town businessman? Are you quite insane?"

"I will spend my life as Dr. Lindenbergis. He insists that I go through with my dream, and keep my maiden name. He supports it. That's what love is, Mr. Sirnis."

The boat was coming back around, traveling slowly as it appeared to be heading for Karlis's dock.

"I told you I was willing to let you go through to be a doctor. I could see to it, that you would get a practice in a very prestigious area."

"But you don't really want me to," Anna said abruptly. "You want me to travel around the country with you like a glorified Gypsy. I'm sorry Valdis. My place is here, Liesma needs me and Larry needs me. I've done enough running from place to place."

Anna turned to watch the boat draw up to the dock. "Goodbye

Valdis, may you be as happy in your world as I will in mine." Anna turned and walked briskly toward the dock just as the boat touched against the bumpers.

Wally wanted to shout after her that she was a fool, but he remained speechless. He remained standing on the veranda watching. Anna climbed into the boat and kissed Larry for a long moment then the boat pulled away and headed out across the lake.

Epilogue

It is now October in the year of 1991, Anna and her son Esa had just arrived in downtown Riga from the airport. Since both the Soviet Empire and the communist system that sustained it had collapsed earlier that year, Latvia had, once again, reclaimed its freedom. Anna dared to travel home again. She had a joyful reunion with Taska as they had kept in touch since Lana had given her the address Karlis had been back twice, even while the Soviets still ruled, and Liesma refused to go even now. Anna was surprised to find that much of the old city had remained intact in spite of the war and half a century of communism. She even found the house in which she was raised. A Russian family, who had lived there for many years, occupied it. As she looked upon the house from the sidewalk and spoke with her son, she thought back over her life with Larry and how things had changed so much from the time when she had started her odyssey. She wondered how she had survived her journey through hell to find her paradise on Earth, and wondered if she had it to do over, would she survive.

Later, she and Esa walked across Cathedral Square. They looked up at the flagstaff and Anna felt a lump inside as she saw the flag of free Latvia flying once again on the mast. The bookstore, the face of which had been once covered with a giant portrait of Stalin, was still there. She had a flash vision of the square filled with German troops. As she pointed out points of interest to Esa, a voice behind her called her name.

She turned, and there stood Wally. His hair, what was left of it, was snow white and his face wrinkled, but she still recognized him.

"Hello Anna," he smiled. "I see you have come home to your roots."

"Yes. I am surprised to see you here though."

"I suppose one gets older and wiser through the years. Besides, since Latvia got its freedom once again there are business opportunities."

"Still chasing the dollar, I see," Anna sighed.

"Well, not exactly, I've retired from that. I'm investing in the future of Latvia. There is a whole generation of people here who have no concept of entrepreneurship. I am loaning my skills so my country can develop a free market economy, and join the European Community. It is the best assurance to keep the Russian bear outside our door."

"That's very commendable Wally," Anna replied.

"It's Valdis again," he smiled. "So, have you led a good life?"

"Yes, I married Larry about two months after I last saw you. We raised two children. This young man you see with me is my son Esa and I also have a daughter named Lita.

"Pleased to meet you, Esa," Valdis said extending his hand.

Esa returned the greeting in Latvian.

"You have taught your children to speak Latvian, I see?" Valdis said.

"Yes, they also know a little Finnish. We were in both Sweden and Finland before we came here. Esa wanted to see the countries where his other grandparents, were born. We named him after his grandfather."

"Larry didn't come with you?"

"He passed away last year," Anna said sadly, "and Lita is busy with her life, though she plans to come to Latvia next year. I may come back with her."

"I'm sorry to hear about your husband. Did you still go on to become a doctor?"

"Yes. I retired a few years ago. And you, do you have a wife and children?"

"No," Valdis said sadly. "After you rejected me, I never married again and my first two marriages were childless."

"But you did well in business?"

"Yes, but while I never went cold or hungry again like we were when we were hiding, I was cold and hungry in a different way. I was blinded by that golden calf and it cost me the happiness I might have enjoyed with you."

"We were not meant to be together," Anna said. "Although we shared some special memories, if one counts the memory of hiding from our would-be executioners special, we were meant to go our separate ways when our time of trial was over."

"You always were wiser than me."

"So now what is your life, besides showing Latvians how to make money?" Anna asked, changing the subject.

"That is my life. All those years that I was a rich American, I didn't care at all about Latvia or my Latvian heritage. I considered it a dead country, and that my past there died along with it."

"What changed your mind?"

"When Latvia became free again this year, I first saw this freedom as a business opportunity. However, after I arrived in Riga two months ago, my past came back to me. I guess you could call it an atonement of sorts."

"So, are you living in Latvia now?"

"Yes, I am refurbishing an old house a few blocks from here. Have you ever thought of returning to Latvia to live?"

"I've thought of it," Anna replied. "My roots are here and part of me will always be here, but my home is Canada, that golden land across the sea."

About the Author

Eric John Brown was born on August 13, 1947 the youngest son of John and Ruby Brown. He was raised on a farm in the community of Magnolia about one hundred kilometres west of Edmonton, Alberta.

Magnolia was, during his childhood, a hamlet consisting of a store, a church and a community hall. The community was a closely-knit one and his family was a warm loving one. During his early grades, he attended a one-roomed school about a mile from home then completed his remaining grades at Seba Beach School from which he graduated. He has always been a keen student of modern history, geography, and science.

Virtually all of his working life has been spent first with Canadian National Railways Signals Department and later with TransAlta at the local Sundance power generating plant.

While on a trip to Scotland to visit relatives in 1971 he met his future wife, Isabella. They were married in Scotland nearly two years later and have since raised two sons, John and Colin.

The author began writing stories when he was thirteen years old but most of his early writings were of the science-fiction genre. Later, as he became more skilled at character development, he turned to standard fiction. He has also developed a keen interest in the ethnic and linguistic background of the vast mosaic of peoples that make up Canada. He, in particular, has focused on peoples seldom mentioned in mainstream literature such as Finns, Latvians, Ukrainians and Scandinavians.

The saga of *Ginny*, his first publication, was conceived when he was only twenty-three years old. At the time however, he lacked the necessary writing skills to tackle a work of this magnitude. It remained, however, in the back of his mind like bedrock, even as he worked on other writings. The details of *Ginny* slowly filled in over the years. Finally after the acquisition of a home computer in 1994, the author tackled this long overdue novel in earnest. As the author set to writing, what was originally to be the story of a community, a strange thing happened. In the author's own words, "the character, Ginny, leaped out of my imagination and took control of the saga making it her story." Since that time this powerful and warm, loving character has captured the hearts of hundreds of readers of all ages.

The result of his literary labours was the publication of *Ginny* on December 11, 1998. From the first day of publication *Ginny* has been well received by readers, reviewers, bookstores, libraries and the general media. With the highly successful publication of *Ginny* via the route of self-publishing, the author has continued to write novels which have found broad appeal on the marketplace.

The author, Eric J Brown, continues to live on the land where he grew up. With his beloved wife Isabella, he has raised two sons, John and Colin, and now enjoys the rewards of grandchildren. With retirement approaching, he hopes to devote his energy to writing and promoting his novels about this great land of Canada.

Ginny
A Canadian Story of Love & Friendship

Ginny is a rich girl from Toronto who dares, against her family's wishes, to elope with Danish immigrant named Marty Polsen to his homestead in Alberta. Ginny faces many challenges on the homestead such as learning how to cook, coping with homesickness, being chased by a bear, and a difficult childbirth that nearly kills her. With the support of both her loving husband Marty, and her dear friends, Ingrid and Gina, Ginny perseveres.

As you trace Ginny's life, from a time when she was a rich girl adjusting to the rigours of the homestead, to a time when she is offering wise counsel to her grandchildren of the baby boomer era - you will come to appreciate that this work is a triumphant story of love and friendship.

The Promise

Full of enthusiasm and patriotism generated by the Great War, young Paul Cunningham enlists in the Canadian Army the day after his 19th birthday. His parents, of a well-to-do Toronto family, are vehemently opposed to his joining, but cannot stop their determined son's call to duty.

With great passion and fanfare, Paul marches off to war and straight into the man-made hell on Earth known historically as the Battle of the Somme - a battle so horrendous, that it consumed a whole generation of young men from both the British and German empires during the summer and autumn of 1916.

As Paul struggles to cope with the horrors of war, he must also deal with a difficult commanding officer culminating in a showdown that threatens to be his ultimate undoing. Away from the madness of the front, two women, his beloved sister, Ginny, back in Toronto and his sweetheart, Chelsea, in England, wait anxiously for him. To both he has promised to return.

Ingrid

AN IMMIGRANT'S TALE

Ingrid is only fourteen years old when she is torn away from all that is familiar including her dear friend, Sigrud. This, because her father had chosen to immigrate from Sweden to Canada in 1910 with his family. Ingrid is frightened at the prospect of having to learn a new language, coming to a strange new frontier land and she pines for her friend left behind. When settled in her new home, Ingrid, is pursued by two undesirable suitors, one is a shy clumsy man and the other a raucous ruffian. When Ingrid finally meets and marries the love of her life all seems well, but tragedy and disappointment still stalk her.

Much of this story takes place with World War I looming in the background and the Great War has its effect on both Ingrid and her neighbours.

To the Last Tree Standing

Following up an article in an outdoors magazine, Freelance writer Jill Tompkins sets out to f nd a mysterious mountain man simply known as Brother Nature or commonly Bro. He is the self-appointed protector of a beautiful stretch of forest in Montana. As she begins her trek into the forest, Jill discovers that there is more mystery here than she bargained for. She is followed by a hit man employed by a ruthless logging magnate, whose mission is to kill Bro and she is watched over by a sympathetic forest ranger. As she plunges deeper into the forest after the elusive Bro, the plot thickens, the mystery grows, and the suspense builds.

Bro is a fast-moving tale of conservation, ecologyand defense of the innocent. It is a must read for all who f ght to save our environment from those who would pillage and destroy our precious natural heritage.

Third Time Lucky

Jane Brody was "as plain as dirt and tough as nails", so her mail-order suitor Ethan Phillips had declared. He also declared that she was "one hell of a cook and could sing like a lark" especially when she sang that haunting ballad *Never-ending Road*. Their many, often humorous confrontations in which her prim frumpish ways clash with his crude sardonic manner , threaten to destroy their precarious relationship at any given moment.

When Jane, the perennial wallflower , becomes entangled in a love triangle with Ethan and the lovable Irish moonshiner, Sean O'Malley, Ethan is at a loss how to cope, and is left to ponder his belief than either bad luck runs in threes or that the third time can also be lucky.

For additional copies of

Anna – Her odyssey to Freedom

Ginny - A Canadian Story of Love and Friendship

Ingrid – An Immigrant's Tale

The Promise

To The Last Tree Standing

Third Time Lucky

Write to
Magnolia Press
General Delivery
Entwistle, Alberta
T0E 0S0

Or

E-Mail mag_press@hotmail.com